Lynne Reid Banks was born in London in 1929. After evacuation to Canada during WWII, she studied acting at RADA and was in repertory for five years before becoming one of the first two female television news reporters in Britain. In 1963 she emigrated to Israel where she married sculptor Chaim Stephenson, had three sons, and taught English for eight years. Since 1971 she has lived in London and Dorset and written books and plays for adults and children, several of which have won awards here and in the US. Her books THE L-SHAPED ROOM and THE INDIAN IN THE CUPBOARD were made into major movies.

FAIR EXCHANGE

April 1989: Judy is a left-wing activist who organises a non-stop picket against Apartheid outside South Africa House. Her life is vibrant with meaning and involvement. Harriet has never fought for a cause in her life, but her religion sustains her, along with a drink or two. They couldn't be more different. But as they go about their separate lives, unknown to each other, the world stands on the brink of breath-stopping change. And as Apartheid and Communism collapse and faith erodes, Judy and Harriet are destined to affect one another's future in ways they could never have dreamed of.

LYNNE REID BANKS

◆

FAIR EXCHANGE

Complete and Unabridged

CHARNWOOD
Leicester

First published in Great Britain in 1998 by
Judy Piatkus (Publishers) Limited
London

First Charnwood Edition
published 1999
by arrangement with
Judy Piatkus (Publishers) Limited
London

The right of Lynne Reid Banks to be identified as
the author of this work has been asserted by her
in accordance with the
Copyright, Designs and Patents Act, 1988

British Library CIP Data

Banks, Lynne Reid, *1929 –*
Fair exchange.—Large print ed.—
Charnwood library series
1. London (England)—Fiction
2. Large type books
I. Title
823.9′14 [F]

ISBN 0–7089–9058–4

Published by
F. A. Thorpe (Publishing) Ltd.
Anstey, Leicestershire
Set by Words & Graphics Ltd.
Anstey, Leicestershire
Printed and bound in Great Britain by
T. J. International Ltd., Padstow, Cornwall

This book is printed on acid-free paper

To Norma Kitson
to whom so much is owed

1

April 1989

'Ach, man!' exclaimed Judy aloud, halfway up Northumberland Avenue. 'I can hear them already!'

A northcountryman visiting the capital stopped in his tracks. A woman talking to herself. And what a woman! He stared after her as she broke into a run. Tall, big-boned, blonde as a Viking, her hair streaming behind her from under a little red tam-o'-shanter with a bobble . . . she moved swiftly in her thick-soled trainers. She was by no means in her first youth.

Women and cows shouldn't run, thought the man, who fancied 'em young and sylphlike, though far from being either himself. Nevertheless he found himself wanting to follow her. Not because he was attracted to eccentrically dressed middle-aged women, but to see where she was hurrying to, in her baggy dungarees and round silver earrings flashing as she ran.

And now that he'd stopped, he could hear it too — a sort of muffled roar coming from the top of this wide London thoroughfare — the Trafalgar Square end. He turned and walked back through the crowd, fast enough to keep the red woolly hat in sight.

★ ★ ★

1

As soon as Judy turned the corner into the Square she could see them. She and the rest of the committee had notified absolutely everyone they could think of, supporters and strangers alike, but still the size of the crowd thrilled her. Must be two, maybe three hundred people, spilling off the pavement into the road. The whole wide sidewalk outside the South African Embassy was crammed; the tiny brave spots of yellow waving everywhere over the heads of the crowd — little earthbound specks of the April sun. It was she who had suggested the daffodils, a token of peaceful solidarity with the prisoners on this thousandth day of the picket.

As she came up with the fringes of the demo, she noticed that many of the daffs had already been dropped and crushed underfoot, their spring-proclaiming trumpets mere smudges on the unheeding London asphalt. Good job she wasn't the sort to see omens in everything.

She'd been due to speak first. Her Northern Line train had been held up for what had seemed bloody hours for a bomb-scare, but one had to allow for that sort of thing nowadays. Basically it was Tina's fault, turning up like that, just as Judy was leaving, spoiling for a row. Tina was driving her crazy, hardly less now than before the bust-up and her departure from the flat — a removal Judy had welcomed but that had subsequently proved more notional than real. Oh, to hell with that, Judy couldn't be bothered thinking about her daughter now.

She tried to push through. It was a good-natured crowd but of necessity packed tight.

2

They were unavoidably blocking the pavement, but were trying, at the stewards' urgent behest, not to block the road. The police had set up barriers, Judy now saw. There was a 'thin blue line', perhaps thirty of them, men and women constables standing with their backs to the white building, and in front of them were the metal crowd-holders, leaving a couple of feet in between to allow pedestrians to pass — only not many were. Everyone who came up to the crowd seemed to be joining in. Well, good, it wouldn't hurt them to listen. They might learn something.

Judy could hear Abby bawling through the megaphone. The police didn't allow any kind of platform, not even a soapbox, but there was Abby's head, sticking well above the daffodils, so someone must have sneaked a bench or something in somehow.

Abby was one of their best speakers, but Judy wouldn't have chosen her for so early in the meeting. She was too aggressive. Abby hadn't exactly favoured the police even before they'd roughed her up in a pork-wagon six months before; the burden of her speeches since then had been saw-edged with fuzz-hatred. She was in full flood right now and it wasn't the moment; she might provoke them to break up the meeting before Judy or any of the others had a chance to make the real pitch. But if that happened, Judy knew it would be her own fault for not getting here on time.

'We all know what we're up against!' Abby was yelling. The megaphone gave her the look of some strange bird with a splayed beak. 'An establishment that pays the police, who are supposed to be the guardians of free speech, to harass and beat up those who are trying to tell this nation what is going on! I am here to talk about a police state, an imperialist racist state, a state run by an authoritarian reactionary government under an authoritarian reactionary leader! Am I talking *only* about the government of South Africa? No I'm not! I'm also talking about Thatcher's Britain!'

Judy glanced uneasily at the thin blue line and saw, in the narrowing of a few eyes, the turning of a few heads, the danger signals she had feared. She wriggled her right arm free from the congestion and tried to wave a signal — 'I'm here!' Abby appeared not to notice, but perhaps she did because, nimble as a circus rider, she swung off her hobbyhorse and on to the prearranged programme.

'Nelson Mandela and all the other political prisoners are what we are here to talk about,' she shouted. '*They* are our purpose. *They* are our pride. These heroic people are suffering for their fight against Apartheid. In their names we have picketed here in all weathers, twenty-four hours of every single day for one thousand days, to draw attention to the horrendous injustices that are being carried out by one of Britain's most important trading partners, against whom she stubbornly refuses to impose sanctions. And — ' her voice pitched up again and Judy's heart pitched down ' — it's not only the weather we have been up against during these thousand days

4

and nights, but those brutal reactionary forces, Thatcher's lackeys, of whom I see so many representatives here today!' And she waved an arm backwards toward the police lines.

Bleddy 'ell, girl, don't start on that again, not till I've had my say! Judy began to shove. She was making no progress until a man who had been behind her suddenly squeezed past.

'Want to get through?'

'Yes.'

'Leave it to me.'

His broad-shouldered figure forged a path for her through the crowd until she arrived, panting slightly, at Abby's feet. Without breaking her speaking-stride, Abby smoothly announced: 'And now I am proud to give place to one of our most tireless committee members, Judy Priestman!'

A swell of applause and 'Viva Judy!'s greeted her as she clambered up to replace Abby on a rickety kitchen chair. The big man who had helped her through the crowd helped her again, with a firm hand under her elbow. She glanced down at him and saw he was grinning up at her good-humouredly. He looked rather nice, healthy and ruddy-cheeked like a farmer . . . but he didn't matter. She forgot him.

While the clapping and whistling lasted, she had time to draw breath and take a quick look round. She spotted a few names: a woman writer, a couple of actors and at least three Labour MPs including the black one. Plus all the usual friends who turned up on special occasions. Unlike the stars and MPs, they came

5

purely because they supported the cause, not in the hope of some publicity.

Well, there might even be a bit of that this time. There were press here for once — she could see them hanging about on the fringes (the event wasn't important enough for them to risk rumpling their clothes or getting their shoes trodden on). They wouldn't stay long, so she had to make the most of it with a few good sound-bites. Photo-bites, she'd been assured, she provided automatically.

The applause died down. She had the megaphone in her hand. She switched it on and began to speak.

'Friends of the prisoners and other victims of Apartheid! I'm here on behalf of West End Group's Perpetual Picket to greet you and to thank you all for your support for our struggle. But I'm so happy today to be able to bring you news which will show you how much that struggle matters, and how much, in real, practical terms, it has achieved.'

She was aware she was speaking too fast, gabbling almost. The good news was not all that good — the slight easing of prison conditions for a few peripheral prisoners in Joburg. But she had to inject a note of hope, and do it quickly. She had seen, glancing to her right in the direction of St Martin-in-the-Fields, a couple of pork-wagons, turning up William IV Street. They passed out of sight, but she knew what they portended.

★ ★ ★

6

A hundred and forty miles to the south-west, another woman, also in her forties but with nothing else in common with Judy and quite unknown to her, took off her gardening gloves and banged them against her fork-handle.

Her name was Harriet Marshall and she was small, neatly built and had mousy fair hair drawn back, showing a deep widow's peak and a high shiny forehead. Her slim legs rose out of green rubber boots like stalks out of flowerpots into the bell of an old full skirt, and her large knee-padded gardening apron overlapped round her waist at the back. The gloves she'd just removed were two sizes too big for her small-boned, childish hands.

The soil in this place, she was thinking, was even clayier than London, and with far less excuse. Since Harriet and her husband Kenneth had moved to Dorset a year ago, they had poured muck into it in a way they'd never been able to in Town, where their only source had been cowboy suppliers with their overpriced sacks of loosely packed stable-sweepings, from which, they sometimes suspected, all manure had been carefully picked out. But then, in Town, Ken had let her buy bushels of good moss peat to break up the soil. Here, where they had the benefit of a local riding stable's well-rotted manure heap for the taking, he wouldn't shell out. The result was that Harriet's back was breaking, her third pair of gloves since October was mud-logged and her nails, despite them, so begrimed that she was going to have to wash her hair two days early.

She'd been moving the strawberries. Ken was deeply opposed. He had that bed earmarked and deep-dug for peas. But this afternoon, while he was off at some local Conservative Party committee meeting, she'd acted on an unworthy impulse and stolen his bed.

The sight of the neat staggered rows of strawberry plants, just budding, countersunk into the newly prepared soil, made her happy, an unaccustomed sensation of late.

She replaced her gloves, crouched, and firmed the first row in. She hated the feeling of the earth under her nails. Not being able, ever, to work the soil bare-handed made some gardening tasks difficult. She fetched the watering can. As she carefully directed the flow around each plant, she could almost hear them settling.

She put the tools tidily away in the shed after scraping them clean. This was a penitent gesture to Ken, who'd organised it so that every implement had its proper place on the wall or the shelves. He liked things to have places, and to be comfortably and safely in them.

Then she went indoors. The cottage was still alien to her. To help make it hers, she polished, washed and cleaned it without mercy, and today in the spring sunshine everything shone and smelt of beeswax and pot-pourri. An American woman who lived in the village had once walked in, paused and cried: 'Oh, I smell popery!' Ken had caught Harriet's eye and countered, 'You do indeed.' Ken was not without a certain dry wit.

Cooking, which had once been a routine, was

now something she used as a sort of therapy. She had, in general, so much more time now. No one to do for other than Ken, who actually got nervy if she cleaned too much, and a house less than half the size of the old one. As for the garden . . .

People in the country thought you must have had a tiny garden in London, but the Marshalls' had been a hundred and seventy feet by forty. There wasn't an inch of it that they hadn't put heart, money and sweat into. She hadn't been able to prevent herself, two weeks ago when she was up for the dentist, driving past the old house, parking, then guiltily sneaking round the back to peer over the fence to see how the new owners had been taking care of her garden.

She'd been rewarded for her prying with the shock of her life. Even now, the sight she had seen had power to rouse something in her far too close to hatred for comfort.

The two cherry trees, husband and wife, were still there, frothing just then like vanilla milkshakes. And the pear. And the peach-tree that had furnished Harriet's family so freely with pink-cheeked fruits in their last August, as if begging them not to leave . . . Yes, they'd left those, the new people. Even barbarians have to eat.

But the wistaria she had planted at the back of the house in the early seventies, when they first moved in, to mark Clem's birth, and which should now be on the verge of smothering the ugly rear balcony with blooms, had been cut down. She could see its poor stump; the sinuous coils of the wood twisting up the rails had been hacked away. And that wasn't the worst. From fence to fence, from top to bottom, saving only the fruit trees in little round earth-circles, they'd laid everything waste with concrete.

She'd raised her head fully above the fence and stared in unbelieving horror. Those damned people had just wiped everything out. Killed the years of loving effort, suffocated the very soil and everything that lived in it.

Despite herself she'd found her eyes fastened to a certain spot now covered with concrete where once her beloved Peace rose had stretched its perfect pink and gold blooms toward the sun. He'd said, the man, that he knew nothing about gardens. She should have taken heed and sent them packing, but Ken had found the cottage by then and fallen in love with it. He'd have sold to Satan for the right money. And money this bunch of turbaned Tamburlaines had in plenty.

So they'd sold. 'Deserted' was the word that came. It was the Sikhs' now, and if they'd chosen to make a desolation and call it a playground for their brood — even while she peered, the view clotted with her sudden tears, a noisy scattering of topknots tied up in handkerchiefs were kicking a football over what had been her rosebed — it was none of her business. But oh, God, how it hurt her. And how she despised herself for going on thinking about it, when she'd said goodbye to the place and *all* it contained, months ago, when she shouldn't have crept back to look,

10

when she deeply believed it was wrong to hate people even when they'd done something *really* unforgivable which this wasn't, by any logical reckoning. And when, to top it all off, she had what she had now.

Absurd to still hanker after it, especially as she'd had the good fortune to exchange that massively demanding old barn in one of London's less salubrious districts for the stuff of most people's dreams — the ineffable *richesse* of the loveliest, most unspoilt part of England.

She cleaned her hands at the sink, where she kept a stiff nailbrush and an orange stick, then wandered to the stable-cut front door and stood staring out at the view. In the foreground lay their beautiful, ready-made lawn and flower garden, left in a state of near-perfection by the previous owner who had employed a professional gardener. Beyond that, a postcard design of hills and fields and trees, rising not only in front of her but all around, 360 degrees of Nature's (and farmer's) wonderland. This the fantasy-money of the London sale had allowed them to buy, and have a lot left over to take care of them until Ken found another job. What kind of ingrate was she to pine secretly for that old Victorian heap, and harbour dark thoughts against its legitimate purchasers?

Instead of making a mug of tea and going to write some letters, Harriet took out the lounging chair and its long cushion for the first time this year and set them up on the lawn. Then she went in again and poured herself a neat brandy, and carried it out, together with

11

the bottle. At the very moment when, quite unbeknownst to her, the police were driving a wedge into the suddenly ruptured and screaming crowd outside South Africa House, Harriet was stretching herself with a little grunt on the damp flowered cotton.

The afternoon was very warm for April and the brandy tasted sublime. The birds sang, the hills smiled down; the tulips, wallflowers, forget-me-nots and bluebells charmed her eyes with their clever colours, and the apple trees were budding almost as sweetly as those they'd planted themselves in the old garden.

I'm an ungrateful woman, she thought, and Ken will never, could never understand it, but I miss horrible Acton. I loved it, with its crunchy mix of people like a good fruit-and-nut bar. What *is* it with Ken and foreigners? Well, whatever, he's shot of them here. Not a black face or a turban in sight. No Italian shrieks from next door, nary a whiff of curry or a Polish shop selling sauerkraut and pickled gerkins and tough seedy bread, in fact nothing that doesn't strictly belong in Ken's stereotyped notion of the English countryside. That's why he's so happy here — one reason. Nothing to grate on him. While I find it all dull, dull, dull. Oh dear. Time for a prayer.

But she had a swig of brandy first. *Holy Mary, Mother of God* . . . Her inner voice went through the well-known formula without her. She was thinking on a much more informal level — she was trying to address the Virgin, but as woman to woman. Even though I shall

12

never fit in here because I don't play tennis and I don't go to the hunt meet and I can't face the W.I. and although I go to church which ought to help, it's the wrong church, and the others who go to it are oddly out of sync with me. But please help me not to get snivelly and low-spirited. To find something to do here, and care about, other than the garden and the polishing. I do not want to get hooked on *Neighbours* or start reading the *Spectator* and the *Telegraph*.

'And just now,' she added aloud, to indicate that she had signed off her prayer, 'I want another little drink, even though it isn't even tea-time.'

★ ★ ★

When Kenneth returned he found her there, fast asleep in the chilling twilight. A bottle which, to his certain knowledge, had been full the night before, wasn't a bit full now. He woke her and piloted her into the house, only a little brusquely. At that point hadn't yet visited the vegetable garden, but even when he did, he quickly got over his annoyance about his purloined pea-bed and refrained from mentioning it. There were more important things to worry about. Finding Harry asleep with the brandy was one of them.

2

About three hours before Kenneth Marshall woke his wife from her tipsy sleep in their idyllic country garden, George, the big Yorkshireman who was visiting London, found himself standing dazed and angry with his big brogues planted on the remains of half a dozen daffodils in Trafalgar Square.

He stood there for some time letting the renewed pedestrian traffic flow past, while he reflected very soberly on the scene he had recently witnessed. Eventually, after wrestling with his practical nature, which was urging him to walk away, he turned abruptly and walked instead up to one of the policemen on duty in front of the Embassy. There were only two of them now.

'Excuse me,' he said tersely. 'Where'd they take 'em?'

'Who, sir?'

'The demonstrators that your lot dragged off.'

'It's Cannon Row as a rule.'

'You mean this sort of — raid — happens often?'

'There are fairly frequent arrests, sir, yes.'

'But how often can they have a big do like today's?'

'Oh, thankfully not often. But as you can see — ' he pointed to a tiny, motley group still clustered round a banner which read HERE WE STAND TILL MANDELA IS FREE ' — they keep a presence here all the time.'

'And get pulled in all the time, eh?'

'If they break the by-laws, which they keep on doing, that's right,' said the young man, seeming brimful of good spirits.

George found his anger, already high, rising. 'Were you here? Just now?'

'Been here since ten this morning.'

'So you saw it?'

'What, sir?'

'Women dragged along the ground. That young black chap kicked.'

The man's face didn't even flicker.

'I didn't see any unnecessary use of force, sir. Certainly nobody got kicked, even though they was resisting arrest.'

'No, they weren't. She said — that lady who was speaking. When the police piled in and she were pulled off the chair, that was the last thing she said. 'Stand firm, but don't resist arrest.' And nobody did.'

The young constable stared straight ahead and didn't answer. His companion remarked equably, 'It's hard to get an overview of crowd trouble when you're part of the crowd, sir. If you have any complaints, you should make them in the proper quarters. Nothing to do with us.'

George turned on his heel, crossed the pavement and hailed a passing tax.

'Cannon Row police station,' he said shortly.

★ ★ ★

15

He was acting in an uncharacteristic way, both in his reaction to the fracas that had brought the demo to an end, and in his impulsive decision to involve himself, however marginally, now. George Reddy was not a man who was easily drawn from his own path, but he was in a rather vulnerable state at present.

His life, though quiet by some standards, had not been devoid of incident. He'd been spared the war, of course; he was only four when it started. But he'd caught the tail-end of National Service and been posted to at least one outpost of the dwindling Empire where he'd seen a few things they don't have on farms on the Yorkshire moors — the Hong Kong police dealing with some street trouble, for one thing. He was shocked inside, but it was really not his problem, and in the Army it didn't do to show that breaking a few foreigners' heads upset you.

Shortly after George's demob, his father died, and he and his brother Derek worked the family farm for the next twenty-five years.

George married at the age of twenty-three, a decent, good-natured local girl called Sally whom he had fancied since they went to school together. She looked as sturdy and durable as one of their upland ewes, born for all the functions of femalekind and destined for survival, but looks are deceptive. The birth of their first baby killed her, and the baby was born dead.

George, who had always thought of himself as a realist first and last, found that the sudden

16

death of his wife and child was, to begin with, too much for him even to believe in, let alone accept. But Derek, and to a lesser extent their neighbours, unexpectedly gave him comfort. The comfort his brother gave came in a strange form — he wept immoderately for Sally himself. It was as if his brother's tears, his overt sharing of the grief, diminished that portion George had to shoulder. After a year or so, the pain relaxed its hold. The immense amount of work he had to share with his brother and their seasonal workers helped.

It was a stolid, rather reclusive life, but there were breaks in it. Derek didn't reckon much to going abroad, but George did. The spell in H.M. Forces had given him a curiosity about other places. Over the years he took package tours to a number of countries in Europe, with France his favourite. He saw something of the police actions against the students in Paris '68, but it didn't have much effect on him at the time. As in Hong Kong, they were not his riots. Although he enjoyed himself abroad and never consciously looked down on foreigners, he never judged them on the same scale of behaviour as English people. At least, not until the miners' strike.

He witnessed parts of that at close quarters. His farm was near enough to a mining town so that some of the miners and their families used the same pubs and shops. One of the wives had gone out of her way to be kind to him, and bring food, at the time of Sally's death. But he didn't realise he felt a particular sense of comradeship with them until things blew up between the miners and the Coal Board in '84.

It was sad and ironic that after so many years of equable companionship, George and Derek's relationship should have foundered over something that did not directly concern them. They developed a bitter running quarrel about the strike. Seated at their scrubbed bachelor table eating their dinners, or tending the sheep, or driving into town in the old van, they argued fiercely over Scargill and the government's intentions with regard to the mines.

'What if she is meaning to shut down some of the uneconomic pits?' Derek would exclaim. 'About time too. She's right — everything's got to be tightened up. How long can the country go on keeping people in work when they're not paying their way? Only outright Commies claim everyone's got a right to a job at the nation's expense! As to a strike, what's that but public blackmail? What if *us* went on strike? Bloody country'd starve to death then! Hope she's laid up plenty of coal stocks, that'll soon stop 'em playing silly buggers!'

Goaded by Derek's my-party-right-or-wrong obtuseness, George decided to lend support to the pickets. He turned out very early one morning at the local pithead. He wasn't able to help much. All he really did was learn that the police in Britain can be just about as malicious and brutish as the ones he had seen knocking Chinese about in Hong Kong, or students in Paris. And this was far worse, because these miners and their wives weren't rioting. They

18

were just defending their livelihoods.

It did something to him, brought him within sight of recognising that the innate superiority, which he had always taken for granted, of his own people over the rest of the world might not be an entirely reliable basis for his own inner equilibrium. He couldn't convince Derek, however. Derek had rejected outright any solidarity with the picketers, whose cause, he claimed — correctly as it turned out — was lost from the outset. As to George's pithead story, he blandly refused to believe in 'bobbies' who came up in force from the south at the behest of a government that was using them like troops, and who lashed out to break up legal pickets; he couldn't conceive of them taunting and jeering at women and kids.

'But I tell you I was there! I saw them. I heard them!' George shouted.

'Folks see and hear what they want to,' Derek said stubbornly.

'And go blind and deaf when it suits them, and all!' George retorted furiously.

From that time on, the two men found it increasingly difficult to share a home. Their relationship had turned sour.

Derek had never married. George, too, after so many years, was in effect a bachelor. Both, as they approached middle age, grew crustier and less willing to compromise. And they were drifting apart in their views, not only political ones. They could no longer see eye to eye on how to run the property. George wanted to see off some of their land for development.

To Derek, such a notion struck at the very foundations of his life. George began to get fed up with the endless drudgery of farming, and hanker for an easier, or at any rate different, life. Derek bluntly accused him of getting old and soft. 'And I don't just mean in the muscles!' And he prodded his finger maddeningly against George's forehead. George wrenched his head away furiously and took a swing at him. Luckily he missed. It was the only time in his adult life when he'd offered violence to anyone. The incident shook them both to their foundations.

Shortly after that, George persuaded Derek, without too much difficulty, to take out a mortgage and buy him out. With no demonstrative goodbyes, George, aged forty-eight, took the money and went off to seek a new life.

* * *

He had always dreamed of buying a place in Devon, so he repaired there at once. The south-west appealed quite strongly after a lifetime of the cold, tough North Country. It felt warm and kind, and aesthetically it filled him with an unaccustomed delight. The people seemed friendly, too. But somewhere deep down he was already missing his brother; he was on the verge of discovering that he was not a loner. He spent most of his evenings in pubs. In the summer of '86, he bought into one.

The brewers had not been keen on a bachelor tenant, and he soon found out that they had a

20

point. Farming without a woman hadn't been easy, but he'd managed because he'd grown up knowing what farming was all about. Being a publican without a woman, when he didn't know B from a bull's foot about running a pub, turned out to be something else. And despite the company of the customers, he still felt lonely.

He decided to look for a wife.

Was it too late? He was knocking fifty. That suddenly seemed to him a terrible age. Not old. Just a terrible, telling age, an age at which a man should have his achievement, and his family, solidly under him like a hill from which he can view the past with satisfaction and the future with some exhilaration. Not an age for starting again, let alone getting down to serious courting.

George wasn't a bad-looking chap for his age, but he was putting on weight and he'd never been a ladies' man. Oh, he had his dreams, why not? A Yorkshire lass, young and slim with flowing hair and a smile to warm him and the customers . . . Rubbish! he knew that wasn't on. What he was actually looking for was a widow in her late thirties. All right then, early forties. But he found it hard to make progress from behind a bar.

That was something he hadn't bargained for. Being a publican was a move downmarket from being a biggish local farmer. He and Derek had never been short of company or invitations, when they wanted to get out and about. They were respected men. Now it was different. The gentry, such as it was, patronised him. To the

21

seasonal grockles from London and abroad, who included the odd nice-looking woman, he might have been invisible. The ordinary locals chatted to him matily enough, but they sensed he was different and soon went back to their own.

He worked all the hours God sent and stifled the knowledge that he was unhappy and had perhaps made a mistake. Distractions apart from work were necessary, some meat for his mental teeth. Derek had been strictly a *Mail* man. Now George read two quality newspapers. He read a lot besides and began to regard himself as well-informed. He loved the radio — loved it. You could keep TV — George preferred to use the screen in his head. And he continued to love the Devon countryside. It was his great compensation. He spent his spare time cycling and walking. That should have kept him fit but he put the lost weight back on with beer, during and after hours. It didn't make him drunk — he loathed drunkenness, and wouldn't stand for it on his premises — but it helped his loneliness.

Then, six months ago, something happened that changed everything. Derek died.

It was an accident, one of those senseless things resulting from a second's inattention during a roof repair. Wick and spry one minute, broken-skulled meat the next . . . The hardest kind of death for a survivor to get to grips with.

When the news came, George walked about for a whole day feeling as if he'd been kicked in the solar plexus. He shut the pub because he couldn't think straight and had to keep sitting down. He'd only been in touch with his brother very casually since the parting. The thought of the years they'd shared, Derek's empathetic good-heartedness when George lost his wife, the stupid political quarrels, and the eighteen months when they hadn't seen each other — the unendurable question of whether Derek's lethal carelessness might have been occasioned by the mental effects of living alone — simply knocked George for six. He hadn't known he cared. That was the truth. The love he must have had for his brother was too deep, too old, too completely taken for granted. Derek had been a year younger than George, who had not reckoned on his ever not being in the world with him.

He went north for the funeral, of course. After it, he went back to the farm and sat again at the old table and put his head on it, and his heavy shoulders heaved with grief.

He had no one to share his sorrow now. His gut-wrenched lonely weeping unlocked his feelings in a way that frightened him. They rose up and threatened to swamp him. Life seemed to offer absolutely nothing, no reason to go on. He'd always thought of himself as a phlegmatic sort; he hadn't known his nature embodied such depths to sink into. In those few days back on the farm, alone as he had never been alone, he realised he had never understood himself, his own feelings and his own needs.

Derek had willed the farm to him. He thought briefly of coming back to it, but he knew that would be the end of him; he would turn into an embittered recluse, if he didn't end up blowing his brains out.

It took him four months to sell to a City gent who didn't care that the land was only good for sheep. What did he know about farming? It was the view, and the 'lovely old house' he wanted. George hadn't realised it was a lovely old house. He was very surprised by the price. Even after the mortgage had been paid off he had more spare cash than he'd ever thought to see in his life.

He'd already offloaded the Devon pub franchise. That added a bit too because, wife or no wife, he'd built up the goodwill. By his own standards he was now a rich man.

What to do with it all? Where to go? Well, south for sure. It was October when Derek died, and George had spent most of the intervening winter months in Yorkshire learning that if one had to live alone, it was better to live in relative warmth, among green hills shaped like reclining women . . . He'd picked this idea up originally from a Maugham short story but it had become his own, like much else he had read. Most people who knew him would have been quite surprised by the constant activity of George's imagination.

On the day he followed Judy to the anti-Apartheid demo, he was in London to register with some estate agents who dealt with decent little farm properties in the south-west.

★ ★ ★

24

'Can I see Mrs Priestman?' Lucky he had a good memory for names.

'Are you a relative?'

'No.'

'I'm sorry, sir, you'll have to wait.'

'Why?'

'She's being questioned.'

'How long's that likely to take?'

'Couple of hours.'

'Sounds more like an interrogation to me.'

'If you'd like to wait, sir, you can take a seat over there.' The duty sergeant indicated a bench, already occupied.

George didn't move. He topped the policeman by five inches.

'Is she all right?'

The man half-closed his eyes and then opened them again.

'Why shouldn't she be, sir?'

'She was rough-handled. Don't tell me she wasn't because I watched it. And that was before your lads got her out of sight in the van.'

'What are you inferring, sir?'

'I'm not *inferring*. I'm not even implying. I'm saying it straight out. The way the police pitched into that crowd was a disgrace.'

'What's your name, sir?' asked the sergeant evenly.

'George Reddy.'

He wrote it down. 'Address?'

With sarcasm in his voice, George said, 'The Savoy Hotel.' It happened to be true — for the one night, he'd given himself a taste of the high-life — but it tickled him through the thick blanket of his anger to see the sergeant's lip curl in a who-do-you-think-you're-kidding sneer. But George's narrow grey gaze obliged him to write it down anyway.

'Were you taking part in the illegal activities outside the Embassy?'

'Illegal? What are you talking about? Since when has peaceful protest and demonstrating been illegal in this country?'

'Peaceful, sir?'

'As far as I could see, it was. At least until your lot come along and turned it into a mêlée.'

The sergeant made another note, indecipherable from upside down. Then he said coolly, 'If you wish to make a statement on the matter, Mr Reddy, it can be arranged. Otherwise I suggest you leave. Mrs Priestman is quite familiar with proceedings here. She can go home when we've finished with her.' He seemed to realise that that didn't sound quite right, and a slow flush of colour rose from his collar. He quickly corrected himself: 'When the formalities have been attended to.'

'She's been here before, then?'

The man permitted himself a thin smile. 'Times without number, sir. Times without number.'

'I'll wait,' said George.

He shared the bench with three youngsters — a pretty, darkskinned girl and two boys. The one next to George had his hair cropped short on top and hanging in limp long wisps over his black leather collar. The ear next to George sported six assorted rings, inserted right through the rim to halfway up. He looked as if he could do with feeding up. George didn't take much notice of the other lad, sitting on the far side of the girl, but he had bushy red hair and seemed to be rather small. George wasn't aware of it, but he had the big man's unconscious contempt for small ones.

The girl's hair was done in dozens of little braids ending in coloured beads, like a short curtain. George elected to speak to her.

'Are you waiting for someone?'

The girl grinned at him sideways and said, too quietly for the man at the desk to hear, 'Same as you. Judy.'

'Were you there?' George asked.

'Course. We just missed getting done too.'

'Specially her,' said the boy with the earrings, indicating at the girl.

'How do you mean?'

He rolled his eyes but said nothing. The sergeant at the desk, responding to what had not been said, looked up to find the black girl's eyes fixed on him. George caught the look of mutual hostility that passed between them — casual and dismissive on the man's part, fathomless and full of rage on the girl's. George shifted his bulk uncomfortably on the bench. More to distract the girl than for information, he asked her, 'Why are you waiting for her?'

The look broke like a rod as she turned away from the policeman.

'Not only her. Everyone that got lifted. We

always have somebody here waiting till they get out, just in case.'

'In case what?'

'Just — in case.'

George felt a cold frisson in his blood. The dawn confrontation at the pithead returned to him, the sneering faces under the helmets, the bared teeth, the provocative, taunting jibes . . . Out there that morning in the semi-dark, in a sort of anarchical no-man's land where no one seemed to be in charge, with a smell of real hatred and defiance in the air — that was one thing. But here in Cannon Row, in broad daylight, why should the police flex their muscles against overintense but clearly decent women and scruffy youngsters who were already under arrest?

'They'd never touch them in here,' he muttered.

The boy next to him and the girl exchanged looks. There was a silence, and then the boy said, indicating the girl with a twitch of his head, 'They strip-searched her last month.'

George was aware that the other boy, the small one at the far end, stiffened and that the face under the ball of rusty hair snapped round, long and pale.

'You mean, policewomen,' said George.

'Course. It was women who did it. But the men stood there. They jeered at her.'

'Jeered?' George's mouth was dry.

The girl's eyes — slightly slanted, unreadable now, George caught himself calling it a black look meaning it was not that of a white person — were again on the policeman.

'At my body,' she said softly.

The boy beyond her made a sound. George caught a rawness of feeling in the inarticulate monosyllable.

George rejected what he'd heard. Everything in him resisted this further jump into disillusion. He was, by nature and nurture, a truster in the basic structure that underpinned his life.

He changed the subject firmly.

'Is she your leader — Mrs Priestman?'

'We don't have leaders,' said the nearer boy and the girl, speaking at once. Then the boy added, 'Not *as such*. Well, we had this leader. She started the picket off when her husband was in jail in Pretoria. Militant, he was, a real hero. Twenty years he done. Then after he got out she started the picket off again in the name of Mandela and the others. Today's the thousandth day.'

'And Mrs Priestman? has she got a husband in prison?'

There was a small silence. The boy started to say something, but the girl jumped in. 'She's very active. She's great. She's been arrested more than anyone.'

'Why?'

The boy rolled his eyes again.

'They don't want us stirring it outside the Racist Embassy, do they? They've done everything they could to break us up. Not just arrests.'

George asked no more. He was having to stop his anger with the police spilling over on to these kids for having caused the frisson, which was still vibrating unpleasantly. He kept irresistibly glancing over his shoulder, and listening, as if he might hear unEnglish sounds coming from other rooms.

3

That same evening, Ken Marshall sat before a log fire in his favourite wing chair with his unfavourite cat on his lap, watching a heavy play on television. Or rather, pretending to watch it. Actually, he was covertly watching his wife Harriet.

He was remembering, uncomfortably, two years ago, when their only son Clem had been fifteen and feeling his oats. It surely wasn't more than that, although Harry behaved as if the world was ending every time she had a bit of a set-to with him.

One day when she was alone in the London house an angry note had shot through the letterbox. It was from some unknown people whose property backed on to theirs, saying Clem had been taking pot-shots in the garden with an air-rifle and had broken one of their windows. Harriet, filled with maternal outrage, had rushed over there and confronted the husband, flatly denying Clem's guilt, saying he didn't have a gun, they wouldn't think of allowing it in a built-up area, and that she resented getting threatening letters without a shred of proof.

The man had responded by declaring he'd seen 'that boy of yours' several times potting at a beer-can on a beanpole. Harriet repressed a start. That pole stuck in the middle of the lawn for no reason . . . She'd kept her end up, but had come home in tears of chagrin and also beset by doubts, which her loyal nature rejected but which her common sense did not. Feeling sneaky, she'd gone up and searched Clem's room, and of course found the blasted gun hidden in his wardrobe.

But that wasn't so bad. Just a scrape really, though Harriet had taken Clem's deceit and her own humiliation bitterly to heart. It was what happened next that had caused the real hassle. She'd had a few brandies, as anyone might to get over the upset, and she was no novice drinker, so she should have known better than to go jumping into the car to fetch Clem home from school just because she couldn't wait an hour to have it out with him. And of course, wasn't it just her luck to foul the kerb, and be caught.

So that was a year when she wasn't allowed to drive. A year when every time the car was needed, she had to call on Ken, or take a bus, or call a taxi. This did wonders indirectly for the original culprit, who was to pass his driving test on his seventeenth birthday, but it did terrible things to poor Harriet. Not least because, although absolutely nothing had happened, she'd gone off on a real king-sized Catholic guilt-trip.

Anyone else would've thought, well, phew, thank God I didn't hit anything more sentient than the kerb, never be such a fool again, et cetera et cetera. Make a bit of a wry joke about the ban to one's closest pals, and carry on. But not Harry.

It wasn't as if *he'd* said a word — well, not after the initial shock — although the whole business was bloody inconvenient, all those afternoons he'd had to get home early to ferry Clem to his tennis or whatever, and Harry to the dentist who naturally had to have his surgery miles away from the nearest bus route . . . but that was life. The trouble was that Harry was really over-scrupulous. In Ken's view, she'd practically wallowed in the old *mea culpa*. But you couldn't say anything. Fatal to try to jolly her out of it, because of the Catholic thing. Difficult at any time, a sort of no-go area — one of several. She'd told him once, before he'd backed right off the subject, that he simply didn't understand about sin. He'd been hurt. Not that sin was a word Ken used — or had ever heard a cradle Catholic mention, come to that — but something he did understand pretty well was guilt. She ought to have known that.

Harriet was a convert. She was very into sin, as if it were a new country she was exploring, not without a certain perverse enjoyment of the fine distinctions, the varying degrees. For instance, for that year when she was banned she climbed so rigorously on the wagon that she'd have considered it a venial sin to so much as put a drop of sherry in a trifle. Tiresome for him too — God knows he was no boozer but with things the way they were at the Bank, his whole department cowering under the threat which eventually materialised, it would have helped, a drink or two at the end of the day. But he felt heartless drinking in front of her so

33

he'd gone on the wagon, too. Well, virtually, He'd reckoned lunchtimes didn't count.

By the time Harry's year was up, the blow at Morgan's had fallen: four hundred and fifty staff shed when the Bank stopped share-trading. Ken had tried the outplacement consultants, at breathstopping cost. Twelve hundred quid down the drain, not their fault, they'd been effectively swamped, and his narrow work experience — twenty-four years in the same field and no 'good back office skills' — hadn't helped. Then at the critical moment his old man had hopped the twig and left them the family house in Barnes, bought in 1948 for six and a half thou, now amazingly worth nearly quarter of a million.

So by the time the ban ended, though Ken was still out of work, life was looking up. There were several good excuses for a celebration, not least having persuaded Harry to move out of London, and having found his dream-cottage. He broke out some champagne, insisted Harry join him, and was pleasantly surprised when she didn't make even a token protest. Penance done, he supposed. That was one thing about 'the Church'. 'Fess up, pay up, and cheer up. They'd toasted each other, the move and the new life, and Ken, an optimist by temperament, put his troubles, and hers, behind them and looked ahead to a happier future.

The end of the ban on both driving and drinking, falling providentially around moving-day, had helped everything along. Not only was it marvellous to have a co-driver again, it stopped her being too uptight about leaving the old house and getting Clem off to boarding school to do his A's. They'd put a fair amount of bubbly away between them over that difficult period. Ken had considered it money well spent to keep them both buoyantly above the scrum. He'd never thought it might — well, start her off again. This afternoon wasn't the first time since they moved to the country that he'd seen signs.

He shifted uneasily in his wing chair, causing the cat to dig its claws warningly into his knees. He yelped and threw it off.

'Bloody animal!' he shouted, making Harriet, who was deep-sunk in the final moments of the play, jump.

'Oh, don't hurt her!' she cried, gathering the disgruntled animal up protectively as if he'd given it a merciless thrashing.

'Who's hurting who? It stuck its claws into me!' he said indignantly, rubbing his punctured knees. Harriet lifted the cat to her face and kissed it. 'Ugh! How can you kiss the filthy thing? It was eating a rat today!'

'Why were you looking at me?'

Now it was he who jumped, at least inwardly. He'd have sworn she had been glued to the play.

'I — ' It was against Ken's nature to dissemble, and despite the bitter price he had once paid for this inability, he still couldn't resist a direct question.

'I'm a bit worried about my Hattie.' He only spoke in this rather soppy voice, and called her pet names, when he was feeling embarrassed or trying to suppress emotion.

'Because, I got a little tight this afternoon?'

'Mm.'

She stroked the cat. Oh, God, don't let her get sin-minded about it! he thought.

'I didn't dream of going near the car. I just sat there in the sun. It was quite harmless, honestly.'

'Of course! I didn't mean anything like that. I'm not reproaching you. Just — '

'Just . . . you don't like me drinking.'

'Drinking alone.'

'But why?'

After an inner struggle, he said, 'Well, you only drink like that when you're not very happy. When you're — tense. I just wondered . . . I mean, down here, everything's so — '

'*Un*tense?'

'I think so.'

'I know you do. You're happy here, aren't you?' She didn't stress the 'you're', at least not that he could detect, but there was an almost maternal note of indulgence in her voice that disquieted him.

He stretched out his legs and watched a commercial without really seeing it. It was one of Harry's inconsistencies to relish certain commercials. This was a Midland Bank one, her current favourite, and when he switched off in the middle he sensed her annoyance.

'I do love it here,' he acknowledged. He was uneasy about saying it. Surely he shouldn't have this terrific sense of wellbeing, of having reached his haven, if she didn't share it . . . But he couldn't really help himself. He couldn't damp down this wonderful energising satisfaction he got from living in the country, couldn't minimise its pleasure even for her sake. He had dreamed of it and desired it for so many years.

He'd been raised in the country; it was in his blood. His roots had kept tugging all through the adult years: university in Salford of all hideous places, later Manchester while he got his early banking experience, then the London Branch.

Ah, the London Branch! Goodbye to the poor provincials, the step up the ladder, the great I-got-there! Marriage, fatherhood, incarceration in a City office, fighting, twice a day, through rush hours that he perceived as a turgid evil-smelling flood like sewage — a constant struggle for survival, a constant battle to subdue his true nature, his true longings. And eventually getting saddled with that huge old-fashioned house with its insatiable demands.

He'd hated that house. Hated Acton. Traffic roared past day and night. They'd lived in a street with a small factory at one end and a pub at the other. The denizens of both, not to mention the big comprehensive school round the corner, streamed past in ones, twos and clots, puffing their fags, filling his front garden with the detritus of their *Sun*-reading, beer-swilling, squalid lives, spraying graffiti on his wall, shouting obscenities at each other in their shrill, awful voices . . . Clem got regularly harassed and occasionally duffed up at the bus-stop; once they were comprehensively and disgustingly burgled. Ken was forever worrying about Harriet, shopping on that grotty High Street, or coming home from the theatre (which she often attended without him) late at night, stubbornly refusing to 'waste money' on a taxi from the station.

The householders all around them — Ken refused to call them neighbours — were nearly all foreigners. Poles, Irish, Indians, German-Jews. Blacks. He kept assuring himself, and Harry, that he had nothing against them, but it wasn't true. Their ways were not his ways, their noises were not his noises, their smells were not his smells. Despite Harriet's genuine efforts — incredibly, she actually relished the multicultural aspects of the area — the Marshalls never had real neighbours-to-call-friends in all the sixteen years they lived there.

And their real friends had to seek them out. Ken had got sick of joking about why they lived in such a down-market district. The real truth was that they had moved in in their early, unplush days because Harry, who at that time expected to have at least two or three more children, had opted for a big house and garden in a ropy district instead of a decent little semi in the suburbs, from which they could have moved on. And by the time they could have afforded to move, she had put so much of herself into the house and garden, making it so much her own, that until the ban, which somehow broke down her resistance to change, she refused to leave it.

Why in God's name had his refined, cultured,

fastidious Harriet loved that godawful place so much? Why, oh why, had she grieved when they shook its dust at last from their feet and headed out of the overpeopled squalor and filth of London into this paradise? And why was she still pining now, if pining she was?

He stood up and came round behind her chair. Leaning over its high back he put his hands rather tentatively on her shoulders. He didn't want to ask her directly, but if she was going to start hitting the brandy seriously, he must.

'And you, Hattie, are you happy here? Be honest.'

She sat very still. Her own hands — those delicate little highbred hands which, so long ago, he had used to watch with incredulous rapture as they condescended to the manual labours of love — were buried in the cat's luxuriant reddish fur, not unlike the colour of his own body-hair. The sight was so suggestive that he felt, for a moment, a shiver of the old desire. But it passed. His body, like his mind, knew the rules and accepted them. All that was done with. Forfeited. Yet still it had the power to leave a sick, sour wash in the pit of his stomach, the residue of loss.

'Ken, don't ask me yet. We've only been here a year — I'm still adjusting. There are certainly things here that I appreciate. Well — love, if you like. It's beautiful, and it's safe, and it's peaceful, and it's — undemanding. Perhaps that's the trouble. I'm not challenged here. And sometimes — ' She stopped.

'Go on, say it.'

'Well. Old friends are a long way off.'

He took his hands away and suppressed a deep sigh. So that was it. The words she had spared him were, *And sometimes I get lonely.*

He went out too much. That was the trouble. He wasn't used to sitting at home. There was so much here he wanted to explore and be part of — he'd joined everything in sight as an antidote to joblessness. He'd been selfish.

'We'll have to do something about that,' he said. And after a silence he added bluffly, 'Now, what about some cocoa?'

'Good idea. I'll take a drop to flavour my brandy.'

He turned in the doorway, his jaw dropped. She was watching his reaction with an eldritch grin.

'ONLY JOKING!' she shouted, like Clem.

He relaxed audibly. They both laughed, and he remembered for the second time in five minutes that they had once had a complete and perfect marriage. And that it was he who had marred it.

★ ★ ★

George had been stuck on the bench in Cannon Row police station for well over an hour, wondering increasingly what he was doing there.

If the police raid hadn't been so brutal, if Judy Priestman's speech had been less compelling and the sergeant on the desk less aggravating, George would have gone off to have his tea long since.

40

Mrs Priestman emerged at last, looking quite unbloodied; in fact, she looked flushed and blooming. Her eyes shot fire. George rose to his feet. The black girl and the boy who'd been talking to him jumped up as well and rushed to hug her, as if she were their mother. The other boy, the one with the bushy hair, stood up too but hung back.

'Are you okay, Judy?'

'Did they give you a rough time?'

'I gave *them* one! Don't worry, I'm fine. Who's this?' she asked, indicating the bush-haired youth.

The black girl led him forward and introduced him. George didn't catch the name. Judy shook hands with him warmly. 'Were you at the demo?'

He nodded; he seemed overcome. He hadn't said a single word all the time, just sat there holding the girl's hand. Now Mrs Priestman said, 'What did you think if it?'

'I thought — ' he croaked, then cleared his throat and said, 'I thought you spoke brilliantly. It was disgusting that you weren't allowed to finish.'

She laughed loudly and cheerily as if they were all at a party, as if the man behind the desk didn't exist. Now suddenly she seemed to remember having seen George before, and she turned to him. 'Hallo, it's you! Did they pull you in, too?' She looked up the scant four inches necessary to meet his eyes. 'I wouldn't fancy being the copper that had to nobble you!'

George thrust out his big hand a bit more

heartily than he'd meant. He squeezed hers harder, too.

'George Reddy. I coom to see if you was all right.' His Yorkshire accent always deepened when he was embarrassed.

'Well, thanks! I am, as you can see.'

There followed a short *sotto voce* conversation. George gathered it was some sort of tactical briefing to the kids about the other detainees. While it was going on, George, standing there awkwardly, suddenly caught himself imagining a scene in which three small policewomen, with the faces of ratting terriers, tried to compel this beautiful strapping Amazon to take her clothes off. When he realised that he was about to let them succeed, he gave his head a sharp shake as if his ears were waterlogged.

In the end she sent the kids off. She gave George a smile and made to follow them.

'Er — can I offer you a lift?' he heard himself say.

Not that he had a car. It would have to be a cab. What was he after? He could see her wondering that, too.

'Well — I want to go home, and it's a fair way, I must warn you. I live in Brixton.'

'Where's that then?'

'Across the river.'

'Sounds nice,' he said inanely.

'My part's the pits,' she returned with a laugh.

He found himself looking at her hair. Honey-blonde, in need of a comb, it lay round her shoulders. The rakish tammy was pushed to the back of her head and her fringe came down to just above the most lovely deep-blue eyes. She wasn't young, she wasn't Yorkshire, and for sure she wasn't small and slender. Her hands looked more capable than graceful. But her smile was right. And her hair flowed. It definitely flowed.

What of it? She was married. She might have a husband in jail for political activities, thousands of miles away. Well. But she was a brave woman, and she was tired, and he had money in his pocket which she evidently hadn't. Couldn't let her ride home on public transport, not after what she'd been through.

He was unaware that a strange, almost strangled chuckle had escaped him. It was the same sound he'd made when triplet lambs were born and they were all ewes, or from the back of a horse on the hunting field when the quarry was suddenly viewed.

'Will you give me a cup of tea if I take you? I'm fair parched, sitting here.' That was right. Keep it light and friendly. Stop staring at her eyes.

'Do you like banana bread?'

'Never heard of it.'

'You haven't lived. Thanks, I shall be bleddy glad of a lift.'

She threw the end of her scarf over her shoulder like a cape, and strode out ahead of him. He heard a muted tinkle, looked down and saw a silver earring on the floor. He picked it up and followed, not seeing the policeman behind him watching with a smirk.

43

4

Clement Marshall stopped growing, knocked a
girl up, and ran away from school, all in the
space of one calendar month. Of course he
didn't know about the first two, or their future
implications, for some time.

Although he was nearly eighteen, he still
harboured hopes that five foot five would not
be the height he was going to have to live at
for the rest of his life. He had, by dint of
ferocious stretching exercises and sheer desperate
mental striving, extended his length by half
an inch over the past year. And that was
real growth — it owed nothing to his other
ploys, such as thick crepe-soled shoes, walking
with a bounce and training his bush of rust-
coloured hair into a well-gelled Lennie Henry
clump. He was keeping up the exercises and
the striving. He also, against his convictions
which were increasingly agnostic, prayed, almost
continuously, for four more inches. He had a lot
of his mother in him, including her height-genes.
Not his father's. It was very unfortunate. His
father was nearly six feet tall. Clem tried not
to hate him for it.

The knocking-up happened on the same April
Saturday as the demonstration in Trafalgar
Square. Until that point, Clem hadn't given
a toss about politics, let alone foreign ones.
But his girlfriend, recently met at a big pop

concert at Wembley for which a party of high achievers had been allowed to travel up from his school, happened to be black and very into the anti-Apartheid movement. Her name, appropriately, was Pleasure — something she hadn't been able to give him much of so far because of his incarceration at boarding school, but the little she had given him had been unspeakably terrific and had changed his entire outlook on life.

This was what he so far knew about Pleasure:

She lived with her mother, whom she sometimes called by her first name, Florence, in Hackney, north London, in a community housing development. Her father had bombed off back to Jamaica some years ago. She was a clever girl — Clem, who was clever too, couldn't have stood her if she wasn't, whatever her other attractions. She had got 8 O-levels, mostly on the science side, just before they turned into GCSEs, at her local comp, and was now in a sixth-form college. She was working for university entrance even though she knew that she might not be able to go because of the financial situation at home, which she described as 'somewhere well south of dire'. She loved her mother achingly but didn't always get on well with her. This, plus some strenuous, but not very advanced, snogging in one of the remoter corridors of Wembley Stadium on the day they had their first encounter, was as much as Clem knew of her until the day of the demo. But in the interim it was enough to prevent his thinking rationally or with any great concentration of anything else.

He'd managed to wangle an exeat for the weekend of the demo after Pleasure wrote to him at school and asked if he'd like to attend the event with her. She enclosed some fiery literature about the iniquities of Apartheid and the collusive, racist, imperialist British government which was all news to Clem, but which he drank up. He was hating school so much that his dissatisfaction spilled out into the wider Establishment.

Of course his parents, whom he'd to involve, supposed the exeat was to visit them. That was a nuisance because he wanted to spend the whole weekend in London, if not *with* Pleasure, at least around her. He told them he'd be down on Sunday and was spending the Saturday with a 'chum' in Town. The word 'chum' nearly choked him when he'd used it over the phone, but it was a conscious and canny choice. It was his father's word and invariably meant a person of one's own sex.

In planning the outing he'd airily decided that he might have to 'sleep rough'; he knew the expression, and that lots of young people did it, but not what it actually involved. He thought it would be an experience, something to talk about when he got back to school. As it happened, it was not necessary.

The day of the demo was a revelation to him, or rather a series of them. He enjoyed every minute of it. First of all, being met by Pleasure at the station, in the purlieus of which they shared a hot croissant and coffee; wandering about London hand in hand with her on a sunny April Saturday provided the most exquisite contrast to the dismal rigours and piety and general disgustingness of school. He felt sure, seeing her again — with her beautiful beaded hair, her skin the colour and shininess of the chocolate poured over the Applause bar in the telly ad, her smiling eyes and best of all, her small stature — she was just half an inch, that critical, hard-won half-inch shorter than he was — that he was truly and possibly even permanently in love.

Then, the demo itself was really fantastic — its anarchic quality, that loud-voiced first woman slagging off the fuzz right to their teeth, and before that the chanting, in which first Pleasure and then he full-throatedly joined:

'CLOSE — DOWN — THIS NEST OF SPIES!
STOP THEIR MURDERS, STOP THEIR LIES!'

It was all immensely satisfying, almost literally intoxicating.

Clem regarded himself as a natural rebel. He'd rebelled at home — buying and smuggling in that airgun, for example, had been an act of pure rebellion, and there'd been others — but it didn't usually feel one hundred percent good because at bottom he knew his parents were okay. But the South African government wasn't okay, and the Thatcher government was obviously the absolute pits, whatever some of the guys at school with posh fathers said. It felt really good to stand in the heart of London outside this huge, imposing building, which had

'Establishment' written all over it, with hundreds of other people, mainly kids in enviously off-beat and scruffy gear, shouting your lungs out in a good, clean cause.

And when the cops encircled them and then broke into the crowd from the rear, and began yanking people off, that was the biggest kick of all. He'd never before experienced the charge afforded by healthy, righteous fury. He saw them kick a black youth while he was lying on the ground, and cart off the middle-aged woman in the tam-o'-shanter who'd been speaking, one to each limb as if she were a sack of peat. The screams and the pressure of the crowd, the sense of unity against injustice — the whole thing had flooded his veins with adrenaline and made him forget the relative sizes and strengths of himself and the police. He wanted to pitch in, hurl himself at them, punch their heads . . . but Pleasure grabbed him and pulled him bodily out of the crowd. He tried to resist, but she had him clear before he could dig his feet in.

He hadn't realised how sexually stimulating that kind of raw crowd-excitement can be until Pleasure led him round the corner at a run, and down the steps leading to the crypt of St Martin-in-the-Fields. There, standing one step below him so that, however temporarily and relatively, his prayer was answered, she threw her arms around him and kissed him with lips and tongue as she had not kissed him at Wembley, and as he had never been kissed before. She was clinging to him as if they'd just escaped from an earthquake.

He promptly lost all sense of where they were. His hand found her breast, albeit through her blouse, and the sensation, coming on top of all that excitement, made him drunk, and sent him (as he described it to himself later) into some wild new dimension of experience.

'I love you!' he almost shouted as he surfaced from the breast-touching like a diver bursting up from the depths of the sea.

'Hey,' she said softly. 'Take it easy.' She drew herself gently out of his arms and made him move aside on the stairs to let some people pass.

'Where can we go?' he asked her, wild-eyed and panting, the second they'd gone. This was it, the moment he'd always hoped would come, when the physical feelings were so compelling that he wouldn't have trouble with his Catholic side afterwards, or at least nothing he felt he couldn't handle.

She smiled at him tenderly and shook her head. He felt shattered. Why wasn't she raging with lust — yes, lust, there was nothing wrong with lust! — the way he was? Yet when she took his hand and led him back up to the street, and made him walk about until his jeans felt more as if they fitted him and his sweat had dried on his face and his breathing became normal — that was something he had to admire. It was just as well one of them kept control. And she talked to him while she did it, about how you didn't say you loved someone straight away when you felt it, but let it grow a bit to make sure.

'But don't you love me, Pleasure?' he implored

her. 'I haven't been able to stop thinking about you since I first saw you.'

They were walking along a broad street now, through sunlight and people and traffic. Pleasure was setting a brisk pace. Her plait-beads twinkled in the sun, blue, green, red, yellow, and made a small jostling sound when she agitated them. She did it now, but he couldn't decide if it was a nod or a shake.

'Clem, you're very nice and you're clever and fun. But I don't want to say I love you yet. That's something I've never said to anyone. And with you it's too early.'

'But you let me kiss you. That first day. And you wrote to me.'

She laughed at him a little. 'Oh, you are a proper Catholic, not like me! We met when the music was strong and I was full of it. I always need to kiss when I feel like that. And when I did kiss you, I liked it better than I usually do — I liked *you* better. Is it bad to kiss when you feel like it, even if you don't really know the person? I felt like it then because of the music, and I felt like it even more just now.'

'I felt like going beyond just kissing,' he said hoarsely, not daring to look at her.

'Well,' she said reasonably, 'that's okay. Why not? We might one day — if everything felt right.'

His heart leapt into his gullet, but he swallowed it down again. *Why not?* Why not just do it whenever you felt like it? Ha! Because you couldn't, you mustn't, it was wrong, it was a sin, it was dangerous.

You could get clap, you could get herpes, you could get Aids, you could get totally stitched, not least with yourself. Clem's upbringing had inevitably given him strong sexual hang-ups, but he was aware of them and working very hard to get rid of them. Just because his mother was a Catholic convert, just because she'd sent him to that lousy school where they were pumping conventional morality backed up with just a whiff of modernised hellfire into you night and day, didn't mean there were to be no cakes and ale for Clem, if *he* had anything to say about it.

Unluckily, now that for the first time there really was something in the wind, all his conditioning raced back upon him. He met Pleasure's eyes, full of the untrammelled joy of life. Okay, he thought, you've put all the possible drawbacks on one arm of the scale, now put just seeing her naked — *just that* — in the other. He did so, and the scale fell over on its side. He threw back his head and laughed. and put his arm round her. He felt crazy, happy and excited. Almost free. Not quite, but he was getting there.

They had turned left off the main road, and were climbing steps up to the entrance of a big building. He stopped.

'Hey, where are we?'

'This is a police station,' Pleasure said cheerfully.

'Wha-at? What are we doing here?'

'Didn't I tell you? I'm on the committee of the picket, and I promised I'd come here after the demo if there were any arrests, and wait for our people to come out.'

'What for?'

'Well, you never know whether the police will thump them about, or if not, they can still feel shaken up — specially if it's their first time. So we always have a couple of people here to wait for them and make sure they're okay. And today they lifted Judy, so I must be here. They really have it in for her.'

'But how long do we have to stay here?' Clem almost wailed. A cop-shop! What a way to spend the little time he had with her!

She smiled straight into his eyes. God! Her teeth were so beautiful, and now he had touched them with his tongue, they belonged in a special way to him and he could feel proud of them. He put his hands round her waist, but she wouldn't have it.

'Not now, Clem. Come on, we must go in. Perhaps it won't be for long. And then . . . '

His mouth went dry. 'Then?'

She looked down at the pavement and he noticed her braided hair in detail, and the brown shiny-clean scalp in between. God! he thought again. She's so *exotic*! He couldn't help this thought. It was part of her appeal. He used to dream of having a jewish girlfriend — which would have driven his dad spare — but a black girl, even in theory never mind the glory of the reality, was twenty times better.

'Then I thought, if I'm not needed, you might like to come back home for a cup of tea or something.'

She didn't mention that her mum was on

night-shift at the hospital, and wouldn't be back till early in the morning. There was definitely something about this boy. She was surprised at herself for being attracted to him, small and immature-looking as he was, with his soft white tender hands and eager eyes. Perhaps it was the contrast to her one serious previous boyfriend who had been big, black, tough and not so gentle. He had initiated her with more energy than finesse, and his sexual activity with her subsequently was quite in keeping with his few words for it, of which 'screwing' was the commonest currency. Pleasure, though headed for a life on the science side, had read other things, including some poetry, and wondered what it felt like to be *made love to*, as distinct from screwed. Whatever Clem's shortcomings (ha-ha), she divined that he was not the screwing kind.

She hadn't firmly decided anything yet, but if he went on being so nice, she might just do it with him — give him a trial, so to speak.

'What do you think?' she prompted his speechlessness.

'Yes,' Clem croaked. 'I could do with — a cup of tea.'

★ ★ ★

Judy and George sat in the taxi and talked all the way to Brixton.

She had been a little doubtful about accepting his offer, but by the time they got to her street, her doubts had vanished. He was a nice, straight,

53

fifty-year-old guy, square as a box and probably out of the Ark politically, but not on the make. The kind she could be doing with a few more of. Most of the men she knew seemed to be under twenty and needing political enlightenment and mothering. She was quite adroit at both but it could get a bit much, or rather, little.

She got out her key while George paid the taxi God knows what. That was another point in his favour; he evidently had a bit of spare dosh, also practically unheard-of among her regular acquaintance. Judy cared nothing for money as such, but there was no denying that twelve years of not having anything like enough made you, ideology notwithstanding, aware of its merits.

Her flat was in the basement of a big peeling-fronted Edwardian house. There was windblown trash in the area near the door. As she opened it, her dog Zulu came to meet her, bent in a U of welcome, presenting both ends, one grinning and the other — oddly indecent, because virtually tailless — waggling itself almost off the ground.

'Oh! You've a dog, I see!' exclaimed George happily. He bent to greet him. 'Till I left the farm, there was always a dog in my life, but never a bald-looking specimen like this. Bull-terrier and what?'

'What *not*? Every breed with horrible looks and heavenly natures. Can I take your coat?'

'Where'd you get him? He's a nice chap. Aren't you a nice chap?' George inquired, rubbing the dog's cropped ears. Zulu gave every sign of concurrence and mutual approval.

'I didn't get him; he got me. You think I went out of my way to land myself with another consumer? I came home late one night, dead beat, and there he was on the doorstep, the answer to a grass widow's prayer. I'm silly about him.'

The big semi-basement room was half-kitchen and half-living room. It was in a fair old mess, and as she progressed toward the Aga, which reposed in a tiled alcove, giving out a beneficent warmth, Judy made a half-hearted effort to pick things up and straighten chairs, rugs and tables.

'Those little fuckwits might have cleared up a bit,' she said without rancour.

'Who?' asked George. He'd already learnt that she swore like a navvy and was trying hard not to be inwardly priggish about it. His dead wife Sally had had a father who slapped any of his children who even said 'damn'.

'The pickies . . . the ones without a place to sleep.' She gathered some newspapers into a rough pile on the floor, and threw two cushions onto a worn armchair. Most of the furniture looked as if it had been rescued from municipal rubbish dumps, especially the chairs — one creaky wicker, others with the square-armed look of the fifties still covered in their original mud-coloured moquette, but all enlivened by an assortment of patchwork, tapestry and mirror-work cushions. The seat of the most comfortable-looking was a white nest of Zulu-hairs. There was some contradiction there, George thought in passing. Surely Zulu shouldn't be *white* . . . ?

'You mean you run this place as a sort of dosshouse for the young homeless?'

'You could put it like that. They're not just any homeless kids though, they're the ones who come on the picket.'

'Can't you make a rule that they clean up after themselves?'

She laughed ruefully. 'Oh, I do. I'm dead firm about it! And they try. But most of them have come from domestic set-ups so deep down disorderly, at every level, that they don't know what clean-and-tidy really means, let alone how to achieve it.'

'Where do they sleep?'

'Can't you tell? On the floor, on chairs . . . in Tina's room now she's buggered off.'

'Tina?'

'My daughter,' she said in a short, let's-keep-off-this-one tone. She reached the Aga and George drifted to a big table, a solid old oak pull-out one with graceless bulbous legs, much scarred with burns and rings. He looked around. Unconsciously he was racking up data about her from the home she'd made for herself, obviously on very little. His eyes were drawn to the dresser, not fashionable stripped pine but painted Muslim blue, with a wild assortment of street-market cullings — ornaments, dishes, mugs and imitation Art Deco jugs among a multitude of other things crowding its shelves and hanging from its hooks. He liked that. Not his taste, but then, as he was the first to recognise, he hadn't much when it came to décor. Everywhere he'd ever lived was just a place to live.

On the walls were a lot of posters. One, which was framed, showed a young, burly-looking black man with sleepy eyes.

'Who's that?' unwarily inquired George while Judy stoked the Aga and shifted a kettle on it.

She turned round, looked, and gaped at him. 'Ach, man, you're joking.'

'No?'

'Don't you know that's him — Nelson?'

'Who? Oh, Mandela!' And after the briefest pause, he compounded his crime. 'I thought he'd be older.'

She continued to stare at him. She really couldn't believe it. It was as if he'd shown unfamiliarity with a portrait of the Queen. Except that, in her eyes, this was an ignorance far and away less excusable.

'Of course he's *older*,' she said, unable to help using a tone of incredulity. 'He's nearly seventy now. That's how he looked before they imprisoned him.'

'I'm sorry,' George said. 'I should have known that.'

'You certainly should!'

She turned away, feeling ludicrously disappointed. She had begun, even so early in the acquaintance, to hope that this solid-looking well-to-do man might evolve into a friend. Not a comrade — that he could never be. (*Thought he'd be older . . . Christ!*) But a friend, a man friend. God knows she could do with one. And here he was, getting off on the wrongest possible

57

foot. It was obviously hopeless.

George sensed the sudden drop in the interest-quotient.

'I'm afraid South Africa's a bit outside my orbit.'

'You've just made that very obvious.'

'I bet you don't know a lot about the conditions of farmers in Yorkshire,' he said, mildly defensive.

'Farmers in Yorkshire may be having hard times,' she said tersely, with her back to him, 'but one in four of their children aren't in danger of dying of malnourishment. They aren't deprived of any political power and shoved about as if they were cattle. They're not being routinely shot and tortured and killed.'

He was taken aback. He sensed the passion behind her words and knew he had blundered seriously; one moment's reflection and he'd have realised that was an *old* photo of Mandela — her hero, obviously. Bloody fool, he upbraided himself. But his male vanity got in the way of a direct apology.

'Not everyone can know about all the wrongs of this world.'

She turned, looking tense, the kettle in her hand.

'I have to say this,' she said, 'and not just because it's my thing. South Africa is an exceptional case. Everyone should know enough about the wrongs of South Africa to be able to know which side of the fence they're on. Only liberals sit on fences on an issue as clear as that. Or make fatuous excuses for their ignorance.'

'What's wrong with liberals? I'm one.'

'Yes, I thought you were,' she said enigmatically, pouring boiling water into two mugs.

'What's wrong with liberals?' he asked again.

'They give themselves righteous airs about seeing all sides, they never actually *do* anything, and when it comes to it they're too busy nursing their intellectual doubts to be able to recognise the last photograph taken of Nelson Mandela before he was put away for life,' she said levelly. 'Here's your tea.' She plonked it down on the table in front of him.

'I take milk,' he said.

'In the fridge.'

He looked round for the fridge, located it across the room, and went stolidly to fetch the milk. Then he returned to the table, hitched forward a chair, poured the milk into his tea and said, 'Do I have to go to the shops to get some sugar?'

She made a noise with her lips, and took a bowl off the dresser. The sugar was a bit dusty but he managed to get at the underneath part and take two large spoonfuls.

'I don't want to seem greedy, but what was that banana cake you mentioned? Or do only illiberal visitors get that?'

He'd been smelling it, a hot-country sugar smell, since he came in. Now she opened the side oven of the Aga and brought out a big baking tin. Grudgingly, as it seemed to him, she cut him a piece and dug it out of the tin.

'It's banana bread, not cake.'

'I repeat: not everybody can know the facts

about everything. And before you chastise me any further, I do know even very good food is not in the same category with politics.'

She couldn't help watching him while he bit into it, and responding like any a-political cook to the grin that came over his face.

'Bread be buggered, it's cake is this, but it's right good stuff.' Subconsciously he registered that it was rather nice to be able to swear mildly in front of a woman.

She sat opposite him across the table and lit a cigarette. She'd smoked all the way home in the taxi. He didn't like that — he'd never smoked and he thought, with all the information there was now, anyone who did must be stupid. But he'd managed not to say anything before and he certainly wasn't about to put his foot in it with her again now, even in a teasing way.

'I'm sorry I didn't recognise him,' he said. 'To be perfectly honest, I don't think I've ever seen a picture of him before. They're not exactly all over the papers, you know. He's been away a long time.'

'Twenty-six years.'

'And nobody knows what he looks like now?'

She shook her head. 'He doesn't allow photos of himself to be taken.'

'Has he got the say on that?'

'He's the most important prisoner they have. He has special treatment. Not at first, of course. When he was on Robben Island in the beginning, they treated him as badly as all the other black prisoners. Terrible things . . . he broke stones for ten years, and froze every winter. He really suffered, in a way the white politicals never do.'

'Like your husband?'

Her eyes flickered. He interpreted this as a reaction to his having found out more about her than she'd told him. But all she said was, 'But it's different now, of course — for Nelson. Now they treat him better. He's not on the Island now. He gets visitors and has privileges. In my opinion they're fattening him up, so to speak, for when they decide to let him out.'

'Why should they let him out?'

'You'll see — they'll have to. If only this country would join in the sanctions, it would happen sooner.'

'Aren't they afraid of his influence?'

'They're more afraid of what would happen if they didn't keep him in good health,' she said dryly. 'And soon enough they're going to need his leadership, to help make the new South Africa.'

George had been racking his brains for bits of information that would make him seem a bit more knowledgeable, and now one surfaced.

'Why doesn't he agree to renounce violence?'

'Obviously because the whole power-struggle is so uneven. If the ANC renounced the armed struggle, they'd be denying their right to oppose violence with violence. They'd be disarming themselves. Peaceful protest was tried, and failed, long years ago. The government just crushed it.'

'In your time? I mean, when you were still in South Africa?'

'*Umkhonto We Sizwe* had been started, as a reaction to years of government brutality, by the time I joined the movement. I suppose you don't know what that is?' she asked, trying to keep the edge out of her voice. 'Spear of the Nation. That was the branch of the movement that undertook what you'd call illegal or violent actions, sabotage and so on.'

'Was your husband part of that?'

'Yes,' she said. 'He was part of that.'

'Is he in for life as well?'

He saw her stiffen. Another sore subject. But why? Whatever the man had done, *she* must regard him as a hero. But her silence lasted so long that he felt constrained to add, 'Of course, I know it's none of my business.'

Judy had an urgent decision to make. How much to tell him? Not many people in this country knew the whole truth. Those who did — Abby, who was the nearest thing she had to a best friend, and the others on the executive committee — well, they had to know; she couldn't conceal vital information from such close comrades. They were sworn to secrecy. They understood. They valued her for what she was, they respected the efforts she made to prop up the lie that underpinned her life with something worthy, something honest and clean enough to outweigh the other, not be tainted by it . . . but this man? He knew nothing about the wider situation which had given birth to the lie. She couldn't trust him with the truth, though it prodded in her throat to be let out.

But she couldn't, she found, give voice to

the lie direct, not to this stolid, bone-straight English ignoramus whom she had already begun — against her better judgement — to like. So she told a half-truth.

'My husband isn't in jail. He's in hiding.'

'In this country?'

She looked into his eyes but she wasn't thinking about him, or even his question. As it happened, her mind had flipped away from her husband Jordan, whom she didn't always enjoy thinking about, and back to Mandela, whom she did. Would he even be recognisable, poor Nelson, after all these years of hardship? She often tried to picture him as he might look now. An old man. Sometimes she indulged in conversations with him in her head. Once she had dared to 'ask' him if it had been worth it. The whole of his middle life, the years when he should have been with Winnie and his family, in the forefront of the struggle, lost, forfeited. He had looked at her with mild astonishment and said simply, like someone answering a child's silly question, 'Yes,' with an 'of course' implied. He had done his duty.

Jordan would not be able to say that.

She gave a deep, hollow sigh.

'I can't really answer your questions,' she said, 'but not because it's not your business. You see, being in hiding means just that — that there's something to hide from, something to fear. I never talk about him.'

'Sorry,' he said awkwardly.

To get over the moment, the put-down even if she didn't mean it like that, he drew towards him a tabloid lying at the far end of the table. 'Good heavens, do you read this?' he asked in a startled voice.

'I do, yes,' she said. 'All us Commies do. It's our newspaper, you see.'

He couldn't help himself. He gaped at her, holding the *Morning Star* in his hand.

'Don't tell me you're really a Communist!'

'I'm a Marxist — Leninist, unrepentant, unreconstructed, unregenerate and unblushing. So you'd better get used to the idea.'

He looked at her for another minute. Then he put his head down on the table with a groan.

'I don't think I'm up to this,' he said in a muffled voice.

'Go home then,' she said. 'I'll call you a minicab.'

Zulu, mistaking George's distress, waddled over anxiously and pushed his long scarred white nose sympathetically into George's crotch under the table.

George raised his head. 'I'm not ready to leave yet,' he said.

5

Clem's parents, Harriet and Kenneth, slept in twin beds.

Even after twelve years, Ken never climbed into his without remembering, however fleetingly, what had become of the beautiful, companionable, sexy queensized double they had had once.

Tonight he thought about it more than usual because of a tiny incident. As he and Harriet were jostling politely for the bathroom basin, he had put both hands on her waist through her thin cotton pyjamas to shift her to one side, and been poignantly aware of the warmth of her once-his flesh. Memories, long marginalised, re-presented themselves.

Clem had been five at the time and Harriet, strictly according to plan (she wasn't a Catholic then, and was not constrained from planning) was pregnant for the second time. Kenneth was delighted but frustrated. Harriet, who had a normal relish for sex at other times, was not keen just then. And Kenneth met a girl — she was Clem's playschool teacher, in fact — and had a brief affair with her.

It was all very oh-be-joyful at first, no commitments, completely discreet, and he would almost certainly have got clean away with it except that, being a closet romantic, he allowed the girl to go to his head. He had no thought of leaving his family, and the girl herself was quite alarmed at the unlooked-for rise in the intensity level, but Kenneth, his priorities turned on their heads, found himself telling Harriet all about it at the first unwary cue she supplied. The thing was, his love for her felt unimpaired. He wanted to be straight with her, and even to get the benefit of her advice. This, and not the affair itself, he was to look back on as the biggest single error of his life.

Harriet took it like a dose of arsenic. She didn't rant and rave or hit him or leave him; she simply fell ill with it. There were times to come when he would have loved to think that in some way she was putting it on, but she wasn't. It poisoned her.

She lost the baby the next night. It was halfway through its term. Her ordeal occurred in the downstairs bathroom while Ken lay sleeping. She never spoke of it beyond the bald words, out of a skull-like face, the next morning: 'I lost the baby in the night. It was a girl.' He was dumbstruck. Literally he could say nothing, not even a word of sympathy, or 'Why didn't you call me to help you?' much less any reference to practical details. He could only imagine — and Ken, not the most imaginative of men by nature, had never really been able to stop imagining — the scene in the bathroom. She had dealt with it alone, presumably in acute pain, and had to handle what would have been their daughter. Where he had always clamped down on his imagination was when it offered him possible solutions to the dreadful problem of disposal.

From then on Ken watched her dwindling, like the light on the TV screen when you switch off; the bright square of her personality, of their relationship, shrank to a dot. For months he thought he was watching her slowly die. She never threatened to kill herself, but each day he went to work believing he might come home to find she had. He was quite convinced their marriage was dead. His anguish was so acute he couldn't even think about the other girl — he never saw her again. The only thing that kept them going was Clem. They both thought they were behaving normally before him.

Ken was almost relieved when Harriet told him about the Church. He had known subconsciously that it would take something cataclysmic to save them. Once he would have been shocked, opposed, fearful that such a radical departure would put a barrier between them. Now the barrier was there, so high they were strangers on either side of it. He felt that if becoming a Catholic gave her back to herself, even in part, some part of that part might hew to him. If that could happen, he might begin to forgive himself.

He read everything he could find about Catholicism, and two things stood out. One, he could never follow her into these arcane realms. Kenneth was not religiously inclined, and took the notion of virgin births and the consuming of flesh and blood in the Eucharist literally; they struck him as at best nauseating, at worst barbaric, at all times totally and fundamentally unbelievable, un-enter-into-able. And, two, no

67

divorce. Marriage 'in the fullest sense' (vide the books) to be stuck to, no matter what. There was hope for him in that. He did not discourage her.

Little by little he watched the trembling dot of light expanding as she returned. Changed: half-stolen from him by this great alien Thing to which she had given herself, with strange tenets and practices he couldn't share or understand. But this was part of the price. He took what she had to give him and was grateful. And little by little he found he had a marriage of sorts left, after all.

Sex was included, at first. It was part of the teaching: marriage whole and complete. Sin was not just doing wrong, but not doing right. Trembling with guilt and hope, Kenneth tenderly did his part. She lay there, acquiescent, unmoved and unmoving . . . After a week he stopped. He did not repeat the experiment.

Then it was she who had to come to him. Irony of ironies!

'But we must. It's part of the contract.'

For the first time — the very first — he cracked.

'I'm making love to you, not a bloody marriage certificate! If you don't respond, I'd rather live like one of your fucking priests!'

She cried then. In all those terrible months he had never seen her cry. He gathered her up, his darling whom he'd betrayed and damaged in his stupid, stupid weakness, and they clung together, drowning in their own deepest natures.

'I can't! she cried. 'Oh, Ken! Please believe

me, I would if I could! I still love you, but I can't feel anything down there, it's all dead and cold!'

Stricken, he let her go. Later, he grew angry. The guilt made him angry. Their baby — her decline — her need of the Church — and now this. Her precious sensuality, the sweet passion that had informed their whole relationship and that had given them, among other joys, their son: with his bit of a fling and his inability to shut his trap about it, he had killed that, too. It was too much for him to bear. The accumulation of feeling in his basically insecure, phlegmatic nature drove him to a seemingly small, but actually crucial, domestic edge.

Even though he knew in his heart that she was not lying, that she couldn't help herself, he had to make some gesture of rage at the disproportion of his punishment. He went out and bought twin beds.

He planned it like a military operation. He arranged for the new beds to be delivered on a Saturday when he would be at home and she would be at a friend's with Clem. The moment she'd gone, he tore the sheets from their marriage bed, and strengthened by despair dragged the mattress downstairs, dismantled the rest with blows from a hammer and carried it, in three separate journeys in and on the Cortina, to the dump. He would never forget the sight of the dismembered corpse of the bed in which he had experienced the most extreme feelings he was capable of, lying upon the giant squalid heap of council rubbish.

The men came with the other beds. Sweating and with teeth clenched, Ken helped set them up, wedging a bedside table between them. Only then did he realise that they had no single sheets and blankets. Clem's bed was child-sized, and the spare bed was a double. The sight of those two bright new bare mattresses and the gap between them filled him with such misery — and terror for what Harry would feel and say when she saw what he'd done — that he felt for the only time in his life that to cut his throat would be a rational action. Instead he wept and got drunk.

But when she returned and walked into the bedroom, there was no reaction. The anticlimax was almost unendurable. She stayed up there some time (making up the beds with double sheets, as it turned out) while he shivered and sweated like a frightened horse below. Then she came down and got on with the dinner.

At bedtime she said, 'I understand why you did it without asking me. I don't blame you — it's for the best really. I just hope you won't mind that I'll have to tell Father Creighton that it's your idea. Otherwise I'll have to confess it every week.'

Kenneth said nothing. He couldn't trust himself to speak. The thought of her telling Father Anybody filled him with such a sense of outrage and betrayal that he wanted to lay about him, smash everything around him, and then go out and smash the priest. Though he hung on to his self-control, his mind was in turmoil for weeks. He himself was now poisoned

70

with hatred — for her, for her bloody intrusive Father Bunloaf, for the Catholic Church, for everybody but himself. Then he realised he was beginning to accept it and he also realised why. Her betrayal cancelled out his.

The most extraordinary thing was that, despite all this, they stayed together. Partly — initially — it was a matter of duty, hers to her new faith, his to his marriage vows and to his guilt, both to their son. But as they got on with life, gradually a kind of normality reasserted itself. Scabs formed, dropped off; the scars faded. They raised Clem, were companionable, shared their everyday problems, made jokes. Ken never went with another woman. The whole idea of sex was soured for him as for her.

He made up for it with constant activity. Against his former bent, which was sociable but basically home-oriented, he joined things. He played bridge. He played golf. He went to football games with Clem, and took up tennis for his sake. A basically all-thumbs man, he studied DIY: he decorated parts of the house and got a kick out of it. He was a model husband. And he stopped, early on, hating his wife and went back to loving her. He loved her because he couldn't help loving her, because, apart from this one thing which he knew he had triggered, he found her lovable.

And now every night, like tonight, they went to bed together, after their fashion. They undressed, jostled for the bathroom, chatted, and climbed into their separate beds, with their separate reading lamps, like a married couple in

71

an old, Hays-Office Hollywood movie; read for a bit, and one by one, turned out the lights and 'tuggled down', as Clem had used to say. A few final, sleepy words, usually including ' 'Night', and off to sleep. That's what they did, all unknowing, while their son was in the process of rendering them grandparents.

★ ★ ★

Pleasure's mother's flat in Hackney was in a six-storey block built in the architecturally regrettable sixties. Clem was shocked by it. It had open balconies running around the sides and lifts that stank.

Pleasure noticed his wrinkled nose, smiled to herself, but said nothing. She had known he would react like this — how could he not? Part of her did, too. But unlike him, she had an overview. She knew that she and her mother were lucky to have a flat in London at all, and extra lucky that it was in a block, and a neighbourhood, where the other residents were a good-natured, mixed lot and where so far they had never had anything other than post and papers through their well-sprung letterbox.

The flat itself was awful too, Clem thought, in a different way. Due to bad ventilation, it smelt of stale cooking (Pleasure did not notice this) and damp. The decor startled him. The narrow front room into which she led him, which overlooked the open corridor, had a different wallpaper on each wall. Once, when they still lived in Acton, Clem had gone shopping for wallpaper with his mother. He had been drawn to the bright-patterned ones but she had poohpoohed them, saying they were ghastly. Now he saw them on real walls and he had to agree with her.

One paper was printed with an ivy-twined trellis. Another had a cubist design. The big wall facing the window was entirely covered with a huge poster-like picture of a bright blue Swiss lake with chalets on its shores and snow-capped mountains shawled in pine trees. The ceiling was covered with polystyrene tiles, painted blue like a continuation of the sky in the picture. There were bright glass and china ornaments everywhere, and framed photographic portraits on the walls, including one of Pleasure. The carpet was brown with repeated orange swirls and tiny white flowers, now grey. There was no fireplace. The focus of all the seating was the television.

He was not aware that he had let go of Pleasure's hand while he took in all this basic difference between their backgrounds, between her parents and his. Now she came to his side after hanging up their anoraks, and touched his shoulder. 'Clem, please don't say anything about my mother's taste.'

He started, and flushed. 'Of course not! I — '

'You're used to the dark and greyness in the weather, and so am I. We were born to it. But Florence and Daddy were used to sunshine and bright hot colours, and bright hot people. I didn't understand myself, until I visited Daddy in Kingston.'

'Yes, I see,' said Clem, who didn't at first, wondering why things should be noticeably brighter in Surrey, but then he realised. He was still staring at the Swiss lake, wondering why it was a Swiss lake and not a scene of palm trees against the truly-blue ocean which would remind them of home. Perhaps there were no wall-sized posters of Jamaica available.

'My room is done up to suit me. Mum thinks it's very dull. Come and see.'

He followed her, trembling inwardly with excitement, into a tiny bedroom, long and narrow like the living room. Here the walls were plain, painted in two shades of terracotta, and the decorations were radical in another fashion — there was a poster of Che Guevara, for instance, and one of a black woman who he later learnt was Winnie Mandela. There was also a framed sign that read:

FOR EVIL TO TRIUMPH
IT IS ONLY NECESSARY
FOR GOOD MEN TO DO NOTHING.

The floor was fawn carpet-tiles with what he failed to recognise as an Indian kelim beside the bed. The whole long wall opposite was lined with shelves, her books and looseleafs gathered within reach of the desk and the rest full of ornaments and photos and soft toys of varying degrees of decrepitude. It was as if she had assembled all the inanimate loves of her short life there where she could see them from her bed.

He reached for a battered rag-doll and shook it in her face. Its wool hair swung like hers. She laughed and rescued it from him, soothing it with her hand as if he'd given it a fright. 'Don't be rough with her.'

'Why is she a white doll?'

'Black dolls cost more. Did you know that? Because they're rarer.'

'That's as it should be,' he said, gazing at her. Her eyes invited him. He took her in his arms, doll and all. As he kissed her, he felt the doll between them.

'Put her back on her shelf,' he whispered. 'She's sticking into me like a big soft sausage.' .

'And what about the big soft sausage you want to stick into me?'

'Who says it's soft!' He snatched the doll and dropped it on the desk, and without any of the difficulty or embarrassment he had secretly anticipated, he shortly found himself naked in bed with her.

How had she done it? — Got his clothes, and hers, off with a minimum of fuss, and slotted them both into her narrow bed, and smoothed him and soothed him (his Catholic part, not the rest) into absolute acquiescence and then roused him swiftly until, much too soon for sophistication, but without the least difficult — like a perfect arpeggio in music — he was inside her.

It was ecstasy, but brief, zooming up like a firework rocket and then petering out in a flutter of stars coloured like her hair-beads. He slipped sideways off her beautiful brown body, gathered it against him, and in an untrammelled trance of happiness, vanished into sleep.

As he was waking up half an hour later, a prickle, then a jolt of unease punctured his wellbeing. He'd done it now . . . lost his innocence. No way back. How would his conscience take it? His left hand was around her, on her silky back. He moved it as if he were stroking his cat, and the prickle went away. What a wonderful thing sex was, he thought. No wonder they didn't want you to try it; it just made everything else seem so unimportant.

He opened his eyes, and found her face six inches from him. Her dark eyes were wide awake, and he knew she hadn't slept and he also knew why. He cuddled her apologetically and said, 'Sorry. I'll be better next time.'

She studied his face. 'Were you a virgin?'

' 'Fraid so.' He could admit it to her as a sort of excuse, but also because he knew he hadn't actually disgraced himself.

'They say a girl never forgets her first love. Is it true of boys too, do you think? Am I imprinted on you for ever?'

'Definitely,' he said, kissing her. It was lovely lying down with a girl, height was simply irrelevant. 'Shall I get imprinted again?'

'You mean, like now?'

'Don't you want to?'

'What I actually invited you here for was tea.'

He didn't know whether to feel insulted or not. But she hugged him and softened it by saying, 'I love your hair. It's like a black person's, all frizzy.'

76

'I suppose you want to put it in little Topsy-plaits.'

'Dreadlocks.'

'Good idea. I'll be a Rasta. Those woolly hats make you look taller.' It was the first time he had given her a hint of his grief about his missing inches. The first time he'd ever been able to joke about it.

'It's ideologically unsound for a feminist to look up to her man.' They laughed without a care.

Only when they were sitting at the kitchen table drinking tea (which he discovered he desperately needed) and eating KitKats, did Clem think to ask: 'Pleasure, are you — I mean, are you on the pill or anything?'

She shook her head. 'Florence won't let me. She says it's dangerous.'

'Does your mum know you — '

'Well . . . I'm never sure. She kind of pretends. I'd be in bother if she came back and found us in bed, but basically she accepts it as something natural. She was quite active that way herself when Daddy first bombed off.'

'So how — I mean, we don't want anything to go wrong.'

'I should've made you wear something, but I always forget. I hate those things.'

A faint misgiving seized him. She had seemed so in charge, she was so obviously the more experienced, it hadn't occurred to him not to trust her to see to everything. Perhaps, as the man, he should have taken the responsibility.

'So how do you know it's okay?'

She shrugged. 'Nothing's ever happened before.'

Uneasily, not really wanting to know, he said, 'Do you do it a lot?'

She laughed. 'No! I've had one boy before you, that's all. But I did it a lot with him.'

He sat up straight. 'Pleasure! You can't just — trust to luck like that! There's always a first time.'

'Oh, okay. I'll get one of those morning-after pills.'

'Shouldn't you take one straight away?'

'No, dumbhead, not till the morning after! Don't worry, I've got seventy-two hours or something. I'll see to it.' She stood up and came round behind him, and kissed his ear. 'And we've got a lot less than that to enjoy ourselves and get you learned how to do it a bit slower.' She crossed her arms over his chest and hugged his narrow shoulders, her face close to his so that he could feel the little cold beads pressing into his cheek.

They went back to the narrow bedroom, to the narrow bed, forgetting the tea cups on the table that Pleasure's mum Florence would assuredly have found in the morning. The only thing was, on that particular morning she didn't return.

As she was riding home from the hospital on her bicycle, dead tired as usual after a night of near-slavery for the NHS, a large container lorry on its way to market whooshed by her too close. Its pressure wave wobbled her against the kerb and she flew through the air, landing heavily on her shoulder on the early-morning-empty pavement. Contrary to assumptions about the indifference of Londoners, she was soon picked up, and a kindly cabby, also on his way home, took her back to her own hospital.

There her broken collarbone was attended to, and her fellow-workers fussed around her and made her feel very popular and important. Her daughter was telephoned and she rushed round at once. Clem by this time was dozing blissfully at Waterloo, waiting for his early train to Dorset and wondering, with some smugness, whether his parents would notice any difference in him. Catholic guilt was, for the moment, nowhere.

What with one thing and another, seventy-two and twice seventy-two hours passed before Pleasure remembered that she had not done that thing which she ought to have done. But she wasn't much bothered. After all, it had always been okay before. She was nature's child, and full of naive faith in its beneficence.

★ ★ ★

George and Judy were in bed too, in Judy's flat in Brixton. Not together, of course. Despite the burgeoning of liking between them, it was not in their respective moeurs, nor did their respective situations dictate such a course as jumping so quickly into bed. Even though each, unbeknownst to the other and unacknowledged even to themselves, would have liked to do so.

They had talked themselves hoarse, sitting in Judy's basement flat consuming pints of liquid — tea, then beer with the fish and chips she sent him out for (accompanied by Zulu) and which he'd thoughtfully bought at the off-licence next to the fish-shop.

Their conversation ran through a number of overlapping phases. They did have the promised political discussion which verged several times on an outright brawl, but in between they talked about themselves. The fey Yorkshire lass of George's dreams wafted away for ever as he leant across the scarred oak table and listened intently to Judy talking. George was not really much of a dreamer, and no dream could stand up to someone as real as Judy.

He learnt that she had lived in England for twelve years. Apparently, Judy had a large, wealthy right-wing family living in South Africa, who had not responded with much fortitude or loyalty to her troubles.

'It wasn't just Jordan being jugged, it was me — becoming a Communist, getting involved in the struggle. You see, they're Afrikaners. Well, half. My father's an Afrikaner, my mom is of English descent but she took her lead from Dad. He was a real hardliner; even Verwoerd didn't go far enough for him. Finding out he had a renegade daughter was real viper-in-the-bosom time. He blamed Jordan, and when he was arrested, and later when he left the country, he expected me to fall back into line, see the error of my ways. I refused. I worked harder than ever. That's why they made me come here — because I couldn't keep us after Jordan wasn't around.'

'How old was your daughter then?'

'She was three and a half. Well, I could have

done, if I'd settled down to being a good little secretary or something, but instead I started voluntary work, organising black women who worked for whites, teaching them to stand up for their rights in domestic service. I helped run courses in civil rights, labour laws, letter-writing, even typing and bookkeeping. And do you know, my father felt that even that very limited contact somehow contaminated him. He couldn't stand the sight of me, as if when I walked into his house in the evenings, having been with black people all day, I was covered with some sort of smelly black grease. I saw then what real racism is. It's a disease of the mind, a virus. In that sense, people who have it can't help themselves. My father loved me, I was his favourite, and I watched him sickening of me, turning away from me. When he looked at me, his mouth twisted as if I'd developed some hideous deformity that he couldn't handle. Only, if it had been that, he could have hidden his feelings perhaps. With this other revulsion, he let it show, because he felt it was quite justified. That's the worst thing. When people are ill with the disease of racism, part of it is not knowing they've got anything wrong with them. Being proud of it. Thinking that the healthy people are sick.'

She didn't tell him what happened when Jordan was suddenly and unexpectedly released, when he came to the house and her father saw him in the condition he was in, and looked at him with the same old, bitter loathing that threw, for him, a sort of ugly mask over Jordan's face so that he didn't have to see — couldn't see — the damage the interrogators had done, damage that might have enlightened him to what he was defending, what he belonged to. He ordered Jordan off the doorstep and wouldn't listen to Judy's frenzied screams of 'Look at him, look what they've done to him!' — went deaf as well as blind, so that Judy left her family home with the clothes she stood up in and never went back while her father was alive. Judy didn't want to tell George about that, because, for one reason, it was the worst day of her whole life, and there'd been very bad ones before and since.

★ ★ ★

The final intake of liquid was hot chocolate with more banana bread at about two in the morning, too late for George to get back to his room at the Savoy, which he was later, ruefully but without real regret, to pay for not having occupied. Judy afforded him more downmarket quarters — a small, vacant bedroom with traces of recent feminine occupancy. The three picketers who were currently dossing down with her were cheerfully ousted to an elderly caravan parked in the back yard.

Judy slept fitfully in her small, cramped bedroom, hemmed in with piles of books and papers. The lie-implied weighed heavily on her. She'd told a lot of truths but the lie lay under them like shifting sands, undermining what was upright and a cause of pride in her life. But the worst was the drubbing George had given her about Communism. She had held her own — like most people, George knew fuck-all about it really — but she was left with a frustrated sense of sadness that he could never be a comrade.

George slept soundly, but towards morning a distended bladder disturbed him and he began to dream of a lazy-eyed black man who wielded a hammer and sickle and claimed to be Judy's husband.

6

The following afternoon, George took them by taxi to Wimbledon Common, saying they could all do with some exercise. More talk, not politics this time, but about his life — his sad life. Not that he made a lot of the sad bits — he had a fine philosophical outlook that Judy liked — but his various trials had caught at her heart. Home for tea and the last of the banana bread.

Munching it, George invented a riddle: 'What has your banana bread got in common with cement?'

'How dare you?'

'Now, hold on! The answer is: they're both binding.'

'How dare you even more?'

'Cement binds bricks, and your bread binds people. It's right friendly stuff, is this. There now, you don't have to hit me.'

George was sitting comfortably before the Aga and behind the *Observer*, with Zulu at his feet snoring contentedly after the best walk he'd had in weeks. The caravan-dwellers were all out.

'Do they live here permanently?' he asked.

'No, they're transients. They're mostly homeless, for the moment. They come on to the picket for company and because they've nowhere to go.'

'You mean they're *not ideologically motivated*?' asked George in shocked tones.

Judy chose not to rise to this bait.

'It's hard to be when you've nowhere to sleep. Then one or other of our people usually scoops them up. They doss down on floors or in attics or whatever, until something better can be found for them — permanent places to stay, jobs, information on their social security entitlements. Most of them are Thatcher's children, just fallen through the net — runaways from a bad home situation, lost their homes some other way, out of work, occasionally you get some kid on drugs . . . No drugs or drink are allowed on the picket, of course, but you can tell. They need a lot of help, that sort, but they pay it all back in spades.'

'Is that a pun?'

'We don't use racist, sexist, ageist, or any other kind of discriminatory language,' she said levelly. 'Not even as a joke.'

'Trouble with the far Left,' remarked George, 'no sense of humour. Now, I've always said, when you can joke with a man about the differences between you, they've stopped being important.'

'Bollocks,' said Judy. 'Joking only proves you're always thinking about it. The differences only stop being important when you stop noticing them.'

'Do you mean you honestly don't notice that blacks — all right to say 'blacks'?'

'Black people is better.'

'Oh, right. That black people are black?'

Judy gave this some thought.

'Of course I notice they're black, the way you

might notice I'm blonde. It just doesn't put them into any special category, that's all.'

'You being blonde puts *you* in a special category.'

She looked at him expressionlessly. 'Oh yes — what category's that?'

He read the signals aright, and said blandly, 'The category *some* gentlemen prefer. Not me. Give me a bald woman every time.'

Her mouth twitched. 'And does my being a Marxist put me in a special category?'

'It does that. Special but not unique. There's dinosaurs in it already.'

She showed no symptoms of amusement this time.

'So why are you interested in me, if the beliefs that absolutely define my life seem to you so antediluvian?'

'Who wouldn't be interested to meet a dinosaur? — especially one that talks.'

'I could get very angry at your dismissiveness. I can feel it there inside me, cold and ready to jump out. I don't know why I bother trying to talk to you. I'm very serious. You and I have nothing in common.'

'We have, you know.'

'Name one belief, one commitment, one premise.'

He sighed and stretched his legs and put his big hands behind his big fair head.

'I'm not falling into that trap. Let me put it this way. You feel a sense of brotherhood — sorry, sexist language — *fellowship*, common struggle and all that, with black working people

86

in your country, and this one presumably. With *all* working people, maybe. Yet the vast majority of 'em you couldn't talk to for five minutes the way you and I can talk. They're your comrades, and you spend your life fighting for them, but what you can't have with them is a real friendship, because at not a very deep level, come a lot of differences that only the struggle can mask. You can claim you're 'defined' by your commitments, but you actually know full well there's other things. Being together. Argy-bargying. Teasing each other, having a good time. It's called companionship. And that's what you couldn't have with a black worker in Soweto, because it's *him*, not me, you've got nothing in common with. You might find common ground in 'the struggle', but I bet you and him couldn't get through an evening if you had to keep off it.'

'Not only could I, but I have — many, many times. You know, George, you are talking the worst racist crap I ever heard in my life. You're as good as saying black workers aren't intelligent!'

Before he could draw breath to retort, the door thudded open and in came Tina.

George looked over his shoulder. In his eyes she appeared rather sweet, with her hate-the-comb blonde hair and her odd, colourful clothes, and her pretty, sulky little face. To her mother, she looked horrendous, but then she always did since she moved in with that little oil-rich bitch who dolled her up to look like a Harrods dress-dummy. 'Slipperies and shinies', Judy called the

87

clothes her daughter wore these days. In Judy's eyes there were designer labels plastered all over her like a patchwork quilt.

' 'Lo, Mum. Oh.'

'This is George Reddy. George, my daughter Albertina.'

'*Tina*. Hi.' She turned her back on him and went into the attack with more vigour than charm. 'Mum, I need some money.'

'Why don't you go down to Camden Market and flog the gear?'

'Funny. Can I have some?'

'How much do you need?'

'*I* don't know Mum! I'm skint, aren't I.'

'I'm pretty much that way myself.'

George automatically reached for his wallet, but one sabreflash glance from Judy and he aborted the movement and turned it into fishing for a handkerchief. Luckily Tina hadn't noticed.

'C'n I just borrow your cashcard — '

'*No*. Not after the last time.'

Tina threw her a look of bitter indignation. 'Last time' was many months ago now and Judy was expected to have forgotten that Tina, officially granted the card and its PIN for a one-off cash withdrawal for Judy, had added £20 for herself which had in due course shown up on the statement. This had been one of the factors leading to her departure from the flat. One of many.

'What's your problem, Mum?' she asked querulously. It was her favourite expression, guaranteed to get under her mother's skin. The instinctive, and routine, answer was, 'You are,'

88

but Judy bit it back this time. She was not about to get into a row with her daughter in front of George, who was already looking uncomfortable. She decided on the soft answer, partly for its surprise value.

'Listen doll, this isn't a good moment.' She cast her eyes sideways towards George. 'You can cope, I'm sure.'

'Well, I can't,' Tina snapped. 'I spent my last two quid getting here. How do you expect me to get *home*?' She laid deliberate emphasis on the word to show Judy that this wasn't home any more.

Judy could feel her temper going. It invariably did when Tina showed her up in front of people.

'I don't *expect* you to do anything,' she said with a cutting edge.'You're no longer my responsibility.'

'Oh, I see! Just like that! Just because I can't pass exams you're disowning me. I'm as good as not your daughter any more, is that it?'

A red mist began to cloud Judy's vision, but she hung on grimly. 'Of course you're still my daughter. You can be my daughter and not be my responsibility. When you walked out of here — '

'Oh great. Now you're going to drag it all out in front of strangers! Typical. Actually I suppose you've told him all about it already?' she asked shrilly, but tears were glistening. She was spoiling for a fight — dying for it. She was a row-a-holic, Judy thought despairingly, and she hadn't scored for two days, since her last appearance on the same errand. It occurred to Judy, not for the first time, that a measure of her own failure with Tina might be that Tina defined their relationship through rowing. For a long time they had hardly met anywhere but on the mother-daughter battlefield.

Judy drew an angry breath, but George's stolid presence behind her extended her short fuse. She walked up to Tina, who stared her defiantly in the eyes with her 'Go on, slap me!' look, but instead Judy put an arm around her daughter. She had the satisfaction of seeing Tina's mouth fall open with surprise.

'Why don't you go to your old room and look in the blue jar you used to empty your jeans pockets into? There were a couple of pound coins in there when you left, and I haven't taken them. That'd get you — home.'

Checkmated, Tina showed her teeth in a soundless snarl, turned and left the room.

Judy stood silently containing herself until Tina swept through the main room again and exited, slamming the front door. Then the tension went out of her shoulders and she turned a rueful face to George.

'Sorry about that.'

'No need.' He'd gone to pour her a glass of wine without her having to expose her need. 'How *will* she get home, wherever home is?'

' 'Home' is an obscenely grand flat in Belgravia, and she will no doubt get there by taxi and borrow the fare from her equally grand friend Leila at the other end. I'm glad I won't be there to hear her explanation, which will show me in a bleddy unflattering light.'

'Ah. So all that about spilling the beans in front of strangers was just a bit of what they call guilt transference?'

'In all the talking we've done in the past twenty-four hours, have I even mentioned her?'

'Once. Briefly. I was wondering.'

She had wanted to talk to him, unload a bit, but something less laudable than family loyalty held her back. Tina was hers, her special, sole responsibility, however she might try to deny it. Judy's bitter disappointment and shame for the way her daughter was turning out, the way she talked and behaved, her recent defiant rejection of any kind of political commitment, and what appeared, recurrently, to be the total, final failure of their relationship, was a constant gall on Judy's heart; to reveal anything about Tina's current situation or behaviour to George would have been to reveal all, and that would prove Tina right, and also show Judy up as what she felt herself to be — a strong contender for the World's Worst Single Mother trophy.

'Where were we?' she said instead, trying to make light of it.

'I don't know where we were, but I know where we're going,' said George. 'Out to get a good dinner. I'll phone a minicab.'

★ ★ ★

Judy had been quite wrong in her supposition that Tina would slag her off to her flatmate on her return. She was feeling far too ashamed

91

and upset about the scene she'd made in front of that burly stranger. She simply hadn't been able to help doing it. She never could, with Judy. Things had got so bad that just the sight of her mother seemed to trigger the very worst in her.

These harrowing compulsive rows made her feel absolutely worthless. Her own mother couldn't stand her — what did that make her? She felt pretty worthless a lot of the time, even without a row. She longed above all for her mother's approval, but it was hopeless. She'd failed her in everything — school, politics, her behaviour, her appearance. Everything was all wrong, all different from Judy and what Judy expected and wanted.

Even her name.

Albertina . . . Being named after the wife of Walter Sisulu, a man her mother considered a great hero, just made Tina feel more inadequate than ever. It infuriated her, as if the name were some huge regal garment she was expected to fill. So she diminished it to Tina and stubbornly refused to answer to anything else. Her mother had gone mad at first. She said furiously that she might as well call herself Tinkerbell.

She used the two pound coins for the tube and walked the rest of the way back to the flat, which was far too grand to be close to public transport. She had to ring the bell. Leila's aunt answered, which was unusual. Perhaps at last they'd given Jojo, the maid, a night out. Subliminally, Tina was relieved. Jojo was black, silent and servile, sometimes to cringing-point, and made Tina extremely uncomfortable. Her whole upbringing since infancy had made her profoundly unwilling to be waited on by a black person.

'Ah, Tina, it's you,' said the aunt, whom Tina called Mrs Salah. She was extremely well-dressed and full of busyness, always hurrying out to her shopping and her bridge parties and her committees. She was obviously on her way out now — she had her chinchilla coat on.

'Where's Jojo?' asked Tina.

Mrs Salah ignored her question. 'Leila is quite cross with you for going out. She says you are to meet her at the Kaleidoscope Club. She left you some nice clothes and here is the money for the taxi.'

'Why do I have to wear her clothes?' asked Tina.

'I don't know, my dear. That is the message. She laid them out in your bedroom.' She patted Tina's arm. 'The Kaleidoscope is a very smart place, I believe,' she mentioned with a glossy red smile. At that moment the Merc drew up to the front steps. 'Don't you girls be home late now,' she chirped, as she waved and departed.

Tina slowly crossed the large hall with its snowy tiles, with just a hint of glint in them, past the vast 'Ali-Baba' jars and the great rubber-plants that climbed to the ceiling, all aglow with faintly pink lighting concealed behind gilded half-shells. The wall-to-wall mirror at the far end showed her herself already clad in a little number of Leila's, worn, she admitted now, to show off to her mother. A crass misjudgement! Tina had seen Judy's eyes narrow with distaste as soon as she'd walked in — perhaps that had triggered Tina to behave so badly. She hadn't meant to go at her like that, to start scrounging money straight away. She'd wanted to talk to her, but of course that stupid stranger had to be there and spoil everything.

Listlessly she obeyed instructions. Well, if her mother didn't love her, she would just have to show her that Tina didn't need *her* to enjoy herself. Oh, but if only she could have seen Tina's bedroom! It was beautiful. Lavender-coloured with a bank of wardrobes (almost empty), an incredible dressing-table with a triptych of gilt-framed mirrors, white chairs with bow-shaped gilded legs, and the bed! The bed! She sat on it now and bounced. She longed to tell her mother about the wonders of this place, but had never dared. She feared it would all backfire, that her mother would throw up if she knew Tina slept in a round bed like a huge pink marshmallow and had the sole use of a sunken bath with gold taps and jacuzzi jets that turned Leila's Body Shop bath-milk grains into fine white froth in which she pretended to be Cleopatra in the warm milk of a hundred asses.

She put on the clothes Leila had picked out. Loose black satin trousers, and a ravishing loose top, solid as chain mail with silver sequins, falling in points at her waist, the upward points between the downward points leaving little triangles of her midriff visible. When all this was on, she found a sequinned bow to match, which Leila presumably intended should

94

adorn Tina's mop of blonde curls, but she drew the line at that. One touch more, and she would have ceased to know herself.

At the Kaleidoscope, Leila and a large crowd of her friends were drinking champagne cocktails in the bar. Leila called to her across the deep-blue room.

'Tina, you look fantastic!'

She came towards Tina, who gazed at her. Leila was not a beauty, but her black hair was gloriously heaped up, catching the blue lights, and her golden-white skin and bright red lips and lemon-shaped, lustrous eyes struck Tina as incredibly exotic. She wore a rather fussy short white dress with a fluted peplum bought from a couture boutique she favoured. Tina happened to know it had cost enough to pay her mother's rates on the flat for four years.

'Where were you all this time? I thought you'd never turn up!' she exclaimed as she hugged her. She turned to the others. 'This is my interesting flatmate. Tina, meet Alex, Melissa, Courtney, James, Achmed . . . ' Tina, feeling shy and vulnerable, found herself tugging the revealing points of the sequin top with her left hand while shaking all their hands with the right. Leila firmly pulled her left hand away.

'Come on, we're just going to the blackjack table!'

Tina felt like an infiltrator into their group. *She* knew she didn't belong, but did they? They seemed not to. Some of them, like Leila, were Arabs. Others were American, two were West Germans, two were Londoners. All were very rich, which is to say their parents were. Tina thought they were wonderfully glamorous and carefree with their expensive clothes, hairdos and habits. She watched an Arab boy scarcely older than herself lose £1,000 in £50 chips at the black-jack table without turning a hair. But that wasn't half as exciting as when Leila won steadily at roulette with a system which involved the rapid and adroit deployment of a great many chips of modest value, on the points where lines on the table intersected. Some of these always seemed to win, and the croupier was getting quite bug-eyed by the time Leila rose languidly to her feet, scooped the huge pile of chips into a plastic bag, and said, 'Boring. Let's go.'

Tina ate in the club restaurant at Leila's cost and obeyed Leila's order to not even glance at the prices — 'That is rude, it suggests you have to worry that your host can't afford.' Tina, who had grown up with the constant constraints of can't-afford, felt in all this spendthriftery the almost sexual thrill of the unfamiliar, decadent and forbidden.

It turned out to be quite a thrilling evening. Tina was glad, now, to be properly dressed for it. She had to keep reminding herself that this was really her. The agony emanating from her feet, clad in a pair of Leila's spike-heeled Italian shoes, helped.

At around five a.m. the whole party, winners and losers, repaired for breakfast to the in-place at Covent Garden, and then split up. At this point, Tina's bubble burst. Tiredness had restored her to herself, like Cinderella — her feet hurt, she was chilled and longing for her pink marshmallow bed, but Leila and Alex, one of the Londoners, wanted to go down to the Embankment and 'visit' the homeless inhabitants who dossed there.

'What for?' asked Tina uneasily.

'They wake up around now because the street-cleaning vans come along,' explained Alex. 'If we get there before that, we can buy them coffee and food, and sometimes they let you sit on their bread-crate mattresses and talk. They've occasionally got spliff, though of course they make you buy it. But the best bit is throwing your plastic cup and other rubbish away in the gutter,' he finished gleefully.

'What's so fantastic about that?' asked Tina.

'Well, the point is I mean it's been driven into one from infancy not to litter, my nanny used to hit me if I threw away even a gumwrapper, but when you're with them it's a matter of when in Rome.'

Tina still didn't get the point, and she thought Alex was being a total dork, but she tagged along. Anyway, she couldn't go home before Leila because Leila had never given her her own key. Besides, she had no dosh for a taxi.

Now the taxis were all full, so they walked. Tina took off the highheeled shoes and carried them. The pavement was cold but her feet welcomed the freedom from pain; she wasn't used to high heels. Alex thought walking in tight shod feet through the West End was 'wicked'. Tina's acquaintance with this set was so new she didn't recognise this as a compliment, but

Leila did. She promptly took her shoes off too, and made Alex carry them.

Halfway to the Embankment Alex steered them into a long detour through Trafalgar Square.

'There they are,' he said. 'Up the revolution! Bunch of crapartists. Let's take the piss a bit as we pass!'

Tina felt a cold wave pass up her body from the pavement. She stopped dead. Her feet simply refused to walk her towards the picket with Alex and Leila at her side. They walked on several yards before they noticed.

Then they turned together. 'Come on, Tina! What's wrong?'

Tina's teeth were suddenly chattering so much she could scarcely talk. Leila, with only a faint exclamation of impatience, came back to her. 'What is it? Why are you standing there?'

'I'm cold. I want to go home.'

'Oh, don't be a spoilsport. Alex!'

He had started to walk on, determined to have his fun with the picketers, whom Tina could see huddled, cold but stalwart, in the early light. She squinted to see if her mother was among them, but then remembered, with relief strong as a blow, that it wasn't her night.

'Don't let's bother with him,' she begged, clutching Leila's arm.

'There's a taxi! Come on, oh do let's go home, I'm knackered!'

Leila was her friend. Anyway, her own feet were frozen.

'Oh, all right, let's leave him. I don't know

why he wants to bother with those stupid people. Sometimes I think he is a bit of a wanker really. Taxi!'

Huddled in the leather depths, the two girls rubbed their cold, dirty feet through the tatters of their tights. 'We can't put our shoes back on now!' Leila giggled. 'Anyway, Alex has got mine. You are crazy — bare feet on those filthy pavements. What if you'd trodden in something?' They broke into giggles.

'Did you enjoy yourself?' Leila asked as she let them into the snowy hall with its pink lighting like a sunset over the Alps. They shed their coats — the central heating was set at 70 degrees at all times. The warm slippery marble felt wonderful to their cold soles.

'Yes, of course,' said Tina automatically. And she had, in a way. At least she had spent a number of hours not thinking about her mother at all. The awful fright she had had in Trafalgar Square, though, had put a great ugly slash across the whole occasion.

'Let us tell Jojo to make us another breakfast,' said Leila. 'Only we mustn't wake Auntie.'

They walked along a wide corridor to the enormous kitchen, expecting to find the black girl already at work though it was only just after six. But there was no one there.

'She wasn't here when I got in last night, either,' remembered Tina. 'Your aunt had to open the door to me.'

'Oh!' exclaimed Leila in annoyance. 'I hope the stupid girl hasn't run away!'

Tina stiffened. 'What do you mean? Why

99

should she run away?'

'Well, I didn't mean that exactly. She couldn't really run away. She's not allowed to stay here — I mean in Britain — except with us.' She became aware that Tina was staring at her with an expression she failed to recognise as one of dawning horror. She took it for idle curiosity. 'We keep her passport, you see,' Leila explained. 'We imported her, to work for us.'

'But why should she run away?'

Leila looked slightly uncomfortable. 'Auntie hits her sometimes when she is slow.'

A ghastly shock ran through Tina. '*Hits her!*'

'Well, she deserves it. She is very slow and stupid at times. Still, I hope she hasn't ru- gone away. Auntie would be furious, and I don't know what Daddy would say. He bought her for us.'

Tina said nothing. Not even goodnight. She went into her beautiful bedroom and took off Leila's sequinned finery, and had a shower and washed her feet. Something inside her was pressing so that she had to keep taking deep breaths. She wanted more than anything in the world to run away herself, back to Brixton, but she had no money, not a penny. And she was dead tired. So she crawled into the marshmallow bed instead.

But the bed was suddenly too soft. She felt as if she were sinking into it, drowning. She wondered what Alex had done to harass the picket. Reactionary prat! She shouldn't have panicked; she should have stopped him somehow — they had enough to put up with. She could never think of the picket without the most terrible guilt. It was two years since she had stood on it.

She lay awake. Now it was Jojo who was keeping her from sleep. '*Auntie hits her . . .*' Tina had heard her crying once. Why had she ignored it? Why had she ignored all the signs? It was too awful to think of. So she turned her mind to reviewing the last year.

Things had not been so bad till she'd failed her A's at the comp. The worst had started at that bloody crammer in Kensington. The worst rows, the worst failure — and Leila. She'd met Leila there. If she hadn't met Leila, she wouldn't be here now, in a household that owned — and abused — a black slave.

Tina had badgered and begged her mother to let her enrol. Only thus, she had said, in a 'structured atmosphere' where people 'had to learn', could she pass her A's and have a hope of university and a reasonable life. In the end Judy gave way. She mortgaged the flat, something she had always just managed to avoid, paid the stupendous fees, and urged Tina to work as she had assuredly never worked before.

It took her less than a fortnight to suss out that the place was a high-class rip-off. The teaching was lackadaisical, and no wonder; most of the kids there were as dim as last year's lightbulbs. They were nearly all rich, spoilt thickos who had failed their A-levels, and whose loaded (and mostly overseas) parents had dumped them there for lack of a better idea of how to keep them off the streets and out of their hair.

To her fellow-students, then, it scarcely mattered that the fees were astronomical and that they were never going to pass an exam, but for Tina it was different. She was living in a rundown basement flat with a mother who lived by the work-ethic and was making a lot of sacrifices to give Tina this begged-for chance. Tina felt, at first, absolutely unmanned by guilt. It rendered her brain almost functionless. She sat in the classes where the others spent the days pissing about, giggling, doing their hair, passing notes, groping each other, and falling asleep, and she tried very hard at first, but it was useless. She experienced the horror of knowing that succeeding in school was not just a matter of structure and being made to learn after all. You had to have brains and you had to have willpower . . . She'd made a terrible mistake and she didn't know how to admit it or undo it.

After school the posh street was a-honk with classy little sports cars or chauffeur-driven saloons. Many of Tina's fellow students had beautiful West End flats. They gave parties and drove around Town to places of entertainment. In the mornings they would exchange endless chat about what they'd been doing the night before. Work didn't enter into it. Nobody was worried, least of all the school, which looked to collect more fees for failure than for success. Several students were doing their third year, on the school's assurance to the absent parents that success was assured this time, or that Samantha or Yacub or Scottie or Jasmin was the mainstay of the class.

Tina started out by despising them; she couldn't help it. However much she rebelled against her mother and her mother's values, they were to some extent built into her, and it was impossible to watch what went on in the crammer, and out of it, without disgust. These kids and the lives they lived, devoted entirely to vacuous pleasure-seeking, was at first such a contrast to what Tina had known all her life that she hovered, poised between two compulsions — to shrink away, and to fly towards. In the end, guilt pushed her from her natural path into the ambit of Leila, who — unlike most of the others, who had Tina sussed as their financial inferior from the off — had always been friendly.

They quit school at the same time. Leila's father, perhaps not as easily duped as some of the others, though no less wealthy, pulled her out when her reports too persistently registered A's for potential and E's for effort. He found her a part-time job in a West End carpet emporium, where she had little to do but sit at a desk and look decorative, and himself went back to Rhiyad to continue making money and, he threatened, find her a husband.

Meanwhile she continued to live in the family mansion flat in Belgravia, under the eye of Mrs Salah, her widowed aunt, who had, luckily, been raised mainly in the States and had progressive ideas, though she concealed these from her brother. She also had her own life and

103

interests, and apart from a few rules, such as no boys in the flat which she strictly enforced, she left Leila alone. She didn't even object — rather the contrary — when Leila invited Tina to share. This came about after Tina, who had also been pulled out of the crammer for much the same reasons, but after a far noisier confrontation with her mother, had left home.

And now it was nine in the morning, and she was lying here in the marshmallow bed, soaked in tears and worrying about Jojo. How could Tina have thought that a set-up like this would employ a black girl and look after her properly? 'Daddy bought her for us.' God. God! She might as well be living with — and on — her fascist-racist relatives in South Africa! If her mother knew!

Tina turned her face convulsively into the squashy pillow.

* * *

When Judy awoke next morning, her first thought was a gloomy one (Shit — another fight with Tina. And it's Monday!) but her second thought was happy and overrode her first.

George.

He was no longer in the flat, which consequently felt considerably flatter than it had yesterday at this time, but he was still in London. He had plans to go round the West End estate agents, on the hunt for a place in the country to buy. Judy, looking out of her bedroom window at the rain-stained backs of other houses, sandwiching a double row of mainly neglected two-by-four gardens or (as in her case) a concreted back yard full of caravan, allowed herself a tiny, romantic dream of the green life.

She would see him this evening. This prospect definitely threw a different and less lupus radiance on Brixton, and on the day ahead.

She had a wash and pulled on the drab concealment-clothes she wore for the office. She worked in Wandsworth for a firm that made and sold stationery. She was expected to do word processing and spreadsheets, mailmerge, the lot, as well as incidental packing and phone answering, occasional receptionist and general dogsbody.

The hours were called 'flexi' but were seldom fewer than nine per weekday. Her boss and colleagues she judged to be boring macho beer-swilling sexist fuckwits who exploited her, made jokes about her accent, and when the spirit moved them, idly tried to grope her. They claimed this should make her feel young and beautiful even though, they freely implied when she yelled at them, she wasn't. She sought redress in vain — there was no one to complain to except her boss, who was as bad as the others. She therefore gritted her teeth, wore her hair pinned up, eschewed make-up and jewellery and wore the most unbecoming (and unnavigable) garments she could find. Her boss then complained that she looked like an old boiler, and kept her out of the front office.

She stayed on because, as she'd discovered

long ago, it is very difficult for a self-trained woman over thirty-five to get a job, and this one paid just enough to keep her and her various 'children' — at a fairly basic level, certainly, but it was a lot better than the dole.

During a welcome break at work, Judy phoned Abby.

'Have you had a chance to look through the papers? There was nothing I could see in the Sundays.'

'Not a bloody thing,' said Abby angrily. 'Not a word — none of them. God, I hate those bastards! They are *all* basically in the pocket of the Establishment. A story like that! A demo in the middle of Town, three or four hundred people, half a dozen celebs, police raid, six people arrested, two hurt . . . what more do they want? The capitalist press! It just makes me *sick*.'

'Who was hurt?' asked Judy anxiously.

'Sophie and Jarvis. Don't worry, nothing serious, but I played it up as much as I decently could when I phoned round a few of our erstwhile 'friends' of the press. They acted as if I had Aids and was trying to jump their bones.'

'They used to cover the picket a lot.'

'No, they didn't. Oh, at first. But after a bit the coverage just dried up and all Maggie's little scrivener rats ran back up her arse. We're too radical for them.'

Judy loved Abby. She was a terrific comrade, absolutely fearless and tireless; in terms of sheer dynamism and driving willpower, it was

106

she, more than Judy, who kept the picket wheels grinding. But the downside of that was this almost fanatical obsession with the Establishment and everything pertaining to it. Judy shared her feelings, but when Abby got started it was like waiting for a small volcano to conclude its eruption before you could actually move ahead.

'Were you 'on' last night?' Judy asked.

'No! I'd earned a rest after Saturday. Don't ask . . . It was bloody awful. I thought the worst of the 'marauding' was over, but we had a real basinful that night.'

'Who — the Nats?'

'I dunno who they were, they don't carry placards. Just a bunch of shitheads having a laugh. After we managed to shake off the skinhead brigade with their 'let's-'ave-a-bash-at-this-bunch-of-nigger-loving-tossers', we just had time to let the smell blow away when along comes a real prat, all on his own. He comes poncing along — clutching a pair of high-heeled *shoes* if you don't mind — all got up, posh accent, they're the worst if you ask me, the so-called educated ones. He pretended to be interested, took a leaflet off me, stood there reading it all solemn, and then turned to me and said, 'It doesn't make sense for me to help to bring the revolution closer, I'd be the first you'd string up.' I said, 'The only people being strung up that we're interested in is black South Africans.' D'you know what the little sod said?'

'What?'

Abby put on a plummy voice. ' 'Sorry and all that, but personally I'd rather they swung there for murdering each other, than came here where we can't even flog 'em for mugging us'.'

Judy said nothing for a moment. Then: 'Worth arguing?'

'Well, I did point out that white people are world leaders at fighting and killing each other. But what's the use, you can't undo twenty years of deep conditioning in five minutes, specially not at sparrow-fart when you've been on your legs all bloody night.'

It was the first time Abby had shown the slightest sign of flagging. But it was impossible she shouldn't get worn down sometimes; she burned up so much energy in the struggle. Judy said, 'Listen, Ab. I met a nice guy on Saturday.'

'At the demo?'

'Yes. Well, after.'

'Is he from home?'

'In my dreams! He's from Yorkshire.'

'Are you sure he's — you know, all right?'

Judy was startled. This had never occurred to her. 'You mean, some kind of infiltrator? No, he couldn't be. If he was, he'd know more.'

'Jude. Take my advice. Don't get too pally with anyone like that. Outsiders. It just won't work. They're like from another planet, you come to the end of them so quickly. Believe me, I've tried.' Judy grunted sympathetically. Abby's marriage to a well-intentioned boring Englishman had just come to a predictably

108

sticky end, but Judy had supposed this was chiefly due to Abby's realisation that she was gay.

At this moment an erk stuck his head round the door of the back room — part storeroom, part office — where Judy had her small, smoke-filled fiefdom.

'Some old twat's come in wants some a them calendars with room to write stuff on.'

'Wall or desk?' asked Judy, covering the phone.

'Y'wot?'

'A calendar that you hang upon the wall, or a calendar that you stand upon a desk,' explained Judy very slowly.

'Dome be s'smart,' snarled the erk. 'Dig out some a both and bring 'em through. Pronto. And knock off the phone calls, darling, or you'll be gettin' a light pay-packet.'

He flapped his hand at her smoke, burst into an overdone hacking cough and went out, slamming the door. Judy gazed after him with muted loathing.

Abby was still talking in her ear. She interrupted.

'Sorry. One of the new underclass just came in with a charm-filled request for my services. 'Bye, doll.'

She sighed heavily and went to dig out the calendars. But while the sigh was still echoing, she recalled it. Tonight after this ballsaching day was over, she would hurry home and put on her own equivalent of 'slipperies and shinies'. George would pick her up *in a taxi* and take her out for another delicious dinner. They would talk more and argue more and she would take a step closer to finding out if she was going to take Abby's advice or ignore it.

7

George was coming to Brixton pretty regularly now.

Of course he wasn't at the Savoy any more. He'd got himself a small service flat in Battersea, which was at least on the right side of the river for Brixton. Brixton itself was a bit more than he could face, for living in. He offered a few ineffectual hints that it was hardly suitable — he meant safe — for someone like Judy, but she turned them off so scathingly that he dropped it.

He thought of himself as courting Judy. It was an old-fashioned Yorkshire expression, and he wouldn't have dreamt of using the term in conversation with anyone, but it was how things were. He wasn't too sure how it was going, though, and he wondered sometimes if he was doing it right.

He had not made a serious pass yet. He felt the time just wasn't ripe. But they talked about a lot of things, drawing closer to each other through speech. He hadn't hidden his intentions, and one evening after they'd been out to dinner and had returned to Judy's flat for coffee, she got up abruptly from the table and came back with a letter. Not to her, but from her — one she had not yet sent. She extracted it from its unsealed airmail envelope and handed it to him silently.

111

To his astonishment it began, '*My dearest Jordan.*'

He looked up at her. 'You want me to read this?'

'Yes.'

'Why? Isn't it private?'

'It's about you.'

'So what?' he asked, still bewildered and unwilling to read it.

'It may help you to understand the — the situation you want to come in on.'

He said no more, but read the letter. It was a very strange one. He had to keep reminding himself that she was writing to a man she had once, presumably, loved and been intimate with in all senses, but whom she hadn't been with, or perhaps even seen, for years. Yet here she was, writing to him in the most open way, telling him she had met a man she liked (himself) and — well, what it amounted to was a sort of asking for permission, for sanction, though for what, exactly, she didn't spell out.

Reading, he felt deeply embarrassed, as if he were spying on Judy in some moment of emotional nakedness. He looked aside as he pushed the letter back to her and muttered, 'By heck, this is an odd situation. What can the poor bugger possibly say? God! I wish you were free!'

'You can cry off and go find someone who is, if you like.'

'I would like. There's nothing I'd like better. But I seem to be stuck.'

'I can see I've embarrassed you.'

'Aye, you have.'

'I want — I have to do more of it. I want to tell you about Jordan. About me and Jordan.'

He stared at the table. 'Must you? I really don't want to know about other men in your life.'

'Jordan isn't other men. He is *the* man in my life, and you can't know me, let alone — '

'Love you — ' he heard himself say, for the first time.

There was a hot silence. They were both flushed and breathing fast. It was a moment, a possible moment, to go round the table and kiss her, but somehow he couldn't. They were physically too awkwardly placed. Besides, it would look as if he were trying to push the Jordan thing away, and he knew it was a barrier he would have to go through to reach her, if he wanted to do so properly. He said, 'Go on then. I'll listen.'

Judy lit a cigarette. She seemed not to know how to begin.

'How did you meet?'

'I've known him for ever. We lived a few streets from each other in Durban, mine a rich street and his, not a poor but a much more ordinary one. We were both in street-gangs, that's how I knew him first. My brothers used to take me out on escapades with their gang. We used to do things — like breaking into ice-cream shops — that if we'd been black, or even working-class, we would have been carted off to reform school or jail for. With us, on the one occasion we were caught, the police brought

113

us home to our parents and told them to take our *broeks* down, which they did to my brothers but not to me, and that was the end of it.

'Jordan's gang was different. It wasn't so delinquent but it was much more subversive. He led them on night-raids into the rich neighbourhood where we lived. They were never caught, not Jordan's gang! Their whole purpose was not to steal ice cream or sweets like us, but leave their mark, to prove themselves by a gesture against our privileged world. They used to TP our front walks or our trees — '

'Do what to them?' asked George.

'TP them. Jordan provided them with rolls of toilet paper and they used to drape it around, especially in high trees, tangling it in the branches so it was difficult for adults to remove. Or they'd form swearwords and slogans with stones on the lawns.

'We met in the streets at night. Not very often, none of us could get out often, but that was how I first knew Jordan. He and one of my brothers had a fist-fight once when we caught Jordan TP-ing the tree on our front lawn. It never occurred to us to give him away, of course, but our property was our property and Barry gave him a good hiding — he was three years older than Jordan. I was sorry for him for getting beaten up, and I admired him. I thought TP-ing looked like great fun — it used to drive grown-ups mad — though Barry would never let me do it. He said it was something only low-class creeps did.'

'Not like breaking into shops.'

114

'Naturally! That was a perfectly respectable entertainment. When we got to high school, Jordan and I were in the same grade. He was very good-looking. We went around together, though I never dared take him home. He was too outspoken. His ideas were unbelievable. I literally couldn't credit that any white person could think like that. He dared to get up in class and contradict the teachers' version of South African history. Whenever the usual talk about stupid lazy kaffirs was going on — we kids used to parrot our parents about the household servants — Jordan used to defend them, and in a very down-to-earth way. He didn't say they weren't lazy, he said anyone would be lazy if they were working for a bunch of privileged shitpots who despised them, exploited them, paid them practically nothing and kept them away from their families. To the rest of the white kids, that was a direct attack on *their* families.

'The fights he got into! The older boys used to knock hell out of him, till he did his growth-shoot and got taller than most of them, then they just stood well back and sneered. He had no friends among the kids of my parents' friends. The teachers regarded him as a ticking time-bomb. In the eleventh grade they found an excuse to chuck him out.'

'He was expelled?'

'Yes. I was stunned. Nobody I knew had ever been expelled. I think it hit me harder even than when he was eventually arrested, because then I wasn't ashamed, whereas when he was booted from school, I was. I was such a little wimp then, I went around saying I'd never liked him, never really had a proper date with him . . . But I kept thinking about him, thinking about the things he'd told me. I'd honestly never thought about the sort of lives black people lived till then.

'My parents had dinned into us that we had to 'play fair' and that not to be 'fair' was the worst crime amongst children. It was a prime value. I began to see the hypocrisy that underlay everything that happened in our house, where the incredible unfairness that blacks endured every hour of their lives wasn't even noticed.

'Being expelled didn't stop Jordan learning. He wanted to be a lawyer. He was put into another school and he kept his opinions to himself till he graduated, then he went on to university. I think he played it relatively cool there, too — he was saving it up. Being expelled had taught him something — lie low till your weapons are in your hands. But I know for a fact, from what happened later, that the authorities had their eye on him even then. I bet there was a case-file on Jordan from the time he was about eleven.'

She was off in her own past world, but she came back to check that her audience was with her. He was. He was leaning forward across the kitchen table, both arms halfway across it, gazing at her intently.

'So anyway, I graduated. High-school, too. I was dithering. He'd unsettled me, made me unfit for the kind of frivolous surface life the women of my family were expected to lead.

116

I went to college too, but I wasn't brilliant like him. I began to be political. I spent more time in political activity than I did studying. I ploughed my degree. I'd like to say somebody up there fixed me, but I'd have flunked anyway. My father was furious but my mother, Dido, just laughed — she'd been against me going. Who needs a degree to land a rich husband? She started straight away trying to match me. I played along when I could be bothered, to keep the peace, but I had a test question I used to ask my so-called suitors. Did they know the tribal name of the household servant who'd been with their family the longest? None of them ever did. They pretty near always seemed to say Jim. So I called all of *them* Jims, though not to their faces.

'While I was waiting for Jordan to get his career started I learnt shorthand-typing and book-keeping. My brother tipped me off that computers were the coming thing so I took a course in them. Nearly drove myself mad, but I thought, Stick at it, Jordan'll need this sometime.

'As soon as Jordan got into a law firm, he started defending civil right cases. I used to read his name in the papers and I always secretly cut the pieces out and stuck them in a scrapbook. You can't imagine how carefully I kept that scrapbook hidden! But you bet my mother finally found it. Dido would find your secret if it was hidden in one of your teeth.

' 'What is this?' she screamed when I came back from work that day. 'Why are you keeping

117

cuttings about that kaffir-loving pinko? I suppose you think yourself in love with him! Where do you meet him? Have you been to bed with him? If you have, you've ruined yourself, you realise that, don't you?' How I'd love to have been able to say 'Yes, yes, we're lovers. I'm going to have his baby, in fact it's triplets — they'll pop out waving hammers and sickles!'

'But the truth was I hadn't seen him for years. I didn't know how to contact him without risking a snub, and all I was doing was keeping alive a kind of crush I'd developed in high school — not even a crush, a sort of obsession. Everything he was doing was at odds with everything I was living, but I hated my life and I lived another life through the cuttings, imagining myself working with him, working for the same things. I think I was already a Communist by then because you have to understand that the only white people who opposed Apartheid seriously then were Communists. Say what you like, Communists have always stood against Fascism. But of course I hadn't done anything about it. To my parents, joining the Communist Party would be the same as joining the Mafia. What am I talking about — much worse!

'He was working for a Jewish law firm called Rosenberg and Rosenberg, and one day I saw they were advertising for a typist. Of course I applied. Some outer-office snotface gave me a typing test. I was jittering with nervousness, hoping and praying every second that Jordan would walk in, that I'd just get a chance to see him, say hallo. Of course he didn't, and my test must have been the worst they'd ever seen — my hands were literally shaking and I couldn't even see the copy through the sweat running in my eyes. Snotface just gave a sort of sour smile, and I got up and left. I felt really bad. But something stopped me running off home. I sat in my car for two hours till he came out.'

'Behold the conquering hero came — at last.'

'Yes. He was my hero . . . If I'd been shaking in that office, you can imagine what a state I was in when I saw him, but I scrambled out of the car somehow and more or less threw myself in his way. And you know what?'

'He didn't recognise you.'

'Oh yes, he did! Right away. And he was glad to see me. And I told him about the test, and even hinted why I'd been so nervous. He took me straight back into the office and said to Snotface, 'This is the girl we're going to hire.' She said, 'But she can't type,' and Jordan said, 'What on earth's that got to do with it? All I want is a secretary with big tits who'll sit on my lap.' ' Judy threw her head back in a burst of laughter. 'Her face! She looked straight at my tits to check, she couldn't stop herself! Of course from that minute on I knew what I felt was real love, not just a crush.'

'So you got your dream. To work with him, to help him.'

'Yes. That was the start of my serious involvement, with the Party and with the anti-Apartheid movement. Jordan and I were

119

never really apart after that. Oh, it was a while before I dared to sleep with him. My free acting hadn't caught up with my free thinking, and I had to go home every night to a mother who could always tell if I'd even held hands with a man, just by looking at me. The deeper in I got with Jordan, the more sure I was that I wanted to make my life with him, the more frightened I got of what my family would do when they knew.'

She paused for breath. George said, gruffly through the ache in his heart, 'This is a great story. Go on.' The ache was caused by the conviction that he could never live up to this, or compete with this paragon.

'What happened in the end was, I told Barry, my adored older brother, the one who used to lead the shopbreaking expeditions, in total confidence, and he promptly blew the whistle. Came straight out with it that night at the dinner-table, in front of Mom, Dad, two aunts, one uncle and a family friend who was a minister of the Dutch Reform Church, a real Africaner hardliner. 'Guess what, ladies and gents? Jude's gone bananas for Jordan Priestman the well-known defender of kaffirs, and she wants to marry him, so shall we crack open some champagne, or just call in the men in white coats?' The silence was something I'll never forget in my life. It was like I imagine that moment just before an axe falls on your neck or the trapdoor opens when you're topped. Why I hate to remember it even now is because it should have been a wonderful moment, a moment of exhilaration and defiance, of breaking free, but it was a moment of perfect terror.

'Before anyone could do or say anything, I had to act. I had to do something completely outrageous to distract attention from this other outrage. So I stood up in my place and threw my dinner at my brother. I screamed at him, 'You dirty little swine, you gave me your sacred word!' And he sat there with gravy and peas dripping from his hair and he looked at me with absolute contempt, and said, 'I don't have to keep promises to a Commie traitor.' '

There was a silence. Then George said, 'After which, no doubt you had no choice but to leave home.'

She nodded. 'Mom tried to stop me but her heart wasn't in it. She was the least shocked — she'd been half-expecting it since she'd found the scrapbook, dreading it rather — but she couldn't go against Dad, against her whole conditioning. You see, Jordan wasn't just a radical or a renegade. Anyone who defended blacks and Communists was seen as an enemy of the white community, of Christianity even, on the side of the Great Threat, the thing every one of them lived in terrible secret fear of. It was the equivalent of a Dutchman helping to breach a dyke, trying to let in the ocean to inundate everything and sweep it away.'

'So you won your man and lost your family.'

'Well, not entirely. Mom came round — I think chiefly because she had four assorted sons and only one daughter, me, when she never liked men in the first place.'

'You said she's had three husbands?'

'Oh well, women like her can't not be married. She married for status and money. All her grandkids are males too, except Tina. It must hurt her to think she's got Jordan's sperm to thank for that!'

George shifted his eyes and felt his face get hot again. 'So what happened when he was arrested?'

Judy got up and went to get a drink. This was the bad part, the part that she'd never told anyone except Abby.

'George, there are things I could never explain to you about South Africa, things you could never understand because you haven't lived them. But this about Jordan, it may just be easier to tell you than it would be to tell a comrade.'

He smiled. 'Don't I rate as a comrade?'

'No. And you never will. And at this moment I'm glad. Now, please, you've been very patient, very sympathetic in your listening, and now I want you to listen and then — then — *not* to say anything bland and Yorkshire like, 'Well, that wasn't so bad,' or 'Anyone might have done the same,' or 'That's nothing for you to be ashamed of.' Because it bleddy well is bad and I am and forever will be ashamed of it, because I love Jordan, we're married and he's part of me. Do you understand?'

'I think so.'

She drew a deep breath.

'Jordan was taken in with a small group

of Communists who were accused of being members of *Umkhonto We Sizwe*. Activists, militants. Jordan wasn't really one of them. He acted for them professionally and he was a sympathiser but he had never taken part in any actions. They — they wouldn't have trusted him with that kind of thing, though he often told me in his fierce, angry moods that he wanted to be part of all that. I was told afterwards, it wasn't that they doubted his commitment. They owed him a lot for helping them in legal cases. He'd stood up to a lot of certain kinds of pressure. He was very brave morally, but they were afraid he wasn't — physically up to it. Not tough enough not to crack if — '

Something got into her throat and stopped her. George put his hand over hers but she drew it away. She was not looking at him.

She cleared her throat, lit another cigarette and went on.

'Well, they were right. As soon as those brute bastards started really hurting Jordan, not just slapping him about like they do to soften prisoners up, but heavy beatings and threatening to throw him out of the window, which was no idle threat as we all knew, he did crack, and names started to come out. He tried to stop himself but he couldn't; he said afterwards it was like trying to stop yourself bleeding. You know, they used to tell us, 'Say nothing, don't give them *anything*. Once you start that's it, you're lost' — and that's what happened to Jordan.'

'Some people can stand it better than others,'

said George. 'Who could blame him?'

Her head came up. Her eyes were glittering with anger, pain and tears. 'I told you *not* to do that,' she said. 'I'll tell you who could blame him, who had a right to blame him — two lots of people: the ones he gave the names of as part of a deal, and the ones who held out. They had the right. And a lot of them did blame him, and for all I know, they still do.'

George was silent, but he held her hand. His mind was afire with awful imaginings.

'Everyone in the movement knew,' went on Judy. 'A big group was rounded up three weeks after Jordan was let out. Well, there were others arrested with him, it didn't have to be him who'd ratted, and I — you can just figure out what I was going through at the time, but at that stage I didn't dream — I couldn't even contemplate that he would talk. I thought he was a lion, a rock, every kind of hero. Torture, a life sentence — it never occurred to me that anything worse than those could happen. I was half-prepared for those . . .'

Her nose and eyes were streaming. He put a handkerchief into her hand and she clenched it fiercely to her face.

'But what they did then, those filthy lousy shites, they cleaned him up and *they let him go*. Like, 'Ach, thanks, man. You've been a real help, so off you go.' And there was nothing he could do but break the Communist oath — you know, the main Communist group promised each other that they wouldn't leave the country, not to escape arrest or prison or anything; they

124

wanted to be examples, to show up the system. Men who served twenty years survived it fine and kept their self-respect and so did their wives. Oh God. How I wish Jordan had been put away for twenty years instead of — '

She broke and sobbed, her head on her arms on the table.

After a while when she didn't stop, George came round and lifted her up and led her to the sofa where he sat with her and held her to him. At last she leant back and blew her nose and became calmer.

'He left the country and went into hiding,' she said. 'I've never seen him since. We write to each other. He's been all over the place. He's in India at the moment.'

'Hasn't he ever visited you and Tina?'

'No.'

'Why not? Isn't it safe?'

She didn't answer for a long time. At last she said, 'I think it would be safe. But I also think he needs to believe he's still in danger. It's strange how shame takes people. It's something you never get over. Countries don't, and individuals don't. Not unless they're dead to shame in the first place.'

'Why don't you visit him?'

'If he wanted me to, he'd ask me,' she said. 'He's never given me a proper address, only postes restantes.'

'Perhaps he doesn't think he deserves you any more. What about Tina?'

'Tina thinks he's in hiding from the South African police,' she said flatly.

125

He stared at her. Nothing she had told him had shocked him like this. 'You've kept it from her?'

'She — she's ashamed of me anyway. Ashamed where I think she ought to be proud. If she knew about her father — the truth . . . I couldn't tell her.'

'Maybe that's why you and she don't get on together.'

She looked at him quizzically. He couldn't read her look. It was as if he had said something either outrageously stupid or the opposite — something that she had never thought of.

'But won't he ever come back — come in from the cold?'

'I don't know. There's talk now among us exiles that Mandela *will* be freed soon, and when he is everything will begin to change. Apartheid is cracking under its own inconsistencies and world disapproval. Britain doesn't disapprove but other countries, including the US, do. There might well be a change in the law in SA, to let banned people come back home, even maybe that we'll get compensation. Jordan's not the only one, of course. There are a couple of men in Zimbabwe, out in the open, running businesses, people who ratted, and they're planning to go back some day and brazen it out. So there's no reason why Jordan shouldn't be — rehabilitated, too.'

'Wouldn't that be good?'

'I don't know. I never have known. Part of me longs for it; another part thinks it's terrible.

126

People suffered and lost so much because of him — I don't see how he can be forgiven by the Movement, by the ones he betrayed, let alone forgive himself.'

'Can you forgive him?'

'Ach, yes!' she cried. 'I forgave him long ago.'

'Do you still love him, though?'

'Yes.'

'And that's why you have to — send this letter.'

'Yes. I can't deceive him about something like this.'

That's love, thought George enviously.

'Meantime, can I kiss you?'

Exhausted with telling, she gave him her mouth and her arms and let him cuddle her and gentle her, and later, she made them coffee. But he still knew that after that, she expected him to leave. She wasn't ready for anything more. And so it had been for the weeks between the sending of the letter and the reply.

* * *

The reply was 'favourable'. Judy read it to George with a strange air of pride. Jordan wrote that Judy must do everything that she could to fulfil herself and be happy, adding that he had 'no right' to stand between her and some companionship, some respite from loneliness. But he added something that struck Judy with a shock of guilt. She didn't read that part aloud.

127

'But keep me and you-and-me in a separate compartment. Don't tell him too much about me. I beg this of you. Don't tell me anything about him and don't betray me to him. You know what I'm asking. No pillow-talk about me, nothing that you know I would want kept secret and private.'

But it was too late for that, and her guilt at having already 'betrayed' him to George kept her from his bed.

8

Only three weeks after the night of the demo, Pleasure bought and employed a pregnancy-testing kit. When it proved positive, she was shocked, if you can be shocked without being surprised. She had known. She simply sensed the change in her body, in her life.

Child of nature or not, she was scarcely overjoyed. She was a free spirit, she'd worked hard at school and she wanted a career; a baby at nineteen was absolutely no part of that blueprint. She was not about to have her life messed up if she could avoid it. She didn't apportion blame. She never saw the point in that. The thing to do was to come to grips with it, decide what to do and do it. That was her general policy which had worked admirably till now.

Sensibly, she didn't do anything or tell anyone for the first few days. She went to school, kept her secret, and got on with things. She even managed to write a letter to Clem without hinting, quite a feat. She visited her mother in hospital (complications had set in — Florence smoked too much, and to the shoulder injury had been added a go of bronchitis) in the same spirit. Clem was allowed an extra week of blithe ignorance. With Florence it was different.

She was a bit of a child of nature herself and she knew Pleasure very well. She said nothing at first; she was concentrating on getting herself

129

better. But when she was allowed home, and had cleaned the place up as well as she could one-handed while Pleasure was at school, she had a look through the sheets in the laundry basket (Pleasure had neglected to visit the launderette for some weeks) and stood there, holding one of them in her hand, giving little, rueful grunts deep in her throat. When Pleasure came home she tackled her.

'Been entertaining, I see.' She showed her the sheet.

'Yes, well, sorry. I mean, that I didn't wash it. Any objections?'

'Only if there's results.' She pinioned her daughter with her eyes. Pleasure met them briefly, then turned away. 'Uh-oh. I thought something was wrong. But you can't be sure yet.'

'Well, I am.'

'You're a bad girl. You are. Sit and have your tea.'

Pleasure sat and had her tea. After a bit, Florence said, 'What you going to do then?' She meant, Who's the boy and what's he going to do?

'Get rid of it,' said Pleasure.

Florence, who had taken the original news quite calmly, fairly flew off the handle now. She jumped up from the table and banged her good hand down on it, making a tempest in Pleasure's teacup.

'You going to do no such a thing! No one made you do what you did, you had your pleasure, now you talking murder! You wicked,

130

or what? God will punish you and if He don't, I will! I'll throw you out in the street if you do that! Stop working for you, stop keeping you, stop loving you and then see how you get on!'

Pleasure watched her in dismay. When she'd finished shouting, Florence fell on the sofa and sobbed, cradling her bad arm. Pleasure came to her.

'Come on, Mum, don't get in a state. It's not like that.'

'So what is it like, tell me!'

'It's not killing a person. It's only a little lump of my own flesh.'

Florence grew a bit calmer. She turned and took Pleasure in her one arm.

'Listen, Pleasure. You know I wasn't married when I started Raymond and Genny.' These were Pleasure's twin siblings, now aged twenty-six. Pleasure knew the story of old, and suppressed a sigh. 'My mama helped me and in the end, when they was born and their daddy seen how good-looking they was, he married me fast enough.'

'Not for long,' said Pleasure.

'For long enough to give them a name and me a few years of happiness. Would I be without them now?'

'You are,' said Pleasure cruelly.

'They leave 'cause they grown up. I don't want 'em hanging around now! But I ain't sorry I had them twins of mine, they gave me something to strive for. I wouldn't have come to England and met *your* Daddy and worked in a hospital or done one interesting, independent thing I did

131

do, if I hadn't had them to bring up.'

Pleasure didn't bother reminding her mother of how often she had bemoaned her lot and wished herself well out of Britain and back in the sunny, simple-life, relation-filled West Indies. Or of the countless times she had seen her chase Raymond around the flat, clouting him on the head and declaring loudly that she wished she'd never had him. Genny'd given her mother her share of grief too, and had run off at last with a very doubtful character, whom Florence suspected of pushing crack. And where were they now? The last card from Genny had been postmarked Amsterdam, and there'd been nothing from Ray for three years. A fat lot of comfort they'd given their mother in return for all her sweated efforts on their behalf.

In fact, thinking of them now, Pleasure realised that being brought up in a (mainly) manless family by a hardworking, unqualified mother was the chief thing that had influenced her to the decision that had only just now surfaced. She felt sure it was the right one. But looking at her mother's face, slit-eyed and determined, she knew that Florence's *laisser faire* outlook, generous as it was, stopped here.

'Well, we'll see,' Pleasure temporised.

'Yeah, we'll see,' said Florence, nodding grimly. 'When December come, we'll see a baby. We better, Pleasure, or you out on your ass.'

★ ★ ★

Clem was astonished and excited when, a few days later, he had a card signed *P.* which said, '*Meet you Sunday at three on the picket.*' He promptly phoned her. Her mother answered.

'Pleasure ain't here now. She's at a meetin'. Who want her?'

'My name's Clem Marshall. Could you give Pleasure a message?'

'Go on then.'

Clem had formed an impression of Pleasure's mother as a wonderful earth-mother figure, full of big-hearted tolerance and without hang-ups. He had no hesitation in saying, 'She sent me a card suggesting we meet in Town on Sunday, but I can't get an exeat.'

'What you can't get?' asked Florence, who had just raked a magazine towards her and scribbled '*Glen Marshal*' across the beaming face of the girl on the cover.

'An exeat. Permission to leave school. Ask her to phone me at six o'clock tonight or tomorrow. I'll stay by the phone — she's got the number.'

'Give it again to make sure.'

Clem dictated the number. Florence wrote it with care. 'I'll tell her.'

'Thanks very much,' said Clem happily, and hung up.

Pleasure was given her message.

'He the one?'

'He's just a guy I met on the picket.'

'So why you writing him and making dates?'

'We've got a special demo on the anniversary of Soweto and we want all the supporters we can get. I've notified dozens of people.' Pleasure was not a good liar, especially to her mother, but she now knew she'd have to become one, and she made a good start. Florence believed her. Nevertheless she did not throw the magazine away.

Pleasure duly telephoned Clem. She said she wanted to see him and arranged to meet him in the village near his school, which was in-bounds. It was thirty-five miles from London but it was on a Greenline bus route. He gave her instructions. She made the journey the following Saturday.

It was a beautiful day. May, Pleasure concluded, must be *the* month if you lived in the country — it couldn't get any better than this. The gardens were something almost miraculous to her London-bred eyes — brilliantly cushioned with aubretia, rockroses, heather, polyanthus. She knew none of these names, nor was she familiar with such bucolic sights, so much quiet and such balmy air, full of lovely smells, and bees. But she knew what she liked, and she liked this.

As she walked from the bus-stop to the little tea-shop where Clem had arranged to meet her, she trailed her hand against an amazing hedge. Some of its little new leaves were like cut-out pieces of bright green silk. Others were opening in a tiny flurry of accordion pleats; still others were shiny and pinkly bronzed, and there were startlingly deep-reddish ones, too. She plucked several and examined them, and smoothed them against her face, feeling them not so much like silk as like cool skin — an elf's perhaps, or some other being who had never set foot in Hackney or its environs. She made a little leaf-posy as she walked along, to give to Clem.

He'd had similar thoughts, only it was wild flowers that he fancied and had picked for her. Late bluebells and pink campion and frothy cow-parsley, and dead-nettles in yellow and white, and trailing mauve vetch. He didn't know their names, either. He spiked them with an assortment of grasses and was very pleased with the result.

They arrived almost at the same time. They stopped and grinned at each other. They didn't kiss, but solemnly handed over their posies. Clem could not get over how beautiful she looked in the sunlight with his flowers held to her nose, the reflection off a buttercup making a golden glow on her cheek. Her hair had been freshly plaited (it must take hours!) and lay close to her head, which had the shape of a woman's in an Egyptian tomb-carving. Her eyes were slightly slanted and the lashes curled back on themselves into almost complete circles. He had relived the scene in her bedroom, the deeds done in her bed, over and over again in the meantime; but looking at her now he could scarcely believe he had held her and moved his hands all over her brown satin body, that he had 'known' her in that special, biblical way. It was quite unthinkable that he should ever want another woman after her.

He touched her hand as she had touched

the baby leaves and carried it to his face for a moment.

'It's so wonderful to see you, Pleasure.'

'I've missed you, too.' A woman with a dog walked by, and glanced back at them, frowning. They did not even notice her, little guessing she would lose no time in betraying Clem to his Head of House. 'Let's go in and have some tea. Do they have those cream teas you told me about?'

'No, that's just around Dorset. The cream here isn't worth eating, it comes out of a squeegie thing and turns into a puddle. But there's cake. Are you hungry?'

'Starving.'

They sat at a little oak table by the window with its frilly curtains. Pleasure asked the waitress, an elderly woman who seemed surprised about something, for a jamjar of water for her flowers. The woman's face, which had stiffened at the sight of her, thawed, and she brought a pretty vase instead and said, 'They fade so quick, the wild ones, you have to get them in water right away. What will you have, then? The sponge is nice and fresh.'

When she'd gone to get their tea, Pleasure said, 'You're dead lucky to go to school in such a lovely place! God, you should see my school, it's a real toilet.'

'So is mine,' he said feelingly. 'I sometimes think I can't hack it another day.'

'What's wrong with it?'

'It's just disgusting. Regimented. And their *minds*! They're always watching you. They keep

136

hinting at things you mustn't do that you'd never have thought of. All that chapel drives me mad, too, enough to put you off for life.'

'How religious are you?'

'Not a lot. Mum's dead hot on it but I think she may have overdone it with me when I was little, all those bedside sessions with the rosary and going off to Mass on Sundays instead of watching *Sesame Street* . . . Personally I think you need it or you don't, and I don't.'

'So why don't you tell her? Just say you want to go to a day school like I do.'

He shrugged. 'Far too late now, with finals coming up. Oh, what the hell.' He leant towards her and squeezed her hand under the table. 'It was so great at your place,' he whispered. 'The other guys cack on about sex but I can tell they know sod-all about it really, not about what we had.'

'Do you join in?' she asked. She let her hand stay in his but it was hard to, somehow. Her secret lay between them and she almost decided not to tell him, not to take that glow of happiness away from him, just to cope alone somehow. For the first time she thought about the morning-after pill she had neglected to take, his virginal state, and knew their responsibility for her plight was asymmetrical.

'Of course I don't join in! You mean tell them about you? You must be crazy! They wouldn't understand — they're just a bunch of pricks. I mean, they read *porno mags* — they think that's what it's about. I couldn't even mention you to any of them.'

137

She thought, Shit. He's serious. It gave her mixed feelings. She didn't know how she felt about him. He wasn't even very good-looking and she was used to a much more robust and practised lover. But there was something about him, something the others had lacked, a sensitiveness that could be really hurt. She stared at the vase of spring flowers on the table and tears came to her eyes.

He didn't notice at first. His mind was on something else.

'Pleasure, I wanted to ask. I keep thinking about that business you said at the police station that day, about what they did to you. Was that — ? Well, I know it was true or you wouldn't have said it, but — '

'It was true all right,' she said in a muffled voice. 'They made me take my clothes off and then two or three police officers came to the doorway of the room, which was open, and stood there sneering and saying I was a skinny little black scumbag.'

He didn't say anything. She glanced at him. The pain was so stark in his face that she was ashamed of having spelt it out to him. That, too, she should have protected him from, kept it to herself. No, she decided, she would not tell him about the baby, she would not. She had made the running, and promised about the pill. It was not his fault.

But he had seen her tears.

'Pleasure! You're crying! Don't, it's all over — ' She met his eyes, biting her tongue, but it was no use. As she had known, so he knew.

He read it in her eyes; words were unnecessary. She saw the knowledge come into his face.

The shock was appalling. He sank back in his chair. She suddenly noticed he had some freckles because they stood out like mud splashes on a white surface.

He didn't say anything, not a word of reproach for the betrayal, the sin of omission, the pill not taken. He just stared at her, his lips open, stunned.

She leant forward and put her hand on his where it lay clenched on the table. 'Don't, Clem! It's all right. I came because I may need some money. I'm going to get rid of it.'

His face went a shade paler, if possible. 'But you can't,' he whispered. 'You can't do that.'

'I'll have to. There's no way I can have it, is there?'

He shook his head, but not in agreement, just in stupefaction. They sat in silence until the woman came back with the tea. 'There you are then!' she said jovially. 'Who's going to be Mother?'

They locked eyes and suddenly they both had an urge, a fleeting, hysterical one, to burst out laughing. 'I am,' said Pleasure. She laid hold of the diminutive teapot and began to pour.

Clem tried to recover himself. 'Perhaps your mother could help,' he said faintly, thinking of the all-coping black Mammy of his imaginings.

Pleasure misunderstood him. 'Yeah, you'd think so, and her a nurse's aide,' she said. 'But she won't, no way. She's a proper Catholic, not like you and me, and she won't hear of it, let alone help. That's my main problem is her, because when she finds out about me getting rid of it, she will absolutely do her number. She says she'll throw me out of the flat if I do it, and she might, too. She threw my brother Ray out for smoking ganja, can you believe? Mind you, he was driving her mad anyway, and I don't. I mean, we argue and that, but she'd miss me if I went . . .'

He said stupidly, 'You've got your finals next month.'

'It'll all be back to normal by then,' she said firmly. 'I wish we'd ordered sandwiches.'

And she proceeded to eat everything in sight, as if she hadn't a care. Only Clem sat there, numb with despair, and couldn't even assuage his raging thirst with a cup of tea, because to do something as normal as drinking tea under these terrible circumstances seemed like singing a pop song at a funeral.

9

About ten days after this, Harriet and Ken were in their garden, discussing with mild acrimony whether they should dig a runner-bean trench one spit deep or two, when they heard a car draw up outside their gate.

There were only four properties beyond theirs up the narrow lane, and one was an empty farm. They exchanged a look, which on the surface said: 'For us?' and 'Must be,' but which actually meant, 'Gawd! Who the hell's this?' (Ken) and 'If only it's friends!' (Harry). Then they turned as one to the gate and saw two heads appearing over it.

Interesting heads, thought Harriet. Bloody strangers, thought Ken. A tall, fair, ruddy-faced man in an old tweed jacket and cap, and a nearly-as-tall woman with dark-blonde hair worn down ('Mutton as lamb,' was Harry's first reaction. 'She must be my age!') and a burnt-orange poncho.

'Hallo?' Ken greeted them in a tone any English person would recognise at once as imparting a goodbye.

Judy, however, was not English. She stared round in approval, then actually opened the gate uninvited and came in, preceded, to Ken's dismay, by a largish very ugly white dog that made him think of Bill Sikes' Bullseye. George of course knew better and stayed in the lane.

'Hi, I'm Judy Priestman,' she said, vigorously shaking hands with Harry, who stared at her. 'We're looking for a place called Bugle Farm.'

'But it's empty,' said Ken. 'Falling down, just about.'

'We're going to look at it,' said George diffidently.

'What, with a view to buying it?' asked Ken, breaking rules but unable to help himself. Neighbours mattered out here, and besides, the farm was a derelict eyesore on his favourite walk. It would be an excellent thing if someone bought it, and this chap looked as if he might actually want to farm it. Part of the property was a five-acre field which ran alongside their garden. Every year at this time it was filled with blowing dandelions, against whose progeny a continual war had to be fought. Ken moved a few steps toward the gate in minimal welcome and George, recognising the signal, tentatively entered and closed it behind him. The cat, meanwhile, had fled up a tree.

Harry was still gazing at Judy. 'Don't I know you?' she asked.

'Well — '

'Weren't you on television the other night? That programme on police powers?'

'Oh, did you see me?' exclaimed Judy. 'Ach, I looked such a *fright*. Today's the first time I've taken the bag off my head. Talk about mutton dressed as lamb!'

Harry suppressed a snort, but hurriedly said, 'Nonsense. you looked very interesting and glamorous. I loved your earrings.'

142

'Thanks, doll, but what about what I *said*?'

Ken's face changed. He'd seen the programme too; it had made him furious. She'd attacked the Metropolitan police in terms he had thought outrageous. She'd called them racists, actually claimed they had too much power, that they were abusing it. Said she should know, because they'd abused and assaulted *her*. And this from a woman who admitted to having been arrested fifteen times in three years! No smoke without fire, she must have done *something* other than take part in a peaceful protest. Damn it all, this was a free country.

To his chagrin, Harry had drawn the newcomer into eager discussion and down the garden, leaving him with the fellow.

'Er — Bugle Farm is just up the lane about five hundred yards,' he said. 'There is a sign but it's too weather-worn to read. You'll see the drive on the right, the gate's hanging off its hinges.' Ken was keeping an eye on the dog, who was relieving himself copiously against an apple tree.

'The agent said it was a bit run-down,' agreed the man. Yorkshire, was it? thought Ken. Yes. Well. No more of a 'foreigner' in these parts than himself. It behoved him to be courteous, but . . .

'I say, could you call your dog? It's — '

'Zulu! Come here!'

The dog obeyed, temporarily.

'Zulu? Is that his name?' asked Ken with a laugh. 'But he's white.'

'Judy would probably reckon that to be a

143

racist remark,' said George, adding cheerfully, 'I knew a dog in Devon called Winston that was a Chihuahua.'

Ken looked baffled and changed the subject. 'Seriously looking for a place, are you?'

'Oh yes, very seriously. And I like the smell of this one.' He flourished some agency details. 'Sounds like a challenge.'

'Have you farmed before?'

'Only most of my life.' George had drifted well away from the gate now.

'Really, where?'

'Up north. Sheep, mainly.'

'It's mostly dairy around here, dairy and arable. Our nearest neighbour grows wheat.'

'Well, I'd raise sheep because that's what I know. What I'd like is to get into rare breeds, maybe Portlands. Zulu! Come off there! Judy, call him, will you? — And p'raps a few horses.'

'Oh! You ride?'

'Yes.'

'Hunt?' asked Ken with a trace of edge.

'Have done.'

'Hunting's a big thing around here.'

George looked at him shrewdly. 'I take it you don't approve.'

After a year in the depths of Cattistock territory, Ken knew better than to rise to this bait.

'Well, it's not my sport.'

'Don't want 'em crashing through your garden, I expect.'

'They'd better not!' said Ken feelingly.

There was a silence. The two men looked after the women, who were at the wild end of the garden, deep in grasses and conversation. Judy was waving her arms.

'Our wives seem to have found something in common,' said Ken.

'She's not my wife,' said George. 'Just a friend.'

'Did *you* see her on that TV programme?' Ken ventured to ask.

'Yes. I was in the audience.'

'Interesting discussion,' Ken fished.

'H'm,' said George. After a moment he added, 'I felt like cheering when she confronted that inspector fellow. Smooth-tongued bugger, avoided every issue, never gave a straight answer to anything. I mean, when you think about it, what are the police for, if not to preserve people's right to protest? Yet now, seemingly, they can pull people in because the officer on the spot thinks they *might* be going to cause trouble.'

Ken suddenly felt contentious.

'Too many marches and demos holding up traffic, if you ask me. Half of them nothing to do with us. Iranians, Indians, God knows what. When I was working in London . . .'

George didn't seem to hear. His eyes were on the women. 'Funny what's happening — one law after another, tightening things up. Once we were the freest country in Europe, now we're the most regulated. I looked at that man and I thought, Living evidence of the new era. Wouldn't fancy being interrogated by him, specially if I was a black. Person,' he

145

added, to Ken's passing puzzlement.

'You're suggesting there actually is racism in the force?'

George came back to him with a look of surprise. 'No doubt of that, surely. Only question is, what forms it takes.'

She's been getting at him, thought Ken. Pity. Seems a nice solid chap. Handsome woman, of course, if she'd dress reasonably. Wonder if they're — But Ken liked to think he was not into sexual speculation.

★ ★ ★

An hour later, George had decided to offer for Bugle Farm. Judy was full of enthusiasm.

'Great, man! It's a gorgeous place. But do you really think you can cope? It needs plenty doing to it.'

'Well, I've no intention of DIY-ing the big stuff. I'll get a local contractor. The milking parlour can just come the rest of the way down, I won't want that. Probably put the dip there. The barn's pretty much okay. Few roof repairs, put up pens inside, I won't need more than that to start with. New fences, they won't come cheap, but you've got to expect that. As to the house . . . '

He was worried about the thatch. Very picturesque and all that, Judy was gone on it, but there was moss and rot everywhere and he knew you had to pay all sorts of money for rethatching. Must have been what put off other buyers, because the rest of the house was all

146

right. Bit old-fashioned, but no worse than his old place; he liked those deep ceramic sinks and wooden draining-boards, and a wood-burning stove was no disadvantage. There was wood on the property, plenty of it — he liked that. Of course all the walls needed painting, and some replastering. Judy had gone crazy about the huge fireplace in the living room and the beams and the views from the bedrooms. The way she'd rushed around the place saying what she'd do with it had given him hopeful gooseflesh.

His putative neighbours down the lane had invited them to drop in for coffee on their way back, at least the wife had. Judy was keen, but George wanted to get straight back to London and put in his offer. Judy said, 'Didn't you like them? You'd better, if you're going to live here.'

'*She* was all right. Funny little wisp of a thing.' He'd already forgotten that he'd once fancied 'em like that. 'Didn't reckon much to him, though. Typical town-to-country squire. Down on hunting, that sort of thing.'

Judy turned and stared at him as if she'd never seen him before.

'Don't tell me you're not!'

'Down on hunting? Course not. It's one of the grandest things on earth.'

'George!'

'Well?'

'Are you baiting me?'

'No.'

'But hunting's terrible!'

'No, it's not,' he said stolidly. 'You don't

147

know a thing about it. Now shut up,' he said equably, as he saw she was about to fly at him. 'There's plenty you do know about, and plenty more you think you do, so just keep out of fights you've got no weapons for, or you're liable to get worsted — and you know how you can't stand that.'

Judy turned her back on him and ran her hand around a deepset window-frame. There was a long silence. Sulking, he thought ruefully. Well, some women do that. Meanwhile he climbed up and checked the underside of the thatch in the loft. When he returned she was on her knees sniffing a skirting-board.

She stood up. 'Damp rot and plenty of it,' she remarked vengefully.

'Well, it's all got to be surveyed.' He came up behind her. They'd driven down with the sunroof open and her hair smelled like linen dried outdoors. His mouth felt dried out too, so he said, 'Come on then, let's get some of that coffee if it'll bring you out of your sulk.'

She turned on him, blazing, 'I have never sulked in my life! I'm not about to start over some fascist farmers frollicking after a fucking fox!'

The spontaneous flow of alliteration and the electric blue of her eyes in anger sent him a bit mad. He had her in his arms and was kissing her hotly before either of them knew what was happening.

When they came out of it they were both flushed and breathing hard.

What's awful, thought Judy bleakly, is that I

148

am not flying down your throat about hunting at all. I'm far gone, farther than I thought . . . Oh God help me, I hope it's only tiredness and sex-starvation! But it wasn't only that, and she knew it, and knowing it, she had to try to bring it out in words.

'Look. Abby warned me. She said people like her and me should never have partners who aren't comrades. But even if we don't share a lot of past, I can talk to you and argue with you and besides . . . ' She was ashamed of her thought, but she voiced it. 'I need you. Christ, I know how feeble that sounds at my age, after all the years of making all my own decisions and doing all the looking-after for myself and everyone around me, but I feel tired and I see you as a sort of — '

'Refuge?'

She nodded ruefully. 'That's not the way you'd like me to see you. I'm sorry.'

'Whatever will work,' he said after a moment.

'And coming here to this place has made it much worse. It's the closest to heaven I've been in since I left SA.'

'South Africa — heaven?'

'Of course. It's my home. It's also the most beautiful country on the face of the earth. What do you think I'm working for, some airy-fairy unattainable ideal? D'you think I'm doing it for the poor down-trodden blacks?'

'Aren't you?'

'Yes, but I'm doing it for myself too, man!' Her accent always became broader when she grew passionate. 'Nothing works if you're only

149

doing it from altruism; you've got to have a deep self-interest mixed up in it, and my prime motive for everything I do is to get majority rule so that I can go back and live there without being imprisoned or without being bleddy well ashamed. It's one or the other for any half-human white South African now.'

'All right, but that's a long way off. I've learned my lesson about politics, I'd never let it come between me and someone I loved again. There are other things in life, even yours, than politics, surely.'

Judy sat down on the windowseat. She reached for his big hand and held it tightly, infinitely comforted by the instant response she felt in it as his fingers closed round hers.

'Of course there are,' she said.

'Like living down here with me, for instance?'

She turned to look over her shoulder, out over the Dorset fields, all balmy in the hazy May light.

To live here, she was thinking, dismayed by the sheer dragging longing behind the thought. No, I'm not ready to quit the struggle, God, no! But to have it to get away to. To be able to leave London and my maddening daughter and all my picket-children who I seem, inexcusably, to love so much more — to have a rest from nightshifts and politics and committees and lawyers and workshops and all the hassle with the fuzz . . . Just every now and then to take breaks from the unending round of work and campaigning, arguing and writing, worrying and being angry — and scared. To wake once in a while to country noises instead of town ones, to a day of bone-idleness and beautiful sights and smells, not to mention the sheer, glorious release of getting regularly and thoroughly screwed! Ach, Zulu would go crazy for it too, she thought, the freedom, poor housebound old sod . . . She could hear him yipping somewhere as if already chasing a rabbit.

She sniffed, snorted and muttered something. George leant closer. 'What?'

'I said I'd love to.' She turned on him and almost shouted, 'I'd love to! You don't know how I need a *rest*.' She was shocked to find her voice wobbling. 'Oh, what am I cacking on about. We can't, of course we can't. Listen to me, I should be ashamed. One sniff of country air and one kiss and I'm going soft inside like a bleddy marshmallow!'

'Jordan gave his okay. Why shouldn't you?'

'It's all very well for Jordan!' she said with unwonted fierceness.

'You mean, he doesn't have to sleep with me?' he asked humorously. 'I wouldn't have agreed, if I'd been him.'

'But you're not.'

'No. There are times when I'd like to be. I wouldn't mind being loved by a woman as much as you love him.'

'You'd need to be a revolutionary to inspire that kind of love,' she said ironically.

'I've been thinking about that. But it's no use. I don't believe in violence, revolutionary or otherwise. If what you call armed struggle means laying bombs and killing people, there

151

isn't a cause left in the world I'd do that for. It's bloody astonishing,' he said as if he'd just been struck by it, 'that you're so against killing vermin, when you'll spend half the night arguing it's justifiable to put tyres round people's necks and set fire to them if they're traitors.'

She started to speak, but he caught hold of her and stopped her mouth by pressing her face abruptly against his stomach. 'All right, all right. I shouldn't have said that. You didn't defend 'necklacing', you just defended Winnie Mandela defending it. This is no time to be arguing political priorities. Just now I want you not to answer yes or no, just to say you'll give it some thought. And come with me and let that dog out. I think I must've shut him into the milking parlour.'

10

That evening, after Harry had put all the tools neatly away and Ken had washed up the coffee-things and glasses from the drinks that had followed, they were together in the kitchen getting supper. Neither of them had yet spoken about the visitors, but both were very full of thoughts about them.

Harry broke the silence on the subject.

'You didn't like him, did you?'

'Did you? Oh, I know you took a shine to *her*, God knows why.'

'I liked them both a lot,' she said quietly.

'Why? They're oddballs, the pair of them.' Even as he spoke he knew that that was enough to explain their attraction for her. 'They won't fit in here.'

' 'Fit in here'! What does that mean? It's like talking about a piece in a jigsaw 'fitting in' when three-quarters of the pieces are missing!'

'What do you mean by that?'

'I mean the place is so thinly populated that there's nobody to 'fit in' with. It wouldn't matter what one was like — I mean, I never see anybody, so what does 'fitting in' mean?'

Ken stirred the soup in silence. With his propensity for joining things, he met plenty of people; he saw the place quite differently. Harry had never expressed her sense of isolation so plainly.

153

'Did you notice the change in her when they came back?' she went on.

'Well, she was quieter, now you mention it.' A welcome reduction in all that flashing of earrings.

'Quieter? She was completely different. You didn't hear her before, chatting away. Then they went off to look at the farm, and when they came back she hardly said another word; she seemed to be off somewhere. Do you think they'd had a row?'

'Possibly. You know they're not married.'

'No,' she said slowly. 'I didn't know that.'

'He said they were just friends.'

They carried their meal to the table. Ken would have liked to open some wine but he decided not to — they'd all had a drink earlier. After a while Harry said thoughtfully, 'But surely he wouldn't bring her here to live if they weren't married. That would cause talk.'

'That's what I meant. I think she'd raise some hackles around here, married or not. I gathered they're both left-wingers. Her antipolice views, for instance, would not go down well in this law-abiding neighbourhood.'

This Tory-Party-in-the-geriatrics-ward, you mean, thought Harry. 'She told me some things that shook me, I don't mind saying so.'

'Do you believe her?'

She blinked. 'Well — yes.'

'That's the whole trouble nowadays!' Ken suddenly blazed. 'Everyone's so damned willing to believe any tale they hear against established authority! When we were burgled in the old

154

house, look how decent the police were. They were there in twenty minutes flat. That young constable even cleaned up the filth for us.' He could not restrain a shudder at the memory of their home befouled by those disgusting yobs.

'Didn't get any of our stuff back, though, did they, never mind catch the thief,' said Harry, reaching for a piece of toast. 'Anyway, we're white and middle-class. We're the sort they reckon they're there for. But they ought to be decent to everybody and they're not.'

Ken felt angry and thwarted. In a few minutes' arm-waving conversation, that weirdo seemed to have subverted Harry. Her arguments were half-baked and absurd, but he'd never been good at thinking on his feet when he was angry and he couldn't immediately come up with a suitably cutting rebuttal.

Just then the phone rang. Harry went to answer it. After a few moments she came back into the dining room, frowning.

'It's Mr Radley. He wants to speak to you.'

'*Radley?*' Ken pushed back his chair. 'What does he want?' Mr Radley was Clem's head-master. They exchanged a look of anxiety. Harry followed Ken back into the sitting room.

'Hallo? Marshall here. Yes, Mr Radley. Well, go on.'

Harry stood at his side for a long time, studying his face and learning only that she should brace herself. He was blinking his eyes as he always did when he was trying to come to grips with something.

At last he said, 'Yes. I will, of course. Yes,

155

I think you're right about that. Not tonight, anyhow, we'll wait till tomorrow to see if he turns up. Thank you for calling. Good night.'

He put down the phone and turned to Harriet.

'He's run away,' she surmised, appalled, every other thought and concern banished from her mind.

'Yes. Sometime late this afternoon. He slipped out at the beginning of prep and they didn't notice he'd gone for a couple of hours.'

'Was he in trouble?'

'Yes, sort of.' Ken pushed his hand through his wiry hair. 'Nothing all that serious, Radley said. He was seen off-limits talking to some girl in the village so they gave him a breaker. That's a punishment, bit military-style, running round a paddock so many times or something, and he forgot to turn up for it.'

Harry's face whitened and narrowed. 'Well, if that's the reason.' she said tightly, 'I don't blame him. I just hope he has the sense to come straight back here.'

The enormity of the thing suddenly hit Ken and made him explode.

'Damn fool, what the hell's he playing at! He'll be in far worse trouble now!'

'There's not a lot we can do except wait.'

'And worry ourselves sick!' He seemed very put about, more than Harry was.

'There's nothing really to worry about, surely. He's got money and sense. He'll turn up.'

It wasn't till they were getting ready for bed, several newsless hours later, that Harry remembered about the girl.

'Who was this girl he was seen with? Was she local?'

'Apparently not,' said Ken grimly.

'How did they know?'

'Well. You know that village. English as ours here.'

She turned round from her dressing-table where she was brushing her hair. 'What do you mean?'

'She was black.'

She let out an incredulous, half-laughing squawk. 'BLACK! You're joking!'

'Would I joke on that subject?'

'Clem — and a black girl? Where on earth did he find her?'

'What are you *grinning* at?'

'I just think it's so funny! You so down on anyone who isn't English you even bristle about a Welsh accent on a radio announcer — ' He turned his back on her and hung up his clothes, furious. After a minute she came to pat him contritely.

'Sorry, darling.'

'How would you fancy him falling for a non-Catholic?'

'I'd hate it. Obviously we don't want him getting mixed up with *any* girl completely different from him. Anyway, I'm sure he's not. Mixed up with her. Probably just a chance acquaintance. Come on, let's plug in the phone in here and go to bed. There's sure to be news in the morning.'

And they did. But neither of them slept much.

Sex would have been balm for both of them, but it wasn't an option.

★ ★ ★

When morning came, then lunchtime, and the phone still hadn't rung, Harry's calm vanished.

At about four, Ken returned from a visit to the local MP's surgery. He had gone there on a point of order about the Council, whose brutish machines were rampaging along the country verges, mowing down the wild flowers before they could seed themselves and raping the hedges while there might still be wild birds nesting in them. Waiting in line behind people all buzzing with complaints about dogs fouling the school playground and suchlike, he suddenly felt the incongruity of his being there at all. The hedges, which had loomed so large on his agenda yesterday, could not but seem trumpery now.

He asked himself, as he drove swiftly home, what was the matter with him. Why did he find it so difficult to turn himself away from a mapped route or preformed plan? He shouldn't have gone. And when he arrived home, Harry promptly and vigorously confirmed it.

'How could you go off to see that stupid old Tory *fart* when we don't know if Clem's alive or dead?' she berated him.

He was brought up short. *Tory fart?* Had he heard aright? He had never known her use such an expression before. He didn't realise until he heard Judy use it much later, where she had got it from.

158

'Darling — !'

'I've been here all alone, just imagining what could have happened . . . I thought he had money but maybe he hasn't. I mean, the school keeps his money. If he didn't plan ahead he could just have run off without a penny!'

'All that to avoid the 'breaker'? It just doesn't make sense.'

'How can you be so crass? What about the humiliation? How could we have put him in a school where they still use military punishments! We're the only country left in Europe that still has schools that openly acknowledge their *failure* by inflicting pain on children. I thought it was a horrible place the moment I walked into it!'

'No, you didn't,' said Ken blankly. '*You* chose it. It was me who hated it. Talk about inflicting pain, all those appalling crucifixes in every room! If that's their idea of goading kids to learn, why not some graphic statuettes of people stretched on the rack or being dismembered?'

Harry gave an exclamation and ran out of the room. Ken poured himself a drink, swallowed it, hid the glass and followed her. He found her out in the garden, on her knees, tearing fiercely at the dandelions around the edges of a flowerbed, with tears running down her face. He looked at her helplessly and did an abrupt about-face.

'Would you like a drink?'

'I've had three.'

'Oh.'

' 'Was that wise?' ' she mocked. 'No, but I needed them. I'm all right and I'm not going to drive anywhere.'

159

'Is that the phone?'

They fell over each other racing indoors. Ken got there first and his face fell. He passed her the receiver with his hand over it.

'It's for you — it's not him,' he said. 'I think it's that woman from yesterday.'

'Hallo? Yes, this is Harriet.' She listened a moment, and then her face relaxed fractionally. 'Oh hallo, Judy.'

Ken left the room, and went into the little study at the back of the house which, due to its north light and tiny windows, he called the Black Hole of Calcutta. He thought of it like that because all he ever did there was pay bills, do his accounts, answer basic and boring correspondence and do what he was going to do now.

Today was the day the *Telegraph* featured business vacancies. He made it a point of honour to apply for each and every suitable job advertised, and had, while in the local town that morning, had a couple of dozen more copies of his CV run off on the photocopier in the estate agent's. He must have got through nearly a hundred in the past year. Every now and then he had to drag himself to London, or Exeter, or once to Birmingham, for interviews . . . It was a weary business.

Why did he go on? They could afford to live, modestly like this, including Clem's school fees which were covenanted for, for some time yet on the proceeds of the two house sales, and for his part he didn't care much if he never worked again. In fact, the thought of actually obtaining a post in the City and somehow having to commute, or get lodgings in London, flooded his whole system with dread. And yet he was only fifty. He wished he were ten years older, then nobody would think anything of his 'retirement' and he could just enjoy country life to his heart's content. Harry didn't say much; she, too, didn't want him to be away from home. It was his accountant with his gypsy warnings: 'It doesn't do to start dipping too deep into capital, you know!' and Clem with his filial digs: 'When are you going to get another job, Dad?'

About Clem, he and Harry, he thought, had swapped positions overnight. It was he who felt philosophical this morning, about everything except that errant girl. The possibility, however faint, that his son had a coloured girlfriend nagged at his mind. He'd lain awake a long time last night, Harry's laughter ringing in his ears. She'd apologised but it hadn't helped. Why couldn't she understand? It was such rubbish to pretend, as she did with irritating success, that there was no important difference between people of different cultures. How could you profess *not to notice* that a person was black, or even Jewish? It was true, her taunt that he got irritable about regional accents on the BBC. The Welsh, the Scots, the Irish — they had their own local radio, why should they intrude upon the English service? Meanwhile the English of even the English broadcasters got worse and worse, more and more sloppy — infected, no doubt, by the general malaise, the lowering of standards,

161

the melting-pot atmosphere pervading the whole country . . .

Well, but not this part. That was another reason for loving it here. Here, the Dorset burr was pleasing, in-place, and besides, most of the inhabitants seemed to be people like himself who'd been decently educated and had come to live here in retirement or because they could afford not to work any more. Harry scathingly dismissed them all as opt-out geriatrics but it simply wasn't true; many of them were only a few years older than himself. He'd met a number of them, in the committees and organisations he'd joined. Like-minded and like-speeched. If Harry would only lend herself a little more to the place, she too would make friends locally, instead of pouncing on the first London weirdo-woman who hove in view.

He had marked up the *Telegraph* and written three application letters by the time Harry came in. 'Writing job letters?'

'Yes,' he said virtuously. 'What've you been doing?'

'Talking to Judy.'

He looked round. 'What, all this time? What on earth about?'

'Bit of everything.' She looked rather uncomfortable, so that he at once asked:

'Did you tell her about Clem going missing?'

'Why not? It's the only thing on my mind just now. I couldn't just chat and not bring it up.'

He stared at her. 'I suppose it never occurred to you that while you were gassing away to your

162

new chum, Clem might have been trying to get in touch?'

Her pale-tan skin flushed red.

'I needed to talk. She laughed — she made me feel a lot better. She said she wouldn't worry if she were me. After all, he's eighteen. She says we're lucky he's a boy. She worries all the time about her daughter. She has a lot of problems with her, apparently.'

'Harry. *I don't care* about her problems with her daughter. I've got our son on my mind. Really, you are strange! You hardly know the woman, and you're blurting out our private affairs like a little child.'

She flushed again. 'You're right. I shouldn't have talked so long. I mean, so much.' She turned abruptly and went out of the study.

Later in the day, Harry's sanguine mood wore off. She grew restive, plaintive, and finally desperate.

'How long are we going to have to just wait like this and do nothing?'

'What do you want us to do?'

'I don't *know*, Ken! Surely the police will have to be notified sooner or later?'

'Our terrible racist police,' Ken couldn't resist murmuring. 'Can we trust them?'

'Trust them or not, I've had enough of this. I'm going to phone them right now!'

★ ★ ★

Clem hitched a lift from the station and showed up at the cottage at nine o'clock that night. The

163

first person he saw as he let himself in was a local police sergeant, notebook in hand. Clem stood in the doorway, the focus of all eyes. Harry rushed to throw her arms round him.

'Darling! We've been frantic!'

Clem, looking over her shoulder into the sombre face of the local constabulary, and the inscrutable one of his father, saw ominous proof of it, but he couldn't stop to think about that now. All he said was, 'Sorry, Mum. Sorry, Dad. Mum, can we talk?'

Harry, half-hysterical with relief, swept him into the dining room without a word of apology and hugged him again. Then she shook him.

'You little monster, where have you been?'

'In London, Mum.'

'Are you hungry?'

'No, Mum. Don't fuss. I mean — sorry, please, I have to talk to you.'

She sat at the table and he sat opposite her. 'Tell me. Go on.'

Now the moment had arrived, he was bereft of speech. How could he tell her, what could he say? All the way down on the train he had mentally rehearsed and revised and rehearsed, but it did no good. He had deceived himself about his own mother almost as comprehensively as he had about Pleasure's, turning her, in his need, into somebody else. Now he saw her in the flesh, the reality of her every hang-up showed ineluctably in the tension of her face, the set of her eyes. He knew she was his only hope but that to achieve her support he was going to have to pass through fires.

He closed his eyes.

'Mum, there's this girl. I've knocked her up.' *Shit, why had he said it like that?* He heard her gasp but in the blackness behind his eyelids he created a different face, one that did not match the gasp, one that showed more love and willingness to help than anger, and forced himself on. 'She wants to have an abortion. She's going to do it, I know she is, that's why I ran away from school. I had to get down to London and try to stop her. Please, Mum. There must be a law that says she can't do it, if I don't agree? I don't expect you to understand about — I mean — but I know you'll agree with me about her not getting rid of it. I couldn't persuade her. She says I can't stop her but I have to. You've got to help me!'

He opened his eyes a crack, but one glimpse of her face made him shut them again quickly. It was going to be worse than his worst fears.

He heard her get up unsteadily and open the door. *Don't*, he squeezed the thought out between his teeth, unaware that he was grimacing with the effort. *Don't call Dad, not yet!* But she had not gone for that. She had gone to get rid of the policeman and to tell Ken to stay out, out, to go to the pub, to leave her alone with Clem. She felt herself a volcano about to erupt and in desperate haste she all but pushed the two men out of the house. Then she rushed back into the dining room, slammed the door, and let go.

What Pleasure had endured from her mother was brief and restrained compared to the scalding verbal lava of recrimination Harriet poured upon the head of her erring son. Her fury fell on him unrestrained; a casual listener might have thought that she hated and reviled him, that she was casting him out of her life for ever. And it was no act. It was, for the moment, how she genuinely felt.

It was quite uncharacteristic of Harry, this uninhibited outburst, but a sort of abscess in her brain simply burst. Everything she had gone through during the whole of Clem's life, all the petty and major crises — these played a part. Her own upbringing and the rigid morality she had imbibed from the teachings of the Church did, too. But the real cause was an unmarked grave on which the Sikhs who had bought the old London house had unknowingly laid the double death of concrete, shutting the little shoebox-coffined body off from her with a finality that she had never completely felt while the roses nodded over it in unhallowed benediction.

Now a new life was coming, a life that Clem — her flesh — had planted. Carelessly, unthinkingly, he had driven his childish seedtrain (this had been her euphemistic approach to the facts of life when Clem was seven) into some equally unthinking and pleasure-hungry tunnel; two children had played this entertaining game together and a human being — which was in itself the beginning of a whole new world — was growing as a result. Soon it would look like that tiny thing that had quivered and fallen still in her hands, the half-finished but very human being that shock and her own inner unacceptance had propelled before its time from her womb. But this one would grow, be born, be a person. Except that, no, it wouldn't. Clem had said it wouldn't, unless she acted.

Even as she was railing at him for his irresponsibility, his lack of restraint, his hopeless selfishness, in another corner of her brain she was searching herself. Did she want it to grow, to be born? How could she, a good Catholic, even ask herself such a question? Yet she did ask, she definitely did. Clem — a father? Tied for life, a perpetual lien on his emotions, his decisions, his earnings, his whole life? Eighteen. *He was eighteen!* His life had barely begun, and already — this. This anchor, this millstone, this time-bomb . . . 'Oh, you fool!' she screamed at him. 'You fool, you fool, you fool!'

She heard a silence and realised she had stopped shouting. Clem was open-eyed now, staring at her with a curious blankness, as if he were no longer here, as if he had removed himself from the blazing merciless harridan she had become . . . As if he no longer knew her or had hope in her. And instantly, her motherlove surged back like a mighty wave and smote her an awakening blow. She looked again and saw her son, her darling, facing the first adult crisis of his life, who had come to her for help.

'Oh Clem,' she whispered, 'I'm sorry. Poor love, poor little boy! What a mess you're in, and all I do is shout at you.'

Her volte-face was too much for him. It had been one hell of a week. He put his head on

167

the table and cried. She reached across and stroked his hair, feeling its rasping thickness, remembering how silky-soft it had once been, remembering his delicious tender babyhood.

'What is it you want me to do?' she asked him at last.

He sat up and blew his nose on a paper napkin left over from supper.

'Come to London, to her place. Talk to her. Persuade her.'

'To have it.'

'Of course.'

'That's really what you want?'

'Mum! Of course!'

She stood looking at him, her expression now transfigured, filled with tenderness and concern. There was so much he didn't know yet, that she would like to save him from ever knowing.

'Have you thought ahead? How is she going to manage?'

'We'll get married,' he said, as if she were being stupid.

'*Married*? Clem, you haven't even finished school! How can you possibly get married?'

'But, Mum, I have to! Don't you understand?'

'Is this what she wants?'

He shook his head. 'No. I told you. She wants to have an an abortion and go on as if nothing had happened. But you must stop her.'

'Clem, I may not be able to do that.'

'You must try. I can't bear it.'

He looked pinched and desperate. She came round the table and put her arm around him.

'Clem, what can't you bear? Losing the baby?'

He frowned, shook his head. 'It's not that. I mean, I don't know about babies, I don't want a baby, any more than she does. But I can't — bear — '

'What?' she asked, gentle now.

'Her to kill — to do anything so wrong.'

To commit such a sin. She straightened up. 'I see.' She was, deep down, amazed. She had not thought she had had this degree of success in instilling into him the Church's morality. She had called him immoral, but he wasn't. He was more moral than she.

'To take it on herself, for ever. She's a Catholic too.'

Ah. So there was that. Another factor. Another complication.

'Mum, what are you doing?'

'What's the matter?'

'You can't have a drink now! You're going to drive!'

'You mean — you want to leave right away? Surely she's not going to do anything tonight.'

'I don't know. When I left her to catch the train, she said she'd found out about someone — '

'Surely she'll get it done properly, on the National Health. And that takes time.'

'I don't know,' he said again. 'Her mother's a sort of nurse, she works in a hospital. But she'd dead against it. Pleasure'll have to creep off somewhere.'

'Pleasure? Is that her name?'

'Yes.'

Harry looked longingly at the bottle in her

hand, and then put it back in the drinks
cupboard. Dear God, she thought, it's the
black one. Ken will die. And I will hate him
for feeling like that. I can't possibly face him!

'All right, darling,' she said aloud, trying to
sound calm and in control. 'Come along, before
Dad gets back. I'll leave him a note, and then
we'd better just go.'

11

They hadn't driven as far as the junction with the A303 before Harry realised the absurdity of setting off for London at nearly ten o'clock at night.

'Darling, this is nonsense. We'd better turn back.'

'No, Mum!'

Clem was evidently no more anxious to face Ken than she was.

'We won't get there till well after midnight. What'll we do? Where shall we go?'

'Haven't you got any mates, Mum?'

'Not that I could land on so late.'

'A hotel?'

Harry reflected. At a moment of hyper-vulnerability she had allowed herself to be bulldozed into this, which was stupid, but when she considered the alternative — going back — she knew why she was still driving in the direction of London. She was afraid. Literally frightened of the look that would come over Ken's face. Her own anger was bad enough, and she had handled it badly enough, but his would be different, alien.

She had only seen Ken really angry a few times. Once, that terrible night she had told him she would have to confess that they were not having marital relations. That was certainly one of the worst, because it involved her own

171

feelings of guilt. But there had been other times. When that Italian family moved in next door to the old house, there was that endless, bitter quarrel about the wall between their properties that fell down after the bad winter. Ken had taken it to the Council, and would have taken it to the House of Lords if it hadn't been settled in his favour. The things he had said about that family . . . Their echoes still lay hooked into her memory, like ticks. It had been a nightmare as bad as finding yourself married to a stranger. And there was the time he had flown at her after the court case, when she'd been banned for a year. It had been brief but burning: 'Serve you right if they'd sent you to prison! Are you turning into a drunk? How could you drive in that state?' She thought he probably didn't remember it, and she tried to forget it too, because of how patient and good he'd been during the year of banning that followed.

These rare fits of rage terrified her in their contrast to his normal phlegmatic calm. A half-black by-blow grandchild! It was absolutely unthinkable to him. How much better if she could . . . What? Settle the matter, somehow, and then . . . What, again? Make something up to explain Clem's odd behaviour? Lie, d'you mean? She asked herself, and promptly and startlingly, the answer came: That's a sin I could live with until my next confession.

But the matter wasn't going to be *settled*, was it, not so that there would be nothing Ken really needed to know. Because of course she was going to do what Clem wanted. Try her very

172

best to persuade the girl to have the baby, not to take its life. Of course she was going to do that. After that the situation would be ongoing; they would all be involved. So why was she running away from something she would eventually have to face?

They drove on in silence for fifty miles or so. Then she gave a deep sigh. 'Clem?'

Clem woke up with a start. 'What?'

'Is she really called Pleasure? I mean, is that her real name?'

'Yes.'

'What — what kind of name is that?' She wasn't supposed to know yet that she was black. She had to draw it out of him.

'I suppose you're asking what her background is. It's West Indian.'

He said no more. She cleared her throat.

'She's black then.'

She said it as carelessly as she could, surprised that it took some effort.

'Three-quarters. Her father's father was an Irish sailor.'

'Oh!' she said brightly. 'Interesting mixture.' Next after 'real' foreigners, Ken hated the Irish.

Clem grunted and seemed about to nod off again.

'Is she — has she got a job?'

He said, with an edge, '*No*, Mum, she's in sixth-form college. She's got her A-levels next month, same as me.'

Oh God, oh God, he may have ruined her life! Harriet thought, feeling herself growing frantic again inside. 'Darling, don't go to sleep, I want to talk. I'm not going to start in on you again, but very calmly, unangrily — how could you have let this happen?'

'I told you,' (though he hadn't). 'She said she'd take care of it.'

'You mean a contraceptive? I thought you said she was a Catholic?'

'Oh, *Mum* . . . ' He always used that tone if he thought she was being priggish or over-scrupulous. 'She was going to take a pill the next morning, but her mother was in an accident and I suppose she forgot.'

'Then it's — ' She stopped abruptly. What were those words which had nearly escaped her? Could she have been about to *blame the girl* for not taking the forbidden pill? 'I mean, how could you have taken such a risk in the first place?'

Clem didn't answer. She glanced at his blunt, Ken-like profile below the bush of rust-coloured hair in the reflected headlights. What a question! What chance did they have nowadays of avoiding trouble? That had been one of her motives in sending him to a boys' boarding school. To minimise the risks of too much freedom, too many opportunities, irresistible temptations . . .

'Is she very pretty?'

'She's not pretty at all. She's absolutely beautiful,' said her son, in the most solemn and grown-up voice she had ever heard him use.

* * *

174

By one a.m. Judy had done only two hours' stint outside the South African Embassy but she already felt pulled towards home and her bed as if by suction.

She shouldn't have let George take her to the theatre after work. She hadn't realised how tired she was; she normally had a kip after supper on picket nights. This time she'd been so keen to have a night out with George. She thought she could cope; she'd get out of the show at ten-thirty, just a short walk away from Trafalgar Square, have a quick, sustaining beer and a bite, and then George could leave her on the picket.

The early part of the evening had been terrific. She'd enjoyed herself out of all reckoning. The play had been a good choice, a real think-piece, the kind — rare now, George said — where you can hardly wait for the interval to end, even though, as intervals go, this was a good one. George had thoughtfully laid on sandwiches (smoked salmon!) and wine, and it had been great, standing in the rich-smelling crush bar talking about the play as fast as they could get the words out past the good food and drink. More of all three — food, drink and talk — after the show, only a little spoilt by the fact that she had to keep looking at her watch. It was a point of principle with her never to be late on the picket.

She had even entertained the faint hope that he might stay and keep her company, though he had never offered to do this after the first time she had coaxed him onto the picket one afternoon. He had not been so much bored as acutely embarrassed.

'What's wrong?' she'd asked, seeing him standing there like a stuffed dummy.

'It's the chanting and singing,' he said gruffly. 'You get a funny look on your face.' This had seemed to her an entirely inadequate reply, but she'd had to accept it for the moment.

So she hadn't been more than marginally disappointed when, tonight, after standing first on one foot then on the other at a significant distance from the little clutch of people round the banner, hands deep in his pockets, staring into space for about ten minutes, he'd edged over to where she was standing collecting signatures from passers-by.

'I'll get off then,' he said uncomfortably. 'Sorry to leave you.' He didn't kiss her. She had asked him not to, where the picketers could see — she didn't want gossip. He gripped her arm secretly for a second and then strode away towards Charing Cross.

★ ★ ★

After midnight the crowds thinned out, and so did the picket. It was a chilly night, though of course this was nothing compared to winter. Judy shared the wide, all but deserted pavement with two regular policemen and three regular picketers: Bobby, who hid his commitment behind a punk haircut and multiple earrings; Doris, a tough Scots lass in a leather bomber jacket who probably did more hours on the

176

picket than anyone else apart from Abby, and could always be called on in a pinch, and Pleasure.

There was also Jack, a staunch comrade of the old school who, to keep himself warm, usually had a couple of brandies before he came on, presently holding one pole of the banner (or was it holding him?) — and Becky. Becky was not exactly a comrade. She was a bag-lady who had once been in music hall. She loved coming, knew all the songs and sang them, solo if necessary, in cracked but carrying tones; but the trouble with her was, she kept sitting down, just slumping onto her behind on the pavement, and when she did that she had to be hoicked up rather quickly or the cops would move in. It was against the rules to sit or lie down on the pavement, and if there was one thing the cops loved, it was to catch the picketers breaking a rule. Judy thought it was what they lived for. Poor sods, she caught herself thinking, though she sincerely hated them as a group. They had no ideology, no songs or slogans or sense of comradeship to keep them from being bored out of their tiny pig-minds as the minutes ticked endlessly past.

There wasn't much sense in trying to collect signatures now. Almost the only people passing after one a.m. were nightfolk, oddballs mainly, the homeless, drifters, drunks, or marauders — Abby lumped them together as 'the outliers'. Occasionally a party group would come along, usually cheerfully and noisily legless, or a group of musicians coming from a gig, sometimes in dinner-clothes under topcoats, carrying their

177

instruments, walking purposefully close together towards some all-night bus-stop. Then Judy would hurry to accost them with her clipboard. A number of them, too, were regulars.

'I've signed about fifty times, hen, but you can have another if it's any help,' said one Scot she recognised, scribbling his name. He must have had a good night because he slipped her a fiver. He knew the drill — the cops mustn't see money change hands or it counted as unauthorised collecting. She sneaked the note into Bobby's pocket; at the end of the stint they'd go round the corner and count the takings. Such donations went to political prisoners' families in South Africa.

A car went past and slowed down. Everyone tensed. The nearside rear window opened and a man's head and shoulders emerged.

'Can we sign your petition, dorling?' he drawled.

Judy didn't move. None of them moved, except Doris, who turned her back pointedly.

'I want to sign all petitions that's in favour of screwing coons! You in favour of screwing coons, dorling? Or maybe having them screw you! Eh, dorling?' His wheedling tone changed to a strident bark: 'Screw you, you bunch of fucking coon-loving slags and poufters!' And through the front windows the chorus was joined as the car pulled sharply away: 'England for the English, and fuck the bleeding lot of you!'

None of the picketers reacted, but every eye was on the policemen standing to their boring night-duty in the portico of the Embassy. They

178

looked at the sky. One of them murmured to the other, 'Look like rain to you?' 'Could be,' said the other. 'Thought I heard some thunder.' Their pipkin measure of wit discharged, they resumed what Abby called their 'bovine silence'.

Doris was an old-stager. Nothing could faze her. Her small walnut face remained utterly impassive, she didn't even exchange looks with anyone, but the way she lit a cigarette and passed the packet around was eloquent somehow — a gesture of defiant solidarity. Absently she offered one also to Pleasure.

'You know she's a good girl. She don't touch it, do you Pleazh?' said Bobby.

'No,' said Pleasure, 'though there's times I wish I did.'

Judy glanced at her. She was very quiet tonight. She was usually one of the ones who kept the picket lively, organising bouts of singing and sometimes persuading people she knew to come along for an hour or so to give a talk or to entertain. In the early days the picket had been a sort of pavement university. Sympathetic lecturers had been known to turn up, though not at night, and once Pleasure had got a pair of fellow-students who did a comic turn to come. They arrived at about 3 a.m. (the picketers' nightly 'low') and burst into view as Kinnock and Thatcher, in bald and fright wigs respectively, and with funny noses. They strolled past, engaged in loud and acrimonious debate, ignoring the picket which almost wet its collective knickers laughing. Even the on-duty cops cracked a smile.

179

Now Pleasure stood holding the other pole of the banner and not saying much. Judy moved closer to her.

'Come on, doll, my turn. Jump up and down or something, you look cold.'

'Jump up and down? Yeah, I might just do that,' she said glumly.

'Start some singing. We could all do with it. What about 'Some Day We'll be Free'?'

'I can't tonight. Especially not that one!'

'Anything wrong?' Judy asked sotto voce.

Pleasure shook her head and turned her face away. Judy took the pole in one hand and Pleasure in the other.

'Spit it out, doll,' she said.

'I wish I could,' said Pleasure in a muffled voice, and added, 'Wrong end.'

Judy had to reflect on this for only a moment or two. Her heart sank. She hugged the narrow shoulders tight to bring the beaded head close to her mouth. 'Ach, Pleasure! You in the club?'

Pleasure, after a moment, nodded.

Oh you silly little rabbit, Judy thought despairingly. But hot on the heels of sympathy came a muffled anger. Weren't there enough kids to whom this happened out of sheer desperation, hopelessness, and a lack of selfhood? *I thought better of you, my girl!* But what was the use, it was done now.

'You poor kid. What will you do?'

'What do you think?'

'Well, it's your choice. We'll talk later if you like.' Judy gave her a comradely squeeze, released her and said aloud, 'It's time for coffee.'

It was early yet — they normally made themselves wait until two before sending off to the all-night cabbies' stand near the river — but the others all looked relieved.

'I'll go,' said Becky, who looked more than ready for a kip over a warm grid somewhere, so you couldn't really rely on her. Bobby said kindly, 'Not you, Beck, you've got your bag to carry. I'll go.' Judy passed him some pound coins (donations of course were sacrosanct), and he strode off, his knees popping through his frayed jeans like alternating small faces.

Becky started singing one of their regular African songs. Her version of the Xhosa lyrics was a secret source of amusement to Judy, but her dear old heart was in the right place. She sometimes brought Judy cuttings, or rather tearings, from newspapers that she collected from rubbish-bins to pad her shoes or sleep under — anything to do with South Africa, or the Soviet Union. 'Somethin' they been writin' that's up our street,' she used to whisper conspiratorially, thrusting the crumpled, stained bits of newsprint into her hands. 'Thanks, Becky! What are they on about this time?' 'Oh, I don't *read* 'em, duck,' Becky would say with her gap-toothed laugh. 'My reading days is over. I just look out fer the key-words like, 'cause I knows you're interested.' Now she put back her matted head, clad in a woolly cap that had been one of Judy's, and sang with fine, wavering street-melancholy about the future of a free South Africa, without understanding a syllable. But it got them all going; and Judy was working up for a good Xhosa click when another car drew into the kerb.

★ ★ ★

Harry and Clem had been heading through the heart of London — eerily easy driving at this hour — in order to find a hotel that would take them in so late, when Clem suddenly remembered that it was Pleasure's night on the picket. He suggested to his mother that they should detour to Trafalgar Square and see if she was there.

Harry was dumbfounded.

'You mean the non-stop picket outside South Africa House?' she asked incredulously.

'Do you know about it?'

'I heard about it just recently, from a woman I met. She helped to start it apparently.'

Clem stared at her. 'What's her name?' Harry told him. Clem gave an exclamation of surprise. 'How on earth did you meet her?'

'I met her at home.'

'*At the cottage?*'

'Her man friend wants to buy that derelict farm just up the lane from us.'

Clem couldn't get over it. 'That's really weird. She's the woman who was picked up by the police a few weeks ago, that Pleasure had to go to the copshop to wait for. I went with her. Pleasure says she's terrific, she really admires her.'

'So Pleasure is involved with the picket?'

'She's involved with a lot of black consciousness stuff. She's very Left. I suppose Dad'll have a fit about that, as well.'

'As well?'

'As well as having ten fits about her being pregnant, and another fifty about her being black.'

Harry could almost smile at the proportions, which were probably accurate.

'Well, one fit extra about her politics isn't going to make much difference then,' she heard herself saying drily.

'You don't mind that side of it, do you? The black part, I mean.'

'I'm too busy minding other sides of it to think much about that right now.'

They came into the Square. It was beautiful at night, Harry thought, easing her heart like an aching muscle by allowing it to respond to her city, and to acknowledge to herself how much she missed it. It was years since she'd seen it like this, in the small, deserted hours, with the floodlighting on the National Gallery and some other noble buildings, the spire of St Martin's piercing the sky and the lions snoozing on guard-duty around Nelson's Column. It had a tranquillity by night that gave her a new way in to loving it.

'There it is!' exclaimed Clem, who'd opened his window. 'And there she is too! By the banner, there, see?' He sounded young and excited, carefree. For the first time it flashed across Harry's mind that he might really be in love, as distinct from just caught up. She turned right with the lights at the foot of St Martin's Lane and drove toward the sound of singing.

'Good grief, there's Judy!' She pulled up level with the banner, opposite the impressive front portico of the Embassy, flanked by two uniformed policemen. 'Judy!' she called out of Clem's window.

Judy left the little group and came to the kerb, peering incredulously. 'Ach, it's you! What in hell are you doing here? I thought you'd come to bait us!'

Clem had jumped out and hurried to Pleasure. Over Judy's shoulder Harry could see them hugging. She couldn't see the girl well, only that she had her hair in those little bead-ended plaits. Judy was urging her: 'You can't stop here. Go around again, park by Edith Cavell, and walk down. You can picket with us, we need everyone we can dragoon! Oh, come on, just for a few minutes, and you can tell me what you're doing kerb-crawling at this hour of night so far from your country estate!'

She seemed delighted to see Harry, who found her ebullience impossible to resist. She followed instructions and was soon sharing a very welcome polystyrene cup of hot coffee with Judy, trying hard not to eye Pleasure too obviously. Judy, chatting away, noticed Harry's eyes swivelling, followed their direction, saw Clem with his arm round Pleasure, remembered the bush-haired youth from Cannon Row . . .

'I don't believe this,' she said quietly. 'Is that your son?'

'Er — yes,' said Harry, and met her new friend's eye. Judy found a vagrant grin, just at the extraordinariness of it all, tugging at her lips, and put her hand up to cover her mouth. It wasn't meant as an 'Oops!' gesture, but that was how it looked. Harry said wearily, 'I can see you know. I only found out tonight. That's why we're here — to see about it.'

'I only found out half-an-hour ago,' said Judy. They looked covertly at the couple, who were standing under the banner also drinking coffee out of a shared cup and whispering together. 'So, 'see about it' how? Or shouldn't I ask?'

Harry said, 'We're Catholics. So there's only one way.'

'*Catholics*?' Judy exclaimed loudly, in the same scandalised voice she'd used when she had said to George 'Hunting!' 'You didn't tell me that.'

'Why should I?' asked Harry with a touch of coldness.

'Well, man! I mean, I told you I was a Marxist. I wouldn't hold back on a thing like that that might put you off.'

'You mean, my being a Catholic might put *you* off?'

'You bet! You're not a convert, are you?'

'Yes.'

'Ach.'

'What's that supposed to mean?'

'Ach? It's what the Boers say all the time. I use it as a kind of joke. It can mean anything you like. This time it means . . . ach. Converts are the worst. Can I be friends with a really religious

185

person, let alone one who'd deliberately joined? I would have said no.'

'Oh dear,' said Harry ironically. 'I had you down as wide-open-minded.'

'I am! Only not about religion. Not about politics. Not about racism. Not about . . . ' She saw Harry's eyebrows go up and stopped. 'Who says I'm open-minded? Ask me, I'm pretty intolerant.'

Harry actually heard herself laugh. 'I'll make a deal with you. Two deals.'

'Go on.'

'The first is, Clem and I will stand on your picket until it's time for you to go home if you'll give us a bed for the night. We've nowhere to go and Ken will kill me if I shell out an arm and a leg for a West End hotel.'

'What's the other deal?'

'I'll put up with your Marxism, you can even try to indoctrinate me — God knows I hate what we've got more every day — if you'll lay off my Catholicism.'

'It's a deal, on condition that only I have indoctrination rights. I wouldn't want you wasting your time. Shake on it.' Harry took her proffered hand. Then Judy remarked slyly, 'It's a very good deal for me.'

'Oh, why?'

'Because frankly I don't believe anyone like you can be really gone on religion: you probably stuck it on like sticking-plaster over some hurt. And,' she went on, 'because my stint doesn't end till six a.m. — by which time it won't be

186

worth going to bed.' Harry's mouth fell open in dismay. 'Cheer up! You've no idea how hungry you'll be by then, and I'm buying breakfast for the four of us. At the best workers' caff in town.'

12

The rest of the night passed uneventfully, at least so it seemed to the regulars. But to Harry it was a five-hour-long adventure.

In all her years in London she had never stayed out in the streets all night. The sense of the great city asleep all around her, except for a few fascinating denizens of the night sharing the adventure with her under the dark sky, inflated her imagination like a shrivelled balloon and set the adrenalin trickling.

She was introduced to Pleasure right away. They were naturally very shy of each other.

'We must talk, I think,' Harry told her, tasting her warm, dry little hand.

'Not now,' said Pleasure, overcome. 'Please, Mrs Marshall.'

Judy edged Harry away to the other end of the banner where by keeping their voices down they could talk more or less privately and leave the kids alone. Harry found herself holding the pole while Judy tried for a signature from a passing man ('Pishoff, you shilly bitsh!' — par for the course at this hour) and after that was not asked to relinquish it for some time. She couldn't help feeling rather daring, holding it, and stared back defiantly at the policemen when they turned their helmet-shadowed faces towards her. How Ken would disapprove!

'How many times did you say you'd been

arrested?' she asked Judy.

'Nine.'

'Were you charged?'

'Of course.'

'What with?'

'Oh, whatever they could cook up. Obstruction. Illegal money-collecting. Lately it's been mainly under the new Commissioner's Rules. They stretch like chewing-gum to cover anyone they don't like the face of.'

'And did you go to court?'

'Sometimes. Sometimes the charges were dropped, if they didn't think they'd stick. I've been to court four times.'

'What happened?'

'Dismissed three times, fined once. Having to take from the prisoners' family fund for legal fees here really makes us *sick*.'

'But why? Why do they harass you?'

'D'you think Thatcher and her cohorts like us being here? We're a political embarrassment. The cops are under orders to try to make us pack it in.'

'But it's a popular cause. Most British people are against Apartheid.'

'Most people in this country, my friend, wouldn't raise a finger for anything with a black skin unless it was a seal or a whale.'

Harry was silent. Funny Judy should say that. She'd posted one of Ken's recycled envelopes only yesterday morning to his pet animal welfare charity; there'd been a seal on the front, albeit a fluffy white one.

189

'Have you ever lived in the city?' Judy was asking.

'Oh yes! We only moved a year ago. We used to live in Acton.'

'The posh part or — '

Harry laughed. 'There *is* no really posh part of Acton, not that I ever discovered. But I loved it.'

'I hate Brixton,' said Judy with sudden savagery.

'Do you really? But I would have thought — ' She stopped.

'Now you're not going to say something idiotic about the joys of living in the midst of a black community, are you?'

'You seem to devote your life to — '

'It's never pleasant, living among people who feel done-down and bitter,' said Judy. 'Even though you can't blame them.'

'Are they — done down?'

Judy gave a harsh laugh. 'In Thatcher's Britain? You're joking. They're at the raw end of every known deal. And to them a white face connotes the doers-down, and raises the hackles of even the most law-abiding. Even the ones who are determined to fit in here are wary.' After a few minutes silence, she said slowly, 'One of my fantasies — I mean, you can have scary fantasies as well as nice ones, can't you — is that one day a gang of the local black youth will burst in through my basement door, which I keep very firmly bolted, and confront me, seeing me just as a White that they want to get back at.'

'What do you do — in your fantasy?'

190

'Oh, I reason with them, I use every combination of words I can think of to try to explain to them that I'm on their side. I offer them food, money, my belongings. But that's not what they're after. They're after something I can't give them, my privileged status in a white country . . . So inevitably they take no notice and start breaking the place up and threatening me. And in my scenario, I watch them with absolute horror and terror and at the same time *I care about them and I understand them*. It's as if I were inside their heads, furious and frustrated, and at the same time I'm inside me, bricking it. And then comes the moment when I have to defend myself. I try not to hurt them, but in the end I always have to pull out every stop — milk bottles smashed over their heads, my dog at their throats . . . It's horrific. Whenever I have that fantasy, if I follow it through I always end up in tears, because it's like fighting my own family.'

Harry was dumbstruck.

'I don't understand,' she said humbly at last.

'Having that kind of empathy with black people?'

'No, *no*! Why you have — fantasies — like that. Why you let yourself.'

Judy looked at her. 'I suppose I need to.'

Harry said, 'If I find myself day-dreaming something unpleasant, I just switch off.'

Judy laughed. 'You make your inner world sound like a TV set.'

'The real world is so frightening,' said Harry. 'I don't think one should frighten oneself.'

'What have you got to be scared of?' Judy asked curiously.

Harry didn't reply; she didn't know the answer. She just knew that she often felt frightened of life, and had for a long time. Prayers didn't do a lot to help. There was a song on one of her musicals records about it; she played it occasionally when Ken was out and sometimes, secretly, wept at the lyrics about the desire for 'someone as frightened as you of being alive' . . . She was always ashamed of being moved by something so trivial, so — cheap. *Was* it cheap? Ken thought so; he groaned, not unkindly, at her taste, at her sentimentality, her easily-got-at feelings.

And now here was Judy, making her ashamed again. At least *her* tears were shed for something — though imagined, perhaps self-indulgent — at the same time real. Her whole life was being spent for something real.

'I suppose I'm just not a committed person,' she said. 'I've never found any cause I cared about enough to go to bat for.'

Judy glanced slyly at the couple at the other end of the banner. Pleasure was now tucked under Clem's arm for warmth.

'I have a feeling that it's about to be your turn at the wicket,' she said. 'What do you think of your daughter-out-law?'

'My what? Oh, I see. Well . . . '

'I envy you,' said Judy suddenly.

'*What*? Now you're being silly.'

'Oh, only in a way. I don't envy you your moral dilemma. It must be terrible to have God looking over your shoulder all the time, to have your rules laid down by people you can't even get at to argue with. But think of that little thing that's threatening to erupt into your unbatting life, defying every prejudice in this racist society. In a few months you could be holding it in your arms, influencing its life — and incidentally shocking the hell out of all your smug county neighbours, saying, 'Hey chaps, get a look, this is my grandchild, so keep any cracks you might want to make about 'darkies' and 'blackies' to yourselves from now on!' '

Harry felt gooseflesh spread up her back and along her arms. She tried not to show how the very thought of such a thing made her quail.

* * *

When Ken got back from his obedient, lonely visit to the pub and found Harry's note, he was abruptly assailed by such anger that he simply stood still for several minutes with every muscle clenched, trying to control himself. When the cat began meowing round his feet for its evening feed, he kicked it out of doors — actually opened the front door and propelled it out with the toe of his shoe and followed its departure with a string of curses that dispersed into the night air, mingling with the cat's outraged yowl.

Then he came in and slammed the door. He stared all round at his deserted kingdom with wild eyes. The fire was almost out. She hadn't even bothered to do that. He hurled some logs into the fireplace viciously, poured himself yet another drink (it wouldn't be Harry after all who would be the family lush if this sort of thing went on!) and sat down to read the note again.

'*Darling, I've gone up to London with C. Sorry I can't explain just yet, let me see what I can do first. He's in a mess but it's nothing criminal. Please be understanding. I'll phone you tomorrow. Love, H.*'

And just what in Christ's sweet name was a man to make of that? That his son — *his* son — was in serious trouble but that he, Kenneth, was not to be let in on it. Was, in fact, fled from in the middle of the night, by both of them. Why? Well, all too obviously because the boy was afraid of him. As Ken would have been afraid of his own father, if he'd been in 'a mess' at that age. How diligent Ken had been to establish a relationship of love and trust with his son which bore not a passing resemblance to the one he had had with his own father (who had been firmly of the 'no tears, shake hands like a man, men leave the kissing and blubbing to women' school). And yet when push came to shove, it had evidently made not the slightest difference.

Whose idea, though, had it been for them to go haring off like that? Good God, it was eleven o'clock at night! Harry must be out of her mind. They wouldn't get to Town a minute before two. Where would they go, where would they sleep, where could he find them? How, *how* could Harry do this to him? Didn't she realise he would be furious and worried and feel relegated to the sidelines in what was clearly a family crisis?

Right, he thought. If that was the way they felt about him, why should he concern himself. He would go to bed, go to sleep and think no more about it until one or other of them deigned to contact him with some information. When that happened he would decide what to do — if anything. Meanwhile he would behave better, more rationally and considerately, than they had.

He telephoned the school, leaving a message on the answering machine to say merely that Clem had come home. Then he went up to bed. He had subconsciously been convinced that his wife and son's behaviour would cause him anguished sleeplessness, but it was not so. He was totally exhausted by unwonted emotion and fell at once into a sleep filled with angry, torn-up scraps of dreams.

★ ★ ★

George, on the other hand, in his soulless Battersea room, couldn't sleep at all.

He spent most of the night prowling about in his pyjamas, trying unsuccessfully to read or listen to the radio, and feeling a complete bastard. He could not wrest his imagination away from Judy standing under that tatty banner.

Why hadn't he stayed with her? Hell's bloody bells, what sort of man would walk away like that and go off to bed, leaving her to stand there the

195

whole night when he could be with her to share her vigil?

Why had he done that, what had taken hold of him? What was there about the picket, and her attachment to it, that he simply found himself unable to cope with? He'd known even as he walked away that he was doing wrong, that he wouldn't sleep, that he would sit up all night wrestling with himself, wishing that he hadn't left her, let her down.

Well, but then he could get dressed at once, call a taxi and go back. She was still there, cold by now, lonely whatever she said about the comradeship of the young picketers, thinking about him perhaps and feeling disappointed. He was in love with her, she was the woman he wanted. And yet he couldn't make himself do this thing for her.

He gritted his teeth and put his heavy face in his hands. He called himself a man, yet he could not face standing there for five hours among those earringed youths, bejeaned tough-faced young women — and have to reckon Judy as one of them, their friend, comrade and mentor. He could not stand there while she chanted and sang those damn-fool jingles and hymnlike freedom songs. The atmosphere of melodramatic dedication repelled him all but physically.

He stood up, had another swig of beer, and banged about the room in exasperation. What was it all for? Who was listening, even by day, and what was it going to achieve? Those bastards in Pretoria were never, not in a month of Sundays, going to let a man of Mandela's stature and influence go loose. The picket with its banner — *Here we stand till Mandela is freed!* would be there till kingdom come. But that wasn't the sticking-point, not really. The worst was, it was alien to him, and it alienated him from her. It actually made him cringe inside. She was not his Judy, that defiant campaigner with the crazy fire of extremism in her eyes.

Judy had never claimed that standing outside South Africa House chanting slogans was seriously going to affect the Nationalist government six thousand miles away. So what was she doing it for? To make the workers in that great white building uncomfortable as they came and went? To raise the consciousness of British people to the plight of the prisoners in South Africa's jails? To alter the self-interested, shameful stance of the Thatcher government on sanctions against South Africa?

The picketers had already collected fifty thousand signatures on their duplicated sheets of flimsy. He'd seen them, gathered into untidy bundles in her basement, tied up with string. When there were a hundred thousand, they were going to march with them to Downing Street. A fat lot of notice the current incumbent was going to take of them. She'd have the lot put straight in the shredder.

They were deluding themselves, chasing their own tails, like Zulu, and like Zulu they didn't really have anything they'd a hope of catching.

He knew himself and his limitations, and this one had old resonances.

One resonance was in Sally. His wife.

197

He didn't think of her very much these days. Long before Judy came along, time had faded her. But he remembered her now for a particular reason. At first he couldn't see the connection, but suddenly he did.

Sally had believed in faith-healing. She'd got it from her mother, a silly woman who believed her life had once been saved by miraculous intervention after a street accident. Nothing George could say could talk Sally out of it. It was just something that was stuck into her when she was a child and her adult skin, so to speak, had grown over it, and now it was there, a part of her. Unreachable.

She used to go off to meetings and come back all lit up, off in some cloud-cuckoo-land and drifting about the place as if in a trance. At first she'd tried to share it with him, to convince him it was all true. He tried to be patient, but when he found out she thought she had a 'spirit guide' — a Chinaman if you don't mind, who'd been dead for twelve hundred years — they'd had one of their rare set-to's. It was his brother who'd stepped in and calmed him down.

Later, he'd had a word with George out in the fold.

'She's okay, is your Sal, what you going on at her for? It's just a woman's fancy, it makes her happy. Leave it, why can't you?'

'It's all a pack of bloody lies, that's why. I don't like my wife falling for a lot of claptrap. How can she swallow that rubbish — spirit guides, I ask you! Fair makes me wonder if she's soft in the head!'

Derek had said nothing for a bit, and then: 'She's none weak-minded, not Sal. Down-to-earth about most things. Just got a crack or two in her head enow to let a notion in that helps life not to be too hard. It's the same reason as us smokes and drinks, to dull the sharp edges of life, like.'

'It's worse nor that, she's deluding herself!'

'It don't harm her health like our soothers. Leave her be — I would if she were mine.'

And George knew even then that Derek wished she *were* his. And he was ashamed of himself, but it didn't help. Every time she got that silly look on her face or hinted about her spirit messages, George would seize up. He felt unmanned by irritation, and try as he might he could not do the kind — the husbandly — thing. He had been a good husband otherwise, but this small occasional failure of sympathy had come back to torture him after her death.

George threw himself down on the bed and screwed up his eyes in an effort to come to grips with himself. Why was he comparing Sally's foolish notions with something as brave, as admirable in its way, as the picket?

A Marxist! God Almighty, how could anyone call themselves that, with all that had happened! Was she stupid, or what? There were times when he simply could not relate to her.

George had not been able to bring himself to lie to Sally, to pretend that he shared or even tolerated her beliefs. He just could not do it. And now he faced the knowledge that if he were going to go on with Judy, he must learn a skill in

199

which he was basically deficient: dissembling. To smile encouragement, to say 'Well done, pet!' when he didn't feel it. About a passion far more a vital part of her than poor Sally's spiritualism.

A passion for a hopeless cause.

★ ★ ★

Harry would not have chosen to have her first intimate conversation with her 'daughter-out-law' in a workers' caff on the Embankment at six in the morning after a sleepless night. But Judy was in charge.

The four of them walked down there together after the morning shift of the picket came on. They were all chilled through and Harry at least was falling off her feet with weariness. But the kids seemed in good form. They, like Harry and Judy, had been earnestly talking most of the night and seemed to have arrived at some kind of plateau, if not of agreement at least of being mutually talked-out. Harry wondered, looking at them walking ahead hand in hand down the hill, whether after all there would be any need for her to say anything. Perhaps Clem had already persuaded her. The thought that she, Harry, might not be called on to influence the issue, brought her a disproportionate relief.

In the steamy café they squeezed into a booth, with a metal-rimmed table on which were two bottles of sauce and a cruet. Judy, evidently well-known to the proprietress, briskly ordered bacon and eggs, sausages, double-bubble, toast, tea and coffee.

200

This preamble over, she said: 'Okay, then, dolls, let's talk about this baby.'

'It's not a baby, it's a foetus,' said Pleasure.

'The baby-to-be-or-not-to-be,' said Judy.

'Not to be, then,' said Pleasure, and Harry knew nothing had been solved in the night.

Clem looked at his mother beseechingly. Harry leant toward the bead-curtained face, close and closed, and said, 'Have you thought it through, Pleasure?'

'Clem keeps asking that. If I was going to have it, there'd be something to think through. I don't need to do more than think of the next year. I have it, that's the end. The end of the whole life I had planned. I won't be able to go to college, I won't be able to get a proper job. I'll just turn into one of those single mothers you see dragging themselves around with pushchairs, clothes courtesy of church jumble sales, with no status and no hope, just adjuncts of their babies, living off the state. It's horrible. It's squalid. And it's not fair on the baby. I want something much, much different.'

'And an abortion's not squalid?' muttered Clem.

Harry glanced at Clem and said, 'Has Clem said anything?'

'Oh yes! He says he'll marry me. Can you believe it? I mean, I never thought I'd think an honest proposal was a joke, but this is. He hasn't got anything — no money, no career, no home, nothing! It's silly. And it doesn't make the slightest difference — in fact, it makes me surer than ever. Just two lives wrecked instead of one.'

'Well, I agree with that,' said Harry. 'I certainly don't think you should marry.'

'Oh!' said Pleasure in surprise. 'He told me — '

'What?'

'Well, that you were very, you know, religious. So what do you think I should do?'

'Have it, and get it adopted.'

Both their mouths dropped open. Then they almost shouted, with one voice, 'Oh no!'

'Why oh no?' countered Harry bravely. 'What's wrong with that?'

'What's wrong with it! You want me to go through an entire pregnancy, and give birth to a full-term live baby, and then give it away? What do you take me for, a robot with no feelings? Sod that. I'm not going to do *that*.'

Impasse.

They ate their breakfast. The kids ate fast, heads down, breaking their eggs methodically into their bubble-and-squeak, using the last of their Mother's Pride toast-crust to wipe their plates clean. Judy, too. Harry picked, sipped her milky coffee, thinking, thinking. At last she said:

'All right, what about this. Have the baby, Pleasure. You won't have to live on the state. We'll help you — I mean, we'll give you an allowance.'

She frowned. 'Who's 'we'?'

Harry tucked her hands under the table, an unconscious habit retained from finger-crossing childhood days.

'My h-husband and I,' she said, holding her

head very tightly on her neck and keeping herself from blinking with an effort.

'Wait a minute, what if Dad — ' began Clem, but Harry forged on brightly: ' — and we'll see how we get on.'

'How I get on, you mean.'

'Well, it's mainly up to you, certainly. I'm afraid that's how things are, were, and ever will be. But you won't be on your own with it.'

Pleasure bent her head again and took up the last of her bacon-grease with her finger. Harry noticed her hands. They were beautiful, pale brown with pink almond-shaped nails. A fleeting image of a baby, the colour of dark honey, held in her arms, passed through her mind, leaving a silky trail there, as of some soothing balm brushed across a ruched, angry area of scar tissue. She banished it because she knew it was instinctive, delusory and sentimental. The baby, to extend the metaphor, might just possibly be the colour of molasses, and would she find it as sweet then?

That she could think such a thing even fleetingly appalled her. Clem had said, 'I'm glad you're not like that,' and she had thought it true. But perhaps everyone was like it when it got this close.

'And what about my exams?'

'You'll take them, of course.'

'What if I get into college?' Pleasure flashed a look up at Harry through her slanted eyes and Harry thought she caught a calculation in the flash.

'Could you put off going for a year? Lots of

people take a year out. You could do that. Then when the baby's six months old or so, you could go to college and put it in a crêche.'

'I probably won't be able to go to college even if I qualify,' said Pleasure.

'Oh, why?' asked Harry, unwarily.

'My mum can't afford it.'

Oh. 'But you'd have your grant.'

'It wouldn't be enough to keep me *and* a baby, specially if they bring in these student loans. I couldn't lumber myself with a massive debt.'

Uh, oh. So that's the way of it . . . Perhaps one can't blame her, thought Harry. *Quid pro quo.* I'm asking a lot of her.

'What if we could work something out about that?' she said, hearing that cosy little 'we' popping out again.

'Like what?'

'Helping financially with your course. What is it you want to do, by the way?'

'Dentistry.'

'You want to be a dental nurse?'

'No, Mrs Marshall,' she said in a dead level voice. 'I want to be a dentist.'

Harry was maddeningly aware of Judy at her side, struggling not to laugh.

'How long does it — er — take to become a dentist?' she asked at last.

'Four and a half years,' said Pleasure clearly. 'Minimum.'

Silence sandwiched the empty plates and the sauce bottles.

13

Tina was sitting in her mother's basement at the bulbous-legged oak table with Zulu (who had been very pleased to see her — nice that someone was!) across her feet, a cigarette in her left hand from which she snatched an occasional sharp drag, writing.

It had started as a letter to her father. After so many years, she wouldn't have recognised him if she'd run into him in the street, but she still tried to write to him regularly. Her mother had told her long ago, 'He needs to hear from us. Whatever you feel, or can't feel, you mustn't deny him his needs.'

So, having arrived and let herself in at a time when she knew her mother would be out at work, she had started a letter to him. But she couldn't write the usual, forced-cheerful platitudes about her day-to-day life. It just wasn't a platitudinous life any more. Had it ever been? Well, in a way. As long as she'd been living here, going to school, standing on the picket, she could write platitudes, because that was a logical continuation of her childhood. One week's letter led on from the last; it was like a diary to which she confided little, just recounted events.

But everything kept changing. When she'd had that horrendous, shattering row with her mother (she had never reported rows in her letters, what was the point?) and she had left to go and live with Leila, it was a quantum leap. She hadn't written since then because she just couldn't explain what had happened and how she felt.

So now she had fled again — leaving a note, written in the heat of her discovery about Jojo the runaway slave, that she kept rewriting, fruitlessly, in her head — just bombed off first thing next morning. Since then she'd been sleeping rough, sneaking back to her mother's flat (to which she still had a key) to have baths and pinch things to eat that she thought her mother wouldn't miss, if only because the pickies were always allowed to help themselves. *They* were allowed, oh yes of course. *They* were politically active, they — the least of them — had more of her mother's respect than she did! And she'd take Zulu for walks, for company. And to prove to herself that she had the willpower to leave again before her mother returned, when all she wanted in life was to stay where it was warm and safe.

None of this could she tell her father, so the letter as a letter soon petered out and she began to just write.

'*I'm all alone at Mom's and feeling shit-lonely. I've just made myself some lunch, not that there was anything much to eat in the house. Mom eats out most of the time since she got her* NEW LOVER *who is a great gormless peasant. I ate some limp Ryvita, squashy tomatoes and dried-out, sweaty cheese. There was half a bottle of red wine but it must* have been open for yonks, pure vinegar. *Still, I drank it. I needed it. I'll have to take the bottle away with me, of course. It's hard, covering my tracks. I've never been so careful about crumbs.*

'*The worst thing about sleeping rough is not just the cold and loneliness and grot, but being scared all the time that something bad's going to happen to you. There's so many drunks and druggies and weirdos and you feel so exposed without a roof or walls. I've only been doing it for a week but it feels like about ten years. I thought it would be different; I thought that you'd just curl up somewhere sheltered with your sleeping-bag and no one would bother you, but it's not like that. It's like every sheltered spot is someone's already. When you get knackered and want to doss down, you either can't find anywhere free, or you curl up and right away someone's shaking you and saying, 'Move on, this is my spot.' There's no comradeship or help from the others either, it's everyone for themselves. Not like on the picket where everyone's supportive. Now I know why so many homeless people wind up on the picket and then here at Mom's. I wish I could. I wish it every single night. It's bloody ironic really, me wanting to be one of Mom's pickies.*

'*I have tried to get work. I'd do almost anything, just to get in off the street, but there's not a lot of casual work going for women, and for things like McDonald's you have to have an address. Of course at the beginning of the week I gave here, but they checked and Mom said* no I didn't live here any more. 'Course, she thinks I'm still at Leila's. Then I gave Leila's address, but she's obviously livid (or else Mrs Salah is — she probably read the note) because she said the same as Mom when they rang her. Maybe I shouldn't have written that about the utter disgustingness of keeping slaves. After all, Leila was very good to me and Jojo wasn't her fault. God, I miss that place! Going from that to sleeping under the arches by Embankment Station is incredible. To think I thought my marshmallow bed was too soft!

'Luckily for me I ran into old Becky, our picket bag-lady, on the third night and she did show a bit of solidarity. And she really knows the drill. I don't feel so scared when I'm with her, but of course we can't stay together all the time. She's got her own routine in the day and she expected me to go off and beg. She gave me a 'homeless and hungry' card and told me where to sit on my sleeping-bag in Leicester Square Station. God, it was so terrible. After ten minutes I'd had it, I was just shrunk up inside. I think I'd almost rather be a tart than beg — at least you're giving something back. I just sneaked away, and when I met up with Beck that evening I pretended no one would give me anything. Not that they had, much, and not that she believed it. Then she shared what she'd got with me (that nearly made me bloody bawl) and we had half a bacon-butty each and some coffee and she showed me where to doss down with her, in her special bash made of opened-out TV cartons near the National Theatre. There

208

was a big bonfire lit and lots of us sat around it and it should have been almost fun but there was no singing. Half of them were dead drunk, we just sat there getting warmed up and then everyone crept off like rats crawling into their holes. I slept with Becky in her bash. It was ghastly, so small you couldn't even turn over, and Beck smelt terrible, of stale wine and dirty clothes. I had to get out after about two hours. It was a nightmare. I sort of lay down outside the bash and slept curled up against it. Some drunk came up to me in the night. He woke me trying to touch me up. God, I was scared! I yelled, and Becky sort of burst out of the top of the bash like a jack-in-the-box and frightened him off.

'Next day she told me about the crypt under St Martin's Church where they let you shower and give you a meal, but of course I dared not go there, it's too near the picket. If anyone on the picket that knows me, saw me, they'd be sure to tell Mom, so I give that whole patch a wide berth. I wonder what Mom'd do if she knew. I have to be very strong with myself to make sure I get out of here in time. I mean, sometimes I find myself pretending I don't know the time, like wanting her to come home and catch me. But I don't think even if she knew she'd take me back.'

Tina stopped writing. She felt it coming, the detailed reliving of the terminal row. She wanted it not to, she fought it off, but it came anyway, horrible and haunting and unalterable, a turning point she would have given anything to unlive.

'I hate Daddy being in hiding!' Tina had cried out at its climax. 'I hate having to explain: 'My father's a terrorist, he's on the run.' I mean, how do you think that sounds?' (She had never, in actual fact, said these words to anyone, and she knew perfectly well that the word terrorist in the South African context was wrong. But frustration and anger turned her tongue into a stabbing beak.)

'Trust you to put it like that!' said her mother, white around the mouth. 'What's wrong with 'activist'?'

'And as for you, standing in the street all night and being arrested every five minutes — why do you have to be involved in all this crap? What for? The Blacks aren't grateful! You can't help them, they have to help themselves. They only resent whites who try to be on their side — it was you who told me about how they turned against the Jews in the States, after all they did for Black Liberation! Most of them hate all of us *honkys* anyway, and if they ever got the upper hand in South Africa they'd murder your lot, all your family, they'd just murder them.'

'Don't you talk such bleddy bullshit,' her mother had said in a dangerous undertone.

'Is it? Is it?'

'When Nelson is free, and takes charge, his authority will ensure there'll be no innocent blood shed.'

'Do you *believe* that? That he can keep control? And who's going to decide who's innocent? Is your mother innocent, the way you told me she treats her servants — is your father innocent with his attitudes? And what if Nelson dies? He's an old man! All you've told me about the shitty people around him — what if there's no one to keep control? How can you guarantee there won't be a bloodbath? You can't! Every newspaper you read — '

'Every newspaper *you* read! Don't bring those Murdoch rags into my house, they're poisoning your mind!'

'No, they are not, they're opening it for the first time! I've spent years listening to you brainwashing me, and for years I believed it, but as soon as I got out of this house I started to find out that the bullshit is right here. Marxism! Who believes in Marxism now? Just a bunch of naive fanatics who refuse to see it's been completely discredited. The Soviet Union — Christ, Mom, would you, personally, go and live there in The People's Paradise? *The people*,' she almost spat. 'You know what 'the people' want? They don't want Marxism, they want what everybody wants — freedom, travel, fun, pop, jeans, Coke, things to buy, *profits*!'

'Do they want unemployment, nationalism, racism, homelessness, drugs, gangsterism, Aids, gridlock — '

'Gridlock? You mean a car for everyone? You bet they want it, and why not? If that's what freedom brings, yes Mom, they want it! You'll see. They want out of Communism, anyway, they all do!'

'What there is in the SU isn't true Communism.'

'You always, *always* say that! Whenever

211

something comes out that shows Communism up, you say that. Well, I say that *is* Communism, a system that goes against human nature — '

'I've told you! *There is no such thing as human nature!*'

'And that's the biggest lie of all! You think human beings can be changed, made perfect somehow, but they can't, I know they can't, because for one thing, look at us! If you and I can't get along, with you wanting me to be one thing and me not ever able to conform to it because I'm absolutely something different, how are you going to change the whole human race by forcing them into *one* political straitjacket? It just won't work, Mom, and you must be thick as two planks to go on kidding yourself it ever will!'

She had heard her voice going on and on, like a lash beating her mother; she saw Judy's face flinch as the blows fell one by one, and Tina's heart seemed to be twisting with pity in her chest but she couldn't stop.

'All your sacrifices for a 'Communist' South Africa, you want to start it all up again there! Well, I'm not South African. I don't care a shit about the bloody place. Let the Afrikaners and Blacks and *Rooineks* kill each other for it, which I'm sure they'll love doing, but if I did care about it I wouldn't wish Communism on to it or on to anywhere, least of all right here. Boy, would I fight to stop it coming here! I'm British and I want to be normal, with lots of freedom to do whatever I want with my life!'

'And what do you want to do with your life?

212

Just fritter it away, doing nothing that matters or calls for the slightest self-discipline? Are you going to be a little parasite for ever?'

'At least that's better than getting mixed up with what you call activism, which is just another name for hurting people! You and your revolutions, if you ever found yourself in the middle of one you'd run a mile!'

'Our work against Apartheid was a revolution.'

'It wasn't a real one, you weren't asked to kill anyone, nobody was shooting at you! And when the going got tough, you did run, just because the police shied a few stones through your window — '

'I left South Africa because they were threatening *you*!'

'Thanks a bundle, so it's all down to me we live like rats in this hole of a basement and haven't any money! Why can't we be like ordinary people? *Why do I have to be ashamed of my parents?*'

And that was when her mother, who had long ago innoculated Tina against ordinary outbursts of irritation, frightened the wits out of her with a barely-contained display of the most terrible anger Tina had ever seen on her face or heard in her voice:

'If you're ashamed of everything I believe in, you're rubbishing my entire life. You don't deserve to be my daughter, or your father's. Get out and go and live somewhere else, you are making me sick!'

★ ★ ★

213

Tina brooded, her chin on her hand, the nicotine staining her fingers as the smoke trailed upward into her hair, filling its uncombed squiggles with cigarette smell.

She thought of writing some of this, just writing it like a play to try to take the vitriol out of it. But she wasn't able to face it in written words.

Anyway it was time to go.

She was so reluctant she had to put both hands on the tabletop and heave herself to her feet like an old woman. She put into a plastic shopping bag her writing things, and everything else, like the tomato-skins and the rind of the cheese and the empty wine-bottle — anything that, even in the waste-bucket, could betray to her mother that she had been there. She spent a last few minutes cuddling Zulu, explaining to him why she had to leave him, telling him earnestly to keep his yap shut about her to her mom.

'You mustn't be an informer, Zool,' she adjured him. 'You wouldn't look so good with a flaming tyre round your neck.'

He licked her proximate nose and she kissed his scarred one.

'I love you,' she whispered, 'Zool the fool, Zool the cool, Zool the drool. Shit.' She had made herself cry with her nonsense. 'I wish you could come with me. Some of the street people have dogs.'

She bit her tears back harshly. She'd bought this. This was her, Tina, making her own mistakes, having her capitalist freedom. As she straightened up and looked around to make sure she hadn't left anything, her eyes fell on the poster of the young Mandela, gazing at her with his enigmatic eyes. For so long he had been her hero, too . . . poor Nelson. Perhaps, like her, he couldn't see any light ahead in the dark tunnel; perhaps, wherever he was, he dreaded the night to come as much as she did.

She went to her room and looked in the blue jar, but it was empty now. She'd have to try to get back to central London by a series of buses, jumping on and off, dodging the conductors, but with more and more of the buses now, you had to have money to get on. Or maybe she'd try to get a lift. She slipped the jar into the plastic bag on impulse. Sometimes Becky nicked some flowers from public gardens to brighten up the bash. They'd look better in the jar than in a stolen milk bottle, anyway. Her eyes lingered on the comforts she had always taken for granted — a pillow, a mirror, an extra blanket . . . But they were her mother's, not hers.

It was past time. She dashed out, banging the door closed behind her. She felt a strengthening awareness that this was the strongest thing she had ever done. She had felt like that each time she did it. But it wasn't much comfort.

As her head rose above the area wall, she noticed a long, shiny car parked in front of the house.

She paused for a moment at the top of the steps, just to stare at it. It was a very posh car, too posh for this street. As she started to walk past it, a liveried chauffeur stepped out and addressed her.

'Excuse me, miss.'

Tina instinctively swerved away. What was this, some new form of kerb-crawling?

He stood in her path. 'Miss Tina?'

She stopped cold. He had a black, smiling face under the flat peaked cap.

'What do you want?'

'Your grandmother sent me to pick you up.'

There was a lengthy pause while Tina tried to orientate herself. She wondered fleetingly if this might be some kind of hallucination or day-dream. It certainly had the weirdness of a dream. At last she said, 'My grandmother is in South Africa.'

'No, miss. She's at the Dorchester Hotel.'

'What's her name?'

'Mrs Diane Ferris.'

'What does she look like?'

'I only saw her for a minute — very dressy lady. But here's proof for you, if you're doubtful.'

He handed her an envelope. She looked at the front of it. It said '*Tina*' in a racy, broken-up handwriting with lots of curly bits. There was even a little heart instead of a dot over the '*i*'. Tina's mother often said that her own mother — Mrs Diane Ferris, sure enough — was functionally illiterate, which was why she did such fancy handwriting.

Tina ripped open the envelope and read the letter, which was so embellished with curlicues she could scarcely read it.

'Lookee-lookee who's in town! Don't tell Mommy yet that I'm here! Secret-secret-surprise! Just come as you are and we'll have DEE-lishus dinnies together in my lovely room! Oh is'nt this too exiting darling I can't wait to see you!!!! Just jump in the car and let the boy bring you to me. I told him to wate till you came out even if it was ALL NIGHT! Wateing for you with OPEN ARMS! Love and kisses, Grandma Dido.'

* * *

The black chauffeur whom Dido had called, typically, 'the boy', escorted Tina through the glitzy portals of the Dorchester and up to the reception desk. He almost had to shove her before him as if she were a sheep going into the dip.

Tina was in a daze. She was also in what could only be described as grunge-clothes: filthy track-suit bottoms, Doc Martens and a dreadful old clapped-out leather-look jacket over a T-shirt that bore a message so basically unappealing to her grandmother's sensibilities (*I Support the Frontline States in Southern Africa*) that Tina clutched the two edges of the jacket together in a spastic gesture of concealment as she was ushered by a bell-boy into a silent elegant lift and thence along a peach-carpeted corridor and into a superb suite overlooking the Park.

And there she was. There she actually, really was, her Durban grandmother, the rich one, the formidable one, the one even her mother was a bit afraid of.

217

'Dido!' Tina croaked feebly. 'Hi.' She made a sketch of a wave with a limp right hand, the false shadow of insouciance, and then resumed her clutch on her zipless jacket-edges.

The tall figure at the other end of the long, magnificent room turned from powdering her nose in the gilt-framed mirror over the marble fireplace. She was pretty magnificent herself, exquisitely dressed in the if-you've-got-it-flaunt-it fashion of her country and station. Her aquiline features were immaculately made-up; her short, crisp mauve hair was cut in a youthful fringe that did not hide her eyes, eyes sharp as lasers that seemed to pierce Tina down the length of the room. Tina could almost see their coloured shafts beaming towards her.

'Alba darling, come get a kiss!' she commanded, holding out arms stiff with red grosgrain that matched her long fingernails. Tina could see the diamonds winking.

She approached her helplessly, drawn by the authority that had kept a houseful of servants, three husbands, innumerable descendants and lesser relatives on their toes throughout a long life. Tina could have found her blindfold by sniffing her way to the epicentre of the perfume source, and as she entered those arms and was clasped to a bosom still rigidly held to attention, the perfume opened doors to the past in her head.

It evoked a lost world, not only of creature comforts but of constant sunshine and all that went with it — Disney-coloured flowers blotting out huge areas of every interior and exterior view, gelatinous sweet foods sticking to her teeth, bodies servicing her wants — hands, feet, smiling faces, all functioning exclusively for her happiness and wellbeing.

With Dido's rings impressing themselves on her shoulder blades, she caught a subliminal glimpse of broad lawns and tropical flowerbeds and turquoise pools, all with sinuous, clean-edged shapes, under topless skies endlessly morning-glory blue, where she had run and splashed barefoot, dodging bees. Until one day her mother had lifted her away in defiance of the natural gravity of a child's selfish hedonism and set her down again on the sweaty greyness of a London pavement.

She drew back. Her grandmother had definitely aged, but she was still autocratic, still glamorous, still she who must be obeyed.

'What are you doing here?' Tina asked uneasily.

Dido refrained, not subtly, from looking her critically up and down. 'Sit down, Alba,' she said in what Judy referred to ruefully as her it's-time-we-had-a-little-talk voice. Tina sat, and saw her grandmother wince at the desecration-by-grunge of the white leather sofa.

Dido placed her small black handbag, with a string of rhinestones for a handle, on the thick glass coffee table, where it looked entirely at home, and sat down concisely on the matching sofa. She smoothed her tight red skirt under her and crossed her legs. Tina could see they were the legs of an old woman, just from that little bony ridge of the shin. But where this ridge ran into the high arch of her instep ('You can always tell whether a woman has good blood in her by her instep') and thence into the low vamp of her black suede pump, the illusion of eternal cosseted agelessness was restored.

'Like my new shoes?' Dido asked, flexing her suspended foot. There were more rhinestones down the back of the high heel. 'Bought them in Jo'burg. Just stopped off for a day's shopping on my way here. Remember me taking you shoppies when you were little?'

'No. Not really.'

'Shame. I suppose you've got no real memories of your birthplace . . . We went to the zoo, you ate a knickerbocker glory and I bought you a delicious pink tulle party frock, like a ballet-dress. You looked like a little fairy in it.'

That 'frock'! But she did remember, not buying it but having it, for years after they had left the shaven lawns and the sundrenched children's parties. She remembered how her mother would periodically take it out and hold it up — pink and crisp and sweet as candyfloss — how it had seemed to light up the dingy basement flat, how she resented having grown out of it before she properly remembered wearing it. She loved it like a favourite doll that never got shabby. And her mother, always wanting to get rid of it, to give it away! She never liked it, she hurt Tina's feelings with her remarks about its silliness, making her feel silly, too, for loving it and refusing to part with it. But for years, Tina won, making Judy put it back in the wardrobe where she could glimpse it every time she opened the door to take out a dreary school skirt or a sensible pair of jeans.

'I kept it for ten years!' Tina burst out now. 'Mom hated it.'

'Shame, flower, but then she would, wouldn't she? Although, you know she likes pretty clothes too, only she won't admit it. Always so serious. Do you smoke, darling? Naughty girl, have one of mine, they're lovely Turkish ones without any nasty stuff in them at all.' They lit up the exotic little black gold-tipped tubes with Dido's crystal lighter, puffed in silence for a minute, and then Dido said, 'How's Mommy, Alba?'

Her grandmother had always called her Alba. The racial associations with Albertina, wife of one of Nelson Mandela's lieutenants, had grated on her. 'Tina' had struck her as common, so she'd invented her own soubriquet which she claimed had 'tender Spanish echoes'. Away from her mother's unspoken scorn, Tina quite liked it.

Since they'd left South Africa, Tina had only seen Dido two or three times, when she had flown to London on a blood-is-thicker-than-water visit. She always wanted to take them out, to 'give them a little treat', and Judy always insisted they eat at home. Only once had she allowed Tina to go out with Dido alone, when she had been heavily caught up in picket-work. It had been an amazing day, full of the things money could buy, but at the same time, awful somehow. Tina had not felt free to enjoy it. She had felt she was being suborned, seduced. There was something subversive to her mother's whole life about the way Dido talked and looked, about the way she was.

'She can't help it, Tin',' Judy said afterwards. 'We don't have to see her much. Try to be nice to her — she's family, after all.' 'But she was horrible to you and Daddy.' 'Yeah, well. That was because of politics. That's racism, that's their upbringing. Her family is all like that, your aunties and uncles and cousins. We have to show we're better than that. I forgave them long ago. You must too. She did buy us this flat.' 'Wow, that was so good of her, Mom, nice lady!' 'Don't you be so snide, she didn't have to do anything. Believe me, I was grateful at the time. We hardly had the *broeks* we stood up in, we'd have been out on the street.'

Out on the street . . .

'I'm not exactly living with Mom any more,' Tina said now, uncomfortably.

The pencilled eyebrows rose questioningly. A waiting silence.

'I — she — well, we weren't getting on, so — '

'But you were there tonight, when the boy came for you?'

'Yeah, well. I go back sometimes, to — to — '

'Visit with her?'

Tina heaved a deep sigh. How much did Dido know? She'd better just stop hedging and tell her.

'No. I go when she's out at work. We had a bad row and — and she threw me out.'

Oh. She hadn't known. Not a bit, or she wouldn't have changed expression like that, gone all pink under the foundation and powder, narrowed her eyes . . . Tina understood why her mother was scared of her.

'She *threw you out*? Into the street?'

'I stayed with a friend. For a while.'

'And now?'

She couldn't bring herself to tell Dido that she was sleeping rough. She would think it was all Mom's fault. She would blame her, as she always had, for everything. Tina said quickly, 'I've got a place to doss, Dido, honest, don't worry.'

'You look as if you've been dossing! In a gutter.'

'I'm sorry. I'd have done myself up if I'd known I was coming to see you,' said Tina miserably, looking round at the luxurious appointments of the suite, which made even Leila's flat pale by comparison. She knew her grandmother was rich — but *this* rich? She felt like Little Orphan Annie at Daddy Warbucks'. Then she remembered vaguely something about the most recent husband dying.

'Your Mom must be very lonely without you.'

'No, she's not. She's far too busy to be lonely.'

'Hm,' said Dido noncommittally. 'And how busy are you these days?'

Tina squirmed uncomfortably in the white leather armchair, making a squeaking sound. 'I'm not actually doing anything much, since I left the crammer.'

'You *left the crammer*?' repeated Dido in

shocked surprise. 'Why does nobody ever tell me anything? Why did you leave?'

'Mom pulled me out because she thought I wasn't trying.'

'And were you?'

Tina looked away. 'Not really, after a while.'

'Why not?'

'I don't know,' she said miserably. 'I just couldn't seem to keep it up.'

'What subjects were you doing?'

'Eng Lit and Art and History seemed the easiest options, but when I got into them I found them dead boring. When I'm bored I can't concentrate.'

Dido blew out a cloud of fragrant smoke and eyed her granddaughter narrowly through it.

'What books were you doing for literature?'

Tina dug her booted toes into the shag carpet with embarrassment. It was horrendous to be catechised like this, fixed with those needlesharp eyes, feeling she had to tell the truth.

'Oh, I dunno. *Mill on the Floss* was one, and some rubbish by Thomas Hardy . . . and bloody *Macbeth*, of course. God, how I hate Shakespeare!'

She glanced fearfully at her grandmother, expecting a rebuke, but instead saw her grinning around her little black cigarette.

'Never could sit through him myself,' she said. 'I couldn't have read Hardy at your age, either. Not that I could now! Why did they make you read such totally unsuitable books? And what about the Art?'

'I have this slight handicap for Art. No talent.'

'And History?'

'If it had only been Modern European, I know a lot since the Russian Revolution, but it only went up to the industrial one.'

Dido stubbed her cigarette out decisively.

'Well, it's perfectly obvious what's gone wrong here, isn't it. You choose the wrong course.'

'I chose the wrong brain,' muttered Tina.

'Rubbish. I've known you since you were born, you're sharp as a tack when you're into something that grabs you.' She stood up and bore down on Tina, who instinctively backed away, sliding along the white leather till she was cornered.

'Get up. Stand straight. Yes, we're just about the same size.' Dido took her by the shoulders and, turning her about, gave her a little push in the direction of a door. 'Go and have a bath while I look out some nice things for you. Plenty of bathsalts. Throw those rags away.'

Oh God. Shades of Leila. 'Dido! I can't wear your clothes!'

'If you can wear what you're wearing now, you can wear anything,' her grandmother said crisply. 'I'm astounded they let you come up here. I'll have to have a word with the desk . . . Now do as you're told, petal, and don't dawdle. I'm taking you out for dinner. After that,' she said meaningfully, 'we'll have to see.'

14

Florence was turning her bedroom upside down in a frenzy.

'Where'd I put it?' she was muttering fiercely. 'I know I kept it. I kept it for a reason! I don't always know what reason I got, but when I keep a paper thing, it always for a purpose!'

She was, indeed, a great thrower-away, not only because the limited size of the flat and her nursely aversion to clutter necessitated it. In particular she threw away everything that was empty, flammable or 'ugly'.

She detested packaging, which seemed to her wasteful and commercially intrusive, so much that she would often be wasteful herself, throwing tubes, jars, boxes and tins away even before their contents were fully used up because the sight of them on her shelves or in her fridge got on her nerves. 'Out, you wheedly devil, I wish I never bought you!' she would exclaim, hurling the offending object into the bin as if she could dispose of the whole design and advertising industry, united in its underhand efforts to take her money.

Her terror of fire was legitimately come by. She had narrowly escaped losing the twins in infancy in a fire at her mother's house in Jamaica, and had only saved them by stripping her dress off — in the absence of underwear, thereby denuding herself — dousing it with water, flinging it over her head and rushing through the smoke and flames while her neighbours, not to mention her man, stood there screaming helplessly. She hardly ever brought newspapers into the house because they were a fire hazard, kept all volatile liquids in a hermetically closed tin box, and of course banned smoking indoors. She could never have borne any kind of naked flame, and had long ago discarded the gas cooker that came with the flat for an electric one, even though it was far more expensive.

Ugly in her terms meant anything that made her unhappy or uneasy. She had got rid of a lot of the detritus of her earlier years, the very things most women treasured — documents, photos, letters — because they reminded her of unhappy times or actions she regretted or was ashamed of, even though to others she always glossed over her mistakes and portrayed her checkered past as all part of the richness of life. 'I'm like that French singer, I don't regret a thing!' she often said to Pleasure. But it wasn't true.

She was ultimately ashamed of both her marriages, because the men in each case had ended up by leaving her flat, and this had to mean one of two things: either she was worthless and unlovable, or the men she had chosen were. Either way was shaming to her and she didn't like to think about it, so she offloaded everything that reminded her — everything she could offload.

Of course there was one reminder that couldn't be offloaded — Pleasure. But fortunately she had no look of her father and was so much her own person and so pleasing to her mother in other ways — her brains for instance, and her personal charm — that Florence easily came to regard her as a sort of fairy-child, dropped into her life by God, effectively cut off from the bad judgment and essential sinfulness implicit in her origins. Florence loved her with a passion, and anything that threatened her roused her mother up till she felt like the angel with the flaming sword before the Garden of Eden. Nobody was going to befoul that happy heaven if she could help it!

And now someone had, and Florence was pretty sure she knew who. It was that boy, the one who had phoned, the one Pleasure had said was just an anybody, but it was him all right who had got her baby into trouble. And now he was preparing to aid and abet her in that crime of crimes, the mere thought of which made Florence shudder deep in her soul, and which she had so categorically forbidden.

She knew it because, though she had her own busy life and in theory believed in leaving Pleasure her freedom, she was on her guard since the pregnancy (her deepest fear was that if Pleasure disobeyed her in this, it might sunder them for ever), and she had stooped to snooping. A week or so after her row with her daughter, she found a letter left trustingly by Pleasure on her desk:

'*Darling Pleaz (how do you write that sound?! Pleash? Pleazh?),*

'*So that's settled! And don't worry, when Mum says she'll do a thing, she does it. Dad'll be sure to get a new job soon, and when he's working he gets paid serious money. So everything's going to be okay. I was so relieved when you agreed, you're terrific, I know what it means for you, at least I'm trying to imagine.*

'God, I miss you! It's hell here. I actually got beaten for 'running away' — archaic barbarians, it was like Mutiny on the Bounty *or something. No, more like the Spanish Inquisition! Funny thing is how popular it made me with the others. They've always treated me like a bit of a wimp, now all of a sudden I'm a folk hero. Now I'm on probation; if I bunk off again or do anything else, even not work my balls off (the cane just missed them), I'm out. If it weren't for the exams, I wouldn't care, but as it is I am working my balls off. June draws nigh . . . AAAAGH! Aren't you dreading it? If only it was all over! Love you like mad, Clem.'*

Florence had read this with growing apprehension shading into righteous anger. She knew what these wealthy people were like — just bought their way out of everything. 'Mum' was going to see to it, was she? In June, which was *now*. So that was their nasty little plan, persuading Pleasure to murder Florence's grandchild behind her back as if she had nothing to say about it! Well, she would show them she wasn't as powerless as they thought.

So now she was hunting for the magazine with the school phone number on it. Her small bedroom, normally kept hospital-neat, was in turmoil, a reflection of what was going on in her head and heart. At last she found it where it had slipped off its shelf, and was wedged behind the chest-of-drawers. She raked it out with a coathanger and struggled up from her knees, panting.

She put on her glasses and consulted the scrawl across the face of the model on the cover. '*Glen Marshal*' she had written. Glen? Well, she must have misheard. And there was the number. She didn't pause to collect herself or to think, she was too upset. She just punched in the long number of the school as if stabbing Pleasure's seducer in the chest with her strong black finger while she told him what she thought of him.

★ ★ ★

Clem had no apprehensions — well, only the mildest — when Mr Radley summoned him. He had been working frenziedly to make up lost time; his mind, now freed of its immediate burden, was focused rigorously on his studies and he had, for the past week, been a model student.

One look at the Head's face, however, put the fear of God in his heart.

'Sit down, Marshall.'

Clem sat. His buttocks were still residually sore enough to make him wince at the possibility of being in trouble again, though he couldn't imagine what for.

'I have received a most unwelcome phone call from a Mrs Florence Swannage.'

Clem felt his eyes widen. He blinked them hastily.

'Do you know her?'

'No sir,' said Clem truthfully, but thought it best to cover himself by adding, 'but I know who she is.'

'And who is she?'

'She's — well, she's my girlfriend's mother.'

'Your 'girlfriend'? Is that what you call it?'

Clem's breathing stopped.

'Did you hear my question?' asked Mr Radley, raising his voice.

Clem nodded.

'Answer it then!'

'She's — my fiancée.'

The Head let out a noisy exclamation. 'I don't think I heard that, Marshall! Your *what*?'

Clem's head came up. He was being mocked — he, who had held Pleasure in his arms, who would soon be the father of her baby. He was not to be made to feel small and humble any more.

'My fiancée, Mr Radley. We're going to be married.'

Radley stared at him as if a harmless chicken had suddenly left its place at his feet and flown up to look him in the eyes.

'Does your father know about this?'

'My mother has met Pl — my fiancée. That was why I left school last week, to sort things out. I don't know whether she's told my father yet, but anyway that's up to her.'

'Your 'fiancée's' mother appears to be in complete ignorance of the impending nuptials. She tells me her daughter is pregnant by you, and that you are planning to aid her in getting an abortion. Is that the case?'

Clem felt a rush of blood to the head and reached out to the near-edge of Mr Radley's desk. It was carved into leaf-shapes. He gripped it with both hands.

'No!' he said loudly.

'No she is not pregnant, or no you are not trying to procure an abortion for her?' asked Mr Radley stonily.

Clem tried in vain to moisten his mouth without saliva. The double question threw him. He didn't find words to answer either part of it.

'There's something else,' Mr Radley said at last. 'Rather delicate.' He examined the tips of his fingers for a moment, frowning. 'I am no expert on accents, but speaking to Mrs — er — Swannage, it occurred to me . . . What are her ethnic origins?'

'She's from the West Indies,' croaked Clem.

The Head's face came up. There was a look on it that Clem couldn't read, but surprisingly it reminded him somehow of his father.

'So your — girlfriend — is coloured.'

'It's called black. So what?' It came out in a whisper, but it did come out.

'Insolence won't help, Marshall. Are you really so naive as to be unaware that this compounds my difficulties?'

There was an infinitely lengthy silence while the headmaster fixed him with a gaze so severe, so redolent of outraged convention and baffled authority, that it eventually forced Clem to look away.

Mr Radley heaved a martyred sigh.

'It is a very unusual, a very drastic thing to interrupt a boy's school career just before his final examinations, for the obvious reason that it will jeopardise his whole future. But in this case the matter is extremely serious. This school is a Roman Catholic foundation, it has governors, it has a moral duty to its students, and their parents. Do you understand what I'm saying?'

Clem stared at him in horrified silence. Radley couldn't be planning to expel him!

'I am going to telephone your father and ask him to come here — '

'Why not my mother? She's the Catholic!' Clem broke in desperately.

Mr Radley was taken aback. 'I meant, of course, both your parents. I will discuss the matter with them, but I warn you, this will almost certainly mean your removal from the school.'

Clem used the desk edge to push himself onto shaking legs. He leant across and shouted in a high voice he couldn't recognise as his: 'You can't do that! You can't! I need those exams, I need a career, I'm going to have responsibilities! You can't expel me!'

The Head stood up and put his hand across the desk to press down on Clem's shoulder. 'Calm yourself, Clement,' he said.

He only used the boys' first names *in extremis*. The effect was the opposite of anodyne. Clem, who had taken his beating 'like a man', now flushed a hectic red and began to pant like a frightened cat. He shook the hand off his shoulder and went on pleading through ground-out sobbing breaths:

'I have to pass, I have to get work and make money, I have to look after her! Just let me take the exams, punish me any other way you like, beat me again, I don't care, just don't chuck me out, Mr Radley, please!'

'Stop this grovelling, you're degrading yourself!'

Clem fell silent and stood shaking and wild-eyed.

'I see the root of this whole wretched situation all too clearly now — you are wholly lacking in self-control. You'd better go.'

Clem left the room unsteadily, leaving the door open.

Mr Radley got up and closed it, then sank back into his swivel chair and reached for the telephone. He sat with his hand across it for some minutes, tapping it with the nail of his forefinger with a slow, regular rhythm like a dripping tap. Sacking a boy just before the exams — and a boy with Marshall's potential — went against the grain, but what could he do? The other boys would tell their parents; there would be a scandal. No, he had no alternative, he'd have to act in the end. Better the pre-emptive strike than be forced into it by a gathering storm.

He lifted the receiver and asked his secretary to get him the number he wanted. While he waited he thought to himself, Is this our failure? All that learning, all those necessary facts, packed into his head, and the main thing we're here for — the life discipline, the doctrine — just nowhere. Down goes the wretched boy at the first fence. But it's his parents' fault, too, we can't do everything. Stupid mess! He ground his teeth, a habit he'd got into in theological college. If only the girl had been white, it might have been got around somehow, but a coloured girl!

★ ★ ★

Ken was out of earshot when the phone rang. He was round the back of the house, erecting, with the aid of a book lying open on an upturned bucket, a small wooden shed to house ducks.

What had suddenly made this move into livestock seem appropriate? Ken would have had difficulty answering this question. He'd probably have said that he wanted to do something to help Harry enjoy country life a little more, to give her an 'interest'. But it had more to do with his own need for vigorous, home-based action, the need to build something and to deflect his inner feelings by hammering in nails with hard blows.

The morning after Harry and Clem had left him to kick the cat and rage alone, he had been woken at seven a.m. by the telephone — Harry, ringing to apologise profusely and to tell him that she was in London and would return as soon as she had driven Clem back to school. He found he could scarcely answer her civilly, even after a night's sleep. His anger was still lodged in him, like a lump of hot food half-swallowed.

Immediately on her return, she'd sat him

down and told him straight out. Clem had got a girl into trouble.

He had sat there unmoving, his anger still stuck in him, blocking all feeling. He was a slow reactor in any case. Now he had no recourse but to listen, and not very carefully or very critically, because he was still numb with the outrage of last night and the shock of the news.

Harry continued in a rush. She hadn't — of course not — meant to deceive him or keep anything from him, it was just that it had all burst upon her last night; she'd been in a terrible state, quite beyond herself with anger and upset. And Clem had been so het up and worried about how Ken would take it — not scared of him, not really, just naturally nervous of his reactions; it had been hard enough for him to tell *her* — that she had just gone off with him, meaning to take him back to school straight away, but halfway there she'd realised it was far too late, so they'd gone to Town to find a hotel that was still open and then she'd taken him back to school first thing this morning.

Ken said nothing as the news trickled through the layers of his antagonism and hurt. He fetched himself a drink, sat down with it, and then watched her helplessly as she got up and fetched one for herself, which he should have thought of. She kept licking her lips, reminding him incongruously of someone else with that mannerism . . . God, it was Mrs Thatcher! His mouth twitched. How could one want to laugh at such a moment? And then all humour left him suddenly as a thought burst upon him with the force of a small depthcharge.

'It's not the coloured one, is it?'

His face and voice expressed more than his innate dismay at the thought. All the wretchedness and violence he had felt last night came out with this first question, which thus sounded far more passionate and disgusted than it need have done.

Harry took a swift gulp of her brandy. 'No!' she said quickly. 'Of course not. It's someone he met through . . . that boy, whatsisname, Jason, that he went to stay with last summer.'

'Not his sister, I hope,' said Ken acidly.

'No. Just a — sort of girl.'

'*Our* sort?'

A spasm of irritation crossed Harry's face and he wished he hadn't said anything that sounded so snobbish. Before he could withdraw it, though, she said brightly, 'Well! She's a very independent sort anyhow. She evidently has no intention of holding Clem responsible.'

'What does that mean? That she's going to pay for the abortion herself, or that she intends to have the thing on her own?'

There was a silence and Ken realised that he was not coming out of this very well. If only last night hadn't happened, he could be behaving much more rationally, much better. He didn't really like this side of himself any better than Harry did.

But she didn't say anything reproachful, only: 'I don't know what she intends. Just that she wants to make her own decisions and doesn't

237

expect Clem to be involved. She says it isn't his fault.'

'Why isn't it his fault?' asked Ken testily. This seemed to him a rather odd assertion for a woman to make.

'Well, it seems that . . . she told Clem she was on the pill, and . . . she wasn't, obviously, so . . . she's taking the responsibility on herself. I think maybe she, well, wants the baby. She's — she's quite a lot older than him,' she added, as if she had suddenly remembered a vital fact.

'How much older?'

Harry took another gulp and said rather loudly, 'She's thirty-one.'

'*Thirty-one!* What the hell does a woman of that age see in a kid like Clem? Is she kinked or what?'

After a momentary pause, during which Ken was again dismayed by the echo of his own words, Harry said in a hurt tone, 'Why, do you think he's so unattractive?'

Ken shrugged irritably and buried his nose in his drink. A new and unlooked-for reaction was stealing over him. Could it be that in the privacy of his heart he was not wholly displeased? Of course, it could have spelt absolute disaster, but this way, with the girl — no, she was no girl, the *woman* — not intending to lumber Clem, what it basically spelt was no worse than a fairly commonplace scrape — and not one that he would necessarily have expected his undersized and rather immature son to get into. Showed he was a man, anyway. One

238

had to worry about that these days, and Ken, watching Clem narrowly through his adolescent years for signs of rampant manhood that never appeared, seeing him instead so small and un-macho somehow, had worried, though he had hardly acknowledged it even to himself.

'Not at all, it's not that.' He coughed. 'Should I have a talk to him, do you think?'

'I don't think that's a good idea, Ken. He's had a bad fright, that's punishment enough, and there's one good thing, he'll be more careful next time.' Ken had to stifle a grin. 'He's got his exams up ahead, better just leave it for the moment.'

'You may be right. It's all over now.'

And he (almost) believed it. Before many hours had passed, the business about the unknown woman had slipped into the back of his mind. Any time it slipped forward again in the coming months, he reminded himself that now, with the pill, women had almost complete control over their reproductive functions. Responsibility for extramural pregnancies were definitely asymmetrical — no, more than that, really 99% down to the woman, surely. Besides, single parenthood — whatever he personally felt about it — was a common-place these days. The woman got social security and all kinds of other help. Whether she deserved it or not, at least there was no need to worry about the welfare of the child. Well, there was damn-all he could do about it anyway, without compromising Clem. Clem came first. Obviously. Nothing wrong about that, any father would feel the same.

Now he could get back to worrying about the pattern of his life with Harry.

The basic trouble was, of course, that there was something unanchored, tenuous, about their relationship. Where there is no sex, there is no safe way to 'earth' quarrels and ill-feeling, no way to keep a woman bonded securely to the marriage and the home.

He had to find a way to give her an anchor, an interest around the place. Something other than him to love and look after, to be tied by. Because he'd already realised that despite his good intentions, he was not going to be able to stay at home to be her constant companion. One of these days he might land a job, and in the meantime he was getting more and more involved in the life of the district. Someone had even hinted he should stand for the Council at the next local elections, something that strongly appealed to him. Joker Brittan had sounded him out rather subtly ('Are you — *harrumph* — on the Square, Marshall?') about becoming a Freemason. Of course he had not responded positively; Harry thought all Masons were the devil's kin and often inveighed against their influence in the police force and so on, but something in him had been gratified by the feeler. Great compliment, surely.

Harry loved her garden but that wasn't enough; you could leave a garden to itself, but you couldn't leave animals. A dog would be an obvious part-answer, but the bloody cat prevented that. If he could get her hooked on poultry, that might just do the trick.

240

At home, in his West Country childhood, there had always been ducks and chickens around the place, and it was his mother who had always taken care of them. They were a tie; you had to shut them up every night. He'd heard some sad tales from neighbours around here about the bloody incursions of 'th' old fahx' and 'Mr Badger'. In fact, Harry had almost suggested keeping poultry herself when the salmonella scare broke.

'God isn't mocked. Keeping them in batteries, treating them like machines! If I kept chickens, they could have a lovely life with everything they wanted, and our eggs would be beyond reproach.'

Precisely so. Ken, in his thoroughgoing way, went to the library, inspected the premises of two local poultry-keepers, asked some advice, bought the timber and the wire netting, the bitumen paper and the nails, and got to work. He'd got the main structure erected on a nicely screed concrete base, and was so busy for a couple of days he hardly missed Harry, who had gone up to Town to consult her old dentist.

'I can't be doing with this local boy, he plays pop music all the time he's fiddling with your teeth, and he's a scaremonger. He says I need a really beastly gum operation and he described it to me — ugh! I'm sure my old chap will tell me I don't.'

So Ken went on banging away at his duck-house. Mr Radley's secretary went on fruitlessly ringing, Clem sat in his sixth-form room in a stupor. Harry went to the dentist in Ealing and had the local pop-addict's view of the state of her gums dismayingly confirmed, and then went off and consoled herself by buying nearly a hundred pounds' worth of baby things.

Florence went to work with her thoughts in two distinct layers: the top layer congratulated her on a duty well and truly done, and the under layer reproached her unmercifully with malicious mixing-in, and tormented her with horrid anticipation of what Pleasure would say when she found out. She stamped about the wards so convulsively, the ward sister had to have a word with her.

Meanwhile George heard that his offer for Bugle Farm had been accepted. He was tremendously bucked. It was fate! It meant his whole life was set on a new, exciting course.

He took Judy out to dinner to celebrate. Judy, to get away from agonised thoughts of Tiananmen Square which had happened barely a week before, put on a bright brittle manner and told him about Clem, Pleasure and Harry (not that she was up to date on the subject). She also talked brightly and brittly about Tina, whom she hadn't seen or heard from in two weeks and about whom she was beginning to feel vague but persistent anxiety, but she made it sound like a sort of running farce.

George put out the antennae of love and soon realised that something was seriously wrong with Judy to make her talk and behave like this. He held her hand under the table between courses and just let her go on and on, not saying much himself.

Then he saw her home and while they were having cocoa she suddenly burst into tears and couldn't stop crying, and for a wonder (as she afterwards reflected) it clicked at once. He had watched the awful scenes on television himself, with his heart going out to her, wondering how on earth she was taking it, for hadn't she carefully explained to him that once the revolution was in place, counter-revolutionary actions had to be put down, by force if necessary, and wasn't that what this, technically, was? The pro-Democracy student movement that was being crushed by tanks and bullets in Beijing had to count as being counter-revolution in a Communist country, but how could she watch without anguish as those brave kids went down?

And here it was. He reached for her and hugged her close to him and without even needing to ask what was the matter with her, said:

'It's the bloody old men, pet, hanging on to power with what's left of their teeth, it's not only the system. Just to stop people from starving in China was a miracle. Those kids might have been able to wrench things back on course if they'd been let.'

She was so astounded — so relieved and grateful — to find him on her wavelength, at least to that extent, that all resistance left her. She threw herself into his comforting embrace, let him kiss her and soothe her and pump her pain away — for the time being — with his big, rather unwieldy and out of practice, but

243

basically sound and loving male member.

But the image of the boy in front of the tank was fresh then, not yet a cliché or a symbol, and even at the moment of her first sexual climax in years, it lit up behind Judy's eyes as if burnt on her retina, and filled them with more tears. These tears weren't only for the tank-boy's gallantry and futility and for all the dead Chinese children of hope. They were for herself and the creeping onset of a great desolating loss.

15

It was Harry who actually found out first that Clem was to be — not expelled, Mr Radley made a great point of that, but 'asked to leave'. There was a difference, he insisted. It was perfectly obvious to Harry even through her fog of distress and shock that the headmaster was impaled on the horns of a dilemma that very simply he was not man enough to prise himself off. She told him as much when she went to see him.

Word had reached her in London, through Pleasure, whom Clem had telephoned in a state bordering on despair. Pleasure contacted Judy (all the younger picketers took their troubles to her as a matter of course) and Judy, with whom Harry had begun to stay whenever she was in London, had broken it to her.

Harry didn't give herself time to think properly or work out the ramifications, nor to muster up any tact, or indeed, tactics. Nor did it occur to her to phone her husband. This was an outrage and had to be stopped, that was all she knew, and just as she had years before about the air-gun, she leapt straight into her car and set off. Luckily she was only drunk with anger this time. She spent the journey rehearsing scene after furious scene. An hour and a half later she was in Mr Radley's office trying to play all of them at once.

It was not a good move. If there was one thing that a man like Mr Radley would never do, it was to give a *woman* the satisfaction of making him back down, especially one as angry and free with her personal animadversions as Harriet Marshall was just then. He climbed onto his dignity and his unassailable power-base, and sat there stony-faced and immovable. Apart from telling her that being asked to leave was not at all the same as expulsion and that he was prepared to give Clem a good academic report, he was adamant. Harry's telling him that she knew all about Pleasure and that Clem really *was* going to marry her, made no difference. Rather, if she had but known it, it made shivers run down his spine afresh.

'The best thing you can do, Mrs Marshall, is to get him into a crammer as fast as possible. He won't be able to take his exams next month — '

'How dare you? Oh, how dare you do this!' Harry interrupted, literally wringing her hands.

' — but he can take them in the autumn, perhaps. Some crammers do summer courses that would keep him up to snuff, providing he doesn't allow himself to be — um — distracted.'

'Distracted! He must be nearly out of his mind!'

'He will *calm down*,' he said pointedly, 'and, I hope, see my position.'

'Your position! If you were standing in a tunnel between two converging express trains, you wouldn't be justified in what you're doing. How can any one man have such power,

246

especially a man as small and *frightened* as you!'

Mr Radley bit his lips until they both disappeared, and rose.

'I should like to terminate this interview,' he said thinly. 'It would be best if you take Clement with you now. I'll get Matron to pack his things quickly. Believe me, I'm very sorry for what has happened, but if you hadn't wished us to maintain Catholic values, you should have selected some other establishment.'

This brought Harry up short. She reined herself in so sharply Mr Radley could almost hear the screech of emotional brakes. She reached shakily into her bag and took out a handkerchief — the tears were streaming down her face unchecked. When she had blown her nose and dried her eyes, she turned and faced him. He had never seen such furious hatred in anyone's eyes, and he flinched.

'As far as I'm concerned,' she said, 'Catholic values include Christian tolerance and a degree of loyalty to those you're responsible for, in times of trouble. If this is not the case, perhaps I should have selected some other *religion*.'

She didn't mean that. Of course not. Her adopted faith was the bedrock of her life. *The bedrock of my life*, she whispered to herself as she sat in the big panelled school hall waiting for Clem and his hastily-packed luggage. These were words she often formed distinctly in her thoughts, as effective as prayer, when confusions threatened. And they'd been threatening quite a lot lately.

It was Pleasure's pregnancy that had reawakened ambivalences that she had thought long since quashed. Her first impulse when she'd found out was one of absolute panic resulting in a spontaneous eruption of pre-conversion pragmatism: 'A lifetime's payment for one mistake! *No. No.* Let things go back to what they were, let Clem not be damaged by this.' Her honesty later forced her to decode this as 'Let her get rid of it!' But this impulse she had successfully suppressed. She had done the right *Catholic* thing in persuading Pleasure not to get rid of it. But now things were going to become very, very complicated.

How was she going to cope with this situation? Ahead lay a miasma through which she could see nothing clearly. But deep down she knew that the miasma was, and could only be, the thoroughgoing deceiving of Ken.

Her marriage as it had stood for the past twelve years was anything but a Catholic marriage. It was actually a mockery of marriage, Catholic or otherwise, except for the baffling fact that somehow it hung together. She was aware that it was harder for Ken to live in this cobbed-up, platonic fashion than for her, because she had convinced herself that she really wasn't interested in sex any more and, although he had never been other than a temperate, English, Tuesdays-and-Fridays sort of lover, she was uneasily aware that he still had needs and that they were not being met.

Her feelings for him were odd — she recognised that. She loved him in a funny, *accustomed* sort of way. She was grateful for the way he took care of the practical side of their lives. He must suit her somehow or other, even though she never missed him when they were briefly apart; even when she was feeling lonely, it was never directly for him.

But she had never lied to him, not real lies. Now a wall of whoppers loomed. Whopping lies to one's husband — a whole open-ended campaign of them, going off into the distance like a forest through which no daylight shows — did not have to be about adultery in order to rate as sins. She was looking ahead to an era where her peaceful *marriage manqué* would become a snake-pit of complex and detailed duplicity, which all the Friday sessions in the confessional, all the penances and false promises of amendment, would not and could not wipe away.

Her heartbeat, which had returned to normal after the scene in the headmaster's office, started racing again, and she could feel the chill across her shoulders from her sweat of anger and distress. She felt exceedingly tired, so much so that she wondered if she hadn't better let Clem drive (if only he'd come, and they could get away from this hateful place!). Then she found that her eyes, which long minutes ago had sought the clock ticking in the empty hall, were actually fixed on the large crucifix just above it.

A memory that she had been blocking sprang back.

It had happened in the run-up to Easter. She'd been in the kitchen cooking lunch, had turned on the radio and heard a talk by some American who described, graphically and with unrelenting precision, how crucifixion had actually worked.

It seemed the usual image was quite inaccurate. You couldn't hang a man up by nails through his hands. His weight would tear the nails out from between the fingers. So the method was to drive the nails ('which would be about five inches long') through the wrists. This would displace the small cluster of bones there, probably go through a major nerve-centre ('extremely painful') as well as damaging other 'sensitive tissues, ligaments, cartilage, etc, etc.'

The feet as portrayed in the classic pose were quite wrong, too, the American expert had continued dispassionately. The legs would have been turned at the hips so that a single nail could be driven through both ankles at once, from the side. Also the knees would be bent. The point of this, he explained, was so that the agony could be prolonged by the victim's inability to lift his torso by straightening his knees, in order to relieve the intolerable pressure on his lungs which would otherwise be impossible to empty. Crucified people 'as a rule' actually died of asphyxiation.

Of course, he went on matter-of-factly, the image on the cross was incorrect in another respect. The five sacred wounds on an otherwise unmarked body would hardly, in reality, have been noticed in the welter of blood. A description followed of the flogging, down to the little spears of bone the Romans customarily fixed into the ends of the thongs to tear the flesh . . . Harry by this time was feeling very strange, nauseated and yet somehow paralysed. Luckily Ken had come into the kitchen at this point, listened for about ten seconds to the American voice, and switched off the radio quite savagely.

'They love it,' he said between clenched teeth. 'All of it. They're aroused by it, and not to piety. Why are you listening to that disgusting beastliness, Harry? It doesn't turn *you* on, I hope.'

She had felt too shaky, angry and upset to answer. It was only ten minutes later, when the strange influence laid on her by the broadcast had released her, that she made a discovery about the state of her body that had disturbed her so much that she had banished all thought of it, until now. Now she thought of it. What did it mean? It meant something too disgusting to think about. Something that, if she did think about it, might taint her whole view of herself as a Catholic.

'Mum? Shall we go?'

She jumped to her feet, breaking into a sweat again (what was the matter with her?). 'Darling! Are you all right?'

He kissed her. 'I'm okay. You look a bit green.'

'Yes. I'm afraid I had a horrible row with Mr Radley, it shook me up a bit. Stupid, ghastly little man! Oh, to hell with him.'

Clem actually grinned. He was feeling better since talking to Pleasure. 'Really, Mum? Actually to hell? Don't go OTT.'

'Don't what?'

'Never mind. The porter's got my stuff out in the drive. Let's go.'

On the way home, with Clem driving — he seemed less shaky now than his mother — they discussed ways and means.

'I've been thinking,' said Clem. 'It's not so bad really. I'll take in November, or, if I'm not ready with all that's going on, next June. I'll need to find some kind of job straight away, and that'll hold me up, but I'll get the exams OK. It only means not taking my year out. I couldn't have gone away, anyway, with the baby and everything. I can go to college next year just as I'd planned.'

'What would you feel about a crammer?'

Clem glanced at her. 'Can we afford it, Mum? Those places cost a bomb.'

'Of course we can afford it. You might even get better marks than you would have done if you'd taken now.'

They drove a bit further and Clem, looking straight ahead, said in a muffled voice, 'I suppose I'm incredibly dead with Dad.'

'Well . . . he doesn't actually know yet.'

'What? What d'you mean? What doesn't he know?'

'He — he doesn't know anything, Clem. I — I just haven't been able to tell him yet.'

Clem drove on for a bit and then abruptly pulled into a lay-by.

'But he knows about the baby.'

'Oh — well, yes. Sort of,' she mumbled.

'Come on, Mum. What's going on?'

She licked her lips and looked down at her

hands, commanding them not to fidget, not to give out the body-language of guilt.

'Clem, Dad's a bit — funny about — '

'Black people. I know. And Jews. And foreigners. He's sort of, a bit of a sort of — racist really, isn't he? I mean, I couldn't help noticing. He's okay in other ways,' he added loyally.

'Well. If you have noticed that, maybe you can . . . You see, I don't think Dad would take it very well if he knew about Pleasure. So I — I've just told him that some girl — well, I made her an older woman actually — was going to have your baby but that she'd gone off. I know it doesn't sound very good — I mean, I did lie to him, which is bad, I know it's bad, but sometimes you can't help it. I — I honestly feel it would upset him terribly if he knew. Sometimes it's a lot more cruel to tell a person something you know would absolutely devastate them, than . . . ' It was sounding worse and worse. His eyes when she glanced at them were full of incredulity.

'Hang about, Mum. Are you saying we shouldn't tell Dad about Pleasure, and me getting the boot from school?'

She thought a bit. She hadn't really had time to consider that part of it.

'No, obviously he's got to know you've left school. But I would prefer it if we could just fudge the reason. You know what I mean. Pretend it was because of you running away before, or say you ran away again. Just so he doesn't have to know you were asked to leave

253

because of Pleasure. Being black.'

There was a long, thoughtful silence. Then Clem said slowly, 'But when he sees the baby . . . '

A shudder ran along Harry's arms. She turned her head away.

'I would prefer it if he *didn't* see the baby — not just at first.'

'Mum, are you scared of Dad? Is that it?'

'Would you fancy telling him you're going to have a half-caste baby?'

'Mixed race. No. But I don't fancy lying to him either, not in the long-term. I mean, he'd be so hurt when he found out.'

He left the rest unsaid, but she said it in her head. *He'd never forgive us.* But she was remembering something: the evening Ken had told her he was having an affair with Clem's playschool teacher. 'I don't want to live a lie with you. I want to be honest — no secrets.' How she had hated him for unburdening himself, and look, look what it had caused! His damned selfish honesty had cost her her daughter, and him — oh yes, it had cost him plenty, too! Was 'honesty and no secrets' the best policy, always? Decidedly, on her own experience, it was not.

But still, to lie like this went against everything the Church taught. She sat silently with that knowledge. It didn't seem to change her profound unwillingness to confront Ken with the facts and to see his reaction. Or rather — and this startled 'her — her willingness to keep it from him. She was not clear at all about what underlay this, but she knew it wasn't just moral cowardice on her part. She had some kind of buried hostility to Ken which made deceiving him possible.

After a long time, Clem gave a deep sigh.

'Look, Mum,' he said. 'You've got to live with Dad, I haven't. I'm so preoccupied with — well, myself, Pleasure — all that. I'm going to be living in London whether I go to a crammer or not. I want to be with Pleasure, we're going to find a flat to rent. I won't be around home much. I can't tell you what to do about Dad. I mean, I'm not prepared to rush off and blow the whistle on myself if that lands you in the shit. Sorry,' he added, glancing at her.

'It's all right.'

'You used to make such a fuss about me swearing.'

'That was before you grew up,' she said.

16

November 1989

One evening the phone rang in the cottage. Harry answered.

'I suppose you and Ken are sitting there drinking bleddy toasts!' she heard Judy yell without preamble.

The baby had been born the day before — a month prematurely, but quite safely — and naturally enough Harry mistook the reference. So full was she of her own concerns that she also missed the note of anguish in her friend's voice.

'Sh!' she hissed sharply. Ken was in the dining room and the door was open. 'Wait a minute, I'm going upstairs.' When she got to the bedroom phone, with the door closed, she continued severely, 'Who told you? Every time Ken set foot outside the house today I tried to ring you!'

'What for? What're you talking about?'

'About the baby. Ken knows *nothing*. Who would I be drinking 'bleddy toasts' with?'

There was a dumbstruck silence on the line. Then Judy burst out:

'Can't you think of anything but Pleasure and her *vervlakste* baby? They're pulling the Berlin Wall down!'

Poland had already happened. Czechoslovakia

had already happened, or was in the process of happening. Ken had indeed been glued to the set, had, indeed, been gleefully cheering on the demise of the Evil Empire. It had all been unfolding in front of Harry's unseeing eyes. They were turned inward to thoughts of Pleasure in her untimely birthpangs, and then, oh, then! — her granddaughter, tiny but perfect, milky-eyed *and* (according to Pleasure herself in an exciting secret phone-call, received, by duplicitous arrangement, at Bugle Farm) with a thick crest of fine hair that, as soon as it was washed and dried, had curled itself entrancingly into little brown feathery circlets all over a head no bigger than a Jaffa orange.

What cared Harry, then, for the upheavals of Eastern Europe? What cared she for the history-making chink of hammers chopping pieces out of that east-west barrier, the crowds pouring west, the embraces and the tears, the ecstatic shopping expeditions by the glamour- and goods-starved easterners, of their glowing return home with bizarre bags full of fruit and toys? Harry was seething with plans for her own toy-buying expeditions, the wild search for a watertight excuse for removal to London in order to bear them to the hospital where Pleasure was lying with the adorable newcomer safe and sound in the crook of her arm, the newcomer who wouldn't have come at all if it hadn't been for Harry — who would have been 'untimely rip'd forth' a lifeless little baby-shaped lump of flesh. She could, she discovered, at last think of what she herself had long ago lost, without agony.

There had been a replacement.

Who, then, had a better right to rejoice, drink toasts, buy gifts, rush to the bedside to take that little brand-saved-from-the-burning in her arms and assuage many years of suppressed hunger with a good cuddle? But all must be done by stealth.

And now Judy, her friend and confidante, with whom she longed to discuss ways-and-means, was furious, and Harry filled with chagrin and remorse.

'Oh Jude, I'm sorry, I'm such an idiot! I just can't take in anything, I'm so full of the baby!' Though she was sure Ken was downstairs, she faced the door all the time she was talking.

'So she popped early,' grunted Judy. 'Well, go on, drool, I'll give you three minutes.'

Harry duly drooled, especially about Clem having been in at the birth. She gave details of weight and length. There was a pause. Harriet heard Judy strike a match, and said subduedly, 'Darling, let's get back to the Wall and all that. I do realise that's much more important, really.'

'It's not about the Wall as such. They're calling it the final collapse of socialism . . . Oh shit, doll, I can't explain.'

'But it's not the collapse of socialism! It's not even the *failure* of socialism. What existed over there isn't even what you call *Communism*, is it? Not your idea of Communism, the way you've explained it to me.'

'Oh, don't be a hypocrite — be honest. You're revelling, like everyone else, aren't you?'

Harry hesitated. 'I'm glad the East Germans

are free. I'm glad the Poles and Czechs are free. Aren't you?'

' 'Free!' 'Free!' Free to join the rottenness, the Coca-Cola culture!'

'That's what they appear to want.'

'And now they're going to get it. And all that goes with it! Unemployment and homelessness, the wheelchair of organised religion — just watch it in Poland! Better Jaruzelski than the bleddy Pope telling them how to lead their lives! Sorry, oh sorry, but he's such a bleddy old reactionary. With his rigid birth-control policies he's probably done more sheer human damage than anyone else living! And then there's crime, drugs, pollution, petty nationalism, antisemitism — Oh God, I could kill them!'

'Who, Judy? The people?'

'No, no! You see, you don't understand! The bastards at the top who corrupted it, who made it all go wrong — the bastards on both sides who deformed it and *betrayed* it! Not the people. Poor fools, what do they know, they just want to fly like moths to the bright coloured lights and they won't know any better till they burn their bleddy wings off!'

Now she was definitely crying and Harry's heart was wrung, imagining, trying to, what she must be feeling.

'Sh, Jude, it had to happen. You can't expect people to put up with being oppressed for ever. That's what it was, you must see that.'

'The oppression, as you called it, was only the outcome of economics, and economics is to do with markets, and markets are what

259

imperialism is all about. Oh, it's no use, you can't understand, you've grown up with the utter, all-corrosive injustice of market forces that suck half the world's share of everything into the great gaping bloated mouths of the other half. You can't see how tragically, vilely rotten it all is — and now another huge area of the earth's surface and hundreds of millions more people are going to be added, split between the plunderers and the plundered!'

Harry had listened for a long time. That night was the worst outburst, perhaps because the sight of the Wall being breached was so totemic, as potent a symbol in its destruction as it had been in its building, which both women were too young to remember.

Later, as that winter — racked in Britain only by meteorological, not political storms, apart from the ambulance dispute and a few relatively minor hiccups — brought its cataclysmic upheavals and eruptions in other parts of the world, patterns exploding and drastically reshaping themselves, Judy and Harry continued to deepen their friendship while covertly watching each other alter in subtler but scarcely less profound ways.

But there was one thing they didn't share.

Harry could sense Judy's unspoken disapproval of her deceiving of Ken.

Ken knew nothing. Nothing at all! Twenty times a day, Harry would remind herself of this delicious fact, which somehow left his share of grandparenthood for Harry, a double share.

Florence had this too. Sturdy, manless

Florence, who had well-beaten Harry to Pleasure's hospital bedside (but then, she worked there, it was no contest!) after the birth, whose fathomless eyes had met Harry's for the very first time across Pleasure's bed, narrow, unreadable at first. Was there a keep-off-Whitey-this-is-mine warning there? If so, Harry had ignored it. She had waited. Let Florence, mother of the mother, keep her hold on the bundle as long as she liked; she had to put it back in the crib eventually, and then it was Harry's turn.

'How do you like her?' Florence had asked, not concealing the mockery. 'Bit of black in her eyes and her lips, her hair look nappy to me.'

'And her skin, you can see it very well in her skin, and she'll probably get a bit darker later,' said Harry between coos.

The eyes with their depths of ancient civilisations, of remotest Africa, opened wide. 'You saying you don't mind?'

'Of course I don't, I'm proud of it,' said Harry. It was a grandmother-to-rival-grandmother ploy, a bit of lifewomanship, but it also happened to be true, and she knew it fully and for sure at that moment. *Thanks, Jude. Bless you forever!* It was a much more spontaneous and heartfelt prayer than any she had recently made to God.

17

February, 1990

Harry reflected — well, no, she was far too excited for anything as placid as reflection, it was more of a mental rocket-burst — that she had never had champagne bubbles in her hair before and that it was almost as good as having them in her mouth.

She found the thought had been accompanied by a joyful leap into the air off both feet. The champagne in her plastic glass flew up and she caught most of it as it came down, like a liquid pancake, and quaffed it off.

Clem at her side was laughing at her, but she didn't care. In the circumstances, such laughter could be nothing but an equivalent form of rejoicing.

'Save a bit for me, Mum!'

'Sorry, it's all gone. There goes a bottle — grab it!'

All around them the crowd was doing as they were, shouting, cheering, laughing, hugging, jumping up and down. The celebratory speeches were going on from the makeshift platform but they were hardly to be heard amid the general crowd-concerto of happiness. Every now and then a new bottle would be popped — the spume would fly out, and the February wind would blow it across the heads of the crowd.

Another deafening cheer, then the bottle would be passed round, being poured in driblets into small plastic bottles, or in gulps straight down excited throats.

'Isn't this great! Isn't it the best moment of your life!'

This from Pleasure, who had just found her way to their side after spotting them from the platform. She had made a speech herself, right after Judy's big one — short, fiercely exultant, full of Black triumph, which had Clem waving his arms in the air with pride at the end. She deserves it, thought Harry. They all did, all the picketers. Day and night, night and day, rain, dark, cold, relentless police harassment and marauding British Nats, non-stop for nearly three whole years! Had they actually, practically, helped to bring about this longed-for dénouement? Did it matter? Harry, grinning like a jester, hugged Clem with one arm and Pleasure with the other.

Her Clem-arm embraced someone else as well, a wide-awake three-month-old baby girl with bottle-brown eyes and golden skin and reddish curly hair. She was suspended in a sling from her father's shoulders. Every now and then he would reach a hand back, underarm or overarm, to touch her. Now Harry touched her too, touched her fluffy head and round rose-silk cheek, felt the little hand embrace her finger firmly as it had when she was first born. Only it was even better now because now there was a smile of recognition, of personhood. Harry felt her soul inflate within her, forcing a profound sigh. This was joy piled on joy. One day she would tell her granddaughter, 'In the hour Nelson Mandela was released, you were in Trafalgar Square, right outside the South African Embassy. You got champagne in your hair, your first champagne.' With her finger she lifted a little froth from the copper curls and put it in the baby's mouth.

'Listen,' shouted Pleasure suddenly above the hubbub. 'Let's leave and try to find a telly. He'll be on and we can see him.'

Harry didn't want to leave. She loved being here, feeling herself an intimate part of this moment, one of the happier and more hope-filled tick-tocks of history. Short of being actually in Pretoria, in the roaring crowd welcoming Nelson out of his long prison exile, this was the best — yes, perhaps it really was one of the best moments of her life, just as Pleasure said. What then must it be like for people like Judy, who had really earned this moment, whose whole life had led up to it and whose future would be rearranged by it? It was only through her that any of this had happened to Harry. She suddenly felt she loved Judy more than any other friend she had, because she had found a way to share with Harry the right — bought cheap with a dozen stints on the picket — to rejoice and be part of this wonderful event.

Harry cupped the baby's head in both hands and kissed her brown button-mushroom nose. Under this specific gratitude lay another, far deeper. Without Judy, Harry might not have been able to look at this beautiful mixed-blood morsel with total equanimity, with unalloyed pride.

She remembered, belatedly, to send up a prayer of thanksgiving for Nelson's release. Even as she composed it and sent it aloft, a doubt flashed out like an arrow and brought it down. If God merited thanks for intervening now, why had He not done so before? Her prayer collapsed.

Now the pull of the crowd was slackening as they turned the corner. Both Clem's hands were behind him, folded in support under the little padded bottom. Harry followed to fend off jostlers.

Pleasure was hurrying ahead, urging them toward a pub that had a telly above the bar.

'What do you think he looks like, after all this time?' she fretted. 'I don't think I can stand it if he looks old — he's got so much to do!'

She scarcely glanced at the baby. Now Harry thought about it, all the time they'd been together in the crowd, she hadn't.

★ ★ ★

Judy stood at the far side of the road, in the Square itself, facing the Embassy. The traffic, crawling through the huge crowds that spilled off the pavements, came between her and the platform, the champagne, the placards, the epicentre of the celebrations.

She had purposely distanced herself after her speech that the crowd was almost certainly too excited to listen to. She'd talked about her

265

aching desire to be there, in South Africa, to actually see Nelson, free at last and reunited with Winnie. Judy felt an enormous love for them both flooding through her. Almost an *in*-loveness.

George had teased her, told her her Communism was just another form of religion, and she had reacted with anger. Because religion was irrational, a superstition, and this was the opposite: a scientific, intellectual conviction in the eventual, inevitable triumph of political good over the evils of exploitation and the basic injustice of capitalism. It was more than a belief in Marx's dictum that power *must* inevitably come to the people after more primitive systems had been worked through; it was a belief in mankind's ability to learn through this process what worked best. When Judy had shouted at Tina that there was no such thing as human nature, she had meant that she profoundly believed in the perfectability of mankind through social improvement.

George said that this was exactly the same as Christians believing that with the help of Jesus they could become as good as He was. According to George, there was nothing inevitable in the historic process; in fact, he believed that history was not a predictable process at all, any more than evolution accorded with any sort of 'plan'. Both were just a series of random turns of events, which at any moment could be twisted by the merest chance into new channels.

When Judy forced herself to understand fully what he meant, she felt a visceral pang of terror. She fought back with a wave of words, unaware how many slogans she was using until he interrupted, no belligerence in his voice, only incredulity: 'How can you still be mouthing that rubbish? Listening to all that discredited claptrap is like digging broken bottles out of an old tip. It's been tried, pet, it's failed, it's killed millions, and now it's broken. What's left is just the twitchings of a corpse. Bury it, for God's sake — just bury it.'

She had rejected this with all her being. For months now everything had been falling apart in Europe, but in the Soviet Union there was still something to cling to. While Communism remained in place there, things could still improve, be brought back on track. It continued to be the only political theory in the world that spoke its basic rightness to her deepest convictions. And yet . . . Events in China, the domino-like collapse in Europe, the horrible revelations in Roumania, the rejoicings in Poland and Czechoslovakia and Hungary . . . all these had affected her so badly that her joy in this wonderful victory in South Africa and the prospect of a whole new and better future there had been undermined. Which was why she had left the crowd and come to stand here, apart, pushed and jostled, hollow-hearted as if some heavy premonition were upon her.

Suddenly she saw Tina.

Judy could hardly believe it. Seconds ago, out of the corner of her eye, she'd seen someone like Tina dash across the road, dodging a double-decker bus, but still she didn't credit it till she arrived, bright-faced and breathless and with her hair exploding round her face like streamers from a party-popper, and said, 'Hi, Mom! Exciting, eh?'

Judy stared at her. 'How did you find me?'

'Caught your speech and watched where you went. Where's your fella? Didn't he come?'

'No.'

'Dido did!' said Tina triumphantly.

She turned and waved energetically across the road. Now to her even greater amazement Judy saw her mother, fur-coated and behatted and standing out in the crowd like a protea blossom in a London windowbox. She raised a languid hand, gloved with the rings on the outside.

'C'mon back to the other side, Mom. Great speech, by the way! God, I'm pissed! Isn't it fantastic?'

Dumbstruck, Judy allowed Tina to lead her back across the crowded road. She noticed that Dido, who, she knew, had bought Tina a whole new wardrobe, had not had her wicked way with her today. Tina was dressed like the other kids in jeans, and her sweatshirt that said '*I Support the Frontline States in Southern Africa*'.

She couldn't believe that Dido had come.

'Hang on, doll. How did you drag Grandma here?'

Tina grinned over her shoulder. 'Aren't I brilliant? I just wanted her to see it — and you! So I bribed her, said I'd have my hair done at Lizzie Arden's if she'd come. She's been on at me for weeks. Be nice to her, Mom. She is paying for my education, after all.'

This silenced Judy. Undeniably, Dido had done miracles. Got Tina into a better crammer on a whole new course that she actually seemed to be enjoying. The trouble was the obvious — jealousy. How could this woman who had practically rejected her own daughter, achieve with Judy's what Judy had failed to do herself?

Brought abruptly face-to-face with her mother, Judy fell back on the same childish sally: 'Hi, Mom.'

Dido pressed her scented cheek to Judy's through a bobbly veil. She looked positively weird in this setting, like something from another era — another world. Certainly another family! *This is my mother*, Judy had to remind herself dazedly.

'So they let him out,' Dido said. 'Well, let's hope he's too old to do much harm now. And look at you. Still haven't grown out of your fiery-speeches phase,' she remarked. 'I would have thought, with all that's been happening — '

'Dido, please shut up,' said Tina, not impolitely, but quite firmly and to Judy's gratified astonishment. Her hand, still somehow holding Tina's, gave it a convulsive squeeze. 'Let's go back to the hotel and watch Nelson on telly,' added Tina.

'Are you still living in that bleddy place?' asked Judy as Dido, with a last glance of distaste at the crowd, sprinted with surprising speed for the kerb to hail a passing taxi, her rhinestone heels a-twinkle.

'Sh, Mom, don't say anything! It's just for the

moment. Please don't look like that, I've got to live somewhere!'

'Out of the frying-pan,' muttered Judy, who still knew nothing of the sleeping-rough interlude. 'Well, I'm not going there!'

Tina turned to face her and gave her a very straight look.

'You know what, Mom, you are,' she said. 'Come on. I don't want to have to bribe *you*. The only way would be to promise *not* to go to Lizzie Arden's.'

Not so long ago, Judy would have felt strong and sure enough to refuse to compromise. Now, though it would have killed her to admit it, the thought of even an hour in the purlieus of the Dorchester Hotel drew her like a magnet. Her flat had developed damp rot and was smelling awful, the electricity kept failing and there was something wrong with the boiler . . . She allowed herself to be drawn to the taxi that was waiting with Dido inside, beckoning imperiously with a glittering finger.

★ ★ ★

As they drove away, the taxi — unbeknownst to Judy, who had thought he was in Dorset — drove straight past George.

He too had followed Judy with his eyes after she had made her speech, which he had listened to with an unaccustomed lump in his throat. He had driven up to London early in the morning, because of an unfightable impulse, a need to be here with her. It was, though he didn't acknowledge it as such, an impulse of penitence. So much did this go against the grain that, even knowing how much it would mean to Judy to have him turn up, he had kept out of her sight.

He had been wrong. Her passionate efforts on the picket had borne fruit. They had released Mandela. Apartheid was on its way out, and those who had fought for that, in however small a way, were entitled to claim their share of pride, success, triumph against the world's myriad wrongs.

It was as if, in Sally's time, her spirit-guide Chinaman had loomed up at her shoulder, visible, tangible, his ancient eyes full of wise reproof, ratifying her beliefs, disposing of George's cynicism, proving there was more to life than his earthbound, practical soul had so far been able to rise to.

18

Harry, her cheery whistling accompanied by the
chink of glass from the boot, was driving to the
local station to meet Judy off the London train
and take her to spend the weekend at Bugle
Farm.

George had asked her to do this for him as
he was busy shearing, and she was very happy
to oblige. First, because it would give her a
chance to chat to Judy before George claimed
her, but also because this small neighbourly
favour, which Ken could not query, gave her the
opportunity to do a little business of her own.

By careful timing, she arrived in the station
yard fifteen minutes before the London train
was due. It was, as she had anticipated, empty
of people — those meeting the train would not
arrive yet. She drew up beside the large, ugly
bulk of a bottlebank which reposed in a distant
corner.

It was full to capacity. The openings always
reminded her of the holidays of childhood. These
had been spent in her wealthy grandmother's
beautiful house on the hills above Weymouth,
but occasionally she had been taken by her
nanny to the sea-front, where she had rejoiced in
lower-class delights including cone-shaped paper
pokes of chips and forbidden sticks of rock

and exciting pastimes like throwing balls into two-dimensional clowns' mouths. You couldn't have thrown anything into these holes, today. Respectively green, brown and clear bottlenecks protruded like dreadfully occluded teeth.

Harry, unaware that she was grinning guiltily, got out and opened the boot. Inside was a cardboard box from which the tinkling had issued. Most of the glass she had to dispose of was jars to which traces of marmalade and mayonnaise still adhered. There were a decorous few green bottles and a small family of squat brown ones that had held Ruggles Real Ale, which Ken, in his settled countryman mode, had recently begun to favour. No spirits. All absolutely irreproachable. Ken had packed the box himself and she had added nothing.

She lifted it out and laid it on the ground next to the bottlebank. She was not alone in having brought fodder for the monster that it was too stuffed to accept. They were a public-spirited and eco-conscious lot around here, but they also put plenty of booze away. With any luck, Harry would find what she was after.

Ah! Two matt-surfaced brandy bottles side by side in a wooden fruit crate, and a vodka bottle sticking out of the mouth marked 'CLEAR'. She glanced round the station car park. An estate Volvo was drawing in — she must be quick.

She hastily picked up the brandy bottles and upended them briefly. She didn't want her shopping bag stinking of brandy. Or perhaps she did. She giggled, pulled out the vodka bottle and upended that too, watching a good measure flow away onto the dusty tarmac. She slipped all three bottles into her bag and stowed it under the rug in the boot, leaving plenty of room for Judy's luggage.

She then repaired to the platform, wandering down to the far end where a fabulous display of multicoloured lupins adorned the bank. The old stationmaster claimed to have collected seeds from his own splendid garden for a lady who had never come back for them, and he had cast them in pique among the nettles and thick grasses on the far side of the road-bridge that spanned the single line. The following year, this superb display had sprung up. Not many passengers walked down that far, and Harry felt privileged to know about this ravishing, semi-secret beauty spot. She selected some pods off yellow and red lupins and stuffed them in her pocket. The blue and pink ones she'd taken last year were ready to plant out in her garden. She felt enormously happy and did not question why.

The train came in. Before it had quite halted, a door flew open and Zulu bounded out, followed by Judy at the end of a taut leash. She saw Harry and threw up her hand in a wave before turning to heave out her usual luggage — a battered nylon camping bag about four feet long.

As Harry walked along the platform towards her she noted her friend's clothes. Judy's whole look had modified. Gone were the dungarees and ponchos. She wore a cream-coloured summer skirt topped by a loose lavender jacket over a white T-shirt. Her hair was pinned tidily to the top of her head, with only the honey-coloured fringe still at liberty. There was no flash of silver, no heavy beads, and her make-up was discreet. The only even remotely OTT thing about her (Harry had long since found out what OTT meant — she rather prided herself these days on being au fait with the latest buzz-words) was the earrings. Painted parrots.

What a difference to the way she had looked on the day, over a year ago, when she and George had first come to view the farm! Harry touched her own ears, feeling there the dangling hoops that Judy had passed on to her when, in an uncharacteristic fit of — what? Bravado? A reaction to the unsophistication of country living and country clothes? — Harry had had her ears pierced. Unexpectedly, it had wrought a change in her whole image of herself. The feeling of the heavy earrings, the fun of buying and wearing a lot of new ones of the dangly type instead of the conventional, semi-invisible clip-ons she had always worn, made her feel excited, dashing, piratical. She had added to the look with more interesting and esoteric accessories — brilliant scarves, coloured shoes, patchwork shoulder-bags, sometimes even whole outfits picked up, not cheap, from the local market-stall that specialised in clothes from South America. Now — how weird! She looked more OTT than Judy!

They hugged each other and emerged from the station.

'How's Surrey?'

Thus Judy's first, mandatory inquiry — the

open-sesame. A casual eavesdropper might have responded, 'I thought we were in Dorset,' but the Surrey referred to was not the county, though the name had been taken from it — that beautiful smiling prosperous county where Clem's school was sited, first visited by Pleasure on the memorable day she had announced her pregnancy to him over the sponge cake and teacups.

There had been some inevitable dismay on both sides of the family at Pleasure's choice of a name, but Clem had forcefully backed her up and now that the baby was nearly seven months old, everyone had got used to it and Judy and Harry privately agreed that it sprang off the tongue very pleasingly.

'More delicious every day,' Harry responded. 'Will you believe she's making talking noises, not to mention crawling absolutely everywhere? She's as bright as new paint. I swear I've never seen a baby like her.' Even though they were obviously alone, she automatically dropped her voice, which took on the gleeful, secretive tone she always adopted when speaking about her granddaughter. Judy smiled. The transfiguration of Harry, she thought, by a little brown baby and a very big secret.

'When did you last see her?'

'Last week when I was up in town for the dentist.'

'How *are* your poor gums?'

The operations for gum-tightening had been viewed in advance with horror and dread by Harry, but in the event had proved a welcome way to put Ken off the scent.

'Oh, the worst's over. I'm still spitting out stitches, have to go up again on Monday to have the rest snipped and that's it. I'll have to think of a different excuse now.'

Before Judy could ask the obvious, Harry adroitly switched the topic.

'Ken and I are having some locals in for dinner tonight. George said okay if *you* want to — you will come, won't you? I think he was secretly quite keen.'

'Of course he was. He's beginning to love parties. Who's coming, anyone interesting?'

'Well, there's the rub, of course. They're all Ken's cronies, or neighbours. The fascist farmer from across the fields — we *had* to, Jude, we owe them! Anyhow I'm afraid Ken likes them. He's awful, no disputing that, but at least he's too outrageous to be dull. He hunts, of course,' she added wickedly, but Judy had stopped rising to that particular bait. In fact, she kept curiously quiet on the subject these days, since George had joined the Cattistock.

'Then there's the Brittans, the local squire and his wife. Well-named, total jingoists. Ex-ex-pats from what they still persist in calling Rhodesia. Their pet-names for each other are Boofer and Joker. Boofer's all right actually. She's not the usual local matron. She used to be a Bunny — '

'A what?'

'There was this thing called the Bunny Club. Bunnies were waitresses. They wore ears and fluffy tails.'

'Never heard of it. Was she some sort of a tart?'

'No one quite knows. Joker always looks embarrassed when she brings it up. 'It was in my soldier-of-fortune days, dulling, when I was on the loose, before Joker rescued me and carried me off to heavenly Africa. I was a Bunnay for the munnay!' As to Joker, you'll have to stuff a napkin in your mouth if he starts on immigration. But everyone's so toffee-nosed, probably all we'll talk about apart from chitchat is the poll tax. Joker's gloating — saving hundreds on his vast house.'

'I'm thrilled about the poll tax too,' said Judy unexpectedly, with a hint of savagery.

Harry turned in surprise. 'You are?'

'Of course. It's going to hang that woman.'

It was the first time for several months that Harry had heard that impassioned note in Judy's voice. It heartened her somehow. The political upheavals of the winter had done something bad to Judy. Driving along with the sunroof open, and Zulu's chops dribbling with rabbit lust on her shoulder, Harry wondered just how bad. She seemed all right on the surface, but something had been driven underground, where — Harry felt uneasily sure — it was doing damage.

'There's one thing puzzling me,' Judy said as they drove through the villages.

'What?'

'Well. The kids've moved into a flat together, and Pleasure's starting college soon. So the allowance has started, right?'

'Mm hm.'

'But you're not earning any money of your own, are you?'

Harry gave her a quick, almost guilty look. 'No. Unfortunately.'

'So where does the money come from?'

'A married couple's money,' said Harry primly, 'belongs to them both. We have a joint account.'

'Yeah, okay. But when the statements come in, doesn't Ken notice?'

'Well, he hasn't commented till now. I expect he thinks I've been spending a lot in London on my gum-trips.'

'But you said all that's over.'

Harry didn't reply for a while. The car crested a hill and all around them a familiar peerless view opened itself, fields smudged with sheep, hedgerows in full mixed leaf, and against the sky a single, beautiful hill, crowned with a special little copse of trees like a peacock's crest that told both women that they were coming into their kingdom.

Harry, her heart high, took the car out of gear and it seemed to fall down the hill in a rollercoaster dive.

'Hey, doll, take it easy, George'd miss me! So what's going to be the excuse for spending money from now on?'

Harry reached behind her and fished out an empty brandy bottle.

'This,' she said. 'He's going to think I'm back on the booze. And that comes expensive.'

Judy stared at her. She had never fathomed Harry's marriage, but now a clear, unambiguous insight came to her. You don't love him, any more, she thought. Or you couldn't possibly do this. The corollary thought that Harry was actually behaving very badly indeed to Ken, was one that friendship kept at bay. Just.

19

At the very moment when Harry was purloining the empty brandy bottles at the station, Ken was staring glumly at the figures at the foot of his latest bank statement. High-interest cheque accounts were all very well, but they couldn't earn much high interest on money that was steadily trickling away.

Well, no . . . not so steadily. It seemed to be going down in jerks. He drew a piece of paper towards him and jotted down some maverick figures from the debit column. What the hell was this £103 in March? He didn't remember spending that. And there were some other odd items, minor in themselves, but adding up. Were these bills? He consulted his cheque-stubs, finding only one or two that tallied.

The first intimations of unease had begun trickling through the hairline cracks in Ken's wellbeing some time ago.

He had always had very strong ideas about things being as they should be, and a need that they should be so. Although his marriage had been technically saved, although it ticked along comfortably enough, of course *it* was not as it should be. The yawning emptiness where his conjugal relations should have been was like one of those big-game traps he remembered from the Tarzan films of his childhood: a great hole with a suggestively phallic spike at the dark bottom of it, covered over with the twigs and leaves of everyday affection and good manners. However well he behaved about it, the awareness of the hole, the twig-coverings that were delicately skirted, and particularly the spike, always underlay the apparent pleasant orderliness of his life.

Of course he was pleased that Harry had lately become much happier and more active, no longer upset about anything, from life in the sticks to the condition of her gums. Ken gave her full marks for fortitude, the way she set off for London and 'The Chair' as she called it, with every appearance of insouciance. He never minded (well, he did, but his relief at her change of spirits far outweighed it) her staying overnight after her treatments, or even for a day or two to see friends and take in a show. But one of the friends, in Ken's opinion, was a subversive influence. Judy . . . Ken did not like Judy, or rather, he didn't like her in relation to Harry. As regards Judy's liaison with George, whom Ken thought a very decent chap on the whole, hunting or no hunting, that was bizarre, but forgivable. Ken, in his sexless state, was inclined to be generous toward other men's exigencies. He just wished she didn't come around so much. Since the fine weather began, she seemed to come down practically every other weekend. And as if that weren't enough, she and Harry did some hobnobbing in London. Other old friends, who could surely have put Harry up in far more style, were passed over in favour of Judy's basement pad in Brixton, of all places, a district Harry cheerfully admitted was 'a bit past a joke' but where nevertheless she seemed to feel at home.

Ken had a shrewd suspicion that if anything was going on that he didn't know about, Judy was to be found at the bottom of it.

What made the financial situation serious was that, despite all the hundreds of letters he had written, and the several interviews he had attended, he was still unemployed. At times he wondered if he hadn't ill-wished his chances by the delight with which he had embraced his new life of idleness when they had first come here. His new friends and acquaintances accepted him unquestioningly in that role. He had no trouble filling his time. Harry said nothing about the necessity for him to get a job, but he did not feel easy about it, if only because his dwindling bank-balance cried out against his unproductive state.

And dwindling was the word.

He became impatient with himself. He had become very sloppy of late. The hard-earned disciplines of early rising, immaculate grooming, orderly routines and the meticulous checking of personal accounts had all begun to break down. Living a life of leisure, being framework-free, made you careless, slack — inefficient. A certain laisser-faire of which he had never approved seemed to be taking him over, blunting his acuteness, making him more imperturbable, less suspicious.

Suspicious?

He sat back, tapping his teeth with his pencil.

So what if Harry was drawing money out of their joint account? It was definitely her money as much as his. With the new individual taxation coming in, he intended to split everything anyway, and give her her own bank accounts in order to save tax; he felt sorry for the men who couldn't do it because they basically didn't trust their wives. It had never occurred to him to question her spending. Just the same . . .

He bent over his desk and added the stray amounts up again on his pocket calculator. They came to a surprisingly large total. What *was* she spending it on? Clothes? He realised he was not strong on noticing what she wore, but £500-worth he'd have noticed. Theatres, meals out? No, she always told him about small extravagances like that.

Perhaps she was giving it to the Church.

This thought stirred the old anger in him. It suddenly became his money. He'd earned it, after all, when he was earning. If she was giving it to those — He bit back the mental epithet with a physical clamping of his teeth.

But there'd been trouble about that before. She'd promised — just one annual donation at Christmas. They'd even negotiated the amount. Besides, these sums were not round figures. No. It was something else.

Drink? Reluctantly he let himself look at that unpleasant possibility.

He'd seen no signs of it, but then she knew better than to let him. Perhaps when she went to London? Perhaps she and Judy . . . ? A fleeting image of them propped against each other in a drunken stupor flashed across his mind, and was swiftly banished. Absurd. Wasn't it?

Well, he would ask her. No harm in that. He would do it very casually: 'By the way, darling, some odd debits are showing up on my HICA statements, I wonder if we could just go over them together; banks can make mistakes, you know.' That sounded perfectly all right.

In unconscious search of a panacea, he got up and went to feed the ducks.

This was another plan that hadn't worked out as he'd intended. At first, when he showed her the house he had made, and brought back a couple of cardboard boxfuls of assorted ducklings, she had been enchanted. She would stand watching them for ages, laughing at their comic gait and their greedy, noisy manners. She dutifully fed them and shut them up. But she was away so much that before long the ducks had drifted out of the purlieus of her routine, into his.

He had dug a pond and lined it with cement and the ducks gave gratifying signs of being well-pleased with it. The trouble was, there was a fox around; Ken had seen him last winter — a big dog-fox with a grizzled mask, sitting bold as brass beyond his fence. Ken fretted. He was fretting a lot lately. A subtle, inexplicable malaise overhung all he did and thought. But now, as he watched the ducks waddling about, eagerly guzzling up the grain and washing their beaks in the pond, the strange discrepancies in his bank-statements hardened in his mind into something solid that he could get hold of, a tangible challenge.

However, there was no opportunity to mention the matter that evening.

As soon as Harry got back, having deposited Judy and her luggage up the road at Bugle, preparations for their dinner party, begun the day before and continued at full-tilt till Harry had left for the station, were resumed. Ken realised guiltily that he had skived off kitchen duties to do his accounts and mess around with the ducks.

'Sorry I didn't get on with the food. Ought I to have been doing the spuds, or — ?'

'It's okay,' she said rather shortly. 'I can manage.' She was scraping new potatoes frenetically. 'You could bring in some herbs if you like.'

'Which?'

'Mint, sorrel, chives — you know.'

He didn't. He could never identify the various plants in her herb-garden. Well, mint, he knew that by the smell, so he plucked a few stems, cut a bit of this and that, slid the pungent, disorganised pile unobtrusively onto the draining-board and was sneaking off when she said, 'Ken, will you lay the table?'

'Isn't there anything else I could do instead?' he asked plaintively. He hated laying the table. He always forgot things Harry considered basic, and to be honest he was never absolutely sure which side things went on. But Harry was adamant.

'And wipe the tops of the salt and pepper

pots,' she adjured him rather bossily, handing him a J-cloth.

He swallowed mild male resentment. If he said anything, she would remind him, justly, that this do was for *his* friends, and she might well add that she didn't think much of several of them. Old Joker Brittan, for one. Incredible old dinosaur, no doubt of it. But he was the one who was putting Ken up for the Masons. God! If Harry knew that!

He hid a furtive grin and got on with the table. After a while Harry came in with some plates and said, 'By the way, do you mind if Abby comes to the party? I hope you don't because I really had to ask her. She's driving down this evening, and she'd be left alone at Bugle.'

'Who's Abby?'

'You know who she is. Judy's fellow-worker on the picket.'

'Have I met her?'

'No, but I've told you about her. The gay one.'

Ken muttered something.

'What did you say?' asked Harry rather sharply.

'Nothing.'

'You said, 'Oh my God'.'

'How many places, then? I make it thirteen, damn.'

'Oh, honestly! It doesn't matter!' She was looking critically at the table. 'I think you'd better lose the fruitbowl, there won't be room, and you've put the glasses on the wrong *side*.

You're sort of dyslexic for tables, aren't you? Are you down on gays, too?'

' 'Too'?'

'As well as all the other minorities you're down on.'

Ken felt a surge of irritation. 'Oh, leave my prejudices alone! Your trouble is, you've got a touch of PPT.'

She looked at him quizzically. 'Do you mean PMT?'

'Not pre-menstrual. Pre-party.'

There was a pause while they looked at each other. Then the hostility dissolved in laughter. It happened like that sometimes. But less and less often. And it didn't last the evening.

★ ★ ★

At Bugle, George and Judy were in their bedroom, getting ready for the party.

Judy was at the dressing-table, which George had bought specially for her, doing her hair. She was pinning it up tidily. George, across the room tying his unwonted tie, was watching her. The dress . . . that must be the one he'd paid for. He'd long ago guessed that she dressed largely out of Oxfam to save money, and a couple of weeks ago he had awkwardly pushed some notes into her hand and suggested that she buy herself a nice dress, something she liked, for this party. And here it was — a 'nice dress' as ordered, but surely it wasn't something *she* liked, but something chosen for this occasion — Ken and Harry's do for the local squirearchy. It was dark blue, very restrained, its soft folds modifying rather than exalting her full bust and hips. Her make-up was subdued to match, and her earrings were quiet little pearly things. He frowned suddenly.

She caught his eye, well aware of his covert attention.

'Yes, it's the one. Don't you like it?'

'It's all right. It's not what I'm used to on you, that's all.'

'I decided it's time to stop embarrassing you with your Tory neighbours,' she said, with a faint smile.

'Are you taking the mickey out of me?'

She turned on the stool. 'No! Why should you think that?'

'I've never been embarrassed by you.'

'You've never shown it. Oh, by the way. You know we were talking about what we could say we were, to each other, to avoid saying 'lovers'? Well, the new word is 'partner'.'

'Don't like it. Sounds like a business. Do I look all right?'

'You look very handsome.'

'And so do you. But I like you to look beautiful and dashing. Where's your red lipstick and your eye-stuff? Why have you tamed your hair?'

'Tamed? Is that how I look?'

He came and stood behind her and put his hands gently on her dark blue shoulders.

'I wouldn't be embarrassed by you, lass, if you came to the party with a tractor-tyre round your hips and a cauliflower on your head.'

She turned to him suddenly and threw her arms round his waist. He bent, turned her pale, bedtime face up and kissed it very thoroughly.

'There, now you can put your make-up on.'

She gave him an unreadable look, a sort of blaze that he had only seen on her face when she'd been on the picket; it sent such a jolt of feeling through him that he wanted to pick her up then and there and carry her to the bed. She turned and splashed on a bright red mouth, and then pulled the pins out of her hair.

* * *

In the spare bedroom, Abby too was looking in the mirror.

She had only 'come out' comparatively recently. Before that, she'd been married, very unhappily. The marriage had ended, not because her husband found out she was a lesbian, but because she had been sleeping with every man she could lay hands on in an effort to prove to herself that she wasn't.

Now, thank God, that was all over. Another woman had got hold of her and taught her the senselessness of self-deception. She knew, now, what she was, and what she wanted, what she had wanted without admitting it for years. It didn't help her much, because what she wanted was Judy, but that was a small secret to keep after the other. She could cope with that. That was just normal unrequited love. Sexually speaking it was hopeless, but not without other joys and satisfactions. To be comrades with the person you're in love with, whether they love you or not, is exciting. Sharing the same goals in the same struggle.

That was something George would never have. It was as if Abby had the entrée to Judy's deepest commitments and feelings, while George was fobbed off with a few transient moments of physical pleasure. Abby basked in the certainty of sharing with Judy her true passion.

But she was already wishing she hadn't agreed to come here for this weekend. That had been stupid, an obvious mistake. Here, Judy was on George's territory in every sense, and Abby was, and felt, the outsider. This party tonight was going to be unspeakable, full of reactionary middle-class arseholes. She should have foreseen that. *Had* foreseen it. So why had she come? Just to see this place, to know where Judy ran away to?

That was how Abby saw it. Judy's sorties to Dorset were escapes, and this disturbed Abby more than she liked to admit. Attuned as they were after all the years of shared struggle, Abby knew better than anyone what Judy was going through, had gone through during the past months since the happenings in Europe. For Abby, these events had hurt, but only down to a certain point, not right to the roots as she feared they had with Judy. Nothing could touch the roots of Abby's Communism. Abby knew her intellectual limitations and was almost grateful for them. She was *defined* by her Marxism. That was what she was, and nothing, nothing that people did to distort it, condemn it, misunderstand it, deny it — even betray it, which was what was happening now — would change its truth for her.

In fact, the more it seemed to be falling apart, the more she stood firm and staunch. The more the comrades argued and wrestled and searched their souls, the more they vacillated and bent with the winds of change, the more Abby was sure.

She pitied them, these waverers, but she despised them too. Marx would outlive all this: his greatness, his *truth*, would transcend it all. This, all this breakdown and chaos, was just one of the stages Marx had predicted, leading to the final dissolution of capitalism: until the whole world went over to capitalism, its fundamental weaknesses wouldn't become obvious and it wouldn't have its final collapse and be replaced by world government and a people's democracy.

At the rate things were changing, in a much shorter timespan than any of them had expected, they would see, the doubters. Judy would see. And Abby would help her to get through this chaotic transition period, as George never could, not in a million years.

Abby, dressed in black leggings under a pair of long shorts, and a mock-leather jacket over a red silk blouse, put on some bright pink lipstick, ran a pocket comb through her newly-cropped hair and hung a single diamanté earring in one ear. She heard them talking through the wall and hoped she wouldn't have to listen to them making love. Well. And if she did, too bad.

She struck a heroic, socialist-realist pose before the mirror.

'Her sawl, you vill neffer pow-zess,' she muttered at George, who despite everything she rather liked, and added: 'You big dumb prick.'

★ ★ ★

The party was only a qualified success. In fact, it was quite a stressful occasion for the host and hostess, who forgot all laughter in the acrimonious discussion later as to who was chiefly to blame.

'It was Joker's fault, of course it was! Getting completely pissed as usual and bawling on about what a pity it was 'they' came over here. I thought Judy was going to explode. The man is absolutely out of the Ark! And the FF was just goading him on.'

'And what, pray, about Judy's dear little chum Abby, bawling even louder about the poor done-down gays? Nobody cares if she's a lesbian, but does she have to make such a song and dance about it? And incidentally, aren't there any lesbians who know how to dress?'

'I thought she was very interesting! At least it was better than all the deadly boring small talk — '

' — And I wish you wouldn't use words like 'pissed'. You never used to. You actually said 'fuck' at the table tonight.'

'I did not! When? Oh, then. Well, it just slipped out. It was because Boofer was gloating away about the poll tax. There they are, living in that vast mansion and they've actually got the effrontery to boast that they're paying so little poll tax, they can afford to pay their gardener's so as not to lose him, and his wife's — and still only be shelling out half the old rates! Who do you think is making up the difference? Working people in council houses, that's who!'

'For that you had to rave about 'that fucking woman'? You're beginning to talk just like Judy. Since when were you so steamed up about the poor old Tories? Anyhow, the dinner-table is no place for strong feelings — or strong language.'

'Nobody heard me anyway, only Boofer, and she swears like a squaddie.'

'Not about the government. She's much more likely to call Neil Kinnock 'that fucking man' — except she wouldn't, at table.'

'What *is* this rubbish about 'at table', as if the fact that you're sitting down with food in front of you ought to change your whole personality and mode of speech?'

'You don't need a table to change your personality — you're changing while I watch you!'

She caught her breath and a silence fell.

'What d'you mean?' she asked more quietly.

'Oh hell, I don't know. The worst thing you used to do was get steamed up about the Church. You never used to care about politics. You never used to swear. *You never used to wear those ridiculous earrings*. It's all the fault of that — that fucking woman!'

She blinked. 'Who, Mrs Thatcher?'

'No! Your precious friend Judy!'

He slammed the door of the dishwasher (quite a difficult thing to do) and a moment later, the door of the kitchen.

Harry stood frozen for a long moment with a dirty saucepan in her hand. Then, frowning, she turned to the sink and picked up a scouring pad.

★ ★ ★

First thing next morning, she walked up the lane to Bugle.

Last night's quarrel had upset her at the time, but a good night's sleep had put it behind her. If her personality was changing, she liked it that way, and if Ken didn't, well that was too bad.

Meanwhile the weather was just what the countryside deserved, golden with early summer sunlight. The froth of hawthorn and the mingled purplish and pink of the bluebells and campion had vanished, to be replaced by long, straggling grasses on the verge and uncountable species in the hedgerows — dead nettles, their yellow and white flowers gone, sprouting high; the sticky-stemmed hops scrambling uninhibitedly through and over everything, blurring the picture with their infinitely delicate but robust web of feathery leaves. Harriet loved them best. Behind the wild flowers, beech and sycamore, stunted by the merciless whirling Council hedgecutters year by year, still with unquenchable optimism spreading their brilliant green and subtle bronze-rust leaves, as if convinced that this year they'd be allowed to grow into proper trees.

George, Judy and Abby were finishing an *al fresco* breakfast in the back garden, which had a hedge around it, giving it a secret, private feel, unlike the main garden with its sun-soaked lawns running down to an islanded pond.

'Come and join us,' said George, rising precariously from a garden chair too small for his bulk. He poured coffee for her into his own empty mug, handed it to her and gave her a kiss and a small, friendly hug. She enjoyed this. She liked George a lot, and thought he looked healthier, happier — and bigger, somehow — every time she saw him.

She was right. George was delighted with life. Buying the farm had proved a wonderfully good move. He loved every acre of it already, and had felt his depleted energies rushing back as he set about its restoration and the getting-in-heart of the land. 'There's nothing that does a man more good at the onset of middle age,' he once said expansively to Ken, 'than to find he can still get really enthusiastic about a new project, and that he's still got the energy to carry it through.'

The weather was not all southerly smiles. The valley drew rainfall and was all too often gloomy and beclouded when a short drive, or even a long walk, would bring you into sunshine. But a good day here — and there were many, especially in spring — beat anything the moors had to offer, or so George convinced himself, looking back as much upon the dark sorrows and loneliness of his past as upon Yorkshire's grey stone walls and greyer weather.

From the depths of the valley, he could walk up onto the chalk-break promontory beyond the nearest hill and gaze all around him at the beauty still remaining unspoilt (keeping his eyes from the clutter of relay masts, and the heavy curving pencil lines running from pylon to pylon across the lovely irregular fields and hills), and breath deep the air that Thomas Hardy breathed, thinking if that writer whose works he loved could stand on this particular spot, he might not be too dismayed by the new monetarists' and motorists' Britain . . .

And then there was Judy. The total opposite of Sally. But more beloved every time he was with her, a challenge, a mystery, a fulfilment.

'We were just postmorteming the party,' Judy was saying now.

'Oh dear,' said Harry. 'I wouldn't have said it died. On the contrary, it was too lively by half for some tastes.'

'Ken's for one, I bet, eh?' chuckled Abby wickedly. 'Men! They aren't born, they're broken out of a conformist mould.'

'I don't think my womb a conformist mould,' said Harry, 'Not if my son is anything to go by.'

Abby looked at her, a sly little look. Her breasts hung down under a floppy black sweatshirt that said, *How I do It Is Not Your Problem* and on the back, *Kill Cause 28.* Ken, thought Harry, should be thankful she hadn't worn that last night. 'How is Clem making out as a dad?'

'He's terrific, the New Man personified. He's

got an evening job as a silver-server in Mayfair, and by day he's Surrey's full-time carer while Pleasure studies. She only has to worry about the nights.'

'When does he start college?'

'Next year. He's taking a year out. He doesn't want anybody else looking after Surrey till she's at least eighteen months. He absolutely adores her.'

'Does Pleasure adore her too?' asked Abby carelessly, stretching her legs with studied gracelessness.

There was a brief, uncomfortable silence. Pleasure was still regularly on the picket (which since Mandela's release was reduced to weekends only) and Abby could therefore be presumed to have private intimations.

'Naturally,' said Harry shortly.

But she wished she were surer. There was something about Pleasure's behaviour with Surrey that troubled her. Oh, she did everything she was supposed to do, but with a sort of casualness — no, more a remoteness, a haste to get it over, to get back to her own things: her studies, her life. When Surrey cried, Pleasure would get irritable very quickly, and if someone — Harry, or Clem — offered to take the baby, Pleasure would hand her over at once and with an air of relief.

She wasn't breastfeeding her. She hadn't even at the beginning. Only on the very cusp of a quarrel, had Harry bitten her tongue about that.

The conversation switched to Tina.

'She's actually doing okay. I never knew she was so bright,' Judy remarked. 'I've got to hand it to Mom. She saw what I didn't. Of course, once Mom gives an order, she expects to see it carried out. I don't think Tina would dare fail now. Besides, she's really interested in her course.'

'Well, *I'm* very grateful to your efficient Mom, anyway,' said Harry.

Dido, in her unstoppable fashion, had looked into the main crammers, compiled a short list and interviewed all the heads personally. Thus she had chosen the crammer Tina was to enter, at Dido's expense, to gain A-levels in Modern European History, Modern Russian History and Politics, all subjects in which Judy had unwittingly steeped her daughter. Harry and Ken had been happy to take advantage of this spadework and had sent Clem there too. He had, without difficulty, obtained two grade As and a B last November, and had been offered places at three universities on sociology degree courses.

'Where's Tina living now?' asked Abby. She still had that little slyness in her voice, making Harry suspect that she knew damn well.

'She's still at the Dorchester.'

'Why doesn't she come back and live with you? Don't you want her to?'

After a brief pause, Judy said, 'Mom took one look at my hovel and declared it totally unsuitable as a centre for intellectual activity.'

What she'd actually said was, it was unfit for human habitation.

'Your mother must really be loaded,' Abby said curiously.

'Thanks to defunct husband number three, she is. But don't worry, she's not paying nightly rates. She's got a job with them.'

'Really? How enterprising! What kind?'

'Publicity department. She used to do promotion for my dad's business in an ad hoc sort of way. Giving parties, mainly. She blew that up into twenty years' experience and a couple of awards from the South African government for services to the state.'

Abby sat up, agape. 'Shit, Jude.'

'Oh well. Most of it was lies, but they took her on. She's not only not paying for her suite, she's getting a handsome salary and enjoying every minute. It's just what she thrives on, endless partying with celebs. Now her great dream is to curtsey to the Queen, and after that, to do the same to Mrs Thatcher. She'll probably make it, too.

'No wonder you're worried about Tina,' said Abby.

'Who said I was worried about her?' asked Judy somewhat sharply.

'All that seductive luxury, and your mother's obnoxious opinions.'

'She won't let herself be suborned by Dido, I can tell you that.'

'Don't be too sure,' said Abby.

'Listen, she's done more on the picket, and incidentally for the British Labour Party, in the last three months than for the past two years before that.' The worm turning against

Abby's subtle jabs, she added with an edge, 'Fancy you not knowing that, Ab, you keep such close tabs.'

'On the picket? Well, somebody has to,' said Abby acidly. 'Mind you,' she added, turning her face up to the sun, 'if you wanted to cop out of the whole scene in favour of more of *this*, who could blame you?'

'She's not copping out!' Harry heard herself say quite fiercely before Judy could respond.

Abby turned her head to face Harry and opened her eyes. 'Well, Harry, who should know better than you?' She closed her eyes again.

There was a baffled silence. The remark had all the heavy emphasis of a deliberate crack, and it wasn't the first, but what exactly did it imply? None of the other three knew. They all sensed Abby's hostility to Harry without understanding it. A moment before, she had seemed to be getting at Judy.

'What's eating you, Ab?' asked Judy uneasily.

But Abby, aware she had gone too far, and not at all sure why, kept her eyes closed and gave only the faintest shrug.

20

Clem was walking a screaming Surrey up and down the tiny living room of the flat he shared with Pleasure in Kilburn. It was nearly three a.m. Florence had declared that the baby was cutting her first tooth, so there was every excuse, but Clem, after five hours of running around a posh restaurant serving posh idiots with silver salversful of expensive food, was practically sleepwalking.

'Poor,' he murmured groggily, and quite inaudibly, patting her back as she arched it and shrieked. 'Poor Surrey. Poor. Sh. Sorry it hurts. It's not just the tooth, mate, it's bloody life. Life's not like a prick, it's always hard, ha-ha. No, I didn't say that. Shhh!'

He carried her into the bathroom and groped one-handed for the oil of cloves Florence had left in the medicine cupboard. He looked at the tiny bottle. Surrey's cries, added to his weariness, were making him light-headed. What did you do with it? She had told him, but he'd forgotten. He carted his daughter through into the kitchen which was in chaos. Her bottle was in the fridge. He'd put it back there after warming it, and trying it, earlier; Surrey's mouth was so stretched she couldn't feel the teat. But he must get some of this clove stuff down her somehow.

He shifted some dirty dishes and found a second bottle. It had some sugar-water in it — another of Florence's remedies. Holding the baby as well as he could, he used both hands to unscrew the cap and poured a little of the oil in. He knew he should sterilize the teat but she was screaming so loud he just couldn't wait. She sounded as if she were in agony, which meant that he was, too. No, this was no good, the sugar-water would dilute the oily stuff . . . Better give it to her straight. He put down the milk-bottle and shook some drops from the tiny bottle straight into her roaring mouth.

She roared on. Obviously wasn't getting enough. In desperation he tried the bigger bottle. When she didn't clamp her lips round the teat, he thought of removing it and giving her the idea by just pouring a bit in. But the baby arched, his hand slipped and half the contents of the bottle went down her throat. Surrey started to choke.

Terrified, he dropped the bottle, which smashed on the tiles, turned her face down over his arm and hit her on the back with as much force as he thought was needed. For an agonising moment she was silent and still, and then the stuff came back up and she started to cry again. Clem thought it the best sound he'd ever heard, and clutched her to his chest, rubbing his check against her hair.

'Shit, I thought I'd killed you. Daddy thought he'd done for you. Go on, yell, I deserve it. God, this is hell. I love you, I love you, please stop hurting . . . '

Suddenly, Pleasure appeared in the doorway

303

in the pair of pants that were all she slept in.

'Clem, can't you keep her quiet?' she yelled above the din. 'They're banging again next door. We'll be thrown out of here!'

Clem stared at her over Surrey's head. The twinkling plaits were long gone. When Pleasure started college she had cropped her hair. It emphasised the long shape of her head and the Africanness of her features. He'd loved it at first. He'd called her his African queen. But now the slanting black eyes were slitty with sleep and irritation, the brown skin puffy, the full plum-coloured lips pinched. Her bare breasts were as beautiful as ever, but Clem was to look back on this moment as the first time he had ever looked at her and not been aware of seeing an object of uncritical love.

Meanwhile he was so gagged with the unfairness of it, he couldn't answer, just pushed past into the living room again. But before he had taken those few steps, he thought of her bare feet on the shards of the bottle, and turned back.

'Look out for the bits of glass,' he said shortly.

'Oh Christ, how did you — ' she began irritably, but he didn't wait to hear her reproach. He went into the bedroom, kicked off his shoes, and crawled, fully dressed, under the duvet. He laid Surrey on his stomach, wrapped his arms around her and rocked from side to side like a boat on a choppy sea. Even when she was driving him crazy with noise, he loved her, and when she was peaceful and he was able to commune with her, he sometimes secretly felt she was all his. He had felt it from the moment he had seen the bloodstreaked top of her head emerging from the birth-canal. He had suffered so much, watching Pleasure suffer, that it really was as if he had given birth to her himself, not in the female way, but as if a baby-shaped bit of his own body had detached itself and winkled its way out from beneath his breastbone.

He heard Pleasure sweeping up the glass and throwing it noisily into the rubbish bin. Only then did he notice that the screams had stopped. By the time Pleasure came back into the room after going to the loo, both Clem and Surrey were asleep.

★ ★ ★

She stood over the bed uncertainly. She ought to put the baby back in her crib, but she couldn't face the possibility of more screaming, so she got into bed cautiously, curling up facing away from them, and tried to go back to sleep herself. But her conscience kept her awake.

She'd been horrible. The nights were supposed to be her share of parenthood, but it wasn't so simple. She was working her buns off in college. When she got home, Clem had to leave at once for the hotel; no time for anything but a quick report and a quick handover. Usually he'd got the baby bathed and bedded down, but sometimes, like tonight, there'd been problems, and then Pleasure had to attend to her instead of getting on with her homework. Tonight she had got hardly anything done and that meant getting up at the crack of dawn. She'd barely had anything to eat, even.

She lay there listening to Clem snoring, as he always did when sleeping on his back. The sound grated on her nerves. At last she couldn't stand it any more, and crawled out of bed and on to the sofa in the living room, her retreat of last resort. They always turned the heating off at night to save money, and it was chilly in here with only her anorak over her. She shivered, fighting a deep superstition originating with her mother: 'Once you start not sleeping with them, that's the beginning of it being over.' Of course it was rubbish, in any case this was a one-off, but Pleasure couldn't entirely shake off her uneasiness. Things just hadn't been the same since Surrey came. But she was not willing to acknowledge that the not-the-sameness might be terminal.

Once you had a baby, you ought not to split. Despite the untidiness of her own family — because of it, perhaps — Pleasure felt that very strongly. The trouble was, she was constantly stifling profound resentment at having been coerced into doing what she had known, from the very beginning, went against her grain.

She hadn't planned to have a baby. She hadn't wanted to have a baby. She hadn't, actually, wanted to live with Clem, or have any of this hassle. She had wanted (still, guiltily, wanted) to live her own life according to her original blueprint, which Clem's mother — and her own — had snatched away from her and torn up, imposing on her another one. The bottom line was, she'd allowed herself to be manipulated. Bought.

She had tried to tell herself the moral imperatives of her religion were the underlying factor, but that was bullshit. She never gave a thought to God except when the going was really tough. Well, it was toughish now. She sent up a half-hearted prayer but it trailed on the ground like Cain's sacrificial smoke. Naturally, why shouldn't it? If religion was true, anything but a genuine prayer would be rejected. But it wasn't true. It was nothing but a childish hangover, a futile reflex. It was silly to believe in a God who gave effortless faith and help to some people and left others out in the cold even when they tried to reach for Him.

And then there was her mother. She'd been a factor, however unwelcome, in Pleasure's decision. Surrey's arrival had sent Florence into paroxysms of happiness, and to be fair, she did a great deal to help. But she had her own life and job, she couldn't be here when she was really needed, in the small hours of the night when the neighbours hammered on the walls and ceiling and when sleep was impossible and you felt at the end of your tether, hating yourself for being so bad-tempered and unloving, but totally taken over by the thought of how you'd feel in the morning, how you felt now . . . . Trapped. Trapped, *trapped*.

Pleasure gave a groan and rolled over with her face to the musty back of the settee. It was only a two-seater and she couldn't stretch her legs. She was shivering. Maybe she'd better go back to bed, put the baby in her cot, cuddle up to Clem to get warm. But then he might wake up, want sex. Pleasure curled forward in a sudden spasm of reluctance. That, too, that early bond, was gone. She couldn't remember the last time she had really enjoyed it.

She began to cry silently.

★ ★ ★

When Harry had crept out the morning after the party and scuttled in the duckpond all the bottles she'd collected, she'd thought Ken wouldn't discover them for some time and that by then they would look more as if they'd accumulated over a long period. Lying in the muck under the water should put a certain patina on them fairly quickly, she thought, but she hadn't reckoned on Ken cleaning out the pond the very next day, just after she'd nipped back up to London.

What really got to Ken as he extracted them one by one and stood them up like skittles, his expression altering from bafflement to dismay to grim incredulous anger, was not so much how stupid she had been, as how exceedingly stupid she must think he was.

The bottles had clearly not been in the water long. And she knew he would find them there. That must mean she wanted him to find them, sooner or later. That in turn must mean . . . well, it wasn't very hard to figure out.

If she had really been secretly drinking, she would not have left the bottles around the place at all. She had gone to the bottlebank only yesterday morning; she could have taken these at the same time. It was clearly a plant. Why should she want to make him think she had gone back on the booze, and in such a big way? Without the smallest mental effort the answer came to him: to explain the disappearance of money from their account.

The fury he had felt the night Clem ran away from school and Harry had taken him up to London with no explanation, returned full force. *Something was going on that he was being excluded from.* His brain, having easily supplied the answer to the first bit of the puzzle, was baffled now. As he grimly scrubbed out the pond and brought the hose round to refill it, hosing the bottles at the same time, he ran through a number of possibilities.

A lover? No, no. He dismissed that at once. Oddly it never occurred to him that his own suppressed desires might have an echo in her. He thought of her now as nun-like in her sexlessness, impervious to the summons of the flesh.

The fleeting thought of an anonymous man was instantly replaced by a woman's face in his mind — Judy's. Whenever, lately, he had had negative thoughts about Harry, Judy was there, lurking in the background. But how?

Something political, that was a real possibility. For some months now, he had known that Harry, who had always voted Tory as he did as a matter of course, was moving, stealthily at first but with increasing velocity, to the Left. It wasn't just things like the police, the poll tax, the government's policy on South Africa. It was things closer to home, less theoretical, such as the steady closing-down of small shops, the condition of the local school, the run-up to the privatisation of water ('Water is everybody's *right*! It'll be air next!'), and finally the drastic tightening of immigration laws which had led to the deportation back to some West African hellhole of a local man who had lived in this part of England most of his life. They argued about everything to do with government policy, as they never had before.

He dated all this to Harry's association with the picket, although it was some time since she had mentioned anything to do with South Africa. Ken assumed that since Mandela's release there had been an end to dissident activity on that front. Yet the odd friendship with Judy survived and deepened. Could Judy be having a serious subversive influence on Harry in some other way? Some way that cost money?

What way? He couldn't imagine.

He would ask her straight out.

No, he wouldn't.

Why not?

It took him all the time until he had cleaned out the duck-house as well as the pond, scattering clean wood-shavings and carrying the soiled old bedding to the compost-heap, where he stood soaking it all thoughtfully, and systematically, with urine (wonderful nitrogenous activator!) to come to some kind of answer to that last question.

I'm unwilling to ask because I don't want to know the answer.

He looked downwards at his drooping, dripping member and thought what a mistake nature had made, combining its functions. How could this pathetic limp little tube of flesh command respect or deserve anything better than the nicknames, 'so rude and so ridiculous' as someone (Noel Coward?) had once said, by which it was commonly known? Who would think, looking at it now, that this same protuberance could leap to life, stand proudly and quiveringly erect, penetrate the body of a woman, flood it with ecstasy, create a new being? How long had it been since *his* had been anything more than an obedient, menial wastepipe?

The thought was an addition to his bafflement and inner distress. He tucked his thing away moodily and zipped it out of sight.

So, that was it then, was it? He was a coward who would rather be kept in the dark, in his unease and uncertainty, than know the truth. Did he, in that case, merit any more of his wife's confidences than she was, these days, choosing to give him? There were men like that, and women too, he knew, who would dodge and evade and play endless, infantile games to keep themselves in comfortable ignorance.

He shook his head sharply as he trundled the wheelbarrow back to base. He must take the bull by the horns and ask her. He must, or he would have no more respect for himself than, back there at the compost heap, he had been able to muster for his thing.

But not yet. Not just yet.

★ ★ ★

It was by now Harry's invariable habit, when she went to London, to make straight for Brixton. Judy had given her a key and told her she could use Tina's old room any time she liked.

She liked arriving and finding she had the place to herself, which didn't happen often. Sometimes the young picketers would be there, foraging, cooking, having showers, sitting about, and Harry found this difficult. So she was relieved today to find only Abby, working on an Amstrad PCW in the barred basement window bay.

She gave Harry minimal acknowledgement.

'Want some coffee?' she asked without greeting.

'I'd prefer tea,' said Harry. 'I'll do it.'

'Nope,' said Abby shortly.

Harry said no more and humped her small case along the corridor to her accustomed room at the back of the house. By the time she returned, a mug of strong milkless tea was standing on the table and Abby was back at the far end of the room, tapping intently. Harry had an idea she was being studiously marginalised. Once, chronically unwilling to be confrontational, she would have stood for it, shrunk into herself, reckoning she deserved it somehow from this busy, committed woman. Now she went up to Abby with the tea in her hands and stood over her.

After a few moments of typing, Abby, bothered, stopped and gave Harry a blank 'What d'you want?' stare.

'I want to know what you've got against me, why you're always either short with me like now, or getting at me, the way you did after the party.'

Startled by this directness from a woman she had always regarded as an exemplar of middle-class reserve, Abby said defensively, 'I've nothing against you, I don't know what you mean.' But Harry just waited. 'Well,' Abby said, 'if you must know, I'm puzzled. I don't know why Jude's so thick with you. You're just not her sort.'

'I think I am,' said Harry equably, swallowing tea.

'What've you got in common with her? Not one thing.'

'We get on,' Harry said. 'We learn from each other. That's enough for a friendship, isn't it?'

'*I* think you have to admire someone to be friends with them.'

'And while you see what I admire in Judy, you can't see the vice versa, is that it?' asked Harry with a wry smile.

Abby stood up and moved away. Her body-language showed Harry that she had got much further under the other woman's skin than she'd expected or intended.

'I suppose you think I'm jealous,' said Abby

without turning. She appeared to be biting her nail.

Such a thought had not occurred to Harry, but it did now. Perhaps it was that. Perhaps it was more than just friend-on-friend jealousy. With her newfound up-frontness, Harry was almost ready to ask, 'Are you in love with her?' but she wasn't, quite; that was not directness, it was bad manners. But the thought enlightened her to a new possibility about Abby. If this was the case, of course she couldn't be blamed for resenting Harry. She'd resent any close woman-friendship.

'No, that hadn't occurred to me,' she said carefully. 'Although if it was that, I could understand it. Your friendship with Judy goes back so far.'

Abby turned. 'My friendship with Judy goes right back to basics, and not just in terms of time,' she said. 'She's shared more with me than with anyone except Jordan, and he hasn't been around to share anything with her for twelve years. If he ever came out of the wood-work, then I think a lot of her friends, male and female, would have something to worry about.'

Harry, who was staring at her, saw a sudden change in her expression. She became perfectly still and her eyes glazed. Harry did nothing to disturb her abrupt reverie, and after a few seconds she came out of it. Unexpectedly, she grinned.

'Oh, what the hell. Judy's got heart enough for all of us. You're right, I'm being petty.' The grin opened into a smile. 'Hey. All that's going on in the world, and here I am being stupid! Good that you said something.' Unexpectedly she came over to Harry and gave her a peck on the cheek. 'There, forget it. Come and give me a hand with this letter I'm writing to the *Guardian* about the new immigration laws.'

★ ★ ★

Later in the evening, when Abby had gone home, Harry cleared up the flat and put a lentil casserole on for her and Judy's dinner. She had settled down with Zulu and a book when suddenly the doorbell rang.

Zulu leapt to startled wakefulness and let off a barrage of barks. Harry, praying, literally, that it would not be picketers seeking shelter for the night, moved to open it, but Zulu's hysteria gave her pause. Judy's self-inflicted nightmare about intruders, black or otherwise, flashed through her mind.

'Who is it? she shouted through the door.

'It's me, Mum!'

'*Clem?*'

She unbolted the door and opened it. Rain was streaming down, and in the heavy drips from a broken gutter above, her son stood bare-headed with a big holdall, and a huge lump on his chest like Quasimodo back to front.

'Darling! What on earth goes on? Come in quickly!'

'I'm so glad you're here, Mum. Can you take her?'

He opened his jacket and revealed Surrey,

her bottom hanging over an outgrown sling, fast asleep. Harry unfastened her and lifted her away from Clem's sodden torso. She settled her on the sofa and wrapped a dog-hairy rug around her. Zulu sniffed her inquiringly, then jumped up beside her and dropped his nose and across her legs.

Clem said again, 'I'm so glad you're here. I rang home and Dad said you were in Town. I was so afraid you'd be out.' He slumped into the armchair, looking done in. His head fell back. There were reddish-brown shadows under his closed eyes.

'Clem, what's happened, what's wrong?' Harry asked anxiously.

With his eyes still closed he said, 'Pleasure's gone.'

Harry didn't say, 'What! What do you mean, are you joking,' or anything of that sort. She sank onto the sofa next to Zulu, took one of his rough back paws in her hand for strength, and just concentrated on trying to take it in. Somehow she had known, deep down, that something — but not this! — was in the wind.

After a few moments, Clem sat up and looked at her.

'Say something,' he said.

'No, you say something. What's the exact situation?'

Clem told her slowly. He and Pleasure had had a row that hadn't started as a row. It started with Pleasure telling him quite quietly, but with passion, how she felt, how she had been feeling for a long time. Trapped. Miserable. Overstretched. Not able to study properly. Feeling her chance of a 'proper life' dwindling.

'I'm not brilliant,' she'd said. 'I know that. I'm no better than just above average. I think I can make it, but only if I *concentrate*. If I can't give all my energy to it, I'll give up, I'll lose out. I'm so afraid of that, afraid of never being anything, just staying down here at the bottom of the pyramid for the rest of my life.'

She said it was no good, she just wasn't the sort who could live for her family. She wasn't the self-sacrificing type. She needed something for herself, real personal achievement. She wanted to have a profession, and Clem and Surrey were standing in her way like a huge barrier that she had to climb up and over every single day before she could give herself to her studies.

'You wanted this,' she had said, trying, Clem could see, to keep her voice calm and rational. 'It was you. You and your mother, and mine too. I knew what to do and I was ready to do it — it was my body and my *choice* but you wouldn't have it. You stopped me, all of you with your damned religion! You never used your imaginations, just imposed your rules on me. And now it's turning out just like I thought it would.'

Clem, feeling some awful threat to his peace impending, had used whatever weapons came to hand. He had told her coldly that without his mother and her money, there was no way Pleasure could continue studying. Then, and

317

only then, Pleasure blazed up like wax on a bonfire.

'I don't want your mother's bribes, I want to manage *by myself*. She can have it all back! I've been to the bank and got a loan. I had to lie to them and say I had no dependants, but it wasn't really a lie. Surrey is your dependent, not mine! If your mother is prepared to pay, and you're prepared to sacrifice your career for the moment, let her pay *you*, and you can look after the baby between you. I had her, now you look after her — that's only fair!'

Harry was stunned. She couldn't believe Pleasure could behave so badly, so unnaturally. Men did this sort of thing, women didn't.

'So where did she go?'

'She went back to her mother's.'

'Florence? Florence won't have her!' burst out Harry.

Clem looked at her curiously. How odd that she knew this! It hadn't occurred to him that Florence wouldn't enfold her darling ewe-lamb in welcoming black-mammy arms, blame him, blame him for everything, as he had begun to blame himself. 'You're right,' he said. 'She threw her out the minute she realised what had happened.'

'How do you know?'

'Because Florence came straight round to me half an hour later in a terrible state, offering me and Surrey a home if I needed it. She's a lot angrier with Pleazh that I am. At least I can sort of see where she's coming from.' He threw his mother a rueful look. 'We did lean on her pretty hard to go on with the pregnancy. She didn't have much choice. A woman should have choice about a thing like children. 'A child's for life, not just for Christmas',' he joked feebly.

'That's right,' said Harry forcefully. Her hand strayed over Zulu's white bulk to Surrey's sleeping figure and Clem saw the almost fierce protectiveness with which she laid it on the baby's back. But he didn't guess her thoughts.

God in heaven, these kids! Irresponsible, selfish, ruthless! How did they get this way? Are we responsible? Did I bring him up to rush into sex? Did Florence bring Pleasure up to be so careless, and now to abandon her child? The opposite, the opposite! All the damned theories blaming the parents are crazy!

'What are you thinking, Mum?'

She told him what she was thinking.

'Well,' he said, 'I must say I don't see that I've done anything so bad. And I'm not going to abandon Surrey — nothing would make me. But I can't live in that flat by myself with her, and work. You are a bit responsible, Mum, like Pleasure said . . . ' He stood up. 'I'm due at work in half an hour. Can I leave her with you overnight and come back and talk in the morning?'

'Yes,' said Harry.

'Everything's in that bag. She doesn't like her milk too hot.'

'Who does?' said Harry, lost in a maze of dire projections.

Clem bent and kissed Surrey's head. Zulu opened one pink-rimmed eye and growled, very

319

softly, almost no more than a clearing of the throat.

Harry said, 'Clem, apart from Surrey — don't you mind?'

He paused at the outer door. 'I don't know what I'm feeling,' he said. 'I think it's a bit like falling off a cliff. I'm just grabbing things as I pass so I won't get smashed to pieces when I land.'

He went out.

Harry sat silently. Yes, this was what mothers were for at this stage, to be grabbed to break falls. But she was thinking of Ken. She shivered. This commitment was beginning to look more and more full-time, less and less something that could be concealed. Like all secrets that will out, sooner or later, this one was getting bigger and more frightening as she pushed it ahead of her, like a dung-beetle's ball.

Nemesis, she knew, could not be too far off.

21

Harry stayed in town for a week after Clem and Surrey came to Judy's flat seeking sanctuary. She phoned Ken every evening in the cheap-rate time and had a brief touching-base conversation with him. 'Can't talk long, it's Judy's phone,' was her invariable excuse. 'Why can't you just pay for the call?' Ken said at last, irritated beyond bearing. 'She won't accept it,' said Harry. This small lie was soon tossed away in the great sea of lies implied and told. She sensed Ken wanted to talk to her. For this reason as well as her own pressing ones, she did not want to talk to Ken.

Judy, when she discovered what had happened, threw open her home to Clem and Surrey. The caravan was cleaned out (a longish job which Clem started and Harry finished), a new, ultra-safe heater installed, everything Surrey-geared.

Judy secretly shared Harry's shock at Pleasure's defection, but she maintained an air of detachment. Pleasure was a comrade; and having been there in the 'caff' the night Harry bribed her to have the baby, Judy could sort of see her point of view. Only sort of, though.

'D'you want me to have a word with her if I see her on the picket tonight?' Judy asked Harry on the Friday.

'Bet you she won't show up. Anyhow, don't. Leave it to them to sort out. You've been marvellous. Don't worry, we won't be in your way long. We're looking for a place.'

Judy fixed her friend with a narrow look.

'Harry, I think we'd better get a few things straight.'

'What?'

'I wouldn't know what to do with an empty flat. I love Surrey, I like Clem, and you're my pal. You can stay here indefinitely, all of you.'

'But you need the place for your 'pickies'.'

'There are alternatives other than the street, you know. A lot of kids who've passed through here now have somewhere to live, not to mention some political direction. But there's another angle.'

'What?' asked Harry warily.

'Ken.'

'Yes, well, that's my concern,' said Harry immediately.

'What's going to happen when he finds out?'

'I don't want to talk about that.'

'You don't want to think about it, you mean.'

'Aren't there things in your life that you're deliberately avoiding?'

Judy shut up. There *were* such things — yes, by God, too many of them.

Harry's troubles — what seemed to Judy, with her innate aversion to lies, the tainted complexity of her personal life — were almost welcome. It gave her a focus outside herself. Having all this *Sturm und Drang* going on took her mind off her problems, which included George.

The truth was, her feelings for him were

intensifying in a way that distorted her sense of herself as an independent entity: she seemed to be seeing everything in terms of him. She knew this feeling, though it was a long time since she had experienced it. She recognised it, with deep alarm, as a symptom of being properly in love. She had never intended this to happen, never thought it could happen. In her letters to Jordan (more and more difficult to write), she was afraid to mention George, because initially she had, through a sort of code dating way back, implied that George was no more than a waystation, temporary support, a palliative for loneliness. But he was by now a great deal more than that. Loving two men at once was not in Judy's image of herself.

She thought of trying to put a little distance between herself and George, and indeed the exigencies of their lives made periods of separation necessary. But it wasn't working. The reverse, in fact: in Judy's case, absence was having its axiomatic effect.

For one thing, ever since Nelson was released, George had changed. He had come over to her side with an unexpected, moving wholeheartedness. He had even, on one occasion, apologised to her for not having believed in the picket initially, for not helping her more in her work.

That was how he spoke of the picket, now that Judy was no longer so preoccupied with it: her work. He treated it so seriously that she felt guilty. The irony of it! George's newfound respect for the picket was putting more pressure on her conscience than Abby's frequent jibes about the falling-off of her commitment.

The result was that often she resisted the longing to go down to Bugle at weekends because it was at weekends that the picket still operated. But since she had to work Mondays to Fridays, that meant she might go for several weeks without seeing George. The pain of this, the debilitating loneliness and sense of half-personhood without him, was what was frightening her. She had not felt anything like this about anyone, ever, except Jordan.

And there was more. More and worse.

Her world, the world of political struggle and alignments, had changed, been turned upside down. And sometimes it did occur to Judy, in small-hours moments of bleak, terrifying honesty, that what she felt about what was happening in Europe was similar to what Harriet would feel if proof started to appear that Christ had never lived. At first she would rigorously shut them out. Then she would shout 'Lies!' Then she would seek counter-proof. At last, confronted by a remorseless, merciless stream of facts, her common sense and intelligence cowering in corners struggling to be deaf and blind, she would fall back on — what Judy was falling back on. Exactly the same. Blind faith.

China was bad enough. The boy in front of the tank, the futile broken courage lying, corpse-shaped, in the streets, the arid cruel triumph of the old men. People — comrades in the struggle whom she had loved and worked with for years — asking her the unanswerable: 'Who are we supposed to be for?' Well, at that stage you could still argue round it and in any case it was far away. But when Communism began to collapse in the Soviet Union — then, oh, then! The fight for some kind of inner survival, the struggle not to be dishonest, warring with an absolute reluctance to acknowledge that all the voices that had been shouting her down, all through the years — not least George's — were triumphant now. But did that make them *right*?

She had gone through several months of intense inner anguish. George had been a help only in one way. While he was actually loving her, actually embracing her, penetrating her body and bringing it to climax, she could not think about anything else.

The rest of the time she worked herself without mercy, allowing as little time as possible for thought. And at night at home, she would sit with Zulu's head on her knees, and stare half-blindly, not at television which offered an all-too tempting 'out', but at Nelson — the young Nelson on the old poster, and support him in her thoughts as she could no longer support Lenin, if only because if you believed in *him*, watching him pulled from his pedestals by the very people he had tried to redeem was too terrible to bear. 'The fallen idol . . . ' Yes, George had said those words, or was it Tina? No, not Tina. Tina still loved her enough, despite everything, not to hurt her in that way. Not now. Not now it was all coming apart.

But Dido had no such scruples.

Dido was back in her life with a vengeance, interfering cheerfully and persistently, triggering some of the old instinctive hostility. But when Dido urged her to stop work and let George look after her, the echoes of concurrence in her own mind confused her. Opposing her mother's demands and suggestions had been a natural 'given' in her life, since adolescence. Now, her mother's saw-edged remarks — 'Your so-called husband's never coming back, darling. And George is such a nice, steady sort of man, rich too — that lovely farm, you know it's what you really want after all these years of *squalor*' — began to coalesce disturbingly with what she desperately wanted to do herself.

As for Tina — Judy stood metaphorically agape. Her erring daughter was practically reborn. Her studies were going wonderfully. Her grandmother would stand for no nonsense. Every day when Tina got back to the hotel (collected and whisked in the limo by 'the boy'), she was given a sumptuous, rewarding tea and then herded to her desk and not permitted to rise from it until her homework was well and truly done. After that, there might or might not be what Dido termed 'bells, balls, balloons and tinsel' i.e. fun and outings, ever Dido's speciality, no expense spared. But not on weekdays — never. A light supper, strictly rationed TV, and bed with a textbook was Tina's lot. One, incredibly, that once the results began to show she did not jib at more than tokenly.

What a change was here, Judy reflected bitterly, not merely in Tina, but from when she, Judy, had been at college! Far from keeping Judy's nose to the grindstone, Dido had treated her studies as a tiresome eccentricity, a mere distraction from real life and vital concerns. 'Oh, chuck it for tonight, doll, I'm off to the movies — it's a musical, oh come on!' Then with a jarringly abrupt change of tone: 'How can I have given birth to such a boring little *swot*?' Flounce, slam, leaving Judy feeling filleted and demoralised.

She'd tackled her mother about this aspect of the past one evening when they were talking on the phone. (Judy refused to go to the hotel and her mother seldom visited the flat.)

'Funny you're so hot on Tina studying when you did everything you could to discourage me.'

'The world's changed, poochie. And being a grandmother is different from being a mother. For another thing, *Alba* knows what's best for her. She does as she's told — something you never did.'

'I would have, if you hadn't thought studying was pointless. If I'd had the least encouragement. All you cared about was getting me married.'

'Ah, but Alba's clever. She must have some personal success. Pity to waste all that on a man. She won't have the slightest problem finding a suitable husband when she's ready.'

'Whereas you thought I would.'

'And how right I was!'

These cracks got under Judy's skin in a way they hadn't for years. They recalled only too vividly the struggles and denigrations of the past. And nowadays she lacked her old resilience and defiance. She felt bruised and adrift. What was the matter with her? All her certainties seemed gone.

She missed her single-minded devotion to Jordan. She missed George with a physical ache. She missed the full-time picket and her work with it. She missed the steady, intense companionship and approbation of Abby, replaced these days by this odd, spiky person Judy felt she hardly knew, full of moods and digs.

She missed Tina. She was surprised to find that, in the thick of all the other missing, Tina stood out. Her clever student daughter, off the fags, beautifully dressed not in slipperies-and-shinies but in clean well-made casuals, her squiggly mop held back by a ballerina bandeau so it wouldn't fall on her books. Her mother hungered for this reborn person whom she hardly got more than a glimpse of when she met her (oddly enough) on the picket at weekends. They were shy with each other. Tina seemed so self-sufficient, so pulled together nowadays. She didn't seem to need her mother any more, and Judy, who for so long had wanted to slough off Tina's needs, now hungered to have them again.

But under all the more admissible hungers, Judy missed something else. She did not dare contemplate what that might be. She was just aware of a dark deep emptiness, where the firm bedrock that had always sustained her, all her adult life, had fallen away. A silly image sometimes flickered at the back of her mind: a cartoon character, a little man with big feet, who walks off the edge of a cliff, and keeps walking in a straight line. It was an old visual joke; soon he would glance down, look up, keep walking, and then suddenly — the panic, the whirling limbs, the plunge, the manshaped hole in the ground. But what if there were no ground, no end to the fall?

All this made Judy irritable. Also, having a baby in the flat was fine in theory, but Surrey cried quite a bit and made sleep even more difficult. Judy was determined not to complain, so she bottled it up and went out a lot. This was unlike her, walking the streets without purpose and with nowhere to go. Once she would have headed for the picket. She felt baffled by her sadness that it was gone. She shouldn't be sad they had won.

The cafés in the district that had once been just lighted windows and whiffs of bacon-or-curry-smell as she hurried past, now became small, cheerful havens in which she ate greasy but comforting meals and sat over Nescafé and a copy of the *Evening Standard* or some silly women's magazine she had guiltily bought, until Zulu's restless grunts and pawings at her foot under the table drew her outdoors again.

★ ★ ★

Harry, preoccupied as she was, was not oblivious to her friend's troubles.

'Listen,' she said one night. 'It's Clem's night

329

off, he's arranged for Florence to Surrey-sit.
Let's go out.'

'Where?' asked Judy.

'A theatre.' Judy pulled a face. 'What!'

'Hate it.'

Harry looked at her, thunderstruck. 'You *hate
the theatre*?'

'Yes, I do!' she shot back defiantly. 'Crap.
Lots of prats and poofters playing pretend-
games.'

Harry didn't actually believe this; it didn't fit,
it was a symptom. She said quietly, 'Okay. What
about a movie?'

'What, for instance? Nothing heavy. Nothing
Japanese.'

Harry reached for the paper. 'You choose. I
don't mind. Afterwards we'll have an Indian
meal — on me.'

'On Ken, don't you mean?' Judy took the
paper and turned it to the entertainment page.

'Why are you so bothered about Ken?' asked
Harry curiously.

'I just feel sorry for him,' Judy said without
looking up. 'Poor bastard.'

Harry stared silently into her lap. Judy said,
from behind the paper, 'D'you mind me saying
that? He is a poor bastard.'

'Isn't Jordan even more of one?'

'Why?'

'Because of George.'

Judy put the paper aside and they stared at
each other.

'Bit of a turn-up. Both of us sorry for the
other one's husband.'

'Why are you sorry for Ken?'

'The way you're lying to him about the baby. Among other things.'

'You don't know him.'

'Has he ever done anything to you to deserve what you're doing?'

'Yes.'

Judy's interest was piqued. 'What?'

'*He* deceived *me*. Once. A long time ago.'

'You mean he cheated on you?'

'Yes.'

'Badly?'

'What d'you mean? He slept with another woman. How bad is bad? Yes, badly.'

'And you've never forgiven him?'

'Could you?'

Judy smiled. 'Jordan travelled a good bit when we were first married. He may have slept with other women. But he never told me about it, so — '

'Ah. Well you see, that's a big difference. Ken did tell me.'

'Being honest?'

'That's one word for it. I thought he was being pathologically selfish.'

'In telling you?'

'Yes.'

'You didn't want to know?'

'*No*!'

Judy frowned. 'That's interesting.'

'The complicating factor was, I was carrying his baby at the time.'

'Clem?'

'No. A second one. A little girl.'

331

Judy sat up, her eyes wide. 'What? You had a daughter? Where is she?'

Harry said steadily, 'She's buried under concrete in a back garden in Acton.'

Judy drew in her breath sharply. There was a long silence. Then she muttered, 'Shit, doll! What do you mean? You — you buried your daughter in your garden?'

'I miscarried. Do you want to hear? It was night. Ken was asleep. When I felt it starting — when I knew it was coming and that I couldn't stop it, I crept down to our ground floor bathroom. It was a sort of instinct, to get right away from Ken and Clem in case I made any noise, and — I realised this much later — because there was a tiled floor there that I could clean. They were so cold, those tiles . . . I was lying on them, rolling about with a flannel between my teeth, trying not to make a sound that might bring Ken. It was terrible, being alone, but I knew I didn't want *him* to come. And when it was over I had to pick the little thing up and wash her and find some sort of coffin for her. I wanted to wrap her in a silk headsquare that my mother had given me years ago, that I really loved — it had flowers on — but I couldn't get back upstairs, I felt too weak.'

Judy was so shocked she turned her face into the back of the sofa. Her hands were tightly clenched.

'I sat with my back against the bath and held her body till it was cold. I think actually I may have passed out . . . But through the fuzziness in my mind, and this great awfulness I was feeling, I remembered I'd bought some shoes that day and the box was in the kitchen bin, so I fetched that, and laid her inside it, wrapped in linen table napkins, and wrote her name on the lid. Early in the morning when I felt stronger, I went out and buried her under a rosebush in the garden. I don't know how I dug the hole. It was very deep. I was so afraid some cat might come and — '

Judy turned a face streaming with tears. 'You poor thing! You poor, poor doll. What — what was her name?'

'Rosy. I've never said that name to anyone before.'

'I heard you say it the other day,' Judy said slowly and indistinctly.

'Yes,' said Harry slowly. 'I do realise I call Surrey Rosy sometimes.'

'Is that why you converted?' Judy asked suddenly.

'I think so.'

'But why did you turn to God? It's enough to make anyone turn away from him!'

'It wasn't God's fault,' said Harry. 'It was Ken's.'

Judy looked at her for a moment, seeing what she'd never seen before — someone who had really been through hell, been scarred by life, known unassuagable bitterness and grief. She was shattered to recognise that until this moment, she had always thought of Harry as her inferior in experience, in suffering. Shallow, spoilt compared to herself.

She stood up suddenly and went into the kitchen part of the room. 'I'm not leaving you. I'm getting us a drink.'

'Tea. Tea would be good.'

Judy moved the kettle on the Aga. Then she said, 'You really blame Ken still, for the affair.'

'For telling me about it.'

'Why did he?'

'I suppose he couldn't hold it in. He told me the way a child tells a heavy secret. You know, some people, if they do something shameful, they twist it somehow: 'If it were wrong I'd be ashamed of it, and if I were ashamed I wouldn't tell. But I'm telling, so it can't be wrong.' Something like that. I think that's perverse. Being too open is a self-indulgence. It causes damage.'

'Keeping secrets does too.' Judy brought the tea and sat down again. 'How long can you go on like this?'

'I look into the near future, and I see a sort of mushroom-cloud. There's going to be fallout. You don't know Ken when he's angry.'

'Has he ever hit you?'

Harry threw her a quick glance. 'Oh no! I'm afraid of him showing a side of himself I hate. And showing me a side of myself that he hates. All that hate is what I've been so frightened of.' They sat close together and drank hot tea.

'You know,' said Judy slowly, 'what you need, what you're going to need, when the bomb goes off, is a job and some money of your own.'

'Do you think I don't know that? That's all

I've been thinking of lately. Living in London. Working. Helping Clem look after Surrey.'

Judy drained her tea. She felt worn out and she wanted to escape, but she couldn't run out on Harry, not tonight.

'Listen. Let's go out like you said. A theatre — anything you choose. *Please*, Harry. I can't just sit here thinking about — Rosy.'

22

Clem had indeed got a night off from the restaurant, but his plan was to make arrangements whereby he could have a night off from baby-sitting too.

While Pleasure had been at home, while he'd *had* a home, he hardly thought about skiving off. Life was serious; so was fatherhood. He had something to prove. He loved Pleasure, he adored Surrey. And besides, he was too tired.

But things were different now. He had a deep gripe inside him, a to-hell-with-it feeling. Pleasure had bombed off. Gone. He hadn't seen or heard from her for over a month. Pleasure — for so long *his* Pleasure — didn't want to be with him and their baby any more. All she wanted was 'a life of her own'. Well, what about a life of *his* own?

At the end of his lunchtime stint at the restaurant, he made for the pay-phone in the foyer and phoned Florence. Florence had told him to contact her any time, anywhere, about anything — so long as she wasn't on duty on the ward. The only thing that bothered him about asking Florence favours was that being near her when she was so miserably ashamed and wretched about Pleasure's desertion emphasised his own unhappiness. But he hadn't asked much of her so far.

'Hallo, Florence, it's me.'

'Oh! How is my baby?'

'She's fine, Florence. Missing her Gran.'

'She miss her mama, is who she miss!' He heard her blowing her nose.

'The thing is,' he said quickly, 'I've got my evening off tonight and I wanted to — you know — just go out. Could you babysit? I'll pay your fares, of course. Please don't dream of coming on your bike.' He had once, only once, since Surrey's birth, offered Florence money for babysitting. Never again would he commit such a crass *faux pas*.

'Yes, I come,' she answered at once, and he could sense her getting herself together. Poor Florence! 'Where you planning to go? Somewhere nice?'

'I don't know yet. I just need a night off.'

'I'm sure,' she said sympathetically. 'You're a good boy Clement, and I like your name too. I wish you called my little girl Honour like I wanted. I like names like that. You mind if I call her Honour?'

'Florence, call her anything you like. My mother calls her Rosy when she thinks no one's listening.'

'I call her Surrey,' said Florence briskly, doing a volte-face. 'Poor child won't know what her name is. What time I supposed to come?'

'I'm going home now. Come any time. And don't forget to use the tube.'

'I go by tube, don't worry, and you know what? When I get to the station I taking a *taxi*. I don't like that district with all them dangerous people you got there! I don't know

337

why you choose to live there and don't come here with me, then I don't have to come miles fighting off druggies and muggies and I don't know what, to help you out.'

'I'm sorry, Florence, I'm — I'm sorry about everything.'

'You not half nor quarter as sorry as I am,' she said, and oddly enough he believed her. He had lost his partner and his baby's mother, but there was always the chance she might come back. Florence had lost her daughter, in the deepest way — by losing faith in her. Could that ever come back? Clem doubted it. Not with Florence. She was like a rock of self-righteous integrity.

He got some more coins from reception and dialled a number he had scribbled down in his pocket diary months ago.

'Dorchester Hotel, how can I help you?'

'Room one-one-eight.'

He waited. Normally he would have been a little nervous about doing this, but all his top-feelings, everything on the surface, was deadened off these days because of the main, big hurt. Everything above that was a to-hell-with-it. The phone was answered by a woman with a high-pitched South African accent.

'Hallo, who is that?'

'Can I speak to Tina?'

'She's still at school, who is that calling?'

'Could you tell her Clement Marshall phoned? She knows me from the crammer, we met there last year, and in case she doesn't remember me, I'm Harriet's son.'

338

'Ah. I know who you are.' Tina's grandmother — it must be her — evidently didn't approve of what she knew.

Clem cared for her opinion only insofar as it might prejudice his chances for the evening. 'I want to ask Tina to go out with me,' he said recklessly. 'Tonight.'

'*Tonight*!' exclaimed the voice, as if a last-minute invitation were the ultimate solecism among people of her sort.

'Yes.'

'Excuse me young man, but aren't you married?'

This was a facer, but what the hell. 'No.'

'But — excuse me again, you understand I'm *responsible* for Tina — didn't I hear that you're — '

'I'm separated. Temporarily. Don't worry, I'm not looking for a replacement girlfriend. Tina's just a friend to spend a fun evening with.'

There was a longish silence, and the phone indicated it wanted more money. Clem dropped in another 10p piece. Then the woman said, 'Well. I'll pass on the message.'

'Yes,' said Clem. 'Thanks.' Hell, 10p wasted.

★ ★ ★

Ken was driving to London along the A303 at 90 miles an hour when he finally saw the police light flashing behind him.

He said the word he had told his wife it was not done to use at table. He'd been saying it rather a lot lately. He pulled in. A large policeman in an aggressive yellow jacket and a flat cap strolled up to the driver's window with pad poised.

'Do you know what your speed has been, ever since the Andover turning, sir?' he said pleasantly.

Ken cursed himself for an idiot. 'I don't know, officer. What was it?'

'Twenty miles an hours over the limit, sir.'

'I'm sorry. I didn't realise. I'll slow down.'

'Yes, sir. I think you will. Funny you not noticing me, I've been clocking you for ten miles.'

So why didn't you stop me before, you smug bastard? 'I'm afraid I neglected to look in my rearview mirror.'

'Got something on your mind, have you, sir?'

Ken said nothing and tried to look suitably remorseful. In his head he was roaring into the man's face, *Mind your own fucking business and get on with it.* His own rage dismayed him. Some colossal fine and a three-point endorsement — what lousy bloody luck!

But worse was to come, because the policeman was now fiddling with something that looked like a colostomy bag. Ken stiffened in his seat and his eyes glazed. Oh Jesus wept! he thought. He had dropped in on the Brittans on his way out of the village, and Joker had forced a double gin on him. *Forced* it — and he hadn't bothered with breakfast. It must've blown away by this time, he thought frantically. I feel fine, perfectly normal; surely it won't show up! Please God it won't show up!

But it did. Ken sat there feeling absolutely gutted with the shock. 'It was only a gin,' he kept muttering hopelessly. 'One gin. Jesus Christ.' It was uncanny — unnatural. There must be something wrong with him, something slowing up his metabolism.

He was put in handcuffs — handcuffs! — and into the back of the police car. They took him to the police station at Andover, where there was a lengthy procedure — it all seemed to take hours. Eventually they tested him again and finding him now well below the limit, let him go. But not before they had warned him and scolded him like a schoolboy. Altogether it was — second only to being made redundant — the most humiliating, degrading thing that had ever happened to him in his adult life.

It must've been a treble. Damn Joker, he kept thinking. Just because he's so pickled in alcohol it would take a whole bottle to put him over the limit! Why didn't I just say no? That Boofer, snoozling up to me. I must have been crazy!

He felt so shaken that he contemplated driving home again, but he found he wasn't doing that, he was driving on to London, fulfilling his original design. There'd been one phone call too many from Harriet.

'I'm sorry, Ken, I know I said I'd be back tomorrow but I've decided to stay just over the weekend and come back on Monday.'

'Why?'

'Well, that's just what I've decided.'

'But what the hell's keeping you in London? What are you *doing* all this time? I haven't seen you for nearly two weeks!'

'I'm going to take Judy out tonight. She needs a break and so — ' She'd stopped herself, but he heard the rest in his head: ' — and so do I.' What did she need a break for, or rather, *from*? She sounded stressed.

'Harry, I want you to stop all this nonsense and tell me what is going on!' he shouted. 'I know damn well something is. Do you take me for a halfwit?'

There was silence. 'Nothing's going on,' she said in a hushed voice. She sounded frightened. Was she in some sort of trouble?

He nearly said, 'I'm coming up,' but bit his tongue. He was quite convinced she was hiding something. In which case, no warnings, he would just arrive, maybe catch her — No, that wasn't what he meant. He had no reason to suspect anything really serious. He wasn't sure what he envisaged or what he expected. He just wanted to know.

★ ★ ★

When he reached the London orbital, he turned south and came off toward Croydon. He got into Town just after six; the rush-hour was in full swing. He pulled into a sidestreet and entered what he thought of as a Paki-shop, a late-opening newsagent, and bought a *London Streetfinder*. He'd never been to the Brixton house. He found the street on the map. Miles

342

away, right in the stews. God! Couldn't he use a drink now!

He went into a café and bought a cuppa instead, and a bit of mass-produced fruitcake. Both tasted horrible. It occurred to him belatedly that whatever Harry was up to couldn't be any worse than what he now had to confess to her. Drunk driving was the last thing on earth he had expected ever to have to confess. A joke in a way, a black joke. One thing only comforted him: he had behaved well during her year of banning, not showing her how he really felt about it. Well, except for that once, outside the court the first day. He had behaved very badly then. Bawled the hell out of her, right when she was most vulnerable. He wished he hadn't. How he wished he hadn't!

Would he be banned? Probably not for being so very slightly over the limit. Thank God he hadn't yelled at the policeman, had looked properly contrite. But it wouldn't be three points, more like eight. Oh, God! If only she hadn't gone swanning off to Town and made him angry and upset and suspicious. If only — !

Not fair to blame her.

He returned to the car and began picking his way through the cheerful, dingy, multi-ethnic south London streets. They made a strange impact after non-ethnic Dorset. So many black faces! Incredible, they were everywhere. And the shops, too. Like a bit of Africa. God, he thought again. I wouldn't come back to this place to live if you paid me a thousand a week!

He was aware that he was still jumpy and nervy. He must get on top of this feeling by the time he confronted her. He must consolidate the advantage of surprise.

At last he turned into the right street, full of gloomy, rundown Edwardian terraced houses, and pulled up outside Judy's.

Only at this point did he suddenly remember that Harry'd said she was going out for the evening with Judy. What if there were no one to let him in?

He got out of the car and fetched his overnight bag from the boot. His hands were shaking . . . This was bloody ridiculous! What was he scared of? What was going on?

Stop it. Pull yourself together.

He went down the steps into the basement area. There were little wild plants growing between the paving-stones, like moss in the bottom of a well, and a bay window with scruffily painted bars in front of it. In the country you could leave your door open; here you went into voluntary imprisonment every time you entered your house. There was a light behind the thin curtains. He breathed a sigh of relief and rang the bell.

A volley of barks erupted behind the door. Oh hell, of course, that great ugly dog that had peed all over his trees.

'Quiet, Zulu!' said a woman's voice. It wasn't a voice he knew, and a moment later a large black woman threw open the door. Ken took an instinctive step back.

'He won't hurt you,' said the woman, keeping

the dog back with her leg. 'Can I help you? You looking for Judy? She gone out.'

'I'm — I'm Ken Marshall. I'm looking for my wife.'

The woman's eyebrows went up and her mouth opened. Then it spread into a wide smile.

'You Clement's father?' she cried, and clapped her hands together.

'Yes,' he said in some puzzlement.

'Come in!'

As he passed closed to her into the tiny dark hall, he stiffened, expecting her to smell unpleasant, and was surprised because she didn't. He passed ahead of her into the main room.

There was only one lamp, a standard, alight. It shone down in a warm circle onto the corner seat of a big squashy many-cushioned sofa where a knitting-bag and some pink woolly object on needles lay. The television was on. The rest of the room was in semi-darkness, but it looked rather untidy and shabby to Ken — very un-Harriet indeed. Yet there, he suddenly noticed, was her cardigan, draped in homely fashion over the back of a chair.

'Sit down! You just drove from the country?'

'Yes.'

'I make you a cup of tea.'

The black woman bustled into the rear part of the room and switched on a light. Something resembling a market stall was illuminated — a bright blue dresser with splashes of other colours all over it: Jugs, cups, candlesticks, plates, vases, statues. Ken blinked, dazzled. There was also an Aga with a kettle and some other pots on it. Ken noticed a carry cot on the table and thought, How unhygienic!

The woman was rattling on.

'I been wondering where you was, why you never come. Harriet talk about you sometimes but when I ask, she just say you busy man. I sort of think you and she is divorced or something.'

Ken's attention focused sharply. Why had Harry been talking about him to this woman? Who was she?

'Are you from South Africa?' he asked. Some hanger-on of Judy's in the 'movement', surely?

But she laughed. 'Me? No, man, I'm from Jamaica, and now I'm from right here!'

She brought him a mug of tea and a piece of cake on a plate. 'Come on, now, you sit down. You want me to switch that thing off? Boring anyhow!' She switched the set off and there was a sudden silence. 'I much rather talk to you. Clement's Daddy! He talk about you, too. Well! You and me, we got a lot in common. It high time we met. You probably guessed, I'm Florence, Pleasure's mother.' And she put out a big black hand to him.

He shook it because he couldn't not. A lot in common . . . What could that possibly mean? What did the words *pleasure's mother* mean? They meant nothing at all to Ken. She might as well have said, 'anger's mother'.

'I'm sorry,' he said rather stiffly, withdrawing from hers the hand she seemed bent on hanging onto. 'I don't understand. What have we got in common? You have the advantage of me.'

Florence opened her chatty mouth — and abruptly closed it again.

She was a thoroughly open, upfront person. But you can't work in a hospital among sick people without quickly internalising the fact that not everything can be spoken about. There are times when the mouth must be shut on what might seem like idle, harmless chatter, or remarks carrying simple information. An instinct born of her work shut Florence up now. She couldn't comprehend the situation, how it could possibly be that this man didn't know who she was. But there was something in his eyes — some sickness, or at least the vulnerability of sickness — that warned her: *There some piece of ignorance here that it not for me to take away.*

'Mr Marshall,' she said, falling intuitively into a kindly and cajoling wardmaid-to-patient role, 'why you don't sit down here and be comfortable till they come back? Clem coming back here too, when he had his night out, so you see all of them.' And very firmly, she switched the set on again. Loud.

Too loud. From the carry-cot came a protesting wail.

'Uh-oh. I woke her up.'

She turned the set down and hurried to the table, where she jiggled the carrycot for a few moments, and when that only exacerbated the din, she gathered the baby — quite a big one, Ken saw — up in her arms and rocked it. She

347

kept her back to Ken, who had still not sat down but was standing, tea in one hand, cake in the other, poised on an edge he could not see but could sense, though he had no idea of its nature. He felt a strange reluctance to move, a stranger desire not to be here. The nervousness, the underlying rage he had felt when the policeman stood at his car window was forgotten, dwarfed by a much deeper fear, a deeper, more incalculable rage.

Suddenly he swung round. 'Is that your baby?' he asked.

A chuckle answered him, but it was cut short. She turned, her face a pattern of incredulity.

'Mr Marshall! You not saying you don't know whose is this baby?'

He felt his hands go nerveless and quickly put down what they held. He walked on shaky legs to where she stood. He said nothing, just looked down at the little angry face, like an overblown orange rose. He saw the hair, abundant, crinkly and reddish, and the small brown waving hands.

Then he looked up into the face of his fellow grandparent, missing in its blackness the tender look of dawning understanding, seeing only something unacceptable that must, nevertheless, be accepted.

'They don't tell you?' she said slowly. 'How could they do so? This is the most awful thing I heard!'

He couldn't bear it. To have her pitying him!

A terrible anger took hold of him. It was not

ungovernable because he did govern it, but he sensed what it made him want to do: to lay about him with the utmost violence. Florence saw it in his face, gasped, and ran from the room with the baby in her arms, but he hardly noticed she'd gone. Because it wasn't really them that his rage was pointed at. It was his wife and son who had delivered him to this horrible moment. He had his fists in front of him and did not realise he was making strangled sounds.

Suddenly he sensed a movement behind him, and turned. The dog was standing there on stiff legs, looking at him and growling.

Ken didn't much like dogs, and he was in no mood to be threatened by this one. In an instant, all the rage he felt against those closest to him fused into a basilisk inside him, and directed itself against this hideous white animal.

'Fuck off out of it, you ugly brute!' he shouted, and kicked out.

Zulu shot forward with a snarl and sank his teeth into Ken's leg.

Ken let out a shout that was almost a scream. In shock and agony, he tried to shake the thing off but it hung on. Off-balance, he fell.

The next second the door flew open and Florence, no longer encumbered by the baby, entered like an avenging angel, made straight for the dog and caught it by the collar.

'Let go, you bad dog! Let go this minute!' She gave Zulu a blow on the head with her hand.

He let go at once. She hauled him clear, and without releasing his collar, removed her slipper and gave him a number of whacks on the rump

349

with it, abusing him all the time. 'Bad dog! Bad Zulu! Why they keep you? Biting people, be ashamed! Now go to your basket!'

She let him go and he crept away under the table, his vestigial tail indenting his rump. A kind of perverse sympathy awoke in Ken. 'It — it wasn't all his fault,' he muttered.

'Never mind whose fault! No, don't get up. Sit where you are. I look at your wound.'

She knelt beside his feet. Ken, meek now, pulled up his damaged trouser-leg. He was shaking from head to foot. The fear had neutralised the rage, leaving his emotions turbid but calm.

'Uh-oh, this is a bit of a mess,' she said. 'Don't worry now, I clean it for you, but then you must go to the hospital. Maybe it need a couple of stitches.'

Ken said nothing. He felt her expert fingers on him in a sudden flood of fatalistic relief. Thank God she was here, was all he could think. The words 'wonderful woman' even crossed his mind. The irony of his about-face didn't strike him until much later. When she asked him to take off his trousers, he obeyed like a child.

23

Judy and Harry walked back from the station, through the dark streets.

They had spent the evening at the Battersea Arts Centre, watching a bizarre play about gays and lesbians on another planet (or perhaps in a future time — the off-the-wall costumes could have been for either), where everyone was gay except a few aberrant straights whose only real function was to produce eggs and sperm for the labs so lesbians could have children without direct male intervention. The 'eggers' and 'taddies' as they were dubbed were heavily discriminated against, and were the butt of heterophobic jokes.

Harry was not comfortable with all this. She found herself roused to the defence of the poor straights. 'They had a biological function, at least,' she said, 'which is more than gays have.'

'Reactionary! Bigot!' cried Judy. 'I'll have to sic Abby on to you.'

'No, really. It's a sterile existence.'

'Abby says the point is that in this over-crowded world they should be respected for their nonproductiveness. I wish we'd taken her along. She'd have loved the stand-up comic in the Working Girls' Club with her raunchy butch-and-femmy jokes, taking off the straights.'

'Yes. I just didn't reckon the eggers and

taddies business, that's all. It's like these cults that make a virtue of eschewing sex. Or pacifism.'

'You've lost me.'

'Well, somebody's got to do it, when it comes to the crunch. Make kids and shoot the enemy.'

'Making the world safe and normal for woolly libs to react against.'

Harry burst into a shout of laughter.

'Judy, honestly! How can you be so anti-everything that everyone else at least pays lipservice to?'

Judy didn't laugh. She had been anti a lot of things, all her life, to which others automatically gave their yes. Harry was being deliberately provocative, looking for one of the friendly confrontations that she was beginning to relish lately. But somehow the words that had always come so readily to Judy were missing. She was tired, and not just because of the long day; for once she felt no inclination to be adversarial. Instead she sighed heavily, tucked her arm through Harry's, and felt the comfort of her companionship on the long underlit walk to the house.

There were no lights on, that was the first thing they noticed. And when they got in, the flat was empty.

Except for Zulu.

He didn't rush to meet them. Judy, switching on the lights and looking round in bewilderment, saw him curled up in his basket. He was shivering all over, and when she went to him he cringed in shame and rolled his eyes at her.

'Zool! What's wrong?'

'Judy! What's that on his muzzle?'

But they could see what it was. It was blood, showing up clearly on his pink-and-white snout. A quick look at the kitchen floor showed where more had been wiped hastily away. The two women stared at each other in wordless fear.

'Where the hell's Florence?' said Judy at last. Neither of them dared mention Surrey. 'There must be a note.'

There was, though it took some time to find it. It had blown to the ground when they'd opened the door. It was scrawled in pencil on a scrap of newspaper:

'*Gone to the hospital* [then there was the word 'with' crossed out]. *Taken Surrey, not her, don't worry. F.*'

'What does it mean? What does it *mean*?' cried Harry shrilly.

'It means,' said Judy slowly, 'that Florence has taken someone, not Surrey, to the hospital.'

'But it says she *has* taken her.'

'She's taken her, but it's 'not her'. She means, she didn't go because of her.'

Harry tried to still her trembling and read the scrappy note again. 'Are you sure?'

'Yes,' said Judy firmly.

She made them strong tea and tried to soothe both Harry and Zulu. The dog eventually slithered out of his basket and pressed his heavy, quivering body against Judy's legs. She washed his face for him and gave him some biscuits and after a while he felt forgiven and perked up.

353

'He must've bitten someone. I've never known him do that,' she said, fondling his long crop-eared head. 'Poor Zool, you didn't mean it, did you, doll?' She was thinking frantically. With the itinerant pickies coming and going, he was not one to lash out at strangers. He had an instinct for the harmless. An intruder? God forbid, with Florence here alone with the baby! Who could it have been? Why had Florence crossed out 'with' and not supplied them with the name?

They waited on tenterhooks. About twenty minutes later, they heard someone come down the area steps and put a key in the door. They both jumped up, but it was only Clem, looking much more cheerful than of late.

'Hi!' he said, pulling off his jacket. 'Had a good evening? Guess who I went to a movie with? Tina. It was good fun. Certainly makes a change, taking a girl home to the Dorchester! How's Surrey?'

They glanced at each other helplessly. He saw it and froze. 'What's happened?'

His mother went to him and took his arm. 'We don't know. Something has, but not to Surrey.' They told him all they knew and showed him the note. He took it in his stride.

'I get it. Zulu bit someone and Florence took them to hospital and had to take the baby along. So that's okay then, she'll be back. Only it'll be too late for her to get home tonight. Judy, please can she stay? She can have the cara., I'll sleep on the sofa.'

'Of course. How do you suppose she got to

the hospital without a car? She must have sent for an ambulance.'

Suddenly, halfway to the kitchen area, Clem stiffened. 'Wait,' he said sharply, and turned and almost bolted out of the front door and up the area steps. Two minutes later he came back, his face white. He closed the door behind him carefully and sat down on the sofa.

The women, braced, stood together, waiting for enlightenment.

'Dad's car's outside,' he said hollowly. 'I saw it when I came past. I recognised it but I thought it couldn't be . . . It's Dad.'

'Oh no,' said Harry under her breath, with an intonation of pleading. She walked unsteadily out of the room.

Judy, left alone with Clem, sat beside him for a while in silence.

'What are you most concerned about?' she said at last.

'Dunno,' he said in the same hollow voice. It was clear he couldn't approach the kernel of his anxieties. His eyes kept going to the front door, even though they would certainly hear footsteps on the steps first.

'Want a drink?' Judy asked.

'Yeah. No. I don't know. Have you got a beer?'

Judy kept beer for George. She opened a can and poured it into a glass. He sat with it in his hand. It was so quiet they could hear the faint popping of bubbles.

'Would you like to be alone with him if he comes? Shall I get out?'

Clem put his head down over the untasted glass and simply shook his head. After a while he looked up and said. 'Why would Zulu bite him?'

'I've been wondering that.'

'Does Zulu react to people getting angry?'

'He might.'

Now Clem began, against his will, actively visualising the scene — his father, Florence, Surrey . . . Cold shivers ran up and down his back. He drank some beer. His face was still ghost-white. Judy put her hand on his knee. He gave her a sideways look of what was intended as gratitude, but appeared as nothing but ghastly apprehension.

Harry did this, Judy thought suddenly. It was her idea. She led him into this catacomb of deceit, and now she's withdrawn. Where did she go? She should bleddy well be here with him. She got up. 'I'm going to see where your mother is,' she said tightly.

'Yes,' croaked Clem. His throat sounded as dry as if beer had never been invented.

'Would you like the television on?'

'Yeah, might as well,' he muttered.

Judy left him staring blankly at the screen with the light from it turning his pale skin a sickly green.

She found Harry in her room that had been Tina's. She was sitting on the bed. Clem was his father's son in looks but white faces and the hollow eyes of fear gave mother and son an unusual likeness.

Judy felt her anger surface. That poor

frightened kid! It wasn't fair, it wasn't on. For once friendship was inadequate to suppress her feelings.

'Harry, this is all down to you. Don't abandon him, go in there and be with him.'

Harry turned smudgy eyes up to her. 'It's not your business to talk to me like that,' she said faintly.

'Like what? I haven't said a fraction of what I'd like to say. All I've said is that you can't leave him in there alone. Ken could come in at any time.'

Harry shuddered and covered her face.

'Oh, *come on*!' Judy shouted suddenly, her patience snapping. 'What the hell is all this big cringe? He won't beat you, even if you deserve it, so what are you carrying on for like a tragedy-queen? You have to face the music, that's all, and whatever will happen will happen and after that you won't have to be afraid of it happening any more. Now get up and get in there, I'm sick of all this. *My poor old Zulu!*' she added furiously.

Harry was looking at her, open-mouthed.

'If there's an innocent victim in all this, it's him!'

Harry got up silently and went ahead of Judy back into the living room. Not a moment too soon. They all heard the scraping of feet on the steps outside, the murmur of voices: Florence's, full of professional sympathy, 'Careful now, the steps is uneven,' and Ken's answering, testily 'I'm fine, I can manage.'

Florence's key in the lock.

She came in backwards, holding the carry-cot in one hand and guiding Ken with the other. He was limping heavily and held, inexpertly, a National Health walking stick.

As one, the three in the room moved forward to relieve Florence of the carry-cot. Clem got there first. He took it, looked at its sleeping contents for a moment and then carried it out of the room. In the doorway he turned.

'I'll be right back,' he said.

' 'So don't start without me',' Judy heard herself add.

Ken glared at her. Judy felt a faint, almost hysterical bubble of mirth and defiance rising in her. *Don't look daggers at me, man, or I'll set my dog on you*, she thought, and turned away to hide the nervous grin that tugged at her mouth. Should she leave? Undoubtedly she should, but for some reason — possibly no better than it should be — she wanted to stay. *Front-row seat* came into her head. She moved into the background near the Aga, where Florence instantly joined her.

'Terrible,' Florence whispered. 'He got mad and the dog went for him. Imagine! Frightened me half out of my life!' She rolled her eyes descriptively.

'Is he bad?' Judy muttered.

'Eight stitches.'

'Oh shit!'

'Why you swear all the time, it's not nice,' whispered Florence reprovingly.

Meanwhile Ken had come limping into the front end of the room and was standing facing

358

Harry who was looking like a rabbit before a stoat.

He didn't speak to her, just stood there leaning on the stick and staring into her face. Waiting. She seemed to be waiting, too — perhaps for Clem to come back. Eventually, after what seemed to the two watchers like an age, he did, having deposited Surrey in the bedroom.

He joined his mother. Ken spoke at last.

'You'd better have something to say to explain what's happened to me tonight,' he said in a low, toneless voice.

Clem looked at Harry helplessly. He didn't want to put it all on to her, even though he felt that was where it belonged. She couldn't seem to speak, though. She just stood there, clenching and unclenching her hands, with a little sheen of sweat on her high forehead.

'We were afraid you'd be angry, Dad,' Clem said.

'I am angry,' he said. 'I'm more than angry. I'm humiliated. But much worse than that, I feel betrayed.'

His voice seemed to choke. He turned to the two women near the Aga and suddenly barked, 'I'm sorry, I know this isn't my house, but can you please just get *out* and leave us alone?'

Florence took Judy by the hand and almost pulled her from the room. Zulu bolted after them, getting tangled up in their legs and catching the closing door on his rump.

They went and sat with Surrey in the bedroom and talked in low voices as if in a hospital waiting room during a life-or-death operation.

Florence took the sleeping Surrey into her arms for comfort.

'Can you imagine, they didn't tell him a word? I don't think he even knew there was a baby! Did you know about this?'

'Yes,' said Judy.

'I shocked at you! Why you didn't say something to Harriet?'

'Not really my business, was it.'

'You her friend. A friend has a duty.'

'You can't force people to do what they don't want to.'

Florence shook her head. 'Poor man. For him, there something worse even than not being told. He look at me like my genes got two heads and a monkey-tail. He deeply colour-prejudice, I can tell.'

'Some people are like that. It isn't exactly prejudice even, it's more like a virus in the brain.'

'A virus? You mean, they can't help it? I don't think so.'

'I know all about it, believe me,' said Judy. 'My whole family has that virus. Half my bleddy nation has it. Sorry,' she added. 'You're right, Florence, I do swear too much.'

'It's for the baby's sake I say it. She pick up bad talk.'

'Not at seven months, will she?'

'You going to stop suddenly when she ten months?'

Judy stared at her a moment, and then said, 'I don't think she's going to be seeing much of me when she's ten months old. I don't think

I'm going to be around much.'

'You mean, they moving out?' asked Florence.

'No. I mean, I'm moving out.'

'You leaving London?'

'I'm leaving England.'

Florence stared at her. 'Ah, I know. You going back. You going to help Nelson Mandela. Help build a new South Africa.'

'That sounds pretty ambitious. Let's just say I'm going home and leave it at that. They're letting us banned people all go back and it would be very bad not to go now. Anyway, I must. I've dreamt of it for so long.'

'And George?'

Judy shrank her head between her shoulders and gripped her hands between her knees. 'I have to leave him for a while. Maybe for good. Probably for good.'

Florence said nothing and her silence spoke volumes.

'Go on then, say it. He's a good man, he loves me, it will hurt him. What about my daughter, what about the Movement?'

'I thinking just, what about the flat?'

Judy indicated the door, through which sounds of a raised voice were coming. 'I think Harry's going to need somewhere to live.'

They fell silent. Ken was shouting. Judy got up and opened the bedroom door.

'This isn't the first time you've shut me out and tried to deceive me! Whatever I've done in our marriage, I've never deceived you! Even *that time* I told you the truth — '

Florence got up and closed the door firmly.

361

'I know it interesting, but it not nice to listen,' she said primly. They sat down again.

★ ★ ★

In the big room, fifteen years of admirable, even successful effort to behave in a decent, civilised way and pretend that sex isn't all that important, were in process of disintegration.

Ken had been unable to let rip with Judy and Florence in the room, but he managed perfectly well in front of his son. Clem sat in silent anguish on the sofa, learning only now that his parents had not slept together since he was five years old, that his mother had miscarried his sister, that the placid, affectionate, *normal* relations he thought he had witnessed throughout his growing up, the partnership he's taken for granted was happy, had basically been a façade. And the façade hid all manner of violent ugly feelings that now flooded over him in a torrent of furious words. All the anger bottled up in both his parents burst forth and half-drowned him in incredulous desolation.

His mother at first seemed well aware of his presence. She tried to calm his father, to placate him with apologies and explanations. Clem saw her as one of those animals in the wild — a vixen perhaps, or one of the cat family — that, when challenged and attacked, lies down submissively to show it doesn't want to fight. She stayed sitting down, her hands clenched in her lap, avoiding her husband's eyes, keeping her voice low. She even glanced at Clem once

362

and signalled him with her eyes to leave, but he couldn't. Later he would tell himself he was afraid for her, staying in case she needed him, but it wasn't that. He was simply stunned and incapable of moving.

'You have lied and lied and lied!' his father shouted. 'You, the saintly Catholic, the sexless, sinless nun! What did you say to the good Father through the grille, eh? 'I'm telling endless porkies to my poor deluded husband about his bastard black grandchild, not for my sake, of course, but for his'? 'Oh, no penance needed. Go ahead, my daughter, keep it up, that's what Christian marriage is all about. If you can't give him his conjugal rights, at least you can make a complete bloody fool out of him'!'

At last, goaded beyond endurance, the vixen abandoned submission, leapt to her feet and gave battle.

'Perhaps you ought to stop heaping all the blame on me and start asking yourself what's so wrong with you that I was afraid to tell you! Yes, Ken, I was terrified! Because what you are, underneath all that hail-fellow-well-met that makes you so popular with a certain type of man, like Joker Brittan and the fascist farmer, is a fanatic!'

'A fanatic! Are you mad? Me?'

'Oh yes. All the things you hate foreigners for — unEnglish excesses — you've got in full measure. You're a racist. Deny it if you can!'

'I don't deny it. I'm a racist the way every other normal human being is. Everyone! We all want to be with our own kind, we want our

363

children to mate with their own kind, and if you tell me you don't feel like that under all your false liberalism I'll call you a liar again!'

'You make me absolutely sick to my stomach when you talk like that!' shouted Harry. 'It's so disgusting! What you actually feel is that Clem has — has mated with something less than human!'

Ken stared at her. 'I never said that.'

'But it must be what you feel, deep down! If it weren't, if you thought black people were merely 'different' but just as good, it couldn't matter to you that much. It's you that's caused all this, by being what you are, and it's you that ruined our marriage, not just sleeping with that wretched little tart but telling me about it like a silly child without strength of will to hold its tongue, not caring how much you hurt me, as if I were your mother or something, not your wife at all!'

'No more you have been, either, for the past fifteen years! Have you the slightest idea how you've made me suffer?'

'Suffer? You're too phlegmatic and sure of your superiority to suffer. Try having a half-term miscarriage on a cold bathroom floor all by yourself and see if you want to whinge about suffering after that!'

'You could have called me — '

'*I didn't want you*! And I don't want you now! If you don't accept Surrey — '

'Surrey? Did you say *Surrey*? What a bloody stupid name!'

'Shut up. If you don't accept her — and you

364

don't accept her and you never will because you are simply incapable of it — then you can't have Clem and you can't have me, because we're on her side, not yours. Now get out and go home because we're staying here — the three of us!'

Clem had seen his mother like this once before. Her flushed face and light-green eyes were infused, shot through with sparks of anger so that she did look like a vixen, a little red furious fox with all teeth bared, her whole spirit roused up and every bit of feeling in her rushing out. Just as it had on the night he had broken the news to her. How ironic, he managed to think, struggling inwardly to put some distance between himself and all this absolute horror that seemed to be breaking something inside him. *Then she went mad against me. Now she's going mad against him. And all about my child. What have I brought her into, what sort of world, when my own parents are like this?*

At this moment he heard the baby crying in the bedroom.

He jumped up. The antagonists stopped at the movement and turned their stranger faces to him. He wanted to yell at them, spill out *his* feelings, too, but the crying sound pulled him so strongly that he couldn't say a word or delay himself by even a minute. He threw them one look of naked reproach and went out.

Judy and Florence looked up as Clem burst in. His hair seemed more than usually on end and his face was distraught, full of a wild confusion of feelings.

'Give her to me, I'll feed her,' he said in a

breathy, furious voice.

'Maybe better if I do it,' said Florence pacifyingly.

He almost snatched his daughter from her arms.

'No, *I'm* going to do it. I'm going to go in there and do it in front of them. And for once I hope she yells her head off till their ears ache, till the roof falls in. I hope she yells so loud they'll have to *fucking well stop!*'

He rushed from the room. Florence and Judy gave each other a look.

'Sometimes you need to swear,' Florence conceded.

24

Ken woke up rather slowly.

He was in his own bed at the cottage, he knew that by his pillow, which was a particular dark green, and by the sound of early bird-song. But he felt distinctly odd. And the mattress felt very strange, lumpy . . . hot. He groped with a hand that was curiously clumsy and half-numb; he must have been lying on it.

He hadn't. Somebody else had. What *he* had been lying on, and still partially was, was Boofer Brittan.

He jerked his head up, forcing open eyes glued shut by deep, satiated sleep and a hangover. Yes. *Yes*! There she was, lying at his side in his single bed, partly under his naked body.

In the dawn light, he surveyed her bemusedly. Unmistakably past her prime but nevertheless shapely — sensual. Her breasts, two soft circular pale puddings with a somewhat faded but sweet little cherry in the middle of each, lay exposed within reach of his arrested hand. Her face, darkly framed by the pillow and tilted towards him was, by any reckoning, still attractive, even with those teasing blue eyes closed in sleep, her mouth (which he now remembered kissing repeatedly the night before) slightly open and lightly snoring.

Ken lay there raised on one elbow and looked at her for some time, trying to orientate himself to this wildly unexpected new situation.

First he had to remember what had led up to it. That wasn't hard. Drink or no drink, he had not forgotten much.

He had driven home from Brixton — not last night, the night before — very, very circumspectly, holding his emotions close in check, concentrating on his driving and on not letting himself think. The pain in his bitten leg, reduced to a dull but constant smart, helped.

When he got back it was nearly four a.m. and he needed sleep as he had never needed it before. But the cat had to be fed, and for the first time he was conscious of being glad to see it (her), glad of some living presence in the house. He'd run out of catfood and ungrudgingly opened a tin of salmon for her. She showed her appreciation by following him up to the bedroom and after claw-kneading him through the quilt for some minutes, settled down against his private parts. He seemed to recall reaching out to touch her several times in what remained of the night and finding her warm softness quite a comfort.

Next day he had to face things, or try to, but it seemed impossible. It was always easier for Ken to face something than nothing — a blank. He had finished it, he knew that. She would never come back, his Harry. No, she was not his Harry, perhaps she never had been, or not for years. She was Harriet, a stranger to his mind as much as to his body. The Church was only the first step she had taken away from him. A new life stretched ahead of him, empty of what had principally filled it till now.

And there was a more immediate emptiness.

Going out early as a matter of habit to feed the ducks, which he had of course neglected to shut up the night before, he came upon a scene of carnage. Two missing, three corpses, one half-eaten, blood and feathers everywhere . . . a horrible sight. He felt a revulsion from the workings of nature that just for the moment ousted all other feelings. *This is the rotten God she prays to, the one who arranged all this predation and terror and bloodshed.* He was grimly burying the remains in the compost when he heard the honk of a car in the lane.

He took no notice. Whoever it was, he couldn't face them now. But he had reckoned without Boofer the quondam Bunny, who after five minutes' search of the premises came upon him.

She took in the situation at a glance and her face expressed unfeigned shock and sympathy.

'Oh, Kenny! The black-hearted little bastard! Did he take the lot? My dear, how perfectly ghastly!'

Ken felt wholly unaccustomed and shaming tears coming into his eyes. He was so taken by surprise at the sensation, which he hadn't had for years, that he could take no controlling action, and the next moment her arms were around him and he was being clasped to that warm and well-formed bosom. Her hair was pressed to his cheek and her expensive scent was floating about him, conquering the stink of droppings and slaughter.

'Poor, poor, poor! Oh, I'm so sorry!'

She persuaded him to curtail the burial and come into the cottage for a drink — his first of the day. Earlier, his leg had started to hurt seriously and he remembered the painkiller tablets he'd been given and swallowed several of them. Only after he began to feel really woozy did he think that perhaps they didn't mix with alcohol. The wooziness was quite pleasant, though, and lasted all day.

Boofer sat there in her trim cream slacks — she had beautiful long slim legs — and a pale blue embroidered blouse that showed her slender neck and hid the telltale tops of her arms. Her hair was short and curly, no longer naturally blonde, but her hairdresser (she travelled to London for his sake) knew his business. She didn't look ludicrously young — just right. Very, very attractive. Ken had noticed it before, only in passing because she was an adjunct of Joker's, but now he noticed it in quite a different way.

And she could hold her liquor. She took it for granted he could, too — everyone she knew could. After a while she suggested she should take him home to her house for lunch, which she did. Curiously enough, Joker was away, some Masonic function in London. They spent the day alone together, eating, drinking, strolling in the garden with her dogs, talking. She was amazingly sympathetic and somehow her swearing, which had always grated on him, now seemed rather flamboyant and dashing.

He didn't spill the full beans of course but

he did tell her he'd had a pretty traumatic 'disagreement' with Harry. Boofer noticed his limp and he told her about the dog and she clucked and cooed over his 'poor leg' and laid a slim, elegant hand over the bandage.

'I'm a healer, did you know that? No, don't send me up, darling, it's true. Shall I give you some healing?'

And she did. She made him lie down and talked to him about his pain going out of a hole in the top of his head while she stroked him gently. To his astonishment, it worked; the pain went away almost completely and so, for the time, did his limp. 'You're putting me under a spell,' he said to her, because the inner pain had gone too. It was as if the touch of her slim fingers, the warmth that flowed from them, drew the pain, physical and emotional, out of him.

And when she drove him home they had some more to drink. Having noted the paucity of his drinks cupboard, she'd brought a full bottle of vodka, a large one of tonic, and a fat lemon. Ice, and rather nice crystal glasses, he could supply. He lit the fire, which blazed up, casting its romantic light on the cottage walls. He neglected to turn on the lights. They sat on his settee in cosy, tingling companionship and suddenly he found himself embracing her, or was it the other way round? He had no intentions in the matter; he could truthfully have employed the old cliché-excuse, 'It just happened,' though from her side it was doubtless a little more calculated. He seemed to recall saying at one rather advanced stage, 'But what about Joker?' and her replying, 'Darling. The poor old sod hasn't been able to get it up for yonks. You can't imagine what this is like for me. You are just saving my sanity, Kenny.'

He was saving *her* sanity! Ken was quite incapable of resistance. As the celibacy of years came to a skyrocketing end, he felt an unaccustomed rush of happiness — of pride, of relief — to every part of him. It emanated from his groin, not his head or heart, but that didn't matter. It reached those parts too, before he dropped off to sleep in Boofer's arms. 'My sweet furry little bunny,' he murmured, last thing. And she, bunnylike, snuggled close to him, warm and yielding. He'd forgotten the sheer, all-obliterating wonder of this feeling.

Now it was morning, the morning-after, but with (so far) none of the negative feelings associated with that phrase. He eased himself out of bed and went for a shower. His heart was high: he cared for nothing, nothing at all — not his wife and son and what they had done to him, not that misbegotten infant or her antecedents, and certainly not poor cuckolded Joker Brittan. Even though this probably meant that Ken couldn't join the Masons now . . . Be a bit out of order, that. Who cared, though? He suddenly realised he'd mainly been considering it to spite Harry and the Catholic Church! What nonsense it seemed, now that Ken had had what he had had. He meant to have plenty more of it, too. It was about bloody time! Remarkable, he thought that he could still do it. And do it, according to Boofer, rather well.

He went downstairs and made coffee, scrambled the last of the duck-eggs, and made a big fuss of the cat. He felt absolutely devoted to her suddenly.

25

Harry staggered home to the Brixton flat night after night after work wondering just how long she could keep this up.

It wasn't the work itself. She'd never actually had any work experience so although it was all new, and Judy had warned her it was dreary and awful, she was almost enjoying the adventure. The erks were agog at her good cheer and the energetic way she went about her duties. They weren't to know she knew sweet fanny adams about what she was doing at first.

Clem, before he started college, had come in with her a few times and surreptitiously showed her how to use the computer. She caught onto it amazingly quickly. She'd done a typing course once, only she'd never used it. It was just a matter of working up her speed, finding out where all the stock was kept, figuring out the filing system, which Judy had briefed her on, and keeping her head down. The first erk who'd tried being cheeky with her received a look of such freezing, haughty contempt, he put the word round that she was not to be trifled with. Her nickname behind her back was Tessie Tightarse, but as she never heard it, it didn't bother her.

No, it wasn't the work so much. It was everything else. The travelling was frightful. She marvelled how people did it day after day, even while she was doing it herself. The cost! How could it be worth working, when out of your miserable pittance of a wage you had to pay a huge whack just to get to and from work? And the queuing, and the shoving, and the rain, and the squalor of bus-stops, the crowded buses, the sheer exhausting grind of it all. No wonder Ken had hated working in London. She'd never realised! If she could have felt anything positive for him after the terrible things he'd said to her, she would have been filled with retroactive sympathy.

She hated leaving Surrey every morning. She was amazed that women, mothers who didn't have to work, chose to do so out of boredom. All she longed to do was stay home and mess about with the baby all day. She loved working on the flat, which was quite transformed already. She and Clem had painted the walls, ragrollstyle, put up new curtains, thrown out the carpets and sanded the floor, though as Surrey's first summer ended they began to wonder if this had been such a good idea. They had big plans for re-covering the shabby old armchairs and sofas as soon as they could afford to, but the cost of everything was horrendous. They were surviving on Clem's wages, plus, now, his grant, and her salary, which didn't leave a lot over for frills, on armchairs or elsewhere.

At the beginning Clem had managed, with great difficulty, to hold the fort all day; Harry took over when he went to work at night. But now he was at college, keeping his waiter's job for weekends only, they'd had to get a childminder and that was unspeakably fraught.

How could you be certain you could trust them? Harry worried about it all day, and she knew Clem did, too. Florence helped when she could, including with bits of money. But basically it was up to Clem and Harry.

'Are we going to make it, Mum?' Clem asked once when Surrey was colicky and they hadn't been getting much sleep. 'How do people get through this? I'm so bloody tired!'

'We'll make it,' Harry said, but grimly.

Sometimes she allowed herself to play with the idea of Clem getting seriously together with Tina. Tina now had money of her own from Dido who, before flying back to Durban ('Of course, we Whites are doomed — we're all going to be killed now these terrible kaffirs are coming to power, but one can't just desert!') had made her a 'sensible' allowance — 'Not enough to spoil you, petal, just enough to give you a bit of independence'. It was evidently a bit better than just sensible because Tina could afford a pretty nice flat on it. But it was quite clear that Tina felt nothing special for Clem, and wouldn't dream of getting involved with a twenty-year-old with a baby in tow. She had too much hope for herself and her future, now, to do that. She was keeping all her options open.

It was all extremely complicated and exhausting and it called for a lot of energy that Harriet was most unaccustomed to expending.

'Tell me something, Clem,' she said wearily one evening while Clem was sitting feeding Surrey and Harry was throwing together something for them to eat. They'd both been moaning about their various hells at work, the low-grade people who bullied and 'shat-on' them, the rotten pay, the 'hierarchical' atmosphere in which every one seemed to be aggressively protecting their own rears. 'Does nobody like their jobs any more?'

'What do you mean, 'any more'? That implies they did, once.'

'It's terrible, though. All this tension and backbiting and underlying fear makes being unemployed seem positively desirable.'

'Of course it is. I wish I could be!'

'No guilt-feelings?'

'I don't know anyone who's out of work who has guilt feelings, it's just a bore not having enough dosh. I'd go on the dole in a minute rather than be ground into the dust by my shitty bosses for a pittance, if I didn't have Surrey to worry about.'

Harry began to improvise a song.

'Surrey's such a worry 'cos she has to have her curry and she really makes me scurry when I'd rather stay in bed . . . '

Clem laughed with an air of surprise. He was amazed at the change in her, and often told her so. 'I never knew you could be like this, Mum.' She had never known it, either, but the trouble was, this new woman didn't know her own limits. How hard could she push herself? Was this constant tiredness just part of working life in a city, part of bringing up a child, nowadays? It had never been like this for her before, and she began to realise, grudgingly, how lucky she had been.

Once, on a Sunday when they were lying in heaps in front of TV, Clem suddenly said, 'You know there's a Catholic church just round the corner, Mum.'

'I know.'

'Why don't you ever go?'

'I'm too tired,' she said.

Of course it wasn't that. In the fairly recent past, it wouldn't have mattered how tired she was, Mass was a must. But something strange was happening to her. She wasn't sure what it was. Part of it — not all — had to do with Surrey. Something Tina had said one evening was the first really tangible clue Harriet had about what was causing her to rethink Church doctrine, reassess her own blind devotion to it.

Tina had been looking at Surrey with an odd expression in her eyes, listening noncommittally while Harry raved on about her. Suddenly she said, 'I think it's terrible to bring kids into the world without the right conditions.'

'Do you. Well, good. That means you won't.'

'Of course I won't. I actually don't think I want children.'

'You'll change your mind.'

Tina rolled her eyes. 'Oh, please! Everyone says that when you say you don't want kids. But it's perfectly logical when you look at the state the world's in. I don't think it's fair to bring kids into it just because you want them. Surrey should never have happened.'

Harry gaped. 'But then we wouldn't have her.'

'No. But how is *she* going to feel about you

378

'having' her? She's not very well-placed to have a really good life, is she? Oh, I know, you and Clem and Florence think you're going to be able to make it up to her, but I don't see how that's going to be enough.' Tina looked at Harry with her new clear-eyed, I-know-the-score look.

'How do you mean? Lots of children — '

'Oh yeah, lots of kids are mixed-race, lots of kids have only one parent, lots of kids' folks are hard up. But how many are all three? Surrey could easily grow up *deprived*. Pleasure should have had an abortion.'

This short exchange haunted Harry.

Abortion — the right thing. Because you shouldn't bring a child into the world if you couldn't give it what it needed. Could that, not preventing its birth, be the real sin? God will provide, said the Church. But it was all too obvious He very often didn't. He certainly wasn't going out of His way to help Harry and Clem not to collapse with exhaustion, or to manage on practically no money. And what *was* Surrey going to think, and ask, when she was older?

And her own, constantly-renewed joy in Surrey — was that just selfishness?

Harry was actually brooding on this one dark October evening when the doorbell ran.

She put Surrey, who had woken up and been brought into the living room for a cuddle, on her blanket on the floor. She switched on the lobby light and peered through the peephole she'd had fitted to the front door.

What she saw made her almost gag

with — what? It felt a lot like fear. Instinct caused her to switch off the light again. To hide. To not be here for this deeply unwelcome caller. But after two or three seconds of standing, tightly clenched, in the darkness, she knew it was pointless, and opened the door.

'Hallo, Pleasure,' she said in a voice that she held absolutely steady and neutral with a mammoth effort.

'Hallo, Mrs Marshall.'

Pleasure was evidently surprised, but not too surprised, to see her. They stared at each other.

Harry knew she should ask her in — knew that she would have to, and that the longer she kept her standing on the doorstep the worse it would look. But it was physically hard for her to move aside.

'Why are you here, Pleasure?' she asked at last.

Pleasure said, 'I wanted to talk to Clem.'

Bizarre. Incredible. *To talk to Clem* . . . Not 'To see my baby, please get out of my way, I want to see my baby.' Yet something deeply tense inside Harry began to loosen and she moved aside and said, as if there had been no telltale pause, 'He's at work. But come in.'

She wished Surrey were not visible, not awake. She had got herself into a sitting position, and was making talking noises, watching the advent of the newcomer with interest. She looked, to Harry's eyes, so adorable, so ineluctably *attractive* in the magnetic sense, that she could hardly believe it when Pleasure did not rush directly to her and snatch her up in her arms.

Instead Pleasure stood looking at her for quite a long time in silence, as if she were looking at a sculpture or a painting that interested her but about which she was not certain how she felt.

'She sits up now,' she said at last.

'Oh, she's been sitting up for months,' said Harry, casually and not quite truthfully.

'Does she crawl?'

'Yes, of course. Everywhere.'

'And talk?'

'She says 'Wozzat?' when you show her something new. And 'dada' of course.'

'What does she call my mum?'

'Gaga. For Granny.'

'And you?'

'She sort of says 'Rara'. It's the nearest she can come to Harry.'

'She should call you Mummy.'

Silence.

'What did you say?'

'Well, you are her mother really, aren't you?'

Harry looked at her in amazement.

'Without you she wouldn't have been born. Isn't that a definition of a mother? And you're looking after her.'

'And loving her,' said Harry.

'That's what I mean.'

Harry sat down near Surrey, and put her hand on her head. She felt something coming she wasn't going to like.

'In my thoughts,' said Pleasure slowly, 'I have to tell you, Mrs Marshall, I blame you for the whole mess. You and Clem.'

'You had no part in it, I suppose.'

'Yes, I did — of course. I was stupid. I was feeble. I should have stuck to what I knew was right for me and not let you and Mum get at me. And Clem, of course. Wanting it so much. All of you telling me that to get rid of it would be murder.' Her voice was rising. 'Well, the truth is I wish I *had* got rid of it. I might have had guilt for a little while but I wouldn't have had it for my whole messed-up life.'

'Is this what you came to tell Clem?'

'I want to be free of it. I want to get on with my life. I don't want to cry all the time. I'm not crying for my baby, don't think it! I don't miss her, I don't want her! *And I don't want her to want me!* I suppose you think that's completely disgusting and unnatural?'

'Shh, Pleasure, don't, you'll upset Surrey.'

'I'll upset Surrey? What about Surrey upsetting me? She ruins my peace every single minute even when I'm asleep! I'm thinking why did I do it, why did I do it, she's here forever now and I'll always have to be thinking about her and feeling bad about her. It's a life sentence! I'll never have any true freedom or peace again and I can't bear it!'

She broke down and turned away, trying to control emotions that were obviously beyond control.

Harry, in her first reaction, did think her 'disgusting and unnatural'. But as she looked at the sobbing figure and sensed the depths of her despair, a sense of personal guilt ousted any criticism of Pleasure.

Yes, it was perfectly true. She, with Florence, with Clem, had ganged up on Pleasure. They had caught her at an intensely vulnerable moment — the most vulnerable moment in a woman's life — and coerced her, bullied her, leant on her until she changed her strongest intention. The intention to do what was right *for her*, for her situation, for her capacities, for the stage she had reached. Perhaps, as Tina had said, even right for the little nubbin of flesh in her womb.

Harry had been so sure she was doing the right thing! And what had made her sure? Was it an inkling of what this little creature would be like when she was born, how passionately she would love her? No, it wasn't that. Harriet had not wanted the baby to be born, either, if she remembered correctly.

She had done it because the Church had told her to. Because Abortion Was Wrong. Full stop. No thinking, no need to weigh pros and cons, no need for decisions, for empathy, for imaginative forward-looking into Pleasure's probable future, or Surrey's either. No need for any of those hard things! Because of course, God and mother-love would take care of all that. Everything would come right if only she obeyed the Church's arbitrary rules. The rules that seemed merciful to the foetus, but were in fact completely pitiless in their rigidity, to the foetus and everyone else.

And this realisation, quite abruptly come by, was not such a shock, after all. The Church — arbitrary and wrong? Was not this the very bedrock of Harry's life shaking and crumbling?

But this wasn't the bedrock. There was firmer stuff under that religious layer, which had been melting away for quite a long time now, perhaps since she had shouted at Mr Radley: 'I seem to have joined the wrong religion!' It had been a cry of defiance, but it had come out of a deeper place than she had realised. Her stuck-on Catholicism had already started sloughing off her, even then.

She was staring at Pleasure with the deepest pity. Poor little thing! If you couldn't help loving, how could you help *not* loving? Harry got up and took her in her arms.

'Don't. Don't. You don't have to feel so bad. You're right. We made you do it and now we've taken over. She's our responsibility now. We'll look after her. You are free, Pleasure. Free to try to be free, anyway.'

'I can't! I can't!' sobbed Pleasure despairingly. 'Look at her. She's mine, my own flesh and blood, she even looks like me, and I can't feel anything for her except resentment and guilt. What's wrong with me, what's wrong with me? No wonder Mum hates me!'

'She doesn't hate you.'

'She does. I've broken her laws. She'll never forgive me. I miss her so much! Much more than I miss — '

'Do you miss Clem?'

'Only in lonely moments. He was too young for me. I wasn't ready for all this, nobody consulted me, it all just happened. I didn't have any *choice*.'

Harry forbore to contradict. She held the

sobbing girl until she grew calmer. Then she said, 'Listen, Pleasure. Surrey's not going to call me Mummy. What would be best is if you keep in touch, if you come to see her sometimes. Then when the time's right we can explain things.'

'How? How can you explain that I — that I didn't want her?'

'We are definitely *not* going to tell her that,' said Harry.

'What then?'

Harry held Pleasure away by the shoulders and looked at her. Clem was right. She was beautiful. Her cropped head had a classic African look. Her skin was silky brown, two shades darker than her daughter's, three shades lighter than her mother's. Her eyes were glossy sloes swimming in brine. Her trim, sexy little body deserved better than to be racked with anguish for the child it had so unwillingly produced. But what Harry saw, primarily, was this lovely creature whose blood ran in the veins of her grandchild, who might grow up to be as exquisite, as sensitive, and also, if they didn't watch out, as confused and wretched as this.

Some of the instinctive protectiveness that sprang up in Harry every time she looked at Surrey, spilled over onto Pleasure.

'We'll tell her that her mother is the best she was able to be and that if Surrey feels like complaining, she should first show she can do better. How's that?'

Pleasure stared at her for a moment, and

then wiped her eyes with the pale palms of her hands.

'Awful,' she said. 'I'll have to think of something else.'

'Then you will come and see her?'

'I don't want her to think I deserted her completely. Only — I know myself — I can't come regularly. Just sometimes. Is that better than nothing, Mrs Marshall?'

A sometimes mother. Was it better than nothing? Quite possibly not; it might even be worse. Harry didn't know. And she had nothing to guide her, now, but the need to protect Surrey and comfort Pleasure. Perhaps, after all, that was as good a guide as any.

'Yes,' said Harry firmly. 'Much better.'

26

On the first of October, which had begun as a beautiful day of sunshine with a hint of crispness, George trailed home from the first hunt of the season feeling rotten.

He was riding a big bay hunter that he had bought himself partly with the profits from his first sale of lambs. He'd done well in his first year, chiefly because the flock he'd bought at auction had proved that he hadn't lost his touch in choosing the best. His ewes had, in due course, presented him with fifteen sets of twins, eight of triplets, nearly eighty lambs altogether, all but three successfully reared. The land here was sweet, wonderful grazing, and his new lambing-barn and buying-in of winter feed had worked out fine. The local man he'd taken on to help with the lambing had been first class and was now a friend.

He wished Derek could have been around, that was all. But he was, in a way. George talked to his dead brother in his head sometimes when he was working. He 'called him in' to help pick his two breeding rams: 'Not that bugger, George, his back's not straight. Look, that one over there, beautiful back legs, jump for you all day long — that's you manny!' He'd said much the same about the horse, using 'jump' in a different sense.

But for all this, George was in a bad mood

now. The day he had looked forward to, his first with the local hunt that he had spent a fortune to join, had gone all wrong.

The hunt saboteurs had been out in force with their banners and their city voices shouting their ignorant slogans . . . Bloody fools. In their besotted care for a few predatory foxes, did they know how many farmers would go out with their guns, poisons and traps instead as the foxes proliferated, threatening their livestock? Nothing sporting about that!

But they were determined and they were ruthless. They'd followed the hunt for miles, or else new groups had been lurking in ambush, rushing across fields with howls like Yahoos, deflecting the hounds. In the end one of them had leapt out from beside a gate George was jumping, causing his horse to shy as it landed. George had come off heavily, half-in, half-out of a ditch. The saboteur — a thin, lank-haired young man in a battle-jacket — had stood above him, screaming with laughter.

George got to his feet slowly, black with mud and fury, and to his own dismay found himself threatening the man with his crop. He was soaked, his breeches were ripped, his hip and thigh were heavily bruised, and the horse, though it had come to no harm, was hanging its head and blowing hard as if it thought it was to blame. The sab ran off, calling shrill Cockney insults over his shoulder. The day was ruined. George remounted with difficulty and headed home.

It was a long way. The sun went in; a thin

rain began to fall. George felt his thigh beginning to throb and stiffen. He was disappointed, angry and miserable. Was this going to happen every time they went out? In which case, why had he spent two thousand pounds on a heavy hunter? There wouldn't be any point in buying horses like this, or even breeding them, if these ruddy sabs got their way.

As he passed Ken's place, going up the lane towards Bugle, he saw what he saw rather often — the Brittans' BMW parked outside the gate. George more or less guessed what was going on. He was no gossip, but it was hard to avoid taking an interest in people's private lives when you lived in a place like this.

He mused on the ironical fact that Boofer Brittan, unlike her husband, was no racist, and would sooner or later probably tell Ken he had overreacted about that little half-and-half that everyone else was so daft about. Couldn't blame them really — George'd seen Surrey for himself and she was a right bonny little thing. He'd given her a cuddle and felt her magic, a sad magic for him. All those ruddy lambs popping out, easy as shelling peas, while his poor little mite had come out dead. She'd have been a grown lass by now, and happen him a grandad. He'd have liked that.

And here was this youngster, Clem, a father by accident at nineteen, having to bring the bairn up with just the grandmas to help him, unless he found a new 'partner', of course. Judy said he was seeing Tina — nothing serious, just playmates. Couldn't be anything else, really, they were still just kids themselves. Nowt so funny as folk.

It was strange to George, all of it, but not boring. In each case, in his present mood of unaccustomed self-pity, there was something he could find to envy. Even Ken — though not if Joker Brittan, with his choleric temper, his shotgun and his Army background, found out — even Ken had his arms full right now, while George was heading home to an empty house.

He dismounted to try to 'oil' his leg a little. It hurt like hell. Limping heavily, he toiled on up the lane and in through his own gate, no longer hanging off its hinges but spanking white and with a brand new latch. He took his horse to the stable-block and saw to him, removing his tack, rubbing him down, and putting a new haynet into his loosebox and a scoop of oats into the corner feeding-bowl. He was thinking with gloom about his own dinner. He quite liked cooking, but it was the last thing he felt like doing now. What he felt like was a long hot bath with some of Judy's Radox and the sort of dinner Judy cooked, when she was here: a spicy casserole, two or three veg and a hot pudding, and then bed, with her, not alone as he would be, with her thousands of miles away . . . *Oh, bugger it all*.

But when he limped into the house through the back entrance, the most delicious smell came out to meet him. He stopped, incredulous.

'Judy?' he bellowed.

She came running. He thought her the most loveliest thing he'd ever seen in his life. He grabbed her and kissed her. His bruises, his anger and his disappointment were all forgotten. He breathed in the smell of her hair along with that of beef stew and wanted to let out a roar of simple, animal happiness.

'How did you get here?'

'Plane. Tube. Train. Taxi.'

'I thought you were in Durban,' he said dazedly.

'I was. I left.'

'So soon? Was it that bad?'

Judy didn't answer at once. She was holding him tight, kissing him through the mud. Zulu was jumping about barking a welcome. Then she stood back a little and looked him over. 'What's happened to *you*? Don't tell me — you've been hunting.'

He wrily showed her his grass- and mud-stained side. He expected her to say 'Serve you right,' but she didn't. He hugged her again.

Over her shoulder he saw something that gave him pause. At the foot of the back stairs were two big suitcases, as much as she could possibly have carried by herself — not the usual here-today-gone-tomorrow hand luggage. He released her, staring.

'What's all that?'

'I came straight from the airport. To stay. D'you mind?'

He gazed at her. 'Mind? Of course I don't mind. But what's going on?'

'I haven't just left South Africa. I've left London.'

'For good?'

'More or less.'

'What about the flat?'

'Harry took it over when I left for SA. I'm sure it's much happier with her in it.'

'What about your job?'

'Harry took that over, too. Not that I'd wish it on my worst enemy, but she needed the money.'

'And your work on the picket?'

'The picket's stopped.'

'What, stopped altogether?'

'We kept it going part-time for the other prisoners. Now things are changing so fast, most of them have been released, there are going to be proper, democratic elections — that fight's won.'

He stared at her, and then a slow smile spread over his face.

'Let me get this right. You're going to be living with me from now on — full-time? I mean — we're a couple?'

'I think the word now is, an item. Yeah, man. That's the idea.'

'Well, I'll be buggered!'

'Ach! Not while I'm around.'

★ ★ ★

Over dinner — she must've stopped off in the village and loaded the taxi with food, God, after that endless journey, she must be half-dead, but she didn't look it — he asked again about Durban. She'd gone off in such a gung-ho mood, the minute her banning-order was lifted;

392

she'd spoken about it always as 'going home'. He'd more than half-expected never to see her again.

'It's gone, the town I knew. I hardly recognised it.'

'What do you mean? Have the black — people — taken it over or what?'

She laughed in an odd, rueful way. 'No. No, that's not what's happened. But it's completely different, all the same. A lot of my aunts and uncles and the older people we knew have died Others have run away. The rest of the whites are living a sort of besieged existence, except that there's no real siege. It's in their heads.'

'Did you stay with your mother? What was that like?'

'Bad.' She dished him out seconds. She wasn't eating much herself, he noticed. 'The white district is called Thekwini. My whole extended family used to live there — my mother still does. Yes, I stayed with her — where else? God, it was terrible! All their big houses, the ones that aren't up for sale, with their double and triple garages and tennis-courts and swimming pools on one-acre plots — they have high walls or huge iron fences around them, all wired up and with heat-triggered floodlights. The security firms are doing a roaring trade. But open those prison gates and walk out in to the treelined beautiful streets, and it's dead. You don't see any people at all. The chief noise in Thekwini — the only noise, it seemed to me, the only sign of life outdoors — is barking dogs. Big, fierce ones.'

'Isn't there some other part of town?'

'Oh, there are lots of parts. The town is enormous now; all the little homely shops and even the big ones I remember are gone. It's all built-up, up and up — high-rise blocks of flats and offices, shopping malls, all the trappings of civilisation.'

She leant back and lit a cigarette, her eyes narrowed, looking through the smoke to her lost city. George knew how much she had missed it, all the years, and tried to gauge how much it must have hurt to find it all changed, no matter how much she'd disapproved of it before. He suddenly wondered if his moorland farmhouse was still there, and tried to imagine it demolished, replaced, the farm built over . . . He would mind. When your childhood home has been wiped away by time, you must feel your past has been stolen.

'If I were Asian,' Judy was musing, 'I might be able to think of going back there. The Indian area is bustling. They have their own world, a mix of classes and of rich and poor, and it's a community, sociable and unscared. *They're* not afraid to come out of their houses and walk the streets. They're well-rooted, confident, not to be moved. Their part of the city is full of life and noise and I liked being there, but I didn't belong, of course. I didn't actually belong anywhere.'

'What about the Blacks? I suppose the Whites have to do their own housework and factory work now. Blackwork become white-work.'

She smiled lopsidedly. 'You must be joking. You think the new democracy has changed the Blacks' lives for the better? The domestic workers are still living in one-room shacks at the bottom of the gardens — the very bottom, as far from the big houses as possible. I visited my mother's servants' quarters. They still haven't got proper floors or ceilings, or light or heat, or kitchens or bathrooms or *anything*. I had this row to end all rows with my mother about it. As to the work, there are fleets of buses and taxis to bring the industrial workers into the city at dawn and take them back at dusk. I kept wondering if they see their children's faces in daylight any oftener than they ever did. That's something that hasn't changed, that I wish had.'

'But why? Can't they live a better, freer life now?'

'You can't eat freedom. In SA any more than in Eastern Europe. That's something all we revolutionaries are having to learn.'

George was chewing his beef, watching her with thoughtful, tender eyes. He was thinking how avidly she had talked about returning to her native place, now she was allowed to, to 'help', to 'build', to be part of the New Age. He wouldn't ask, he wouldn't poke her wounds by asking what had happened about that. But she answered his unspoken question by herself.

'Tina was right.'

'About what?'

'About how superfluous we Whites are in a Black country. Oh, not economically, unfortunately, but — I don't know how to say it — we're just an irrelevance to their proper development. Worst than that, we're a distorting factor. They don't want us exiles back

395

with our eager-beaver desire to help them. They want us out, and although they 'need' Whites, as long as we're there black Africans will never be able to normalise their country. Three weeks was enough to show me that what they most need from us is our space.'

'You might be able to affect things.'

'How?'

'Get your mother to give her servants better conditions, for a start.'

Judy lit another cigarette from the stub of the last. 'She won't. She insists they wouldn't want them, that if she turned that shack into a proper home it would set them apart from 'their kind', make them too comfortable, make them not want to work any more. I tried to persuade her to leave, to come here, but she just laughed and said, 'What, and live in a hotel again with a wardrobe full of co-ordinating umbrellas and have no one to play bridge with?' I tell you, George, there is *nothing* for me to do there. Even politically. That's not a pretty picture either. Who was it who said, 'When the despots go down, the scumbags rise to the top?' You can't imagine the sort that are gathering around Mandela now, people who've betrayed every principle we fought for. And he hasn't even got Winnie to help him. I will never,' she added fiercely, '*ever* believe the things they're saying about that wonderful woman!'

George held his tongue, quite literally between his teeth.

But after the apple and blackberry crumble and clotted cream, it came loose.

'Are you still a Communist?' George heard himself ask suddenly.

There was a long silence. Then she stirred, put out her cigarette and said flatly, 'Probably. You can't dig out your own bones. But I don't want to call myself that; I want to de-label myself. I think that's why I want to be with you. If I were with a comrade, I wouldn't be able to do that.'

Later, when, full of good food and contentment, he was getting ready for bed and Judy was unpacking, George watched her carefully extract a framed poster from her suitcase and hang it on an empty nail on the wall opposite the bed. It was a different photo, one taken recently. Of course there was no problem of identification this time.

'Oh, so you brought Nelson with you?'

'Yes.'

'I have to share my bedroom with him, do I? Make love to you with him looking on?'

'Yes.'

'Good luck to him, he'll need it. Our bedroom's the most comfortable place he's likely to find himself in for the next few years.'

In bed, he almost hugged the breath out of her. 'I'm so glad you coom home to me. I wish I had words to tell you. I'm going to make damn sure you stay and are happy with me. I'll even give up hunting if you like,' he added heroically.

★ ★ ★

Lovemaking made George sleepy. It had the opposite effect on Judy.

While her lover, his big, warm body fitting snugly against hers from behind, breathed deeply and steadily, Judy lay wide awake in the dark. It was the darkest dark she had ever experienced. In Brixton — in Durban — streetlamps, bright-windowed buildings and reflected car headlights, the constant day-in-night of the city, had provided a varied pattern of light which, by contrast, made the total absence of it in the country disquieting. Frightening, almost. When Judy had confessed this to George early on, he had taken her out and shown her the astounding myriads of stars that hung over the uncompeting farm, whose numbers and brilliance she had not seen for years. She saw the Milky Way for the first time since childhood — when it had stretched above her in the Southern sky like a vast etheric twist of voile, with a mysterious hole torn in it — and stood in the silence, staring upward. George's hand in hers, reassured, enchanted and consoled.

But this consolation deserted her now.

The line of tall spruce trees outside blocked off starlight, and her wide-open eyes could barely discern the oblong outline of the window. Even with George's arm around her, the blackness and silence were engulfing and oppressive. Perhaps, she thought, because they reflected a blackness and silence within her.

She carefully identified all the sources that should give her well-being. She was warm, satiated, companioned and safe. She need never — until she chose, or until death intervened — be alone again. A part of her had craved this for a very long time. It meant that the pain of all the lost battles would be muffled. What was wrong, then? Why did she suddenly feel so hollow, so *deprived*?

She didn't even have to formulate the question fully. The answer lay there, curled up and deadly as an unborn cobra in its egg.

Warmth, comfort and safety — even the presence of a loved one — were no substitute for real living and real feeling, which, for Judy, meant participation, commitment and struggle. Without those, she would dwindle to the condition almost of an animal that instinctively seeks only a mate, a warm secure lair, a full belly. The ultimate bliss, beyond which no goals exist.

Judy had always felt set apart from people who were animal-like in that way, who lived on that simple, selfish level, committed only to their own creature needs. Harry had been like that; but no longer. She had joined the struggle — not Judy's of course, but her own. After forty years of being spoilt, protected and privileged, she had found her cause and become a live-er, a do-er, a fighter. She was on the frontline. While Judy felt herself, in the midst of her happiness and relief, defeated and pushed to the margin. *Her* fight was over.

It was a fearful thought. Was she to blame, as Abby had hinted? Was she just too weak to stick to her guns? Abby would never quit. But then Abby didn't know when the battle was lost.

Judy put her hand over George's as it lay on her breast. It felt good, but not right. Something so safe and protective could never feel right. The hand was like a barricade, with Judy crouched in its lee.

Her thoughts flew to Jordan. He would never have let her come to this. He would have kept her on the barricades, even against all common sense — he would have needed to. If he ever came back, he would rouse and challenge her again, if by then her fighting spirit had not completely withered away. Where would her loyalties lie then?

She must try not to think of him any more. She had made her choice. She must live this happy half-life now, and forget the rest. It was the way of the new world.

Epilogue

Jordan Priestman sat in his room in a rundown but respectable guest-house in Trivandrum, smoking a *beedi* and reading a letter.

He was forty-nine years old, but looked ten years more than that. His tall thin frame was slightly stooped, his once-black hair now reduced to a thick fringe of grey round the sides and back of his head. He wore old shorts and a washed-out shirt, both freshly returned by the *dhobi-wallah*, and a pair of ancient sandals.

For fifteen years, ever since his arrest and what followed it, Jordan had been moving about, never settling anywhere for long. Mainly he had stayed in Europe, with a preference for Eastern Europe before the fall of the Berlin Wall, and now he was in India where the living was cheap. He had used up every penny he'd managed to save, or could borrow, to get here.

Money had always been a problem. It had been impossible, since he left South Africa, to practise law in any regular way, though sometimes he gave advice and sometimes even got paid for it. For the rest, he did whatever came to hand. Freelance journalism was a useful option, and he did this in several countries under a variety of pseudonyms. Once he ran an obscure left-wing bookshop in Paris for several years.

401

That was the nearest he'd got to London, and the most uncomfortable he'd ever been.

Apart from that, it hadn't been so bad. He was a natural soldier of fortune. He chafed chiefly at the shapelessness of his life, the lack of any cutting-edge political component, the fact that the world — his world, and especially his country — was proceeding without him, times and events washing over him, leaving him rolling uselessly under their waves. He didn't mind the hardships, or even the loneliness. In fact, they helped with the guilt.

He minded the guilt. But he found out that there's a device built in to everyone's head to deal with guilt. Jordan's worked by telling him he had paid: with exile, with the loss of his wife and child, the loss of his profession, comrades, his purpose in life. He did not betray his political creed (though in some locations he had to keep quiet about it) and he did not become, even to a minor extent, a law-breaker. His integrity, broken once, remained in its original shards. It was not broken further.

He stayed out of sight because he assumed he was still on some people's wanted list. Judy wrote several times that she thought few, if any, even of those he had named, were after him. But the need he felt to keep his head down gave him — though he would never have acknowledged it, even to himself — a perversely desired sense of the importance of what he had done. If it was not important, if it was now forgotten, then the past fifteen years had been meaningless.

He kept in touch with Judy out of duty,

now, more than anything. He wrote on the assumption that she needed his letters. Judy's to him, picked up habitually from whatever poste restante address he had given her and answered when he had something safely neutral to write, meant very little to him any more; in fact, her continuing political activities — the chief subject of her letters for some years now — troubled him in a deep place. *She* was still part of the struggle.

But he loved Tina's letters. He still loved Tina; he loved what he had bred into her of instinctive dissent. He would read every letter several times, longing for little intimacies that were seldom there, look long at the snaps she sometimes sent, and then stand them up around whatever shabby lodging-room he was occupying, little coloured windows into a different world. To his occasional visitors he would say, 'Did you notice my beautiful daughter?' Sometimes he had secret fantasies of meeting her in the street, knocking on her door, telephoning her — not always telling her who he was. In his more dramatic moments he even fantasised about saving her life, having her thank him tearfully and when he announced his identity, fling herself into his arms. In these fantasies he tried hard not to end melodramatically, Hollywoodishly, with her crying, 'Daddy! Daddy!' But in his rare moments of weakness and sentiment, she sometimes did.

He always kept one photo in his wallet, a token of what he had forfeited. Sometimes he looked at the photo not for pleasure, but to punish himself.

When, months ago, Judy had written and told him she had 'found someone she wanted to live with', Jordan's first reaction was relief. This had surprised him. He never expected the best of himself any more. He himself was too conscious of his fugitive status, and his self-respect was too low, to ever get seriously involved with a woman; he had lived all these nomadic years essentially alone. So, surely, jealousy or resentment might have been his natural reaction. But when the first small shock was absorbed, he was glad. That she had found someone at last took a weight off him that he hardly realised he had been carrying.

It never occurred to him that her writing such a letter was an unusual thing for a woman to do. Complete honesty in all important things was part of the creed they had shared — it was that which had impelled him to tell her the truth immediately they had let him out of prison. Before he had even greeted her, while she was still staring in horror at his bruised and swollen face he had told her: 'They broke me. They broke me easily. I ratted.' How could things ever be the same after that? She did her best, but they were both secretly convinced that the police would never have broken *her*.

When Mandela was released, and the logjam that was South African politics began to break up, Jordan felt a strong frisson of excitement. He foresaw, almost at once, that this radical change might result in an amnesty, official or unofficial, for people like him. Perhaps, in the new South Africa, some lines would be drawn under the past. Perhaps, sometime soon, he would be able to — dare he think of it? — go home. Though he had stopped dreaming of his wife, he had never stopped dreaming of South Africa.

And now this unexpected letter had come.

Dear Mr Priestman,

We've never met, but maybe Judy's mentioned me. I've been her friend and comrade on the picket since it began. I'm a South African exile, like her, though I'm from Joburg. My name's Abby Brown.

As you may know, Judy went back to Durban a few weeks ago, but I heard from her today that she's planning to return to Britain. I got a shock, but I can't believe she's actually coming back here for good. I know she's been through a political crisis, like a lot of people, but I am certain that she is still staunch in the struggle. Judy will never give up. And the place to wage the struggle now for people like us is definitely in SA.

If Judy's banning order was lifted, yours will be too. I think it's quite safe now for you to come back into the mainstream. The word is out that even people who committed every horrible crime in the book under the Nationalists stand a chance of being rehabilitated and forgiven, so someone in your position has absolutely nothing to worry about.

We have to rebuild the Party in the new SA and make sure that the Mandela government, when we have one, will move in that direction. I needn't tell you how things have degenerated, including in the ANC and the SACP, in the bad years. Apart from Nelson himself, you just don't know who to trust. Even Winnie is tainted now, and some of the people around Nelson are very dubious; one fears their influence on him. I feel strongly that people whose politics are sound should stick together and try to overcome the past. I'm going as soon as I can sell my flat and wind things up here.

In case you're wondering why I am writing this (or how I got your address — I'm afraid I pinched it from Judy's desk some time ago) I will explain when we meet. I urge you to come back and stand at Judy's side. That will give her the strength she needs now. Let me know if there's anything I can do. Money for instance. I'd be very glad to help.

Yours in comradeship,
Abby Brown.

PS You know that Judy took a lover, but you shouldn't let that stand in your way. It was an any-port-in-a-storm thing. They've got nothing in common. She'd never have gone back to SA if there'd been anything in it, and I'm sure her coming back now has nothing to do with him. In spirit I know that she's been utterly faithful to you.

Jordan sat over this letter for a long time. At last he got up, stiff from sitting too long on the hard wooden stool. He remembered his friend Jeremy Rosenberg, a partner in the law firm in Durban, saying, 'Your trouble is, you got no *sitzfleisch*, Jordan! Maybe if you had more to sit on, you wouldn't run around so much and get into so much trouble.'

He went into his dingy, grey-tiled 'bathroom', ran water from the single tap into his tin basin and washed the latest layer of sweat off his face, neck and arms. He examined his chin in the frameless mirror, smoothed his remaining hair and went out on to the sunbeaten concrete walkway that fronted his room. He didn't bother affixing the large padlock to his door. One heard a lot about thievery but he didn't credit it, not among these gentle, self-sufficient, leftwing southerners. His need was to trust them. Anyway, what did he have worth taking? Only his battered old portable, which he kept under the bed. What little else he had of the slightest value — his watch, his passport and a few rupees — he carried with him.

He'd managed to get a job teaching English at a local private 'English Medium' school. The salary was so meagre the job was virtually voluntary, but the school paid for his room, his laundry and his lunches. He needed very little else. And he liked the work, though he often felt that teaching English to these children, relatively untrammelled so far by western influences, might in a small way be invidious. What did they need English for in Kerala, where the Western rat-race seemed so blessedly far removed?

Now he walked down the steps and out into the crowded, dazzling street in search of a brief change of scene. It was incredibly hot. That was the one bad thing here, but the sea was at hand. He often took the jam-packed public bus to Kovalam beach after his day's teaching, swam and lay on the greyish sand, ignoring the cloth-sellers and other touts as well as the awful girls from northern Europe who saw nothing wrong with taking most of their clothes off in front of the young Dravidian men, who far from ogling them, averted their eyes in embarrassment. Here, among the foreign pederasts who gathered young boys around them on the beach, and the backpackers who trailed about looking grubby, sweaty and unkempt, wholly unaware of the contrast they made with the locals in their beautiful saris, combed and beflowered hair or freshly-ironed shirts, Jordan sometimes wondered if he ever wanted to return to the civilisation that had bred such brash, ugly-spirited, insensitive people.

Across the street, high up on the side of one of the jumble of buildings, was a large permanent 'poster'. It showed, in red on white, crude but recognisable representations of three male heads, each many feet high: one broad-cheeked and bearded, one bald with a goatee, the other heavy, with thick hair and a big moustache.

Jordan wondered how many of the multitude continually passing below, even the Communists, could name these representatives of Communist iconography, or knew that for years now they had been discredited everywhere but here. Kerala was like an island where dropout soldiers lived, not knowing the war on the mainland had been lost. He could never look at this bizarre token of outdated ideology without a sense of bitter disappointment.

He bought tea at a stall, watching with muted pleasure the *chaiwallah* pouring it from a brass pot into the tiny glass. He thought about food. The only cooked food he could afford was rather sloppy vegetarian *thalis* on partitioned tin trays. He disliked eating with his fingers, yet to eat with a fork seemed to set him apart. He bought a couple of slices of fresh pineapple instead, and sat down on a wall that held the roots of an enormous peepul tree. He munched the fruit with relish, swallowed a mouthful of the syrupy tea, then took out the letter again.

Abby Brown. Yes, the name rang a bell. Everyone Judy mentioned in her letters except Tina was a name without a face, one-dimensional, meaning nothing to him. But now here was this woman, part of Judy's world, who clearly had designs of some sort on him.

What was her game? 'I'll explain when I see you . . . ' Explain what?

She wanted him back in Judy's life. She wanted them both in South Africa, where she was going.

Was there something fishy here? Possibly dangerous?

The stuff about the corruption of the ANC was very disturbing. Nothing worse than your own side behaving badly. Now when things should be coming right, all that shit, all that mess — clawing for advancement and prestige, cover-ups for the blunders and cruelties of the past, betrayals within betrayals . . . At least his betrayal had been a thing of the flesh. Not for money or revenge or power. The thought of people who could do that *now*, when so much was at stake, made his soul shudder.

He drank his *chai*, frowning. Here was an invitation to come back into the mainstream. He wanted that, didn't he? Or did he?

Life, ironically, was remarkably simple when you had been in hiding for so many years that the difficulties and drawbacks had become routine. Now, to barge back into the life of his family . . . To find, almost certainly, that there was no niche for him, that they *didn't want him*, that he was an intruder. That he was being manipulated by some Abby Brown who had her own agenda. It must be important for her to hint that she would bankroll him.

He sighed, rose, and went back to the tea stall to return the glass. There was no bin for the pineapple crusts, which joined others of their kind in the kaleidoscopic gutter. Gutters in this poorest state in India demonstrated paradoxical plenty, bright with fresh fruit-skins, the bounty of nature, affordable by all. Thanks in part to the Indian Communist Party, few were truly poor in Kerala, or caste-ridden, or illiterate. Here, if nowhere else in the world, one could continue to cherish some faith in the Party. But here the Party hadn't even been sensible — or ruthless — enough to make sure they couldn't be voted out of power! What would Stalin, still dominating the main street, have to say about that? Or Abby Brown. Or Judy?

Judy. His intense, passionate, doctrinaire Judy, full of fight to the bitter end, not even knowing the end had come. She probably still had Marx and Lenin on her wall too! Judy would never give up, never allow doubts to weaken her, never turn away with a shrug or take the easy path. Oh irony . . . Perhaps it was his memories of her as the eternal, unshakable comrade that had made him stay away so long. Once he had been her mentor. Now he knew he couldn't match her. His own certainties had long since broken down, his ideology become rat-eaten by reality. Could he face her blazing, naive, *transcendent* certainty? Could he face it and tell her, as he had once told her that the interrogators had broken him, that life had changed him so that he was no longer sure of anything, and never would be again? That he had become the thing they had both despised — a liberal?

He found his face twisting into a wry smile at this extraordinary realisation.

As Jordan was crossing the teeming space between the tea stall and his lodgings holding the unfolded letter in his fingers, he paused.

He saw himself arriving back in cold grey Tory England, which Judy had once, after one of her arrests, described bitterly as 'this green unpleasant land', with its built-in hypocrisy and willful ignorance of the way things were run to protect the powerful, the horrible degrading contrast between those with power and those without. He thought of what was likely to happen in South Africa, the bloodletting and the mayhem that he felt sure was going to be the price of any transfer of power. He reflected for the thousandth time on the fight he had lost against his body and his interrogators, and his disgrace, a disgrace he didn't know if he could ever live down if he went back . . .

He thought of Tina.

She didn't know the truth about him, and if he went to London, he would have to tell her. He would have to tell her everything, to justify himself — stain her young mind not merely with the things that had been done to him, but with the clear realisation of the damage he had caused to others. She would not cry 'Daddy, Daddy!' and fling her arms around him then. She would lift them, in instinctive self-protection, to keep him at a distance.

He turned away with an involuntary clenching of his innards. No. Not now. And if not now, almost certainly never. He tried to tell himself this in terms of face-saving philosophy. *The young ought to be allowed their illusions. The old, their failures and shames. The middle-aged, their right to hide their faces, or to begin afresh* . . . But it was really, he knew, just old-fashioned cowardice and inertia after all.

He tore the letter from Abby into small fragments and let them fall among the orange mango-stones and the green shells of drinking coconuts, and went home to prepare his lessons for next day.

LEGACIES
Janet Dailey

The sequel to THE PROUD AND THE FREE. It is twenty years since the feud within his family began, but Lije Stuart, son of the Cherokee chief The Blade, had never forgotten the killing of his grandfather. Now, a promising legal career beckons, and also the love of his childhood sweetheart, Diane Parmalee, the daughter of a US Army officer. Yet as it reawakens, their love is beset by the beginning of civil war.

'L' IS FOR LAWLESS
Sue Grafton

World War II fighter pilot Johnny Lee had died and his grandson was trying to claim military funeral benefits, but none of the authorities have any record of Fighter J. Lee. Was the old man once a US spy? When PI Kinsey Millhone is asked to straighten things out, she finds herself pursued by a psychopath bearing a forty-year-old grudge . . .

BLOOD LINES
Ruth Rendell

This is a collection of long and short stories by Ruth Rendell that will linger in the mind.

THE SUN IN GLORY
Harriet Hudson

When industrialist William Potts sets himself to build a flying machine, his adopted daughter, Rosie, works through the years as his mechanic. In 1906 Pegasus is almost ready, and onto the scene comes Jake Smith, a man who has as deep a love of the air as Rosie herself. But Jake sparks off a deadly rivalry, and the triumph of flight twists into tragedy.

A WOMAN SCORNED
M. R. O'Donnell

Five years after the tragedy that ruined her fifteenth birthday, Judith Carty returns to Castle Moore and resumes her flirtation with its heir, Rick Bellingham. The tragic events of the past forge a special bond between the young couple, but there are those who have a vested interest in the failure of the romance.

PLAINER STILL
Catherine Cookson

Following the success of her previous collection of essays and poems, LET ME MAKE MYSELF PLAIN, Catherine Cookson has compiled a further selection of thoughts, recollections, and observations on life — and death — together with another collection of the poems she prefers to describe as 'prose on short lines'.

THE LOST WORLD
Michael Crichton
The successor to JURASSIC PARK.
It is now six years since the secret disaster
of Jurassic Park, when that extraordinary
dream of science and imagination came to
a crashing end — the dinosaurs destroyed,
and the park dismantled. There are rumours
that something has survived . . .

MORNING, NOON & NIGHT
Sidney Sheldon
When Harry Stanford, one of the wealthiest
men in the world, mysteriously drowns, it
sets off a chain of events that reverberates
around the globe. At the family gathering
following the funeral, a beautiful young
woman appears, claiming to be Harry's
daughter. Is she genuine, or is she an
impostor?

FACING THE MUSIC
Jayne Torvill and Christopher Dean
The world's most successful and popular
skating couple tell their own story, from their
working-class childhoods in Nottingham to
world stardom. Finally, they describe how
they created their own show, FACE THE
MUSIC, with a superb corps of international
ice dancers.

ORANGES AND LEMONS
Jeanne Whitmee

When Shirley Rayner is evacuated from London's East End, she finds herself billeted with the theatre's most romantic couple, Tony and Leonie Darrent. She becomes firm friends with their daughter, Imogen, and the two girls dream of making their names on the stage. But they have forgotten the very different backgrounds from which they come.

HALF HIDDEN
Emma Blair

Holly Morgan, a nurse in a hospital on Nazi-occupied Jersey, falls in love with a young German doctor, Peter Schmidt, and is racked by guilt. Can their love survive the future together or will the war destroy all their hopes and dreams?

THE GREAT TRAIN ROBBERY
Michael Crichton

In Victorian London, where lavish wealth and appalling poverty exist side by side, one man navigates both worlds with ease. Rich, handsome and ingenious, Edward Pierce preys on the most prominent of the well-to-do as he cunningly orchestrates the crime of his century.

THIS CHILD IS MINE
Henry Denker

Lori Adams, a young, unmarried actress, gives up her baby boy for adoption with great reluctance. She feels that she and the baby's father, Brett, are not in a position to provide their child with all he deserves. But when, two years later, life has improved dramatically for Lori and Brett, they want their child returned . . .

THE LOST DAUGHTERS
Jeanne Whitmee

At school, Cathy and Rosalind have one thing in common: each is the child of a single parent. For them both, the transition to adulthood is far from easy — until their unexpected reunion. Working together, the two friends take a bold step that will help them to become independent women.

THE DEVIL YOU KNOW
Josephine Cox

When Sonny Fareham overhears a private conversation between her lover and his wife, she realises she is in great danger. Shocked and afraid, she flees to the north of England to make a new life — but never far away is the one person who wants to destroy everything that she now holds dear.

A LETHAL INVOLVEMENT
Clive Egleton

When Captain Simon Oakham of the Royal Army pay Corps goes A.W.O.L. immediately after a suspicious interview with the security service, Peter Ashton is asked to track him down. The key to it all is an embittered woman whose unsuspecting knowledge of a lethal involvement makes her especially vulnerable.

THE WAY WE WERE
Marie Joseph

This is a collection of some of Marie Joseph's most outstanding short stories, and is the companion volume to WHEN LOVE WAS LIKE THAT. With compassion, insight and humour, these stories explore the themes of love — its hopes, joys, disappointments and reconciliations.

EXTREME DENIAL
David Morrell

When CIA agent Stephen Decker is sent on a sensitive mission to Italy, his partner is Brian McKittrick, the incompetent and embittered son of the former chairman of the National Security Council. Disobeying orders throughout the mission, McKittrick makes one final mistake: sleeping with the enemy.

THE WOOD BEYOND
Reginald Hill

Seeing the wood for the trees is a problem shared by Andy Dalziel and Edgar Wield, the latter in his investigations into bones found at a pharmaceutical research centre, and the former in his dangerous involvement with animal rights activist Amanda Marvell.

RAGE OF THE INNOCENT
Frederick E. Smith

The first of a trilogy.

Young Harry Miles clashes with Michael Chadwick, son of a wealthy landowner, and sows the seeds of a lifetime's conflict. When the 1914 – 18 war breaks out, Harry is driven into volunteering and finds himself under Chadwick's command. Taking his revenge, Chadwick makes Harry a machine gunner . . .

MOTHER OF GOD
David Ambrose

Tessa Lambert has just created the first viable artificial intelligence programme — a discovery so controversial that she must keep it a secret even from her colleagues at Oxford University. But soon there is to be a hacker stalking her on the Internet: a serial killer who is about to give her invention its own terrifying and completely malevolent life . . .

THE ANDROMEDA STRAIN
Michael Crichton

When *Project Scoop* sends satellites into outerspace to 'collect organisms and dust for study', one of them crashes into the town of Piedmont, Arizona. Soon after, all but two of the inhabitants are found dead from a strange disease. The scientists must trace what is causing the horrifying virus before it spreads . . .

TO WAR WITH WHITAKER
Countess of Ranfurly

When World War II broke out, Dan Ranfurly was dispatched to the Middle East with his faithful valet, Whitaker. These are the diaries of his young wife, Hermione, who, defying the War Office, raced off in hot pursuit of her husband. When Dan was taken prisoner, Hermione vowed never to return home until they were reunited.

IN PRESENCE OF MY FOES
Frederick E. Smith

Sequel to RAGE OF THE INNOCENT.
Harry Miles is now recovered from his war wounds, but a mysterious and compelling urge drives him back to the Front. He faces the menace of Michael Chadwick, his commanding officer and life-long rival, and the fearsome German offensive of March 1918.

YEARS OF THE FURY
Frederick E. Smith

The third volume of the trilogy which began with RAGE OF THE INNOCENT and continued with IN PRESENCE OF MY FOES.

The First World War has ended and, with Harry Miles back from France, he and Mary are hoping to settle down to their married life at last. But they have not taken account of their two unrelenting enemies.

FAMILY TREES
Kate Alexander

Catherine Carew fills her life with good works and is a pillar of the community. But in her distant university days she was a very different person. One night's indiscretion leaves her with a burden of guilt and regret that overshadows her later years — until a stranger appears on her doorstep . . .

INDIAN SUMMER
James Mitchell

Mixed blood courses through Veronica Higgins' veins, resulting in an exotic beauty. But to the expatriates in India at the height of the British Raj she is just another 'bloody chee-chee'. When her Aunt Poppy falls in love with an English industrialist, the three set off for his homeland. The arrival of one of England's richest men with two exquisitely beautiful women causes a flurry of excitement . . .

VANISHING POINT
Morris West

When Carl Strassberger, the son of an old New York banking family, renounces his position in the business to become an artist, his place is taken by his brother-in-law, Larry Lucas. But when Larry disappears, Carl must put himself at risk as he investigates those who live 'on the dangerous edge of things'.

THE RUNAWAY
John Grisham

In Biloxi, Mississippi, a landmark trial begins routinely, then swerves mysteriously off course. The jury is behaving strangely, and at least one juror is convinced that he is being watched. Is the jury somehow being manipulated or even controlled? If so, by whom? And, more importantly, why?

SHADOWS OF THE PAST
Palma Harcourt

When Christopher Grayson, a young Oxford don, decides to trace his family history, he learns that during the Second World War the de Mourvilles were condemned as Nazi sympathisers. Even worse, his grandfather was accused of crimes against humanity. But someone is on Christopher's trail, willing to kill in order to keep a tragic secret.

NOT JUST A SOLDIER'S WAR
Betty Burton

For Lu Wilmott, the call to Spain is irresistible. Signing up as a driver, she breaks the last link with her past and becomes Eve. Her work takes her close to figures of many nationalities, but it is the country and its people in the struggle against Franco that have the greatest effect on her.

THE WITCH OF EXMOOR
Margaret Drabble

The Palmer family and their children are coming to the end of an enjoyable meal. As usual, their conversation is brought back to their eccentric mother, Frieda, who has abandoned them and gone off to live alone on Exmoor. She has always been a monster mother with a mysterious past. What is she plotting against them now?

LEWIN'S MEAD
E. V. Thompson

The sequel to the bestselling novel BECKY
When artist Fergus Vincent forsakes the Bristol slums of Lewin's Mead he leaves behind him Becky, the street urchin whom he loved and married. After Becky is struck down in a cholera epidemic, she is cared for by Simon McAllister, a blind musician. But she never gives up hope that one day Fergus will return.

YEAR OF THE TIGER
Jack Higgins

When Paul Chavasse looks out of his window on a November evening, he is unaware that the figure standing opposite knows a great deal about his past. Back in 1961, Chavasse — now chief of a little-known section of British Intelligence — had been captured by the Chinese. When he had at last escaped he knew that he could be taking with him the means of his betrayal.

THAT CAMDEN SUMMER
LaVyrle Spencer

It is 1916 and Roberta Jewett has returned to the town where she was raised. But in Camden, Maine, a woman divorced is a woman shunned. Only Gabriel Farley treats her with respect. Although the chemistry between them is undeniable, they fight it. Then, a brutal act of violence forces them to aknowledge the powerful feelings that have grown between them.

PASSIONATE TIMES
Emma Blair

When Corporal Reith Douglas was injured during the Second World War, he lost his memory. But once he returns to his wife, Irene, in Glasgow, he gradually recalls the joy of his early married life, and the pain he suffered when Irene declared her love for a renowned villain. Little does he realise that he could well recapture the passionate times of his past.